something like
Sunflowers

something like Sunflowers

a novel by **Elsie Bea**

CONTENT WARNING
While light-hearted with a happy ending,
This work is intended for a mature, adult audience.
This work may contain content unsuitable for
readers sensitive to the below topics or themes.
Please note that reading content warnings
may lead to plot or character spoilers.
Read at your own discretion.

Content Warnings: trauma, emergency hospital care, addiction, child loss, PTSD, alcoholism, sexual assault, anorexia, body dysmorphia, teenage pregnancy, motor vehicle collision, child neglect, animal neglect, foster care, bondage, light-BDSM, violence, underage drinking, reference to underage sexual activity and/or violence; explicit language and graphic sexual content.

For Mom.
To more people than you knew,
You were everything.
You were a Polly.

For my husband.
Thank you for believing in my stories.
And loving me for me.

And for my children.
With you, my heart sings.

Chapter 1

Devyn

alm your darn britches! I huff as my hands curl into the edge of the sleek metal chair, willing myself to relax before I ruin my newly manicured nails. I snatch my hand back, noting how the rounded tips still sparkle with the sunflower-shaped, jewel-encrusted finish that I just had done last night, and I breathe a sigh of relief.

I haven't been this nervous since my first pageant. In fact, I don't get nervous. So, the butterflies that have taken up residence in my belly are entirely unwelcome.

I've been waiting my whole adult career for this moment, the chance to work for a company both female-dominated *and* that happens to be the retailer of my absolute favorite line of country-chic clothing. There isn't a single girl in my hometown who doesn't own one of their shirts or bags—the ones with puppies and cows sketched in pinks and lavenders.

I own more than I care to count.

This isn't an interview for just any position, either.

This is for their new Marketing Outreach and Influence Branch. It's not even an established department yet, so their goal is to find someone to build it from the ground up.

A thrill shoots through me as I plan a future for myself that's…for once in my life, something *I* choose.

This could finally be my opportunity to throw my creativity into something again, and I can't let anything jeopardize it.

But things have tested me today, that's for sure.

I barely even made it here on time because some absolute d-i-c-k, the size of a linebacker, bumped me, spilling my piping hot caramel macchiato on not only me but a poor older woman—who had amazingly gorg Condora-Suede Stiletto Louboutins, by the way. I almost cry thinking about it again. My coffee absolutely ruined those shoes.

May they rest in peace.

He who shall not be named—mainly because I didn't catch it before he dematerialized—ended up just glaring at me as if *I* were the one who bumped *him*. I mean, completely gawking at me through his stupid camo sunglasses and sexy blondish-reddish scruff of a beard that he absolutely should never shave, and then he just left!

He didn't even say sorry. Definitely didn't help me clean myself up. And that poor woman…

I hope she didn't think I was rude.

I was so distracted by Chad Michael Muscles and his lack of apologies that I didn't get a chance to explain myself. Or check on her shoes, more importantly.

Oh, well. I made it here. Despite one heck of a morning in this crazy city.

And the only thing that matters is that I land this job.

I don't hate my current job, exactly. It's just…

I already quit.

I tend to do these things, just jump right on in and hope

to God there's a lifeboat or some sort of saving grace at the bottom of the watering hole, rather than thinking things through and making plans. It's not the best way to live life, if I'm being totally honest with myself. But it is effective in enacting change, that's for sure.

I haven't told anyone aside from my brother. I have especially been avoiding conversations with Dad.

But it was so boring day in and out, showing up at the station for hair and makeup at two in the morning, running through mic checks and lighting checks and sound checks, and pantyhose-sticking-to-the-back-of-your-skirt checks…all of it to just stand there for an hour and tell people about the ten-mile delay on I-95.

I can't stand it anymore.

I thought I'd be covering *real* stories, doing something fun or exciting or even dangerous, but I'm over it. I've done nothing but traffic jams and crime kickers for four years now, and I'm not even sure I like being on the news anymore. I don't want to waste my life on stuff I hate just because I'm *Devyn Lynn, the Girl with the Facts before Five.*

I've made a cutesy little name for myself here in the news circles, because for some reason everyone just *loves* my accent. Honestly? I didn't think I had one. But a few *bless your hearts* too many, and Channel Five basically declared me their personal Annie Oakley. Now I can't end a single segment without saying, "This is Devyn Lynn and that's been your Highway Ho-down!"

It's taken me a long time to realize this, but a huge part of me misses the love of life that I had before I ever moved to the city.

Before I was a commodity.

I'm only a stone's throw away, but it's not quite the same. It's the pageants and the nightlife, the community, and the rodeos. It's horses and manure and entire fields of flowers.

It's kissing a boy in a truck, and the only lights aren't made of chandeliers or cameras flashing in your face, but the lights from stars.

Stars so bright they burned out centuries ago, but never stopped showing their fire.

I huff a breath that blows my bangs away from my forehead. *Maybe I'm homesick.*

But that isn't completely true, either. As much as I miss those things, I don't miss home. Things are always off with Mom. We split ways so long ago it never seems genuine when we try to reconnect. We weren't exactly on great terms *before* I left.

And it's not like I can talk about Dad.

It's always nice to see Shana, but everyone else…they made it clear there's no place for me in their circle years ago. Shana can say it's not like that all she wants, but it is. And it has been since I left home.

That's not my friend group anymore. That's not my home.

Even if I do miss it.

Honestly, I don't belong anywhere right now.

But that is exactly why Classy Country is the perfect next step for me. They aren't just a business; they're a family. A sisterhood. They go on retreats and team building vacations, and I mean *huge* gatherings of women empowering women to achieve their goals. The outreach influencer will oversee everything from social media promotions to community fundraisers. It feels like I've finally found something that combines my business and communications degree with my grass roots and the things I value. I'll meet like-minded individuals who want to succeed in their careers *and* form friendships.

And when I remember those things, my insecurities about quitting the station fade away.

This position is mine. And let's hope I'm right, because I've got a sudden taste for some Condora Suede Stilettos right about now.

Chapter 2

Hunter
Twenty Minutes Earlier

Yeah, *sure as shit, that was Devyn.*

Did she recognize me?

I can't seem to shake the feeling that she didn't. I shouldn't give two shits what the Farmhouse Barbie Doll thinks about me, anyway. And I don't.

She made her choice long ago. As did I.

My chest burns, memories ripping from within my heart with just one look at her eyes. There was a time in my life when I had different ideas about my best friend's little sister.

There was a time when we were different. But everything can change in one single breath.

I thought she'd be better off in the city. With fame and stability. Away from people like me.

But the way she is now? She's either faking it for her *image*, or she's gone completely. Because the Devyn I see on the television each night, the one in the Internet photos I swear

I won't search…she isn't the girl I knew. And that's the same one I just saw on the street, glued to her phone, taking selfies, fixing her hair in her camera. Wearing that *dress.*

Why the hell she thinks she's allowed to walk the streets of the city wearing a hot pink loincloth is beyond me, but there's a strict brother's best friend code that I'm going to have to abide by, or so I tell myself as I snap a quick picture of her and send it to Dusty.

HUNTER: What the fuck is Dev wearing?

DUSTY: Where are you?

HUNTER: On a corner. In the city.

DUSTY: What is she doing wearing THAT?

HUNTER: Dunno, but I wouldn't want MY sister wearing things like that in front of guys like me.

DUSTY: You don't have a sister.

HUNTER: I could have your sister.

DUSTY: And you could have two less balls.

<middle finger emoji>

A grin forms on my lips. *He's too easy.*

A horn blares, rattling the insides of my ears as exhaust blows in my face, and I'm instantly reminded why I hate the city. It's the constant *noise.* You don't hear that in Pine Forest. We have our share of noises out there. But it's crickets, cicadas, maybe roosters. All that stuff's supposed to be there. None of this sensory over-load bullshit. If it weren't for the corporate sponsorships Classy Country could bring to my youth farming program, I wouldn't be within fifty miles of the stench of this place. Factories and ATMs on every corner. It's like the whole world's forgotten how to live *with* the land instead of consuming it.

I stumble on the corroded sidewalk beneath my feet for the third or fourth time, and I shake my head at myself, feeling right stupid for poking fun at Devyn being glued to her phone earlier when I'm distracted by mine right now.

Looking at *her* picture. *Fuck.* I shove my phone in my pocket because I do not need to be looking at *that.*

Seeing her always has this effect on me. And it'll undoubtedly be weeks before I get the image of her in that dripping pink fabric out of my mind.

I didn't mean to run into her and send her coffee flying through the air, but I can't say I regret it much, because even though it must have been scalding hot—judging by the scream of the older woman who was doused with some of it—Devyn had just enough fire under her skin to ignore the burn and cast me a glare that could damn me to hell right where I stood, those green eyes blazin' somethin' fierce.

And with them, a fire I thought was long gone.

I just stood there, stunned, unable to move as the wet dress clung to her tight little body like a candy wrapper, and that is so fucking far from being an appropriate thought I had to drag my eyes from her and walk away. As far away from her as possible. As fast as humanly fucking possible.

Because Devyn is complicated. She's bratty, spoiled, self-centered, and half the time she's so far stuck up her own ass she can't see in front of her face. She pushes my buttons, gets under my skin, and *fuck,* she's like a human version of water torture, ya know? She's just there…drip, drip, drip, drown, repeat.

Devyn is an addiction.

If you don't have her for a while, you can detox, forget she exists, move on.

Even if the taste of her never does quite leave your lips.

But I've slipped up now. I've seen Devyn. I've seen the fire still burning in her stare. The one that tells me maybe she isn't all bubblegum pop and Prada like she leads the masses to believe.

My girl is still in there somewhere, and I can't unsee her.

I grind my teeth as my boots pound against the pavement in the opposite direction of where I need to be going, breathing, and reminding myself of reality. It's been ten years since we did this dance, and I *know* I shouldn't wrap myself up in that kind of thing with her again. Especially with the way things are now. What my life has become. It feels like a knife slicing through me with that realization, but it's true.

What we once had is forever gone. I made sure of that. And her presence in my life wouldn't only affect me this time.

That doesn't change the ache in my chest when I see the spark in her eyes again.

Because Devyn Lynn is and always was two things.

Off limits. And *mine.*

Chapter 3

Devyn

My heels click on the white marble floors…well, more like *clunk*. I suck in a breath. Part of it must be how nervous I am to finally meet the interview panel, but my footwear probably doesn't help. I'm slightly regretting the Miu platform booties with the block-heel ankles, as my every single step echoes through the cavernous hallway of bright whites and muted grays that seems positively endless.

The trim and chair railing lining the walls are purposefully weathered to match the rustic but clean aesthetic of the brand. Braided hemp-roping coils around the sconces that decorate the walls, and each one is adorned with a tiny barn star at the base. We seem to walk—well, *clunk*—forever, and I wonder how this all fits in the building that seemed a lot smaller when I was on the outside of it.

Studying the floors in hopes of silencing my clunking just a tad, my eyes trace the gold flecks patterned into the marble, swimming around and tying in the golden embroidery of the thick, sage-colored curtains that feature the Classy Country emblem displaying four gold rings linked together to form a clover with a simple CC in the center.

"Here we are," the receptionist, whose name I learned is Bella, chirps as we stop outside a huge set of barn-style sliding doors. She's a pretty girl, skinny and tall, with cream colored skin and freckles all over her face and arms. Her naturally red hair curls around her cheeks, spilling free from the tight bun atop her head. Her dress is very office-chic, like something you see on a Macy's ad, and the muted lavender pansies peppered along the collar and waistline look both basic and professional. I peer down at her hands, clasped tightly around her cellphone and stylus. She picks at her cuticles with her nude-polished nails as we loiter outside the doors.

"Molly Preston is just inside there," she whispers. "She will conduct your initial interview, and then you will meet with Claudette and James for the remainder of the time. Do you need anything? Have any questions?"

She pulls at her sleeve in a show of nerves, which is crazy because she already has a job secured here, and I'm the one about to walk into the shark tank. At least it feels like it. I still can't shake how anxious I am for this. I never used to get nerves before a performance or a pageant. Never once before a segment at Channel Five. So, why now?

"Devyn?"

I've been letting my mind wander like a dandelion again. I straighten the neckline of my dress. It still smells a bit like caramel and coffee grounds, but I think I used enough of the vanilla-scented foaming hand soap in the bathroom to make it seem intentional. *I hope.* I couldn't get the big stain off the center of my dress even with the detergent pen I carry in my clutch for emergencies such as this one. But despite the universe's incessant attempts to thwart my success today, I'm here, and I plan to put my best self forward and show the executives just who Devyn Lynn Campbell is.

Or wants to be.

"Right as rain!" I assure Bella. "Nothing I can't handle." I force a very practiced pageant smile, the one my mother habit-forced into me with ten years of Vaseline and Pixy Stix. I hated it then, and I hate it now.

It feels fake. Still, Bella exudes sincerity and takes my lie of a smile to her heart all the same.

I envy how nice she is. It almost annoys me. And I can't figure out why.

But I'm prettier than she is. We can't have it all.

As soon as I let the thought hit my skull, I regret thinking it. My skin prickles with shame.

I think things like that a lot.

I only recently noticed how bad it had gotten when I was talking to my brother last month. Even though we don't see each other often, we still talk on the phone every week and text almost daily. Sometimes it's just never-ending strings of reels back and forth for weeks, but last time we chatted, he basically spelled it out for me. I'm a bitch.

DEVYN: I hate when people who don't deserve it, get all the good stories.

DUSTIN: Like you? <Thinking Emoji>

DEVYN: I'm serious! I worked so hard to pitch the story about the school board corruption in Valley County. You read my pitch! And they loved it so much that Megan Chamberlain gets to cover it. MEGAN CHAMBERLAIN.

DUSTIN: She's hot, tho.

DEVYN: Her nose is so big it could cover the story on its own.

DUSTIN: Chill out, Dev. It sucks she got the story, but you still did some great work on that pitch.

DUSTIN: I'm sure you'll get the next one.

DEVYN: Well, I'm quitting so…

DUSTIN: Don't quit just because you're salty.

DEVYN: I'm NOT salty. I'm JUST. I deserved that story.

DUSTIN: Did it ever occur to you that Megan might have written a killer pitch, too?

DEVYN: Whose side are you on?

DUSTIN: I used to be on my sister's side, but I don't know where she is lately.

DEVYN: wtf is that supposed to mean?

DUSTIN: You figure it out. Just know that you tend to quit and run away when things get hard.

DEVYN: Eff you. You know why I left.

DUSTIN: Still not sure why you haven't come back, though. My little sister is still in there somewhere. Don't lose her in the city.

<Dustin has been blocked>

I was madder than a rattlesnake after that conversation. Who the hell does he think he is, spewing bull-crap about quitting when things get hard? Things never got hard for him. He didn't lose anything. He got to stay. But as my brother, he's the only person I ever really believed. The only person who knows the real me.

The only one I can count on, at least.

So, I'm facing the truth about myself. For the past month, I've been identifying when I suck as a human, and I'm sure that's a start to something.

The Twelve Steps to Not Being a Bitch?

Because I *am* kind of a bitch.

Dusty's right.

I wasn't always like this, but somewhere between being whisked off to private school in the city in an insane custody battle, separated from my only brother…among other people, and becoming a reigning pageant queen turned news anchor, things got complicated.

Things happened before all that too.

Life got harder.

It's not like I try to be a bitch. I'm nice to people. At least to their faces, so that should count for something. Dustin says it's my fault. That I put up these walls, as he calls them, and quite literally force people out of my way. I'm starting to think he's on to something.

And apparently, in addition to being a bitch, I'm also a personality masochist because I can see just how horrible this all is for me, but I'll continue to pick apart this girl *Bella* in my mind.

She's got this job at a place I want to work, and this nice girl thing going for her. But my boobs are pushed up higher, my hair is longer, and my lips are fuller. My car is top of the line, my shoes cost more than her paycheck, and my nails are baller right now.

I instantly feel better about myself. Isn't that shitty?

I know it's wrong, but I'm not hurting anyone by *thinking* things.

And Pollyanna over there has no clue as I smile brightly on the outside that I'm one hundred percent Wednesday Addamsing on the inside the longer she pays attention to me.

"I'm a big fan," she suddenly says, using her stylus to push her glasses back in place. "People tend to view pageant queens as vapid, but you are a huge role model for so many of us women who just want to change the world for the better! The work you do with the kids at the library is so important," she gushes. I feel my pulse quicken, my body becoming sticky and heated.

I'm putting my best face forward, but I'm uncomfortable, extremely so. Despite what people might assume about the once spotlit pageant queen, I don't like people telling me they like me. Or that I look beautiful. Or that I'm a great person, most of all.

Because I know what they don't.

I'm not.

And the actual knot…the "things I'm *not* knot" in my stomach, gets further mangled and twisted the more she falsely elevates me as some sort of revered humanitarian savior. Because the work she's talking about was all for PR purposes. It was press-motivated. Scripted. Fake.

Just like me.

"After your segment at that inner city elementary school, I signed up for weekly reading sessions with the kids in my neighborhood. I just wanted to say thanks for inspiring me. And I'm rooting for you!" She smiles brightly and gives me a thumbs up before turning away and leaving me by the door with my heart in the pit of my stomach.

Emotions, they say, are like a tidal wave. And mine slam into me full force.

Everything about me is fake.

Just like that entire conversation with Bella. I sat there and picked her apart in my mind—made fun of her looks, her personality, her hair. I fancied myself as better than her in all the ways I could think up just to make myself feel like a nicer person.

No. To make myself feel better about *not* being a nicer person.

And all the while, she was a "fan" of mine, this great philanthropic pioneer who singlehandedly delivers a love of literature to the children in her community and runs puppy adoptions at the local grocery all before the evening traffic report!

I'm a fake and I'm a bitch. I don't deserve this job. People like Bella do.

But if I know this and *want* to change, doesn't it count for something? Maybe I can't be the Classy Country employee they want me to be just yet, but I can do what I'm good at.

What I've been raised to do my whole life.

I can smile and fake it.

And pray they like the smell of caramel macchiato.

Chapter 4

Devyn

Oh, Devyn! I absolutely love your sunflower nails. I'm so happy we're finally meeting in person! And I'm thrilled we might get another fashionista around here. There are a few of us, but there are equally as many non-creatives in the business place. And we love them, we really do, but what can ya say? They aren't always flaunting the most interesting of seasonal wardrobes, now, are they?"

Molly Preston stands behind her desk in a bespoke Tiffany blue, pinstripe, two-piece suit with ruffle lapels. Pinned neatly to her left lapel is a small gold CC emblem, and a pink belt with matching Tiffany blue cattle printed across the leather is secured neatly around her waistline.

Molly Preston is breathtaking. She's not only one of the three co-owners of Classy Country, she's also the lead investor's only daughter. She's two years younger than I am, and plenty richer.

I want to be her friend. I might want to be *her*.

I smile widely as we shake hands across the desk. Positioned before me is a picture of a little girl with blonde curls and a Classy Country T-shirt that's so big on her, it's practically touching the floor. She's holding Molly's hand as they laugh, and a pang of jealousy hits me.

"She's cute. Is she your little sister?" I don't know why I ask her this. I know how old we both are. I also know it's not her sister. It still hurts when she confirms it, though.

"My daughter, actually," she says, blinking. "I was an only child, I'm afraid. I always wished I'd had a sister or brother. Do you have any siblings?"

My shoulders ease with relief at this question. Partly because she did me a solid by not making my daughter/sister question more awkward than it had to be. And because it's something I have an honest answer for. Something I don't have to fake.

"I do, actually." I say, sitting up straighter. "A brother. His name's Dustin. We're nothing alike. He's the caveman, stern, broody type. Barely speaks, but always seems to be in my business." I roll my eyes and offer a laugh.

"Oh? Younger?"

"Older, actually. By two years. He was always giving me a hard time growing up. Super protective. Like, he was on the rodeo team, and God forbid one of those cowboys even looked at me too long."

"Wait, back up to the rodeo team and cowboys. What school did you go to? We just had football and cheerleading at mine."

I forget sometimes that rodeo teams aren't normal outside of Pine Forest and our surrounding counties.

"Pine Forest High?" I shrug. "Rodeos are kind of the highlight of the town there. Think Friday night football craze, but with more horses and less padding."

"And your brother…I guess he wouldn't let you play in any

cowboy games with his rodeo pals?" She wiggles her eyebrows, and I sputter a bit at the implications there. *If only you knew.*

"He tried his best." I smirk and leave it at that. Where it should rightfully stay.

"Okay, cowgirl." Molly blushes and fans herself. "I'm a sucker for a good romance, and that sounds exactly like a book I'm reading. A super overprotective brother and his hot best friend. I'm going to DM you the name of it after the interview. You never know when you might get lucky and need the instruction manual." She winks, and we both laugh.

Molly's warmth is contagious, and her passion for books and fashion makes me feel at home. It reminds me of what it was like having actual friends back in Pine Forest.

Before everything changed.

I suddenly want to know more about her, to get this job and become friends with her. With people *like* her. Whatever I need to do, I'll do it. And anyway, she seems super on board with me joining the team, so I only need to convince a couple more execs, and moments like this—potential friendships— might not be so fleeting anymore.

The stress I felt from my encounter with Bella sheds from my body like a fur coat, and I can finally feel the air surrounding me again. I'm no longer nervous while Molly paints a picture of what this life could be like for me. Who I could become.

"Claudette and James should be here any moment, along with the other candidate," Molly says, eyeing the hot pink watch on her wrist that I am low-key in love with. "But before they come, I wanted to ask you something."

My nerves creep in again with the formality of her question, but it's okay. I remind myself she's been friendly so far, so snapping the hair-tie on my wrist, I keep my walls down with her for now.

"Shoot," I manage.

"We, I mean, *I* love your personality and your fashion choices." She stops and briefly eyes the stain on my dress, raising an eyebrow.

"Coffee mishap." I scrunch my nose. This seems to make sense to her, and she continues, "I think your creative energy would fit in well here at Classy Country. And with your social media following, you'd be sure to have a huge success in launching your own fund-raisers and events…"

She pauses and purses her lips like she isn't sure how to phrase the rest of her statement. Wasn't it supposed to be a question? Regardless, she's stalling, and I sense a "but" coming.

"…but," she says…*and there it is,* "we are aware how things work at the news channels. Most of the population might think it's all genuine, but we at Classy Country are in the marketing business. We know these ideas are very rarely, if ever, the news anchors' ideas. And most of them are just photo ops. We *want* to want you. But none of us is sure we know you. The real Devyn Lynn Campell, that is."

"What if I don't know her either?" I ask. Dead honest. And I'm not even sure why. I'm fake with everyone I know, even my own family and friends. But for some reason, at this moment, this interview means enough for me to be real with Molly.

She studies me for a quick minute, and then swallows and folds her hands below her chin. "I think you'd be a good fit, Devyn, despite what you do or don't know about yourself yet. And I'd be willing to give you a chance. Now, you need to convince Claudette and James. And they…" She scrunches her nose and eyes my stupid coffee stain before flipping her eyes back up to my face with a tight smile. "Well, they are going to eat you alive, sweetie."

My mouth pops open because I most definitely wasn't expecting her to say that after her heartfelt declaration of confidence in me.

She senses my shock and puts a hand over my own. "It's okay." She beams. "You got this! Just fake it till you make it."

You haven't the faintest idea.

Molly gets up from her desk and moves to the coffee table in the far corner, and I finally get a glimpse of her shoes.

My mouth pops open. I'm honestly surprised. She's wearing plain old cowboy boots. Not unlike the ones I keep in my blanket chest and can't seem to throw out, despite not having worn them in almost a decade.

Something like warmth curls around my heart, but only briefly, as I'm brought to the present by a solitary knock on the door before a rush of people come tumbling in.

"Bella, dear, send a message to Abigail in marketing. We need the finishing edits for the wording on the spring collection ads by three p.m. today, and there will be absolutely no exceptions this time. Got it?"

Bella, who I thought was pale before, gets whiter than a lamb's tail as she jots the vivacious woman's instructions down on her tablet screen. "Yes, Claudette. No worries. I'll make sure she has the message."

"Good," the woman, who is apparently the Claudette who'll eat me alive, as Molly put it, says, "and Bella?"

"Y-yes…Claudette?"

"You don't have to fear me, dear. I'm not going to bite you. Now, stop picking at your nailbeds and type my email." Bella's face goes from white to red in a matter of seconds. She stops fiddling with her nails, nods politely, and makes a beeline for the door. It isn't until Claudette rounds the corner of the desk and Molly stands to greet her that I realize just who this woman is…

God is full on cackling right now. He's clearly got nothing better to do with his time today than throw some vinegar in my coffee pot, and he has delivered. Massively so. Long black hair spills down her "impressively fit for her age" body, and with the royal blue maxi dress that hugs the curves of her hips and ends just above the knee, she looks like an actual pin-up model.

A pin-up model with Condora Suede Louboutins.

"You," is all she says. But the squint in her eyes and the purse on her lips say more. So much more.

I stand immediately.

"I am so sorry for what happened on the street. I wanted to check on you, but there was so much going on. I know how much those shoes cost and will one hundred percent be replacing them. I'll even host a vigil for them if we must. I just feel *so* bad."

Claudette eyes me suspiciously, discerning whether I really care. She must decide I do, and for real, I do. I'm not being fake about this. I want this job, and I want to be a new me. I'll scream it from the hallways of this giant building, so it echoes louder than my shoe clunks, if it'll prove it, but this means everything to me right now.

I need this change.

"I'll accept your shoes," she finally says. She doesn't smile, but her mouth curves just slightly enough that I figure that's about as close as she probably gets to smiling anyhow. "But I'll decide on your apology after the interview."

I find myself beaming back at her, and she huffs out an almost-laugh that I accept as a win. "I hope I won't let you down," I say. "There won't be any smoldering cowboys to knock over my coffee during the interview, I presume?"

I start to laugh at my own joke, but Claudette just sips her tea and gives me the faintest hint of a smirk.

Just then, the ground shakes, knocking the teacups around on the table, as two large, mud-covered boots carry in a thick set of denim-clad thighs that make my mouth physically water.

They could crush my neck, I think, for no appropriate reason whatsoever.

Claudette stares at me. I can see it from the corner of my eye, but I can't seem to direct my focus back to her. Nope, just me over here…the job applicant who can't stop staring at how tight that zipper looks on this random man's Levi's.

You, Devyn Lynn, are a complete perv. Snap out of it and impress these people!

With the strength of a hundred men, I find a way to pull my eyes away from his inseam and up to his face where Jesus, Mary, and the whole damn manger know it belongs. His camo sunglasses look back at me, and my breath catches, because he's annoyingly gorgeous, yes…but also because I realize… he's the man from the street who caused this whole predicament. *He's* the reason I'm, quite literally, groveling at Claudette's feet.

And then I'm angry, because he isn't groveling at all. He's standing here, hand on the side of his face, about to remove his hat and glasses, calm as a freakin' cucumber. And when he finally notices me staring, he looks me up and down…full on checks me out in front of everyone in this room. And then the asshole has the audacity to lick. His. Lips.

Heat rushes to my lady parts, because bless their sinful little hearts, they know not what they do. He's *hot.* I can't even help it.

But I've got to shake myself out of this spell, reminding myself he didn't even apologize, and that is most certainly *not* hot. I'm more used to men like him than he probably realizes, anyhow. Wanna-be cowboys who think they know everything? Been there, done that. Good old boys who mansplain their days away and think the sun rises in the mornings just to listen to them crow? Check and check. I might not be giving him a piece of my mind right now, in front of the executives, but you can bet your bottom dollar this cowgirl will be dishing out a stern whiplashing once these heels hit the parking deck. He owes me an apology.

It doesn't matter how good his body looks shoved… so perfectly snugly in those blue jeans. *Damn it.* I clear my throat and wipe off my hands, which are sweating for reasons unknown, and remind myself to be super polite to this…*bubba.*

Don't kill him, and don't jump his bones.

I'm honestly not sure which would happen if I let myself loose on him, and I need to save face, if only for the sake of this job.

But when he takes off his sunglasses and my eyes meet his, my heart stops dead in my chest. And time seems to stop alongside it, before it explodes like a firecracker, spreading electricity straight to my core. He's older. Scruffier. And I'm not sure how, but swear to God, he's sexier. And I don't for a single second believe everyone in this room doesn't hear the needy, breathless whimper that escapes my traitorous lips when I hear the deep bass rumbling of his voice for the first time in ten long years.

"Hey, Dev."

Chapter 5

Hunter

I turned thirty this year. And I don't know about anyone else, but thirty feels old to me. Like I should have lived a thousand lives by now.

And maybe I have. I've been a thousand different men, and that's the truth.

Maybe I've been hanging around horses too long. Heck, they don't live to be much older than thirty, even if you are lucky, like I am with Beau. He's the best fuckin' horse there ever was, and I might just lie down and die alongside him when he goes. I don't remember a day in my life without him.

There are only two people alive I've loved longer than my horse. One of 'em's my best friend, Dusty. And the other one?

That would be his little sister. And she's standing right in front of me.

Lord knows I put up a valiant fuckin' effort to avoid her this morning. I didn't even stop to help her, or the woman I now know is Claudette, right themselves before I shot outta there like a horse at the starting gate. Makes me sound weak, I know. But she weakens me.

I'm not stupid. I know why.

I know I'm still in love with Devyn fuckin' Lynn.

I never stopped loving her. How could I?

No amount of glitz and glam, rumors and tabloid head-lines…no amount of time could change that. She could burn the world down, and I'd still worship the way the flames light her eyes.

It doesn't matter who I love, though. Dustin, her father, the princess herself, and even my own damn self knows we're over. However, my stupid fuckin' cock was not afforded the memo, and he's sittin' pretty, prancin' straight in the Barbie Doll's direction.

I can't blame him if he knows what he likes, but damn it if it ain't harder than hell to make the damn thing obey me when she's over there plain as day looking at my bottom half like it's the cheeseburger her mama never let her eat.

A crease forms in my brow with that. She looks too thin. Funny how stuff like that can be second nature to consider, even when taking care of her hasn't been my job for a long time. I take my time as I look her up and down and feel a low growl start in my throat when I let my mind drift to past conversations we'd had about her health. All the times I snuck a happy meal through her bedroom window on pageant week.

About everything else.

I'm certain my girl still has no idea who I am, and damn if that doesn't sweeten the pot. She doesn't know she hates me yet. And I'm enjoying the way her eyes roam my body. I've bulked up since the last time we tangled, and I never used to grow a beard. That's something I started for TikTok. Sometimes when you run a non-profit community farm, you have to…

I film thirst traps. Plain and simple.

It gets me sponsored by big farming equipment companies, and that way I can run the youth farm and rodeo with no cost to the parents in our low-income area. And all I have to do is take my shirt off while I do completely normal farm shit. I might spice it up from time to time, flirt with the camera a bit. It's nice to feel appreciated.

For whatever reason, the ladies of the interwebs go crazy for it. I gained almost twenty thousand followers after the first month, so I keep doing it. Why not?

People might call me a playboy, spin tales of OnlyFans, say I'm a porn star…that's my particular favorite. In a small town, people love to talk, but I don't give two fucks who thinks what about me. Let 'em think all they want. My nine-year-old niece and her friends know how to raise livestock and lead with sustainability, and their parents don't have to worry about where they are and what they're gettin' into after school. My farm is a safe space for most kids in our town. And if taking my shirt off on the Internet so bored thirtysomethings get their cowboy fix is what keeps the kids in my community from behind bars like the rodeo did for me, then so be it.

I've worked too hard to make this town something for people to be proud of. I want generations after me to say, "Yeah, I'm from Pine Forest, that's my hometown." I want them to go off and get jobs and come back to raise families here because this is home to them. Like it is to me.

So, I do what I can. I donate. Give back. Sponsor community events. Take my shirt off while I chop wood from time to time and get a free cultivator for it. Doesn't make me a playboy.

I don't care about any woman on the Internet, anyway. I haven't dated anyone in a long time. It's not fair to give them half of my heart when the other half will always belong to the girl next door.

No, I don't care about any of those women. The ones who

send me late night texts, hang all over me at bars, soccer moms with phone numbers stuffed in coat pockets on the sidelines. I don't give a lick about any of 'em but the one standing right in front of me. Never have, and I reckon I never will.

I've been thinking about her since I bumped into her on the street. I've mulled it over. I've weighed the damn pros and cons. And you know what?

I don't really care why God saw it fit to put her in my path again, but I'm not dumb enough to fuck it up twice.

I came here for a job I don't even need.

They reached out to me.

I could give two fucks about Classy Country and their frilly fabrics, and as far as I see it, the only thing that's piqued my interest here in the city came from the country to begin with.

And as I watch the girl of my dreams do nothing short of make an ice cream sundae out of my body right in front of the whole damn interview, I lick my lips and decide right then and there.

I'm gonna make this woman fall in love with me. *Again.*

Chapter 6

Devyn

H i," I breathe. I think I breathe it, at least. I'm trying super-duper hard to make words for, like, sentences. But that's Hunter Isaac.

My stomach is doing loops, because of course on a day as important as this one, there would be obstacles. I just didn't think they'd be two-hundred-pound, six-foot-two obstacles that quite literally walked out of my bedroom fantasies. Still, I have a job to land. And now a few questions waiting on the tip of my tongue.

The first being, "Why are you here?"

I don't realize my sentence making abilities have returned until after I say it. I also don't mean for it to sound so hateful. It's part of my bitch curse, I'm sure.

Molly, Claudette, and a man in a cat sweatshirt and chemically distressed jeans, who I guess I'm supposed to assume is James, all stare at me like I'm an absolute lunatic, but Hunter just works his bottom lip between his teeth while his eyes say barrels of inappropriate things to me with a single glance. My thoughts betray me, and I can't help but imagine running my own teeth over those stupidly gorgeous lips and…

"Fuck. Me."

Oh, my God.

My hand shoots to my mouth at the same time as James' pops open, in what seems to be the only moment he decides to pay attention. *Of course.* We all watch his pastry crumble to the floor, and as the cherry filling splats on the cow-print rug next to Claudette's already-ruined-shoes, my stomach leaps into my throat.

This is not going well.

Suddenly, the room is hot. And not the good kind. The "I want to rip my shirt off and sit in front of two fans or else I might pass out" kind. I'm beyond embarrassed. And all at once, it hits me like a ton of bricks that I am one hundred percent not getting this job now.

What will I do? What will I tell Dad?

I've never had a panic attack before, but I might be. I'm lighter than air and the room is so bright. And I'm *hot.*

I don't like feeling so out of control, so against the odds.

Like a failure. *In front of everyone.*

"Breathe, Ponygirl," Hunter whispers beside me.

I'm safe in his command before I even feel him.

Ponygirl.

I meet his gaze, and for a split second, we're just kids playing tag in the very sunflower fields that inspired my nail design.

The deep vibrations of the voice I've only heard in my dreams for years float around me and hold me so close that I forget we aren't alone. Hunter's arm is wrapped around my waist, where it feels natural. The hand that presses against my back guides me gently to my chair, as the scent of pine and sandalwood seeps into my soul and fits around me like a life-boat. I feel instantly at ease beside Hunter. I'm not freaking out.

And that freaks me out.

Molly's gaze bounces back and forth between us before she narrows her eyes.

"So, you two are already acquainted, it seems."

"I've known this girl for a hundred years," Hunter purrs, making me squirm. When did he learn how to purr, though?

I really shouldn't like it.

"*Woman*," I correct. "I'm not a girl, and you very well know it." I stutter on my exhale, and Hunter studies me, winking and making my skin prickle.

"How interesting that you're now competing for the same position," Claudette says, her lips curving up on the edges.

And there it is. I stiffen.

I knew something was up, but this? Of all people to be competing with for the job, it's Hunter Isaac.

The man couldn't dress himself if you gave him one option and a picture diagram. I know. I've tried it. Heck, he's wearing a fishing T-shirt to an interview for a multi-billion-dollar fashion empire. What does he even do these days? Works at the lumber company by day and probably spends his nights drinking at Cowboy's Paradise and chasing after college tail looking for a ride on his—

Hunter throws his arm around my shoulder and tousles my hair like he's my older brother. Like he used to do when we were in junior high, and I give him major side-eye, because he knows how much I hate it. I know what he's doing, trying to lighten the mood for the interview. But I'm not the little girl he remembers. If he thinks he can flirt with me and get me all gaga for him while he takes the job I deserve out from under me, he's got another think coming.

Brick by brick, I shift my wall back in place and commence operation Destroy Hunter Immediately.

"Competing?" I snort, and even though I intentionally sound like a bitch this time, Claudette shoots me approving glares from across the table. I think she hate-likes me, which might be a positive in Claudette standards, so I dig my nails in further. "The only thing we will be competing in is who will be first to get my brother to text them the Netflix password." I turn to face Molly and James now too. "You can't possibly be considering Hunter, of all people, as the face of your outreach. I mean, look at him."

"I am looking." Molly says, far too appreciatively. I whip around to face her, but she only raises an eyebrow at me in challenge, and Hunter starts to snicker.

"Ladies," Claudette says, cutting through our weird stand-off and giving me a fragment longer than I'd like to consider why I even care about Molly looking at Hunter.

I heave a sigh and turn my attention to Claudette and James, who is still shoveling pastries into his mouth. It's clear he doesn't care who gets hired, and it's probably best to direct my efforts toward Claudette at this point since Molly is too busy eyeing my man…er, ex-man…to be of any help to me.

"Devyn." Claudette nods. "Hunter. You have been selected as our final candidates for the Marketing and Outreach position. We at Classy Country feel you both demonstrate a level of social, personal, and career-based excellence that will help our company grow and thrive."

"Both of us?" I ask, and James chokes on his pastry. How on earth is he still eating that thing? How long does one dessert take to consume?

Molly's been far too quiet as she treats Hunter like her own personal copy of *Gentleman's Quarterly*, and I really dislike how unprofessional that looks on her, so I roll my eyes when I think she isn't looking, but Hunter catches it.

"Careful, sis. Your bitch is showing," he whispers.

"Don't call me sis." I elbow him. "You aren't my brother."

"No," he says, curving his mouth up and nearing my ear. He puts his lips so close that his breath feels warm against my neck, and damn if that doesn't make my nipples respond. "Neither of us would want that, now, would we, babygirl?"

The way my body reacts to this man is absolutely illegal. Or it feels like it should be. I've never hated someone so much yet wanted them to push me against a wall and defile my mind, body, and soul all at the same time.

And it's not fair how confusing that is.

Claudette clears her throat, but it seems she's the only one who saw that freaking soft-core just now. I shove my body a considerable distance away from Magic Mike and turn to face Molly, whose twisted lips tell me I'm two seconds shy of being the gum on the bottom of her boots here soon. I cringe internally at the energy shift since we had our little girl-talk earlier.

"Maybe you've been banned from bubby's rodeo pals too long, Devyn," Molly says as she looks between Hunter and me. He raises an uncomfortable eyebrow to me as she continues to check him out like he's a steak dinner while she goes on. "This man is a walking cowboy thirst trap. Exactly what our brand could use. Even if we do like you—"

"Hey!" That's not okay. He may be an actual, living rep-resentation of Adonis, but she is not allowed to objectify him. "You can't talk about him like that! He's more than a sexy body shoved into a pair of stupidly tight, but frustratingly attractive jeans!"

"Thanks, Dev." Hunter smirks.

Oh, God. What am I doing?

All I had to do was impress two people. One of whom would have been impressed if I'd just brought him some Little Debbies, it seems, and the other just wanted me not to spill my coffee on her. It hasn't even been a full news segment's length of time, and I've already made the one person in the room who did like me question it. And now Hunter Isaac, of all people, is sitting two feet away from me smiling like he's the cat that's got…not just the cream, but the whole sleeve of cookies too.

"Devyn," Molly snips, "come to the hallway with me for a quick second, all right?"

Here it is.

Now is the moment she will tell me it was nice to meet me, but they're going in another direction, and I'll have to walk out of here and into Dad's office with my tail tucked between my legs and tell him the truth.

I take a deep breath and look at Hunter one last time before I get up and follow Molly out of the room and away from my dream job and any possibility of a new life.

My heels are still clunking as I exit Molly's suite, but this time I can't hear them over the fear of disappointment and shame.

That, and one repeating word on a loop in my head, over and over and over.

Babygirl.

Chapter 7

Devyn

Devyn," Molly starts on me as soon as the door closes, "I am not your enemy. Stop treating me like your rival in there. You do know I'm married, right?"

My arms unfold themselves from across my body as I put meaning to her words. She isn't hitting on Hunter, then?

"I'm trying to help you by playing devil's advocate in there. Your ex—"

"He's not my ex!"

Molly raises a brow. Even to a total stranger, it's an obvious lie.

"Okay, he's my ex. We literally dated my whole youth."

Molly smirks and leans against the doorjamb, as if to settle in for a bedtime story. "I mean, we didn't date as kids, but we did…in a way. I don't know. It's never clear to me whether the years before fifth grade really count when you calculate that sort of thing, ya know?"

"Mm-hmm." Molly grins.

"Why is Hunter even an issue, anyway? You realize this is a fashion empire, right? He cleans his fingernails with his hunting knife."

"Well, for one, you're still into him."

"I'm not into him."

"You are."

"I'm not."

"Well," she says, pressing her body away from the wall, "let's just say, for the sake of this conversation, that you are still into him. And you want to land this job and shove it in his cocky little belly dancing face."

Belly dancing? I narrow my brows, but her version of this ends with me getting hired. That's the goal, after all.

"I really like you. In fact, you were my recruit. We each got one, and I chose you. James, on the other hand, is a very loyal follower of your man's—"

"Not my man."

"Sorry." She smirks. "James is a huge fan of Not-Your-Man's TikToks."

"What do you mean, his TikToks?"

I'm not on social media much, but when I am, it's on Instagram where most of my followers live. TikTok is a mystery to me.

"Oh, my gosh, you don't even know, do you?"

I don't love the entertained look Molly has in her eyes. She's far too excited to show me whatever has her tapping and swiping like a madwoman across her phone screen.

But a few heartbeats later, I understand.

Hunter's eight-pack abs are rolling up and down while he grinds himself against the air. Each and every ripple of his muscles is highlighted for the camera as he bends down so low the hollow of his tight backside is peeking from the top of his skin-tight work jeans, covered in filth and absolute sin as he raises his body and lifts a hay bale. Before the clip ends, he pokes his head around the side of his tractor and winks at the camera, looking the viewer up and down in a way that makes me feel like stabbing the eyes out of anyone who's watched it.

"Sixty-four thousand views?"

Too many eyes to stab.

Molly snaps her fingers in front of the phone screen. "You okay, hon?"

She slowly retrieves her phone and slips it back into her pocket, biting her lip.

"You didn't know he filmed those, huh?"

But I can't respond.

"Well," she finally says, "now you see who you're competing against. He has the credentials, he has the followers, and he bought James a Dunkin' Donuts gift card, so you've got some work to do. Now, we're going back in there, and you're giving Claudette reasons you should be the top choice, so I can beat James, got it?"

Molly might be as big a bitch and a fake as me. But that doesn't mean everyone will be. *Land the job. Start your new life.*

We enter the room again, and I can faintly hear the end of a conversation between Hunter, James, and Claudette, which is awkward, even if I'm not still thinking about those videos of him half-naked on the Internet. Or why he's doing that. Who he's doing that for.

Does he spend time with any of the women who watch them?

My stomach feels queasy.

"And they say it never hurts to show up for the community, so that's my life's work," Hunter says, and I almost cackle. Show up for the community? By filming videos for the Internet to ogle? Sure, bro, sure.

I've been thinking my new bitch program needs steps. Step

one is not to say everything I'm thinking. Especially not that. So, naturally, I roll my eyes at Hunter instead.

He narrows his in response, because apparently my judging his half-naked extra-curricular is offensive to him.

Whatever.

"I know what you are now, Hunter. And I won't be fooled by your buttery smoothness." I cringe.

Shit. Why did I say that?

"My buttery smoothness?" He grins, making me grind my teeth and shoot him a death glare. "By all means, tell the interview panel how smooth my butter is, Dev."

Molly chokes on her drink, sharing an inquisitive look with Claudette. But my eyes never leave Hunter's as I find my seat. "I'm going to win this job," I whisper to him as I lower into my chair.

He seems surprised by that. "Oh, yeah? What am I, then, Miss Winner, in addition to buttery smooth? Isn't that how you put it?"

"A player," I deadpan. "Not much has changed, I guess. Has it?" I don't mean to sound saddened by this revelation, but I'm a shit actress when it comes to hiding things from Hunter, and he probably would have felt it even if I pretended.

He looks like I just shot his dog. Which I didn't think would make me feel like I just shot my dog too. And now I feel like an asshole, and everyone's dog is dead.

See what I mean about not saying what I'm thinking? Yeah.

"Ehem," Molly clears her throat and laser beams her eyes at me, "I was just telling Claudette about your charity idea, Devyn."

"You were?" I say, turning my body decidedly away from Hunter's.

He scoots his chair away from mine too, and while I thought that wouldn't affect me, my heart crumbles a little, like a road that can only take a few more bad storms. And maybe that's exactly what my heart is.

"The Charity!" Molly repeats, abrasively enough that I stop letting what Hunter's thinking distract me and slap my news anchor face back in place. It might be the fake me, but at least it's a me who isn't totally affected by Hunter Isaac and… hay bales.

"Oh, yes," I say, "the charity. We were thinking about doing one…" I look at Molly for more guidance, but she looks like she's about to pop a gasket if she loses to James, so I just wing it. "Whoever gets more money for their charity…gets the job?"

Molly's eyes are wide now, but she's smiling and nodding with a twinkle that says she likes this idea a whole lot more than whatever her original plan was. James isn't concerned, go figure. But he has moved on to bigger and better things, such as his Sargento cheese stick. Who knows how long that will keep him occupied.

"I like this idea," Claudette finally says. "But we need some rules."

Hunter isn't smiling anymore. He's kept the same stone cold, neutral face since I called him a player, and even though I think it was justified—I mean, just look at the evidence all over the Internet—I also think I feel bad.

"Rule Number One," Claudette begins, "you must use your existing social media platforms to promote your charity so we can follow along and track your progress."

"Shouldn't be hard for Playboy over there," I mumble. I expect Hunter to tousle my hair or elbow me. To say something snarky. Anything. But he doesn't, and I feel uncomfortable with that.

Regardless, he's my competition. I must think of him that way, and only that way.

"Rule Number Two, you will have exactly three months

to promote and conduct your event. Rule Number Three, you must hold your events in the same area on the same day for us to get accurate results where marketing and audience statistics are concerned. You are from the same hometown, so that should be easy enough."

My eyes widen, but Molly shoots me a glare that says to keep my lips sealed, so I do. I don't know why I keep trusting her, but so far, I'm failing on my own, and I need to learn to trust someone if I'm going to get where I want at this company.

"At the end of the three months, we will all fly out to Forest Prairie—"

"Pine Forest," Hunter and I reply in tandem. The whole room falls silent while Molly, James, and Claudette exchange glances. I shift my gaze to Hunter, but he averts his eyes, and suddenly I feel like someone stole the wind from within me. Deflated my lifeboat. I'm sinking.

But no! This is *my* interview. *My* life.

We had our chance. And he proved that when life got tough, he could move on from me however easily he wanted to. However much it broke my heart. Now this? This is *my* chance.

I turn to Claudette and clear my throat, outstretching my hand and giving hers a quick, firm shake. "It sounds perfect. I can't wait to show you just how much money I can raise with the Classy Country image in mind. You won't regret it."

"I bet I won't."

Hunter, who's been dead silent since I called him a player, finally perks up and pastes on the most fake smile I've seen since my own damn face on last week's news. I'm almost charmed myself, but only momentarily because when he speaks, I remember how much I hate him.

How cocky and full of falsities he is. How easily he lies, and how pretty it sounds when he does it. I want to clobber Hunter Isaac.

"Miss Claudette, thank you for the opportunity to put my little program on the map. I'm honored. I'm already working with the youth rodeo team, and Classy Country's designs can be featured on our competition wear and merchandise." He leans in and pulls a handkerchief out of his stupid T-shirt pocket and wipes at the non-existent sweat on his brow before lifting the hem of his shirt, waving it in and out and showing more skin than I feel was legitimately necessary for the temperature.

"It's hot in here, don't you think?" He winks at Molly and James and then turns to me, licking those lips like he seems to fancy doing.

I can play, too, Isaac.

"That's awesome, Hunty," I say, my words dripping in sugar. He tries not to show it, but I get the satisfaction of seeing the cringe sweep across his features. He hates when girls call him Hunty, so Hunty it is. "I'll be at the fair working on my charity, too. Guess we can see once and for all which of us is better."

"Oh, Little Devy Campbell," he twists his lips, eyes glinting in mirth, "you said that once upon a time at a lemonade stand, and I'll be the first to remind you, I won that day." He twists his chair to face me head-on and places his hands in front of him on the table. "Bet I'll win this time, too. It just feels like tradition, ya know?"

At that, I place my hands on the table to mirror his body. Everyone is still present in the room, but I'm not paying attention to everyone. I'm only paying attention to the cocky-ass cowboy in front of me. "You won't beat me with a bunch of stupid horses and ropes."

He grunts. "And I suppose you'll be winning with the Little Miss Rodeo pageant, then?"

I hate him so freaking much right now, I don't even think twice about my answer. Sure, why not? I'm a national pageant queen. I won the Little Miss competition for three years running. I headed the charity council for years before I moved away. It's not like they would turn me away if I asked to help this year. Especially if I come bearing exclusive Classy Country patterns to use. What better way to show Claudette what I can do than by dominating at what I know best?

"You better believe it," I say. "And my multi-talented girls are going to put your little pony riding babies to shame."

We both just stay like that for a minute, breathing the fire that has been scorching between us for a decade, waiting to consume its other half.

I hate Hunter Isaac.

No. That's a lie.

I hate how he makes me *feel*.

"Sounds like you're up for playing dirty, Dev," Hunter finally says so low that only I can hear him. "Lucky me. I like you better that way."

He sounds angry and wanton at the same time. Like he isn't sure whether he wants to hate me or date me, and I breathe in his scent on a gasp. Seems we aren't so different, then.

I don't respond, though. I have better things to do than let Dustin's stupid friend—the same boy who rubbed his body in sugar water and let the hummingbirds feast from his abs for homecoming king votes—weasel his way into my thoughts and intimidate me. I need to keep my guard up and get to work if I want to beat him. And I cannot and will not entertain being with him.

Ever. Again.

After we nail down the details of the competition, we all stand and make our way out of the suite. Molly grabs my hand before I leave and squeezes it. "It really was great to meet you in person, Devyn. I'll text you later."

I smile, but I'm suddenly not so sure how I feel about Molly. Or any of this.

Hunter walks a few paces ahead of me. It's weird now because lots of emotions and feelings and words happened back there. Buckets of unspoken things were splashed about, and before I can process them, I need space from Hunter. I can't be three feet behind him walking to the parking deck.

We enter the elevator together, which is even more unnerving because now it isn't just the two of us and our thoughts. It's the two of us, our thoughts, and his cologne permeating the only air I can breathe until we reach the lower deck.

"I hope you know what you're doing," he says, leaning against the elevator wall with his arms crossed.

Jerk.

"I do."

"Well, I guess I'll see you around town, then. You gonna stay with Dusty?"

"Shana, probably, not that it's any of your business."

"Oh?" He wrinkles his brow in confusion, but I'm not sure why. Shana is my best friend for all of time. Of course, I'd stay with her. I mean, I haven't asked her yet. Hell, I didn't know about going home until two seconds ago when Molly concocted the plan, but of course it'd be Shana's.

"You can stay with me. If you need to."

"Why would I do that?" I say before I can stop myself, true to Devyn fashion. "Sorry. I mean, no. I think Shana's would be most appropriate."

"Most appropriate? Who are you, Mary Poppins?"

"Shut up. You know what I mean."

This elevator is taking forever, I think, as I avoid eye contact with him. *Jesus, take the wheel. Or the pulley system…or whatever makes this thing move and move it faster, please!*

"Look, I just think it's a horrible idea, okay?"

He scoffs. "You can't just deny me when I offer you a place to stay and tell me it's a horrible idea, Devyn."

"But it is."

"No, it isn't."

"Yes, it very much is."

"Why?"

I heave a most annoyed sigh. At least I hope it sounds as annoyed as I am, so he gets the message. I am not going into this with him. We can't be together. He knows why. He knows what we've both been through. We can't return to the past. There's too much pain between us…pain that quite frankly took enough out of me the first go-around, and I won't stand here explaining this to him because fate stuck us in this strange vortex of chaos together!

"Stop it, Hunter. We're competitors now. And honestly? I just want this job. So, stop flirting with me, and start competing if you want it, too."

He whistles and rubs the back of his neck. Then I notice he's been holding the elevator stop button this whole time. We haven't been moving. I step closer to him and box him into the wall, raising my chin and looking him square in the eyes. I'm not falling for him this time. I'm not getting myself hurt again. We can't be. Just when I'm inches from his face and his eyes shift to my lips, I shove his arm away from the wall and release his hold on the stop button.

When the doors open, I rush out, but he stops me, grabbing my hand and turning me around. The wrinkle in his forehead says plenty. He's hurt. I hurt him. I can see it on his face plain as can be that he thought I was going to kiss him.

And even though I'm the one who knew it wasn't going to be a kiss, it still hurts me, too. Hunter stiffens and stands taller. He puts his hat and glasses back on like we didn't just share the most awkward last hour together and nods.

More pieces of my heart crumble away, knowing he'd have kissed me back. He'd have taken my hair in his hands and threaded his fingers through like it was some sort of handle he'd placed there himself just for moments like this. But we both know very well how that ends, and I'm sure he's realizing it too since I'm watching his face the moment he shifts. He goes from heartbroken to heartbreaker in a matter of seconds when he, like I do, puts his fake-self back in place. He gives me a onceover and releases a breathy laugh before he shakes his head like he's realizing the same things I've been thinking. Then he gives me that cocky sideways smirk that apparently over sixty-four thousand women get to admire daily via their social media subscriptions…*still too many to stab.*

I fiddle with my key fob as he throws a Pine Forest Rodeo Team hoodie over his upper half, which is good because it distracts me from his lower half. It's a new sweatshirt, crisp and green with bright white lettering, and it makes me smile because it means he bought it recently to support the kids. That's very…grown up of him.

"Devyn? Good luck with the pageant." He winks. "I look forward to seeing how you pull it off."

Chapter 8

Devyn
Thirteen Years Ago

top freakin' out!" I snap at Shana through my teeth. My eyes stalk Shane Porter, the eleventh grader on my brother's rodeo team who winks at me every day when I pass by his locker. Dustin would kill him if he knew he even looked at me, let alone winked. But it makes my heart beat super-fast when he does it. Besides, what my brother doesn't know won't hurt him.

An eleventh grader and a ninth grader, especially one like Shane, who won the Tri-County Rodeo championships two years in a row…it's unheard of. In his freshman year, he beat a thirty-seven-year-old record, too. I'm not in his league no matter how much he winks.

Shana's hands are shaking around her Solo cup because she gets nervous anytime we do anything remotely fun or exciting, but I managed to drag her to the party tonight anyway. She has a thing for someone on the Rodeo team, too. Only she won't tell me who.

"I'm not freaking out, Devyn, I'm just saying that if we aren't home by eleven-oh-one, my dad is going to call your dad, who's going to realize we are not, in fact, in your bedroom watching TGIF, and we will be grounded for life when they both find out where we are." She runs out of air at the end of her lecture and takes a deep breath. "That's all I'm saying, okay?"

"Okay," I tell her. Because it's fine. I have no intention of staying here past eleven, anyhow. I set my cup down on the counter, but then think better of it and throw it away altogether. I'm going to be away from it for long enough that I won't be able to know if someone's put something in it when I return. I didn't want to drink, anyway. Beer is nasty, and I'm here for one thing.

I stand on the hearth and scan the living room, but I don't see Shane down here. Or any of the other wannabe cowboys, for that matter.

"Shana, upstairs!" I shout over the music. She nods and follows me.

I've been around my brothers and his friends long enough to know the hangout spot at Robbie's house, where the party is right now. Robbie's parents are loaded, so there's a fourth-floor renovated attic that is totally soundproof and has a full bar and entertainment system.

Everyone worth knowing at Pine Forest High will be there. And they will be…making out. Or whatever. That's why I'm here.

I want a first kiss.

And if I'm being honest, the boy I'd rather have it with is never going to happen, so before ninth grade gets all crazy, and before I see Miss Priss Lemon Perkins at the regional Jr. Miss Pageant and she rubs her stupid baseball champ boyfriend in my face again, I will have had my first kiss with the star rodeo champion of Pine Forest High.

Take that, Lemongrass.

I know I shouldn't care about this stuff, but I'm almost fifteen and haven't kissed a soul. I'm a minority, honestly, an anomaly. In my friend group, at least. And I'm tired of waiting around for it to happen with someone who's probably off kissing other girls and will never ever think of me that way in one million years.

If I'm gonna kiss someone, might as well be someone I can use against stupid Lemon Perkins.

As we walk up the second and third flights of stairs, Shana gets uneasy. "Devyn, where are we going? The party is down there. The only people upstairs are going to be doing something shady like drugs or…having s-e-x."

"Don't spell sex, Shana."

She's always acting like such a baby, and it drives me nuts. The crazy thing is, she's already had her first kiss.

Again, she won't tell me who, because she's mortified it even happened, I guess. Who knows? Her parents never let her watch cable, and I blame that for her unusual level of innocence in times like this.

Still, she should understand why I need to get this done. "I have a plan, so just relax. Your crush might be up there too, for all you know."

She blushes but keeps her head down while she follows me up the steps.

"I wish you'd tell me who it is. I could see if Dustin could talk to them, and—"

"What are you doing, Devyn?"

"Huh?"

"What are you doing? What's your plan? You're just going to, what? March up there and see Shane and kiss him? All to prove to some dumb pageant queen—"

"Princess."

"What?"

"Princess. You said queen. She's not the queen, because she hasn't won…and I fully intend to win the crown myself, so she's a princess."

Shana stops walking but keeps her hand on the rail until I turn to face her. She blinks at me like she intends to challenge my snooty behavior, but she gives up.

"You are aggravating sometimes."

"My plan is to catch them playing a kissing game, and as long as Dustin doesn't get cut from his shift at work earlier than he's supposed to, I can insert myself next to Shane, spin the bottle just a tad too poorly, and finally get my dream first kiss."

I stare off into the fake sunset to add to the dramatics for Shana, but she does not seem impressed.

"This is a stupid idea," she says. But we keep walking. "I don't even think you like Shane. I think you really like—"

"I can't, Shana. He hates me. You know that. Besides, it doesn't matter if I like Shane or not. He's hot and popular, and kissing him can only help my high school status."

The attic is at the top of the last flight of stairs behind a locked door, but as fate would have it, it is unlocked today. I turn the handle and open the door, expecting to smell pot or beer or something worse up here, but it's neat and tidy, aside from five or six pizza boxes and a few opened drinks on the bar. I scan my eyes around the room, appreciating the layout when I hear Shana gasp beside me.

"Ew. People are humping up here. Let's go back."

"You go. I'm staying. I can tell it makes you uncomfortable, so if you don't want to wait around, it's fine. I'll find a ride."

"Suit yourself," she sighs. "But I'm not leaving you here. I'll be right downstairs waiting. If you don't come back down in thirty minutes, I'll send a hired hit for Shane."

"Shhh!" I whisper and shove her to the door as we both giggle.

I click it shut behind her, only to be yanked back roughly by my hair and pulled into a hard body. My breath hitches slightly, and I tense up, ready to break away from whoever this is that has the actual nerve, but then I recognize the smell of him.

I hate that I like it.

"Ponygirl? What are you doing here?" He scans my body with an irritated huff he has no business huffing, the asshole. "Wearing that?"

I yank my hair free and whip around, shoving Hunter away before he can feel the goosebumps that I loathe come from his closeness. I'm not surprised he made an appearance at Robbie's tonight; I just didn't expect him to come ahead of my brother. They usually travel as a set. Dusty won't be far behind him once the Sugar Stable closes in an hour or so.

Which means I need to lose Tweedle-Dumb over here, find Shane, and act fast on the kissing plan.

Hunter takes in my jean skirt and cowgirl boots and snickers. "You better get out of here lookin' like that, kiddo."

"Don't call me kiddo!" I snap, enraged that he even thinks he gets a say. "You aren't that much older. And I can wear whatever I please, thank you."

I throw my hands on my hips to show him I mean business and he can take his skirt comments somewhere else. I'm in high school now. I'm not the little tween tagging along that they seem to think I still am. I can take perfectly good care of myself, and he and Dustin need to get used to that.

He frowns at my lack of obedience and tugs off his hoodie. "Here. You can wrap this around that piece of fabric that's barely covering your ass." He wraps it around me just like he says and then he ties the sleeves so tight around my waist that my stomach might burst. Or maybe that's just how I feel whenever I'm around him. He makes me so mad sometimes.

I look down at the sleeves dangling in front of my jean skirt and cock my hip to the side. "And what are you gonna do if I don't wear your nasty, smelly hoodie?"

His jaw clenches, and he gets up close and personal with my face. From a distance, I'm sure it looks like we're flirting, not fighting. But then, I never can tell the difference when it's Hunter.

"I'll tell Dusty you're here. Bet he doesn't know, does he?"

I try to hide my reaction, but I suck at hiding anything around stupid Hunter. I guess because, aside from my brother, he's known me longer than anyone. He can tell when I'm lying, and that freaking sucks. It's like having two brothers rather than just one.

Only, that doesn't feel right. Hunter's not a brother. And I don't like thinking of him like he is. Which is why it annoys me when he tousles my hair and keeps his arm around my back possessively as we approach the bar like he very much is my older brother.

"Hey, guys, look who came to hang."

We veer to a smaller hangout area with three couches and a game table in the center. A few people are playing cards. One person is unidentifiable since they haven't unlocked lips with their partner since I entered the room with Shana five minutes ago. Ew. And the rest are a handful of rodeo team members I half know from being around the competitions. Most of them are juniors and seniors, and—

Bless my stars. I smile widely and shove away from Big Brother 2.0 as I lock eyes with none other than Shane Porter.

Hunter
Thirteen Years Ago

Of all the girls to walk into Robbie's, how did it end up being Devyn? And of all the things in the world she could be wearing, why did it have to be a teeny skirt and a top that barely qualifies as fabric? Every single eye in the room is on her, and I don't like it for one second.

She's Dusty's little sister. She's basically mine to protect when he's not around.

Mine.

And it's not the first time that word has dropped into my mind when I've been around Devyn. I shove the feeling deep down every time, though because again, she is my best friend's little sister, and I've known her since she was in Barbie pajamas. It's not a thing you do. You just don't mess with someone that close to you. Someone with so many possible ramifications.

And if we did have something? What would happen if we broke up? Would I lose both Campbells? My best friend, too? I couldn't risk that.

Still, Dusty isn't here, and therefore, per bro-code, she's mine to protect until he arrives.

She could have made the job easier by not being the prettiest girl in the room.

And the least dressed. I sigh and rub my temples as I get the sudden urge to put more space between Devyn and the guys, but before I can, Shane plants his huge ass between the two of us.

"Hey, Isaac, who's your friend?" He lets his eyes roam her body and smiles at her the way I've seen him do to hundreds of girls before. I don't like it. "You're Campbell's little sis, aren't you?"

I don't like it one bit. I especially don't like how pink her cheeks get when he asks if she has a date for the dance yet.

The fuck?

"She does," I blurt, and Shane and Devyn turn to me like they've just noticed I'm here.

"I do?" She folds her arm across her chest.

"You're going with me," I say, because I honestly don't know what else to do. "As friends," I add, feeling like I have to establish some boundaries. If not for her, then at least for me. I'm not sure I should be making my own decisions all of a sudden. I just asked—no, told my best friend's little sister I will go to the damn dance with her.

Dusty's gonna kill me. And Devyn knows it, too, because she smirks and clicks her tongue at me in that sassy ass way I hate that I like.

"You must want your ass kicked. But I'll play." She turns to Shane, and I almost think I see regret cross her face. "Sorry, Shane, I forgot I have to babysit this loser over here." She shoves her thumb over her shoulder at me.

Shane looks confused, but that makes sense. This is all very strange.

"Okay, well…are you two a thing, or…?"

"No!" she shouts before I can say anything. "We're not. We're just friends." she says it the same as I said it a few minutes ago, but it feels like a sting coming from her. I don't want her to think of me as a friend.

But I don't want her to think of me as a brother either, if I'm being honest.

Shane winks at Devyn, making her chest pinken and my knuckles clench. "Well, then, Miss Campbell, we were about to play spin the bottle. Wanna join?"

I don't miss the way her eyes light up at his question. She really wants to play. She wants to play with him. I'm not sure what to do because this isn't a short skirt and I can't just wrap my hoodie around a multi-player make-out game, but I also can't let Dev go swapping spit and getting felt up by guys from the team and not do something about it. Dustin would literally kill me. No, dismember me. Remove my balls at the slaughterhouse and feed them to the pigs.

I shoot him a quick text to see when he's coming, but he doesn't reply before the game begins. Devyn is still wedged between Shane and Garrison, a senior, and I'm on Shane's other side just waiting for this nightmare to end. A few people go, and none of them land on Devyn, but then it's Shane's turn, and just before he reaches out to grab the bottle, I see him wink at her and then again at Garrison.

It happens so fast I almost don't see it.

But I do.

Shane exchanges a look with Garrison, who nods back. You'd hardly notice if you weren't looking, but I'm look-ing. I've seen them use this method before…the pair of them. They'll work together to make the bottle land on whichever girl they want.

It's not right. Regardless of whether a girl sits down to play and wants a kiss, something feels off about rigging it to land on certain ones. It's dishonest.

My hands clench so tight my fingernails are causing bloody little crescents on my palms, but I don't care. All I care about is what happens when that thing stops spinning.

Shane sets the bottle down, and it's not like I can stop him. What am I supposed to say? I'm sweating bullets, but why? I'm pretty sure Devyn wants this fucker to kiss her. She came up here all dolled up looking for precisely him, and she can't even argue that. She talked him up all summer long. It's no secret she's got herself a little crush, but I didn't think she'd be this bold.

I also didn't think he'd bite back. Fuckin' shithead. She's a freshman.

It's Dusty's sister. He's our teammate. She's off limits.

And if she's off limits to me, then she is absolutely off limits to Shane.

I scoff at myself for even thinking like that. Devyn is most certainly off limits to me. And everyone in this room. And as the bottle stops abruptly, pointed at the girl in question, I lose it.

Shane leans in, angling his head, and I see her. She looks at me for one quick moment with a question nestled in her stare. A dare.

And that right there is all I need.

Shane will not kiss my girl tonight.

Abso-fucking-lutely not.

Devyn
Thirteen Years Ago

Before I know what's happening, Shane is shoved to the ground, and I'm thrown to the side of him. My shoes crunch against the floor as I stand, the table flipped, and the bottle shattered all over the floor where two bodies are throwing punches at one another.

I don't even need to see him to know one of them is Hunter. But why?

I don't understand.

I came up here for Shane. I wanted to kiss Shane. Shane wanted to ask me to the dance, and Hunter stepped in the way. Then he blocks my chances at a first kiss with the star of the school?

"She's Dustin's little sister, bro! You can't mess with her," he shouts before throwing a punch into the side of Shane's nose. I hear a gross crack and a growl as Shane spins and shoves his elbow into Hunter's side.

"I don't care whose little sister she is, Isaac. I think you're just jealous she wants some of this," he kicks Hunter in the gut and then rips his shirt off and does a quick belly roll show of his abs while some of the others in the room cheer him on, "and she doesn't want any of that." He gestures to Hunter, who's sadly crumpled on the ground, and I cringe.

Why I care is beyond me. Shane might be as dumb as a doornail…and he's certainly acting like a d-bag right now, but I knew that about him beforehand.

Hunter, on the other hand, has no excuse for his completely immature behavior, coming up here and fighting for me like he's my boyfriend or something.

I pause at that. Because something about it makes me even angrier. And I don't know if it's anger that he acts like my boyfriend or that he isn't my boyfriend. And I hate that. I hate how confusing he always is. Like this summer at the lake when he acted like something more was going on between us, and then became a total ass to me whenever my brother was around.

No, I know where we stand. It's about time he knew, too. "Just go, Hunter!" Both boys stop throwing punches, but they don't release one another as they look up at me. I'm still wrapped up in Hunter's hoodie while I step up on my soapbox to reprimand him. "Stop treating me like I'm your responsibility. I'm not some little girl who needs to be taken care of, and it certainly wouldn't be your job if I were."

Suddenly, the room is dead silent. But the crowd is no longer looking at me or the shitshow on the floor. Eyes wide, flip phones out snapping photos, jaws dropped…they are looking behind me.

"No, that would be my job," my brother's voice booms.

Shane backs off as soon as he sees Dustin. Hunter pushes himself up, covered in blood and bruises, and it bothers me that it bothers me. Screw him for being a caveman; that isn't my fault. It's his own damn fault if he can't handle a guy kissing me.

But it's in the moment he's looking between me and my brother, still dripping in sweat from fighting for my dignity that wasn't even his to fight over, that I realize…Hunter Isaac has a crush.

On me.

Chapter 9

Devyn

"He's impossible," I tell Shana through the Bluetooth of my 2024 hot pink Jeep Wrangler Unlimited that is absolutely the only good thing to come of my news anchor career. I can't say I would have been able to afford this baby before I joined Channel Five, and the materialistic side of me says it was probably worth the sacrifice. This little thing is a beauty.

I know pretty much nothing about cars...*internally,* so to speak. You know, engines and gears and stuff. But I know a ton about color hues. And the shade of pink coating my pretty little ride is Dragon Fruit Sparkle, a limited-edition color that happens to match a real nail polish color available in the Dicon Nails summer collection.

People can call me a ditzy fashion doll all they want—and they have—but I love that I can match my nails to my Jeep, or my Jeep to my shoes, for that matter, and I don't care who thinks it's stupid.

My brother never cares what anyone thinks of him, and whenever I feel down on myself for being too girly or too…I don't know, too me, I remember that about him.

But when I think of him, I think of Hunter.

Just about always.

"I just don't understand why he must pop into my life all these years later and mess with the one thing I want. He doesn't even like fashion! So self-centered."

Shana chokes a bit over the phone, but it doesn't sound like she's eating. *Hmm*.

"You don't agree?"

"Um," she starts awkwardly, "I do agree that it's crazy he popped back into your life and all, it's just…"

"Shana, just spit it out. Rip the Band-Aid off and tell me how it's my fault."

"Devyn, stop." She sighs like I'm exhausting her. People do that often around me.

"Nothing is your fault."

"No, I'm sure it is. It usually is."

The people in my life are always telling me the things I'm doing wrong. But what about everyone else? Yes, I left. But I came back. After a shitty fucking year, I might add. And they can think they know what went down all they want, but nobody ever points fingers at their own faults. Where were any of them when I returned and needed love and hope and home?

I slam on my brakes as I realize I'm at a stop sign. It's a new one that never used to be there, and it caught me totally off guard. This is Mullins Road, named after Albert Mullins, the town founder who emerged here in 1922 and built the first convenience store off the main road.

Mullins Road was always a straight through with a yield sign on the cross street. I could have caused an accident with the car in front of me at the new four-way stop if I'd been any less aware.

"Are you okay?!" Shana yells into her phone. I must have screamed and not realized it. For a second, there, I was gone, encased in a memory I've buried as far down as it will go.

"I'm fine!" I say, taking a few deep breaths. "I've been gone for longer than I realized." I finally pull forward, slower now. "When did they put a four-way stop at Mullins?"

"Um, six years ago?" she muses. She can't even remember. That's how long it's been since I've been back home. Shana and I have seen each other only three times since then, and every time, she's come to me. Because I'm a terrible person. Again, the realization hits me of what I need to work on in life.

The leaves are grasping at orange and pink, because it's early September and school's already begun in Pine Forrest. I smile as Shana goes on about something I should really be paying attention to as a new and improved, non-bitchy person, but I'm not. I'm thinking about how it is back home this time of year. Spring chickens will finally be laying cartons of eggs, rodeos will be in full swing every weekend, and the Sugar Stable will be the place to go on a Friday night after football games for some shitty burgers and a strawberry shake.

These are the reasons I miss home.

"Can you hear me?" Shana shouts. "I don't know if your phone is breaking up, or you're just doing that daydreaming thing you do. Did you hear me ask where you're staying? I'll come by and get you later for drinks so we can catch up in person. There's some stuff I think you should know, Dev."

I pause, mulling that over. But before I can even process, my mind snags on what she said before. About where I'd be staying. I'm five minutes from her doorstep, but I never asked her.

I just assumed.

Oh, my gosh, I really am a self-centered bitch.

"Um, I was going to stay with you?"

"Oh," she says. That's all. Just oh.

Shit.

I look in my back seat. I didn't exactly pack light. I thought I'd have Shana's whole guest room to stash my stuff for a few months. Does she not *want* me to stay with her?

I should have asked.

I tense, readying myself to break the silence, but thank God she does it for me.

"I want to say yes, Dev, but there's…" She pauses again.

What the heck?

"What are you not telling me, Shana?"

"What? No, it's just…dang it, Devyn. Don't hate me for not telling you sooner. It's just, there isn't much you can do from out there in the city, anyway, and you always seem to have a lot going on, so I…I didn't want to burden you with the news."

She sounds like she's about to cry, and it breaks my heart because something is going on, and my best friend in the world has been holding it in because I'm busy.

"What's going on, Shay?" My hands grip the steering wheel tightly, but before she can tell me, I hear a loud honk coming from behind me, making me jump in my seat.

"What is—"

Honk. Honk, honk, honk, honk!

"Really? Shana, I'm so sorry. This feels super important, but some asshat in a white Ford is laying on his horn to get my attention. Pick me up at Dustin's later, okay? We have some catching up to do. In person."

"Sounds good, Dev. I'll see you tonight. Say hi to Hunter for me."

I barely have a second to reflect on the end of that before I jump again, my ears ringing.

Honk! Honk! Honk!

Seriously?

I pull my Jeep over to the side of the road, checking my makeup in the mirror before swinging my door open. This asshole is already on my shit list as I click my matching pink stilettos onto the cracked and weathered Pine Forest asphalt and whip my annoyed-as-shit face around to get a glimpse at whoever needed me to stop everything at their convenience.

And it's him. Just like Shana said.

Of course.

It's always him.

I roll my eyes and brace myself for the fireworks, because here we go again.

Chapter 10

Hunter

Dammit, woman! Just how many times, exactly, were you gonna make me honk before you pulled over?"

"At least you're acknowledging I'm a woman now." She sighs with an air of snobbery that I want to cover with my mouth.

I knew it was her the minute I got behind her car, and not because it looks like Pepto-Bismol on wheels. Because only Devyn Lynn would spend thousands making her car match her nails just to drive around with her muffler dangling by less than a shred of metal.

This girl makes me so mad sometimes. Doesn't she know how dangerous that could have been for her? I suck my teeth because I don't think she does. She's certainly not acting like I've done her any favors, cocking her hip to the side and crossing her arms defensively as if I'm inconveniencing her.

Somehow, I'm obsessed with this woman.

"Last time I checked, pulling over for crazy jerks in pickup trucks who won't stop honking at you was dangerous for girls like me, so you're lucky I stopped at all."

"Oh, dangerous, is it? Kinda like driving around with your muffler two seconds short of falling off?"

She furrows her brows and looks to the side at the pink monstrosity she calls a Jeep, then huffs at me like a horse that finally got broke.

"The muffler?"

I scrub my hand down my face. "For Christ's sake, Devyn, you don't know where the muffler is, do you?"

She scrunches her nose, and it's annoying how cute it looks. "Um, no?"

"Fuck...all right, let me just—" I'm halfway through taking my shirt off when her sass stops me in my tracks.

"Um, excuse you! We are not messing around, if that's what you think's gonna happen while I'm in town. I hope you're aware of this."

"Are you kidding me?" I peer at her through the neck hole. "I'm gonna get under your car, baby, not attack you with my glorious muscles. Don't get your panties all twisted. Unless you like that sorta thing."

"Ew! Glorious muscles? I can't even with you."

"No, I guess you can't, can you?"

Well, shit. I don't know why the hell I said that to her. Fuckin' stupid.

She backs away, and she has every right to. It was a dick thing to say to her, considering everything between us.

"I'm sorry."

She nods, casting her gaze away from mine and slicing little cuts in my heart.

That's my own damn fault.

I move past her to get the ramps from the back of my truck. I don't normally have these in here, but I feel a smile tug at my mouth thinking about how Aunt Sarah used to say, *God knows when you need intervening.*

Last week, my pal Bobby's car needed some work, and I loaned him these ramps. I picked 'em back up a few days ago, just hadn't gotten 'em back out of the truck yet.

Aunt Sarah would say it was divine intervention, God putting us back in the same place together like this. To face our issues and…then what? Come together again?

I'm a God-fearin' man and all, but I'm not like…I don't believe he's got an individual plan for each of us like some do. What about choice? Devyn didn't choose me. She *couldn't* choose me.

But she could now.

If she wanted.

We're not the same people we were as kids. Could it be that simple?

I wish Aunt Sarah were here to answer that for me, and I feel that painful tug in my chest being reminded that she isn't. Even if she were, she'd give me some rhetorical or metaphorical bullshit, anyway.

You'll know what's in your heart when you start paying more mind to it, that's what she'd say.

Right now, my heart's outside of my chest, Aunt Sarah. It's five-foot-seven with blonde hair, a spattering of pink everything, and eyes that shine like emeralds when she's mad.

Yeah, she's what's in my heart, all right. I just need to unfreeze hers. And who better to unfreeze it than the asshole who put the ice there in the first place? If I can just convince her to give us another chance.

I toss the shirt at Devyn, and she catches it. A smile pulls across my lips and warmth floods me with that one action of hers. She doesn't totally hate me. She watches my body while I get down under the Jeep and check why the muffler's come detached. I wouldn't exactly say that I'm making a show of working just for her, but I might flex my arms more than necessary. Just a little.

"Are you sure you know what you're doing down there?"

"Do you?" I ask from under the Barbie-mobile. Seriously, even the metal on the undercarriage is rose gold. I smirk at how simultaneously stupid and cute that is, but I give her shit all the same because I can. "For a girl who spends money on a ride to be custom made just to match her life aesthetic, you sure don't take very good care of it."

"First of all, not a girl. I'm a woman, as we've already established on more than one occasion. I'd prefer not to see you regress, thank you very much. And okay, so I didn't know about mufflers. Most people don't! How do you even know? Is that something else you film in your undies for your little page?"

She might think it stings, but it doesn't.

She's always been a tease, and I've always liked it.

I roll out from the Jeep and meet her stare with a lick of my lips and a onceover of her sassy little body just to make her squirm like I know it does.

"You're suddenly so concerned with the amount of clothes I wear on the Internet. Jealous, baby?" I wink at her, snag my screwdriver, and roll back under the Jeep before she can reply. "It's not my real job, by the way," I shout from under the carriage. "It's just a side hustle. I learned to work on cars and tractors on my farm."

"Your farm?"

And that, right there, puts our situation into perspective. She's been out of my life so long she doesn't even know about my life's work. Shit, the whole town knows about Friendly Farms. It practically *is* the town these days.

"Yeah, I, uh…have my own little stretch of land now, just

past the Presley ranch. You know the one, that bend by Piper Creek?"

I can't see her, but I hear the gasp, the wonder in her voice, and that wonder pulls at every bit of hope I have for us, for every bit of hope I've had this whole time she's been away.

"That old farmhouse that was back there. From when we were kids…is that…you actually bought it?"

I roll out with the muffler in hand and rise to my feet to look at her, really look at how fucking beautiful Devyn Lynn is.

"I did."

I turn away from her. I can't see her face. I don't want to be disappointed by her reaction to something so important to me. Those are memories and feelings I won't give up even if she does want them back.

"What are you doing with the muffler?" she says from behind me. I walk to the bed of my truck and place the muffler into it. She follows me and pokes at my shoulder.

"Earth to Hunter! Helloooo. The muffler? Will my car be okay without it attached?" She eyes her Jeep with concern, and it's cute that she thinks I'm letting her ride away in that, so I give her a few minutes to live in that fantasy before I burst her bubble.

"Nope."

"Nope?"

"You heard me."

"Well, how am I supposed to get home, then?"

I stop and turn to her.

"Home?"

It seems like we stay locked in each other's gazes for a full sixty seconds while we both muse over the word *home*…and its possible meaning.

"Yeah, um." She fiddles with the balled-up T-shirt I'm pretty sure she forgot was mine. I can't help but smirk at that.

She can keep it, for all I care. I wish she would. "I'm staying at Dustin's, I guess."

"What happened to Shana's?"

It's kind of cruel that I ask because I already know. When she initially mentioned Shana's as the place she'd be staying, I realized she didn't know about Shana's dad. I have no idea why she wouldn't tell her best friend about Randall's stage four pancreatic cancer, but it seems Shana has some secrets she's been keeping.

And it's not my job to spill them. So, since I don't know how much Devyn knows, I tread carefully with the information I have.

"It seems Shana's spare room is occupied. I don't know. I'm catching up with her later at Cowboy's Paradise. Anyway, is my car okay to drive, or do I need to call an Uber?"

I whistle through my teeth at this little princess. She never ceases to amaze me with her bullshit. "You musta been gone way longer than anyone realized. You know better than to think there's a ride share within fifty miles of this town."

"I just assumed you guys had risen to levels of advanced civilization by now." She puts her hands on her hips and lets out a groan as she looks to the sky. "Whyyyyy?"

I swing the passenger door of my truck wide open and nod at my girl. "Get in, drama queen."

"You wish. My days of climbing in your truck are long gone."

Is that so? "Well, go on, then, take your chances hitchhiking out here so far from town. Sure hope you don't end up abducted and put in a box under some creeper's bed."

"Oh, fuck off, Hunter." She stares down at her phone. "Google says it is fine to drive within thirty miles, but to get the vehicle serviced at the soonest possible time thereafter. Looks like I'll be driving myself to my brother's. Not in a box."

I stomp ahead of her and block her way to the Jeep, because there is no way in hell she's driving that thing all the way to town with the emissions blowing back at her.

"Seriously, Dev, you could get carbon-monoxide poisoning. You're not driving it."

"Really?" she asks, nose scrunched as she scrolls through her phone to confirm the validity of my statement. "I don't see that here in the article. It just says—"

"Cut the shit, babygirl. You and I both know there ain't a chance in hell of me lettin' you drive yourself away in that poison pumping gob of bubble gum, and there isn't a chance in Heaven that God didn't put me here in the same place to help you out, so just pop your trunk so I can get your bags and get in my damn truck."

She looks mad as hell, but damn, it's sexy.

"Fine."

"Fine."

Fine.

Chapter 11

Devyn

Don't smell his shirt. Don't smell his shirt. Don't smell his shirt.

Ohmygod, that smells so good.

Fuck.

Chapter 12

Devyn

"I can carry my own bags, you know." I roll my eyes because I certainly don't at all enjoy watching Hunter hoist a third Classy Country zip-up tote onto one of his biceps. It can hold a lot of weight. It's really freaking strong.

As thick as my thigh? Quite possibly.

Moving my eyes down to *his* thighs, I appreciate just how much he's changed since we were teenagers. He's Hunter, but he's so much more now.

He's all man.

And muscles.

With a farm.

I stare at the boy I once loved, no longer a boy. He's a real-life cowboy. Just like he always said he'd be one day. And that makes me so damn happy for him. Maybe this is pride?

Pride and lust are feeling like sisters right now, though. It's hard to tell them apart while he keeps making semi-grunting sounds in his throat that I'm not even filing away in my sound bank for future sordid purposes *at all*.

Two more bags go on his other arm, and he pulls me back to the real world.

"Babygirl, I'm not sure you can carry your own bags when you're too busy checkin' me out to realize I've emptied the whole trunk already."

Shit.

He walks toward the house, but not before he gives me one of those thirst trap winks of his, and I'd be lying if I said it doesn't make me really freaking thirsty.

I need him to leave so I can be far enough away from him to remember to stay Far. Enough. Away from him. I shake away the goosebumps he just caused and pray my body behaves as I follow him up the stone path to Dustin's front door.

A smile breaks across my face when I take in the front porch. Some things never change. The door is still bright red. My brother liked how it made the house pop. It was the first thing he did when he bought the place at eighteen. He and Hunter were roommates at the time, and it was covered in take-out boxes, protein powder, and empty bags of Doritos. It was pretty disgusting. I only saw it a few times before I left for the city.

Dustin's made some updates to the place over the years. They take my breath away. It's the new siding, the picket fence that lines the perimeter of the tomato plants, the wraparound porch that was most definitely not there before…*damn, this place looks good.*

I walk in behind Hunter who seems to act like he still lives here—*great*—and just waltzes in without knocking. Before I know it, we're standing in the living room and Hunter's chucking my bags onto the floor by the sofa. I stand in my brother's house, wide-eyed and breath stolen from me as I take in the gorgeous mahogany flooring and pinstripe siding beneath pristinely painted white chair railing.

Did my big brother do all of this?

"Yo, Dusty!" Hunter shouts, breaking me away from my daydream yet again. "Found something that belongs to you on the side of the road!" I punch him in the arm, and he snickers.

"What? It's true…not my fault you seem to find yourself in messes on street corners lately."

"You asshole." I punch him again. I think he likes it.

I think I like that he likes it, smiling at me with those bright blue eyes, winking at me again like he's lost his damn mind. It makes me smile back.

Shit, shit, shit. He's the enemy, Devyn, Get your shit together and enemize him!

Okay, I know it's not a real word, but it's my new mantra when it comes to Hunter. I need one. I need an anchor before I get pulled all the way under and love how fast I drown.

Enemize. *Enemize.*

"If I recall, you are the reason for my mess on the First Street corner, and—"

"Ew!" I suddenly hear from behind me.

"You're not home even five minutes and you're already crawling out of this asshole's truck?" Dustin teases.

"That's not—"

"And I do not need to know about whatever messes you guys are making together on street corners."

My face heats, and I'm about to go full-blown bitch on them for ganging up on me, but then they share a look that I'm all too familiar with, and my eyes widen as I start to back away.

"Oh, no…don't you two even think about it!" I shout, looking around for something I can use against them. Nothing practical seems to be near, so I grab a pillow and start slicing it through the air like a sword. "I'm stronger than I look these days! I take Pilates!" But they don't care. They never have. They know they can overpower me, and just like that, I'm transported to my childhood when they go from both sides and squish me in the biggest hug I've ever felt, throwing our heap of bodies onto the couch.

"Devyn sammich!"

They proceed to tickle the shit out of me until I'm laugh-crying, kicking, and swatting.

"Not fair. You two are solid muscle!"

But they don't stop.

They never did.

Dustin gives me a shit-eating grin from my pinned stance beneath him, then pulls me up and into a real hug. "I'm glad you're back. Welcome home, sis."

I stay in the comfort of my brother's arms for a moment, and for once, I do feel at home. With Dustin…and Hunter.

Why do I feel so weird about that?

"Thanks for the ride, Isaac," I make a point of using his last name to keep it casual, even though it feels far from where Hunter's involved. "I guess your friend will just call me when the Jeep is ready?"

"I'll bring it to you."

I fiddle with the cuff of my cardigan and look at my brother, who quickly averts his gaze and beelines to the kitchen. I guess he thinks I want a moment alone with Hunter.

Maybe I do? Fuck, this is already getting complicated.

"Devyn?" Hunter breathes so quietly I can barely hear him. "I've missed you."

And then he's gone. He says bye to my brother, gets in his truck, and drives away, leaving me to stand here with his smell all over me and his declaration ringing loudly in my ears.

I've missed you, too.

Chapter 13

Devyn

I always thought coming back home would feel overwhelm-
ing, but honestly? It's the opposite. I worried being around
these people and the associated memories would cause
some sort of cataclysmic explosion that'd knock the wind right
out of me, but that's not been the case at all.

I can finally breathe. And breathing, instead of suffocating
for once, is much preferable. I inhale and fill my lungs with
the smells of home.

Manure smells.

Farm smells.

Flower smells.

I tear open the guest room curtains, and I'm pleasantly
greeted by the endless rows of wheat as far as the eye can see. The
sun touches the tips of the grass horizon as dusk creeps in, and
it charges me in a way. I'm refreshed, eager for what's to come.

Springing onto the guest bed, I fumble through the notifications on my phone. I haven't looked at this thing since I

hung up with Shana on Mullins Road, and like, one-million-and-two people have sent me things.

After a couple of minutes sifting, it's mostly just group chat messages from Channel Five that I forgot to remove myself from. I tap on the photo attachment and see it's an announcement from Chad, an anchor I dated for a few months before leaving the station. He was nice to look at, but he was equally gropey and full of himself. He also checked his reflection more than I do, and that never would have worked for us long term.

I didn't really grieve our breakup, so to speak. It was mutual. But I still stall when I read the cutesy pastel banner—*Chad and Brittany's Baby Shower!*

They are getting married next month; they tell us in the text that follows.

Wonderful for them.

Not only is that just *wonderful for them*, I think as I gag myself, but it also means they were likely screwing around while I was with the jerk in question.

I twist onto my stomach and shoot Chad and Brittany a quick, "Congrats," that's not a lie, but also not sincere. What I should do is tell them I have syphilis or something. That would serve him right for sleeping around.

Upon further consideration—and self-reminders of the Bitch Program—maybe it's best to remove myself from the group chat altogether. It's annoying getting a million dings back-to-back about stupid stuff, anyway.

Distractions seem to come in bountiful amounts here in Pine Forest as it is, and my most recent one is still lingering in my mind.

God, he's so much prettier to look at than Chad.

Hunter Isaac, the boy who threw sand at my face and pulled on my ponytail.

'*Breathe, Ponygirl.*'

Who knew he was going to be about eight thousand muscles hotter than he was when we were kids?

Newsflash—I did.

There's an inside scoop for ya. I knew he'd be everything, and that's why I stayed far away for all these years.

But not far enough away from his social media, apparently. Because before I realize what I'm doing, I'm typing in his name and scrolling through his posts.

Oh, my God, he's fine. If he could just leave shirts off altogether, the entire female—and some of the male— population would be cured of depression. He's a shot of dopamine in a tall, dark, smooth-talking son of a glass that I want to drink all the way up.

I tap on a video of him with an axe on his shoulder and roll my eyes. *He would.* Still, I snuggle down into the mattress as I watch him slowly move his hand down the handle. He caresses it like…like it's my skin.

Before I know what I'm doing, my hand is under the covers, fingers trailing up my thighs just like his move across the smooth wood of the handle. His fingertips brush the part of the axe where the metal wedge meets the wood, and with great precision, he takes his other hand and *licks his fucking palm.* His eyes never leave the camera, and I swear to God when he winks, it's for my pleasure alone. I gasp when he slaps his hand down hard on the side of the wedge, and then he swings the axe above his head, giving a clear show of his triceps, ridges and all, before I hear the smack of the metal on the wood pile beneath it.

My hand snakes between my legs. But it is no longer my own.

It's Hunter's.

His arm muscles bulge as he slams the axe into the wood, splitting it in two. He pries the pieces open, inspecting the slit like I want him to inspect me. Between my legs. I whimper, hanging my head back. My eyes close, and I'm wholly given in to my fantasy as I pump my fingers inside myself, swirling slick circles over my clit—and it's him—Hunter. He's on top of me, his hand over my mouth with those piercing blue eyes of his, blazing into my very soul and embedding themselves there. As if they finally found their way back home. I gasp as he licks the shell of my ear and whispers in that deep, rumbling voice that haunts my fantasies, "Look how well you take me, babygirl."

My legs tense, my core pulses, and before I know it, I'm breathing in quick gasps, as I come so hard, I swear I see stars. Stars and planets and entire galaxies. All for him.

I just did that, I think, staring at the ceiling fan and lying there with Hunter's video on the mattress beside me. In my brother's house. On a bed Hunter most definitely uses as a crash pad often, based on the decor around the room I'm just now taking in. Oh, my God…this was *his* room…when he lived here. *His. Bed.*

Shit.

A knock sounds at the door, and I know it's Dustin. I scramble to get my dress tugged down and hop off the bed, closing out of Hunter's TikTok and praying to God my brother didn't hear and know I was watching one of them.

"Hey, Dev, want some chili?"

I pull open the door and smile awkwardly. "Sure, I'm starved."

I make my way past him, but before I reach the stair railing, he grabs my wrist and twists me back around. His eyebrow rises, just the one, and I know he knows. "Are you catching feelings for Hunter again?"

"What? No!" I shove away from him and continue my walk to the kitchen so he can't see my face. And the lies written all over it. "He was just helping with my car, and we're doing this work competition thing now, so—"

"Then why are all of his videos getting liked by you back-to-back?" He holds up his phone.

I whip around to face him with my hands on my hips, not bothering to look at his phone of lies. "That is both none of your business and wildly untrue."

"You're into him," he deadpans, towering over me at six feet and looking me in the eyes. "Just admit it so we can all avoid whatever shit show's gonna happen when you don't. And keep in mind, he's had a whole life here without you in it. You may be surprised by what you find."

"I'm still not *catching feelings*. And there wouldn't be a shit show. You're being dramatic."

His eyes go wide, and he laughs. "Okay! Fine, don't listen to me. I'm only the one person who knows the two of you better than either of you will ever know yourselves. And I'm the *one* person who knows you both never stopped obsessing over each other like dumb, lovesick puppies or some shit. It's actually super gross, and you should fucking thank me for even caring because the last thing I wanna see is my best friend all over my sister, you know? But you're both adults now, so honestly, I just want you both happy. And if you're both gonna be around here all the time again, you're going to need to talk through some shit with him first."

I huff at that. "One of us is an adult, you mean. The other one gyrates to Luke Combs songs while he shovels horse shit, is what it looks like."

My brother's jaw sets. He doesn't seem to like that, a wave of serious energy replacing our earlier banter as he looks to the sky, like he's praying for help. And in this part of the world, that means someone's only got but a few more fucks to give you, so you better listen.

"Sorry, go on." I drop my shoulders, meeting his stare.

"You need to admit you still have feelings for him, Dev. Hunter already has."

I pause. I was prepared to listen to what he had to say, but that? That's his grand piece of wisdom? That's bullshit.

He wants me to admit it. *Admit* it? Admit that the one man I've always loved has been here getting hot as fuck and putting on little muscle shows for women on the Internet while I was off reinventing myself in a new school, a new city, with no friends, divorced parents, and made to dress, act, and behave like everyone's pretty little princess—all while getting over fucking heartbreak? Let's just throw in an eating disorder for good measure, but I'm supposed to just be okay with it all now because time has gone by and this cowboy with a Chippendales complex makes my hoo-hah tingle?

No.

"Whatever, Dustin. I can't do this right now." I walk away, but he stops me. He pulls me into a hug, and I hug back. I have to. It's my brother. I know he just cares, even if he really doesn't get it like he thinks he does. And he really does show it when he chews his bottom lip and sighs like he wishes he could fix it all for me. It's a sigh I've grown to know over the years. Because he does love me. Dustin's always been in my corner, even when things got seriously messy way back when.

"I know you haven't had it easy. Trust me, I know. I was there, remember? I just want you to be happy. And Hunter's my best friend," he says, steering us to the breakfast nook. He pats the chair beside him, inviting me to sit. "He's a good guy, you know? He's changed a lot. He's grown up, he even raises—"

"It's fine, Dustin. Just stop."

He listens.

And I don't sit.

Until I do.

We eat our chili in silence for a few minutes, but what he said is itching at me. Catching feelings for Hunter is a horrible idea. Because when you love someone the way I love Hunter, you only end up torn and destroyed when it inevitably ends. And I've got to protect my heart this time.

Because I do love him. Not because I don't.

And he should do the same.

We both need to focus on the competition. Which reminds me, I need to get hold of Clara's number and see about getting involved in the pageant. I don't seem to have a working number for her in my phone anymore, which is weird. I could have sworn it was a landline.

"Dustin, do you happen to have Miss Clara's number?"

His eyes go wide like he's seen a ghost.

Oh, no. My heart stills. She isn't…

My brother scrubs his hand over his face and furrows his brow. It tells me the answer before he even voices it.

"Clara died five years ago, Dev. She was surrounded by her whole family, but you know, she was eighty-two."

"Eighty-two? There's no way." I shake my head in disbelief. Tears are starting to pool in the corners of my eyes, but I hate crying in front of people. I won't do it. I push them back until they sting, but I don't let them fall.

"Yes, Dev. You've been gone ten years, you know?"

And that stings worse than the tears. It stabs me raw right in my gut, because while I've been off getting manicures and attending social events in the city, trying to make a name for myself that would shine so bright I'd forget how much I hate being me, trying to destroy Devyn Lynn so I didn't even recognize her, Shana was hurting, Hunter was changing, people were dying, and I've not even been aware.

"What about the pageant?" I suddenly blurt through my anger and sadness. "Who runs it now?"

I know from the look he gives me that I'm not going to like his answer, and when he confirms my suspicions and says, "There is no program anymore," that sadness and anger and excitement and confusion that have been swirling inside of me since Hunter Isaac spilled my stupid macchiato on that street corner come crashing together in the cataclysmic explosion I'd warned myself about.

Then it hits me.

Good luck with the pageant. I look forward to seeing how you pull it off.

Hunter Isaac isn't playing by the rules. He's playing dirty.

What he doesn't realize, though, is that two can play at that game. And if he wants dirty, he hasn't seen a thing yet.

This cowgirl's about to get filthy.

Enemize.

Chapter 14

Devyn

Why didn't you tell me they transformed Cowboy's Paradise into a badass nightclub, Shay?" Shana's curly brown hair bounces in waves down her back as I follow her to the dimly lit booth on the dining side of the new…*rave hall,* it seems.

Cowboy's Paradise used to be a hole in the wall bar that only locals knew about. The seats were that sticky kind of plastic that you try not to think too hard about if you're gonna eat without barfing.

This? This is not Cowboy's Paradise.

But it is.

There's the cowboy boot the original staff hand-signed when the bar opened years ago, under a glass display by an axe throwing station that used to be the rusted gumball machines that routinely stole your quarters. This is more what paradise should look like than the alternative I keep recalling. Looking around for merely a few minutes already tells me a ton of money went into the renovations here. There's an entirely new sound system, new flooring, paint, beautiful glass panel roofing over the center of the building lined in petite fairy lights just above the dance floor, and the most spectacular difference I spot is the *life*.

There are locals, yes, but also professors and students from the college an hour north of us, and other random faces I can only imagine must be tourists.

Tourism was shot when we were growing up. The railroad line that used to go through Pine Forest was out of commission for decades, and there wasn't much to bring folks out to our little town aside from those who traveled in the rodeo or racing circles.

This place must bring in bank for our town.

"Wow, Shana. This is insane!"

We're seated and given actual menus. They used to be crumbled and grease-stained card stock. "Who funded all of this? What happened here?"

Shana's cheeks redden. Her complexion is a lot like Bella's from Classy Country, aside from the red hair, that is. Shana's is a deep, silky brown, but she's just as pale as Bella, and all her emotions tend to show when she blushes.

"All right, what aren't you telling me?" I level, but we're interrupted by—

"Lemon?" I don't mean to sound mortified, but I'm taken aback. The last person I thought I'd run into today was my childhood nemesis serving me food. Wasn't an ex-boyfriend enough for one week?

"Hey, Devyn!" Lemon says, much too cheerily for being, well, Lemon. It's not normal.

I clear my throat. *It's just Lemon*, I remind myself. I'll deal with her, and then get back to why Shana is being weird.

"It's good to see you," I force out.

I eyeball Shana awkwardly, but she's just smiling brightly like this isn't super uncomfortable. *What the heck?* I turn back to the strangely welcoming Stepford Lemon and clear my throat again. "We'll just take water, thanks."

I smile and turn back to Shana, effectively dismissing Lemon.

Or so I think.

But she doesn't leave. She and Shana share a wide-eyed look before they both burst out laughing, and then Shana scoots over for Lemon to—*sit.*

With us.

I'll wait. Surely, they will explain their…closeness.

But they just stare at me and smile. They smile like they're—

"You two are friends now, aren't you?" But I already know. I moved away, and I was replaced. By Lemon Perkins.

And Shana doesn't know how to tell me.

First Hunter, now Shana.

Lemon probably lives in the spare room and that's why I can't stay. My skin prickles and my fingers toy with my wrist to find the hair-tie I know will be there. The one I put there for purposes like this. I find it and pluck, the sting that usually calms me doing quite the opposite right now. It spurs me on.

"You could have just said something on the phone when we were talking, you know?" I spit out, before I can remind myself of Step One of the Bitch Program—not saying everything I think right when I think it. "You didn't have to lie to me. I thought something horrible happened."

I suck in a quick breath, trying to calm myself down, but failing, my mind spinning circles of words around on a wheel that only seems to grow larger with time and never ceases to slow down. Words like unworthy, fake, bad friend, *bitch.*

I swallow, my eyes swerving between the two of them and landing on Shana like a dart. Meant to pierce.

"You sounded like you were going to cry on the phone, Shay. And I was all worried about you. You made it seem like someone was dying." Shana's face sours, and Lemon's eyes widen, shifting back and forth between us, as if she's concerned.

I'm aware, as my tear ducts burn with promise, that much of my anger is laced with emotions entirely unrelated to Shana and Lemon and more assuredly stemming from my dealings with Hunter, my learning of Clara's passing just another pin in the cushion. I wipe my hand across my eyes, hiding any evidence of imperfection.

And right now, the hair-tie and the other stupid tricks are not enough. I should stop myself before I say something I shouldn't, but I'm a fully-fledged bitch, remember?

"I was so worried about this mystery of yours, and here you were just afraid to tell me you have a new best friend. Or maybe roomie?"

Who also happens to be the worst, most evil version of myself. Someone who made life a lot harder than it needed to be when we were younger.

Shana knows all about my issues with Lemon, too.

That's what hurts most. How could she?

She furrows her brow, like she's disappointed in me. Maybe I deserve it, but I don't know. I'm too sad to know. I don't have a place here, any more than I did in the city.

I breathe through it because no matter what, there's nothing I can't handle. Strong women don't give up. That's what Miss Clara used to tell us girls. If I'm going to have a change, I must make the change myself. I wipe the tears from my cheeks and stomp away before I can say more bitchy things. Before I'm too close to them to hide my feelings. I really am trying to be a better person, despite how I behave when emotions take over.

"Devyn, you don't understand. It's not even about Lemon. You're being dramatic," Shana shouts. She keeps going on, something about me never listening and always making everything about myself, but I can't hear her over the pounding in my ears. I'm so angry, but it's not even at Shana.

It's at myself. I'm so fucking sorry for myself, and I hate it.

What right do I have to feel sorry for myself?

I made myself this person.

Tears bead like glass over my eyes as I think about the girl with the long, unbrushed hair, who used to ride horses barefoot through the dandelions as a wannabe cowboy chased behind her with a water pistol on his hip. *I won't give up. I'm still that girl, aren't I?*

Storming through the dining halls, I push open the double doors underneath a blazing Exit sign. But it isn't to the parking lot.

It's to the bar.

I don't normally drink, but I'm damn sure drinking tonight.

I click my hot pink Jimmy Choo kitten heels across the floor and march straight for the bartender. He holds his head back and checks me out, but not sexually. I know that look; he knows me, somehow. But not like people in the city do. Not because I'm micro-famous, or whatever people are calling it these days. Their word, not mine.

No, he probably knows me from here. Home. I squint, scanning my memories. He does look familiar, but also not.

"Devyn?"

"Yeah, yeah," I say, waving whoever-he-is off, "good to see you again, too. Look, what's a super strong drink?"

What's-his-face hesitates but finally answers me, "Whiskey?"

"I'll take that," I say confidently, even though I've never had whiskey before. "And keep 'em coming."

I hand him my card to start a tab, and he takes it, but super-duper slowly, still eyeing me the whole time like he's waiting for something.

Weird.

I swivel around on the stool and watch the crowd. I recognize half of these people, and it's so damn awkward as their eyes take turns picking me out, the look of discovery on each one of their faces like old wounds cut back open. Their knowing stares are half the reason I left this place. I wanted to be alone.

You are never alone in a small town. Everyone is so damn nosy. A few are pointing and whispering. Some are flat-out staring at me. This used to happen in the city too, but it was because they recognized me from TV, not because I was some blast-from-the-past car crash that made local headlines and gossip trains for years to come.

Someone clears their throat. I turn my head a bit to see it's just Jeremy, returning with my drink.

Wait, Jeremy?

"That's who you are!" I say, spinning around with a smile. The first genuine smile I've felt all day. "You've changed so much, Jer Bear!"

He places the whiskey in front of me and wrinkles his nose, much the same way I'm doing to him.

"I was about to be offended if you didn't realize it soon, babe." Jeremy makes his way through the opening of the bar and pulls me in for a bone-shattering hug. He may have lost a hundred-something pounds, but he still hugs like he hasn't, squishing me in his tight embrace.

"What the heck happened to you, Jer? Someone kidnap you and feed you a liquid diet?"

He gives me a sassy look and rolls his eyes as he goes back behind the bar and makes work of sorting receipts. "It was honestly a lot like that, yeah. My partner, Corbin, and I did this healthy booty camp thing. It was mad expensive, but his company paid for half of it as some sort of health insurance write off." He sets up a pirouette and ends it perfectly with a cock of his hip. "As you can see," he gestures down his body, "it totally worked, and I look irresistible."

"You looked perfect before the weight loss, too." I really mean it. Jeremy is a beautiful soul inside and out. He was the best male cheerleader in our high school, even if he was the only male cheerleader. He emceed all the county pageants, and he was also in every one of my classes since kindergarten and was there for me when not a lot of other people were. We used to share loads of gossip. And anyone would be lucky to be with him, no matter what he weighs.

You know that one friend you have that you can just exist around, but it never feels forced or planned? And when you catch up, it's on a deeper level than most? It feels like old and new coming together. Effortless.

I tell him about Lemon and Shana, and how Hunter screwed me over with the pageant, and he tells me all about his honeymoon in Cabo, which sounds like everything you could want and more. But after a while, he has to help some customers, so I turn back around and sip my whiskey, feeling slightly better than before.

Whether that's because of Jeremy or the whiskey, I'm not sure.

But the longer I sit by myself, staring into the lights reflecting off the metal jukebox across from me, the longer I think maybe it's the whiskey. And maybe I'll just rehash my entire night and pick it apart obsessively.

I might have been wrong about Shana. I might have been a bitch.

Okay. Upon further inspection of my words and actions, I was a bitch. To her and Lemon.

So what if they're friends? I should be fine with that. Am I really so insecure that it would bother me for my friend to have someone to confide in and hang out with? I don't even live here. I haven't been home in ten years.

Of course, they've all moved on.

It's just…why Lemon? I whine internally, thanking God that at least in my own thoughts, I'm allowed to be mopey about it without anyone knowing. I'll have to apologize to them both if I want to be the better person I claim I'm trying to be, though.

Just as I'm thinking about closing my tab and finding Lemon and Shana again, someone taps my shoulder. I'm feeling pretty good from just the one drink…was it one?

And someone smells pretty good too, as I turn around to face him.

"Hi," I beam. Hmm, I think I'm beaming, I might be tipsy. But he's beaming.

A man, five years or so older than me, I don't know…maybe more—tipsy age is questionable—anyway, he's right here in front of me.

"Hey, there, lood-gooking," I say. And then I face-palm. "Ohmygosh, I mean good-looking."

His eyes crinkle at the edges when he laughs at my joke. I bite my lip, embarrassed by my slip-up, but also taken aback by how handsome this man is. He smells nice too, like fresh linen and mint. He holds his hand out to shake. There's something familiar about him.

"You're lood-gooking, too, Devyn Campbell."

I offer him my hand, but instead of shaking it, my body heats all over when he presses my skin to his hot lips. Things are a bit wobbly as several thoughts rush into my head in one single stream.

Have I had too much to drink?

Wait, how did he know my name?

Maybe I should leave and find—

"There you are!" I hear from beside me. And like some sort of magic, Lemon Perkins is perched on the stool beside me, smiling at Mr. Someone, but I don't think it's sincere.

"Isssnot sincere, is it Lemon?"

"Excuse me," she says to the stranger who might know me, "I have some personal business to discuss with my associate here. Will you please leave us?" She bats her long eyelashes at him.

She's so pretty. And I feel really bad about earlier, so I just have to tell her.

"You're really pretty. I didn't drink lemonade when we were kids because I hated you so much, but I actually love lemons. They're yellow and bright, like your haaaaair! Ooh! Is that why they named you Lemon?"

"Oh, my God, Jeremy!" she shouts, climbing over the bar like she owns the place. Maybe she does? "How much did you give her to drink? Jesus, she's drunk as a skunk!"

"I am not! I had one whiskey."

"Three," Jeremy interjects. Lemon and I shoot him a glare, probably for different reasons, but he just shrugs and sips his water through the straw.

Lemon huffs and throws her hands in the air. "Well, there ya go!"

"I jusss don' drink much." I shrug, searching the room for the handsome man in plaid who Lemon just scared off. He did look familiar, but doesn't everyone here?

"She's a lightweight. It makes sense now," Jeremy says, giving Lemon another reason to swat his shoulder.

"Ow! It's not my fault. She asked for something strong."

Lemon sighs and turns to me, rubbing her temples. "This was probably my fault. She never did get to order any food before I ran her off."

"What did you want to say to me?" Now that I've had a moment, I'm feeling a lot more lucid. I take the water she shoves my way and sip it. "Can I have some French fries, Jer?"

"Cheese?" he asks me with a sympathetic smile, and I nod. He's a good man. There are good people here I forgot about. And that makes me sad again.

"Look," Lemon says, twirling a straw in her own water glass from across the bar. I remind myself to ask her if she does, in fact, work here later. "I'm sorry we bombarded you. Shana was afraid you'd hate that we've become close, but I told her we were just kids back then. It was a stupid pageant rivalry. I don't even do pageants anymore. I mean, I know you did for a while there and all. Congrats on the whole Miss American Rodeo thing, by the way. And Devyn?" she says, biting the edge of her lip and looking away. "I'm sorry I shared your secret with everyone way back when. It was wrong of me to use that against you for the pageant. Blaming it on being a bratty teenager feels like a cop-out, but I hope you'll give me a chance to show you I'm not that girl anymore."

I look up at her from under my bangs and see she's gen-uinely smiling.

"Thanks, and I'm sorry for throwing a tantrum like a child. I was wrong. Shana's allowed to have friends who aren't me."

"Shana's been through a lot lately, you know? Becoming friends was just a bonus, but being able to stay at her place and help take care of her dad is the only way she isn't drowning."

Lemon's going on, but I stopped listening.

"Wait, what do you mean, *take care of her dad*?"

Lemon's face pales. "You don't know. She hasn't told you yet?"

I'm mad right now. I'm *really* mad. And I'm worried. I don't like how tight my chest is. How out of control I feel. And I definitely lose my shit a bit when my stupid hair-tie snaps in half with the force of my tug and falls from my wrist to the floor.

I'm the last person in the room to know what's going on with my own best friend.

"What is going on, Lemon? Tell me straight."

"Ugh, this is awkward and HIPPA-violation-y now, but *shit*." She blows out a huge gust of air, her words rushing out like a wave. "Randall has cancer. I'm a nursing assistant. I moved in to take care of him. He's stage four, Dev. That's…" Her eyes shift to the ground. "He's not doing well."

"What?"

I don't know what to say. I'm not super close to Randall, but it's still Shana's dad. I grew up with him always being there. Being fine. Spitting lines of Shakespeare to us over breakfast pancakes when I'd stay the night. Vibrant. *Alive*.

Not dying.

My sorrow right now is wholly for my best friend who has been dealing with her father's declining health, in her own home, for who knows how long.

"He has a year or less. She didn't want you to think she needed you. Kept saying you had enough problems."

"Lemon, what I said to Shana about someone dying…I didn't know. I feel so—"

"I know." She places her hand on my shoulder, coming around the bar to sit beside me. "Shana is fine. She went home after she sent me in here to check on you."

"She did? Why you?" I stumble on my words. "Sorry, I didn't mean it like that. It's just—she knows how we used to be."

"Because I understand what it feels like to be isolated and misunderstood. After what I did to you in junior year, I lost a lot of friends. All my friends." She turns away slightly, maybe not wanting to meet my eyes. It's not exactly an apology, but I can't be sure with Lemon. Not this new, strange, different Lemon who honestly seems like someone I wouldn't mind being friends with.

"I deserved to lose friends after what I did. I've never been proud of kicking you when you were at your lowest."

I hold up a hand to stop her. Not because I don't accept her apology, but because that past, the one I thought was scarred over and covered up, keeps getting poked and prodded and reopened the more time I spend here in Pine Forest, and honestly?

It's exhausting feeling sorry for myself.

I shove the twentysomething French fry into my mouth. They're so warm and crunchy. I didn't realize just how hungry I was.

Maybe it's time to put rivalries in the past. I could use someone on my side right now. Lemon twirls a straw in her clear, plastic water cup that I'm pretty sure she just stole from behind the bar and filled up herself, and I find myself entranced by her, in awe of what time can do to people and relationships alike.

"If Shana thinks you're good people, you probably are," I say, earning an ear-to-ear grin and a squeal of delight from Lemon, who is bouncing up and down on her toes.

"Jeremy," she yells, "we need a round of truce shots."

"You don't mean to tell me that Lemon Perkins and Devyn Lynn Campbell are calling a truce? This is worthy of Paradise pinkies!" Jeremy shouts the name of the drink into a megaphone, and the whole bar erupts into applause, chanting, "Pinkies! Pinkies! Pinkies!"

"What's a pinkie?" I ask. But nobody tells me. They just smile and nod, like they can't wait for the fun to begin.

I'm suddenly regretting remembering Jeremy.

Looking out into the crowd is always how I've grounded myself, and this time as I look out, I see that man. The one from before who I called *lood-gooking*. I mentally roll my own eyes at myself. He really is, though. That isn't whiskey goggles talking. The French fries seem to appreciate him, too. He's built, with broad shoulders and tanned skin. Blue eyes, like someone else I know.

He sees me, and my heart skips.

"He looks just enough like him." I don't mean to say it out loud, but I'm thinking that didn't work out how I intended because Lemon's looking at me like I have three heads.

"What?" She whips her head in the man's direction. "You mean Garrison?" Lemon shakes her head. "No, that is the worst idea possible for you, babe. Trust me."

"That is *Garrison*?" I rub at my eyes, thankful for smudge-proof setting powder and waterproof mascara, as I squint for closer inspection purposes. "There is no way that pimply heap of skin and freckles grew up to be *that*."

He looks like Hunter on steroids.

The crowd rumbles as Jeremy comes out from the back with two pitcher sized goblets on a silver, mirrored platter. "What do you mean, he'd be the worst possible decision for me?" I ask as I watch Jeremy work.

He's fancy with his bartender moves, slicing strawberries and popping bottle caps into the air.

Casting another quick glance in Garrison's direction, our eyes meet, and he cocks his head at me in invitation.

"He seems good enough for a one and done to me."

"You're bad!"

Lemon slaps me, like we're friends. Maybe we are? I smile, but only just a little, keeping up my walls and all.

"Still, can't you find someone else? He's—" she pauses, "well, let's just say I know stuff about him. He's battling demons within his soul that no woman can fix. He's broken, Dev. And he just drinks his days away. Barely even takes care of his farm."

"Who cares when it's a one-night stand?" I argue. "Did he kill anyone?"

"No."

"See! It's fine. Besides, he has to look right for me to get this out of my head and move o—"

Whoops, I've said too much.

"Has to look right for what?" Lemon eyes me suspiciously, but of course she already knows. I try to avoid the subject either way.

"The pinkies!" I say, changing her focus to the obnoxiously large beverage before us. I'm sort of confused why they aren't, well, *pink*, but the cheers from the crowd get louder, and I certainly can't ask Lemon over the noise.

We each have a giant blue drink that's a mix of rum, grenadine, and fruit. Jeremy lights the liquid on fire then throws a handful of cinnamon on each drink, making the flames spark up around us and the crowd roar.

It reminds me of the Fourth of July. The display of lights and colors, while the whole town surrounds one another and cheers for the sake of cheering.

The crowd whoops and hollers before they break off into a mix of line dancers and table minglers, and finally, it's just Jeremy, Lemon, and me as our drinks light the bar. And when we pour the lemon juice Jeremy gives us into our drinks, they turn from blue to bright pink before the fire is extinguished. We clink our giant glasses together and chug them down.

Then, Lemon Perkins and I do something we've never done before.

We hug. And it feels right.

I peer into the sea of tables resting beneath the neon lights, and somehow, I already knew who I'd see in the far-right corner beside the pool tables. He doesn't look my way, and that annoys me. He knows I'm here. The whole bar was just chanting our names so loudly, he couldn't have missed it.

I shouldn't care. I won't care. He didn't care when he tricked me with the pageant.

I continue to feed myself lies, but we all know I do care. It's Hunter. And I have some lessons to teach him. Then a light bulb sparks as I realize Garrison might be able to help me teach those lessons. But first, I'll need bait.

"Hey, Lem? Wanna dance?"

Lemon smiles at me and links her arm with mine.

"I thought you'd never ask."

Chapter 15

Hunter

I'm not an idiot. I know what she and Lemon are doing right now. I know they're trying to get me worked up dancing all over Gary and his friend. Devyn, rubbing up on him in her tiny fuckin' dress and legs for miles. His hands on those legs.

I grind my teeth, flicking my gaze when I see her look my way. She can dance on him all she wants. I'm not playing her games. If Devyn wants my attention, she can come get it.

I'd give it to her freely.

At least, that's how I wish I could react, but I can't keep my cool if he keeps touching her like that, getting more handsy by the minute, rubbing across her hips and thighs while they sway to the music. He spins her and throws her into a pathetic excuse for a dip before pulling her up and barely managing to get her steady again.

Lemon doesn't seem impressed by him, but that's because she knows him like I do.

He's a snake. And I wish I could say it was his own damn fault, because it's not like he was a saint when we were kids or anything either, but it isn't only that. I'm unfortunately tied to Garrison Presley in a way I wish I never was. In a way where he and I understand one another.

And I'm pissed at Lemon for not steering her clear of him to begin with. She might have had a rivalry with Dev when we were kids, but she and Shana are thick as thieves now. Come to think of it, over the last few years, she's become one of my best friends too. She wouldn't mess with Devyn like that.

Still, it doesn't seem like she's done a very good job of warning her off him. Probably hasn't gotten stubborn-ass Dev away from him long enough to listen.

She knows nothing of my history with that man. Of the way he took his own tragedies and allowed them to harden over his heart, taking his pain out on the community who tried to offer him a helping hand. And he made it clear to me how he feels about my family. My name.

But you don't get to take your anger out on others. Not when everyone's out here fighting their own personal battles in this little town and finding a way to get by.

To love.

A community I'm trying to rebuild while he continues to do stuff that puts us right back where we started. Hell, I could throw that asshole out of here right now if I really wanted. I own fifty percent of this bar, after all. Because it brings tourists here, which brings patrons for shops, gas stations, hotels, and more. Our town lights up on the map now, when before nobody knew its name. And the money I make from my investment profits? I pump it into the community farming program.

Devyn has no idea that this fucker shoots his animals up with steroids or cages them inhumanely. She doesn't know how he lets his waste run directly into the spring that contaminates everyone's drinking water, with no repercussions because he's the governor's nephew. Doesn't see how he treats his own kid. I don't even think Garrison can see it through the liquor that's probably replaced the blood in his head.

But Devyn just sees a pretty face willing to spin her around on the dance floor. She has no fuckin' clue.

She seems into him.

Oh, hell naw.

I stalk to the dance floor, tugging Lemon away from Garrison's creepy friend.

"Thank you." She lets out a sigh of relief. "That guy was so gross. His hands were sweaty." Her nostrils flare, and she shoots a quick glance at him over her shoulder, shuddering.

"Just what the hell is the princess thinking?" I ask Lemon in a hushed whisper. "And what are you doing letting her feel all over him? You know what he is to me."

Lemon shoves me away from her face but keeps dancing with me for show. "It's your fault, Isaac. Don't blame me. If you weren't such a liar, letting her believe the pageant was still a thing, she wouldn't be all hellbent on finding someone who looks enough like you that she can—and these are her words, mind you—fuck you out of her system."

My mouth drops open.

"She's gonna…what? With him? He looks nothing like me!"

"Um…" Lemon hesitates and then sucks air through her teeth. "Yeah, he really does, hon. Like, your identical twin or something."

"Evil twin is more like it. Please, Lem. You have to help me get her back. She can't fuck my evil twin."

Lemon thinks, tapping her purple fingernail to her chin and chipping away at my patience with each long, agonizing second. She's as bad as Dev.

Are all women born this sassy or is it just the ones in my life?

"Come on, Lem, please!"

"Do you still love her?"

"What?"

"Do. You. Still. Love. Her?" She claps…annoyingly, I might add. "It's a simple question. And it matters because I'm not wasting my time or Devyn's helping you if it's just for shits and giggles. She can have a fling with Garrison if that's the case, and everyone will be better for it."

"He can't have her," I growl, and I can't rightfully tell you what's taking over me, but the thought of her with Garrison Fuckin' Presley makes me want to knock him the fuck out.

Right here. Right now.

Him and his stupid sweaty-handed friend.

"She's mine."

Her violet eyes light with a twinkle. "That's what I needed to hear." Lemon pats my shoulder, reining my neanderthal in a little. "I'll help you. But we do it my way."

I hesitate. Lemon's ways are usually unconventional. But what choice do I have?

"Deal."

She smiles and moves aside, giving me full access to Devyn and the asshole known as Garrison Presley.

"You need to swoon her," she says. "She doesn't know what you're like now. She remembers the boy who wasn't in a good place when she left. She remembers someone who got under a lot of women to get over her." She casts me a knowing look and offers a small smile. A smile that pierces me with guilt.

I never fucked Lemon Perkins, Devyn's childhood rival. Just made it look like I got with her two best friends from Valley High right after Dev left.

And when she came back.

I recognize I didn't handle the breakup well. I was fucking seventeen. I lost just as much as she did that day. I didn't have any other options like she did.

I've changed.

Lemon places her hands on my shoulders and fixes my shirt. It's a T-shirt, so I'm not sure what there is to fix, but she seems to find quite a bit, fluffing my hair and then tilting her head for a final inspection before she nods in approval.

"Good. You're all set. Now, go woo her!" She turns me around and uses all hundred and ten pounds of her tiny five-foot-two body to shove me in Garrison's direction.

Lemon's a boss.

"Garrison." I announce myself, earning a huff and a nod from the man of the hour.

"What's it to ya, Isaac?" The edges of his lips quirk up, but he sighs as if I'm inconveniencing him. "Crop season been good?"

Devyn stops dancing but doesn't move from Garrison's side as she eyes us back and forth cautiously. I wink at her and watch the pink spread across her cheeks, and that gives me every bit of motivation I need, because it means nothing's changed. Not really. Not when her body says otherwise.

"Crops been fine. I got a different problem right now, Gary. I'll be plain and simple." I cock my head to Devyn. "I need a word with my girl."

Devyn gasps, her eyes widening to huge discs. Garrison shifts his gaze back to her.

He steps forward, handing his beer out to Devyn like he's plum ready to fight me for her, and my skin prickles with the challenge in the air. He knows it, too, lifting his chin in invitation because the bastard thinks he can bait me.

She doesn't take his beer, though. She purses her lips, narrowing those forest-colored eyes of hers. She doesn't want to be on my side, but she so the fuck is.

Because she doesn't want me out of her system.

"Come on, man. Doesn't have to be a fight, Gary."

Wouldn't be the first time I took a punch in Dev's honor, but I clench my own fists at my sides and force my body to keep them there. I'm no longer that kind of man. And he hasn't really disrespected her honor.

But it's Garrison, and he doesn't give a shit what I say. Once a teammate, someone I swore to stand beside, he's nothing more than the town drunk now. His nostrils flare, and he stalks toward me, rearing back, and I decide I'll let him. If he wants to, I'll let him.

I tense my face as his fist swings out and slams into the wall behind me. "You look like your fuckin' brother."

"Whoa, whoa, whoa!" Devyn interjects, throwing her body between us and shoving us apart, Garrison's chest heaving possibly as fast as my heart. "I was having a very nice time with…" She eyeballs Garrison and squints for a moment.

"Sorry, man. Looks like she doesn't even remember you. Can't say I'm surprised. I hardly recognize you either, these days."

I grab Devyn's hand and tug it lightly. "Come on, Dev. Have drinks with Lem and me. We'll catch you up on—"

"I'm sorry, what?" She tugs free from my grip. "You come over here like some sort of caveman talking about crops, like a touch-her-and-die romance, and all of a sudden, I'm not allowed to fuck who I want?"

"Fuck?" Garrison chokes on his drink, and then smirks triumphantly. "Your girl, Isaac?"

I shoot a look at Dev, pleading with her through a mind-channel only she and I seem to share, but she's got my damn number, twisting her lips into a coy little smile and linking her arm through Garrison's, even though she knows good and well she's not going home with him tonight. I see the game she's playing.

What she's forgotten is how attractive I find just about anything she does. Including throwing herself at another man who—I clench my jaw even admitting it in my head—looks like me.

I'll play along. I look her straight in the eyes and turn my mouth up in amusement. Her eyes widen, but the slight parting of her lips when she looks my way and the twinkle lighting up her eyes tell me her anger is thickly coiled in an entirely different emotion altogether.

One I have every intention of exploring.

"You aren't gonna fuck him, and you know it," I whisper as they meander back to the dance floor. I try my best to ignore the intentional sway of her hips, taunting me and ensuring my eyes follow her every move.

As much as I hate seeing her within the slightest proximity to Garrison Presley—or any other man, for that matter—I can't deny how much I love this little game she has going on.

Because I see right through it.

She's teasing me.

And that means she wants my attention. Whether she realizes it or not, I've already won.

I'm still smiling wide like this is the best damn day of my life. And that right there makes her madder than hell, huffin' and puffin' like she always does when she's worked up. I love it. Probably why I fuel the fire.

"You never did like it when someone told it like it was, did you, babygirl?"

Devyn spins on her heel, hair whipping against her face. "Stop calling me babygirl!"

She licks her lips, narrowing those sexy little eyes to dangerously sharp green points.

Come at me, they say.

We find ourselves in these standoffs far too often. Always have. And I'm gonna do now what I always did then.

Fight for my girl.

Thirteen Years Ago

et home now, or I call Dad." His voice shakes the floor. So much that people have started coming upstairs and peeking in from the doorway.

Dustin turns away from his sister, who's tugging on my hoodie like it's her lifeline. It only makes me want to hold her, but that's what got me into this. I was right. I shouldn't have been making my own decisions tonight.

My best friend is solid muscle and force. The fact Shane even thought it was a good idea to try anything when he knew Dustin would find out eventually, is beyond me. He looks at my bloody face, and the hoodie around Devyn's waist, and his eyes narrow.

I don't think my secret is a secret anymore.

But he doesn't call me on it. No, he turns abruptly and gets right up in Shane's face. Shane looks like he might shit himself, and I would, too. Shane might be older and the best on horseback, but my boy, Dusty? He's got anger issues and a juvie record. Granted, it was only six months, and the bully he got in trouble for putting in his place had it coming. My man might have anger issues, but he's fair.

Fuck around and find out, they say. That's Dusty.

He looks between Shane and Garrison and rolls his neck so every pop is heard by the whole damn room, and then his voice is low. It's scary. I kind of want to be his sister, too. Nobody'd ever mess with you.

And that's what he reminds us as he slams his fist down on the bar top and shoves his way to the center, taking his time circling the room and making careful eye contact with each and every one of our teammates.

"If I catch any of you fuckers so much as breathing in my sister's general direction ever again, mark my fucking words, I will put you in the ground."

"How could you!" Devyn shouts from across the room. Tears run down her pretty face, washing her makeup off in streaks. But she's still the most beautiful girl I've ever seen.

Dustin whips his angry glare toward her, and I can feel the energy coming off him in waves. He's rightfully worried. There are some shady guys on the team from not-so-great upbringings. Devyn loves with so much of her heart, but you can't just trust everyone in our little town. Dustin…well, he and I both, we've always protected her from that, even as kids.

I feel kind of sorry for her. She shouldn't have been up here, no. But she's not a little kid. Not in the way her brother just made her feel. If I'd told her how I felt by now, she'd already be with me.

Tears like those would never touch her face.

"Not a single fuckin' one of them is good enough, Dev," Dustin spits out, disgusted, it seems, that she'd even consider it. "And if you don't get your ass home—"

But she cuts him off before he finishes, slamming the door to the hangout.

Dustin rubs his hand across the back of his neck, kinda like how my dad used to do before he'd rip us a new one. He chats with Robbie for a bit, gesturing to the table we just shattered.

They must come to an agreement, because they bump hands before Dustin makes his way back to me.

"Thanks for looking out for her." He helps me to my feet. I pull my shirt off with a groan that I feel over my whole body and wrap it around my busted knuckles. There are little pieces of glass embedded in my fist, and no matter how I hold my hand, it's going to feel like hell until they come out.

"Shiiit." I wince. "This is all my fault."

"Your fault? Are you kidding me?" Dustin squeezes my head in his hands and checks my eyes, like he's worried I'm concussed. I might be. Shane hits hard.

"I should have taken her downstairs the minute she showed up. I thought I could protect her, ya know?"

Dustin furrows his brow like he's holding something back, and it isn't the first time I wonder if he doesn't know my secret.

That Devyn is more than just his sister to me. So much more. Even if she can't be.

Even though I know that.

"Why'd you hit him?"

I open my mouth but don't immediately answer. We both just let the silence sink in. It does a good enough job of saying what I can't seem to get out in words.

The room has cleared out now, and it's just Robbie and a few senior girls from the cheerleading team, cleaning up the glass and wooden splinters I created. Dustin clears his throat, breaking our silence.

"Did he kiss her?"

"He would have."

"And would that have been so bad?"

"Bro." I step back. "It's Devyn…and Shane!"

"I know." Dustin smirks. "But I'm her brother. I'm supposed to wanna hit a douche like Shane if he tries to kiss my sister."

I look at him.

Yeah, without needing to say it, he knows.

I always felt like letting that out would feel huge. A secret I've kept since we were kids.

I'm in love with my best friend's little sister.

"You knew?"

"For pretty much ever. No ten-year-old boy in his right mind gives away that many of his holographic Pokémon cards to a girl without motive."

That makes me laugh. Yeah, I did that. And I'd do it again.

Truth be told, I'd give her anything she wants.

"So…" I clear my throat, avoiding as much eye contact as possible and pretending to inspect my injuries.

Shit, this is so damn awkward.

"Go get her," Dustin says.

"You won't put me in the ground?"

He shoots me a glare that tells me maybe he will if I don't stop while I'm ahead, so I throw out my palms.

"Just needed to double check. I kinda like it where there's oxygen and all."

Dustin laughs, running a hand through his hair.

"You're my best friend." He wraps me in a hug and squeezes my shoulder, looking me straight in the eyes with green ones that match hers. "Just don't break her heart."

I bro hug my best friend tighter than I ever have before, because he knows, and he gets it. He knows how much I care about Devyn.

And soon she will, too.

I run down the stairs, out the front door, and onto Robbie's street as fast as I possibly can.

"Devyn!"

I spot her a few mailboxes up and run ahead, but she keeps a steady pace, putting considerable distance between us.

"Devyn, stop! Can we talk?"

She whips around and stalks toward me with full force, and damn, I thought she was gorgeous before, but she lights the world on fire in an emerald blaze when she's angry.

"And tell me, Hunter Isaac. Just why would I listen to a word you have to say? First, you tell me I can't hang out in the big boys' club. Well, newsflash, I'm all woman now!" She yanks off my hoodie and throws it at me, hiking up her skirt as high as it will go without showing her actual private parts, and holy…I hold my hands over my eyes…I mean, I peek too, because we're in the middle of the road and all, and I can't help that she did that, but I wait to really take my hands down until I hear her scoff at me and finally tug her skirt back to a normal place on her thighs.

I run my teeth over my bottom lip and shake my head at her.

"You're definitely not a little kid." I watch my words hit her, lips popping open on a shiver as the wind blows her hair around. "I didn't mean it like that."

"Well, you sure said it like that," she crosses her arms over her chest and takes a power stance that would be hot as hell if she didn't want to kill me right now.

"And you cockblocked me." She huffs.

I choke at that.

It's something I love about her. She's never let being a girl…woman…stop her from doing anything. She's a force who demands to be heard on her own terms, in her own way.

"I…cockblocked you?" I force out. "With Shane?"

"Well, whatever the kissing version of that is." She steps closer, her brow creasing. "You told me you liked me at the lake."

"Because I do," I say.

"Then what's with all the games?"

"I was scared to ask you out." It's true, even if there's more to it than that.

"Scared? To ask me out?" Her brow remains creased, and I can tell it's insane to her that I would need courage for that. But I do.

"I've always needed courage when it comes to you, Dev." We walk in tandem for a moment, and when she grabs my hand, my heart takes over my whole chest. It's warm. It's strength. It feels so damn right.

"Because of my brother?"

I nod. We stop walking to face one another.

They say when you feel something with all your heart, you're supposed to listen to that feeling. I never knew what they meant until this moment right here, standing in front of the girl I've dreamed about my whole life.

"Tell me that if we do this it won't ruin our friendship, Dev. It's not just Dusty I worry about. It's you, too. I can't lose either of you."

"You wouldn't lose me," she whispers. Her lips are right beside mine. So close. Closer than they've ever been before.

I want to kiss them. I want to claim them as mine. I want Devyn Lynn Campbell to be my girl.

"Do it," she breathes.

"But—"

"I dare you."

Chapter 16

Devyn

If Hunter Isaac wasn't six-foot-two with eyes that bore into my soul like ice daggers with one glance, it would be really freaking helpful.

"God, I understand you're trying to get me to learn something and change my ways. You don't throw us anything we can't handle, am I right? But look, I am so freakin' tipsy right now, I actually might be drunk. And I'm so sorry, God. I'll be not-drunk next time, promise. But look, I absolutely cannot be trusted with this plan of yours tonight, so if you could just, like, make him dissipate, distract him with a burning bush or—" *Ow.* I'm jabbed in the shoulder by Hunter's elbow, and I realize God is not, in fact, budging on his plan.

Well, I hope you're ready to pop some popcorn then, Big Guy, because this is gonna be one hell of a show.

"What're you doing?" He snickers at me. I don't like it. We are not on good terms, and he isn't allowed to snicker like we are. So, breaking one of my Bitch-Step Program rules, I say what I think.

"You aren't allowed to snicker at me like we're friends." I sit on the stool, spinning away from him, and fold my hands beneath my chin, my elbows resting on the bar.

That's that.

But then I decide, in my alcohol induced wisdom, that I'm not done talking to him, so I whip back around, using the stool to propel me toward him with emphasis. It makes me kinda dizzy, but it also makes a point, so it was totally worth it.

"And for your informationnnnnn," I drag out the n for dramatic flair, "I was praying for guidance. You should try it sometime."

"Praying?" He laughs. "In the bar? Babygirl, you got your priorities all sorts of mixed up. I don't think the big man's scrollin' through drunk-girl prayers on his iPhone before bed, do you?"

"You said you wouldn't call me babygirl anymore!" I shove his shoulder, effectively backing him up. It's then I notice Garrison is gone, and I whine in frustration. "You ruined my night."

"See," he says, pointing out my whining, "you don't want me to call you a baby? Stop actin' like one." He sticks his tongue out at me like he's ten years old, and I lose it.

"Me? *Me?* I'm acting like a baby? You are the one who went along with the whole charity competition and let me think I even had a shot at my dream job, and you knew good and well there was no pageant anymore. Did you even think about how much it would hurt me to find out like that Miss Clara died? Or are you just a selfish, lying, fake, Hunter Isaac?" I hold up my hand. "Never mind. Don't tell me. I think we both know the answer to that."

Whoops. I stop and inhale sharply as I take in the wince of hurt on his face…and the streams of tears down mine. I didn't realize I'd let them fall.

"I'm sorry. I didn't mean that." I wipe my eyes. "I think maybe this is too much for me." I gesture widely around the room, insinuating it's not just the conversation that's too much for me, but the whole *home* thing in general. And that thought hurts…not having a home. "I'm gonna go."

I wipe my face and start toward the ladies' room.

"Wait, Dev." He scrubs his hand down his face like he does when he's stressed out. How is he stressed, though? This is what he wanted. I walked right into his little game, and the only one who wins from here is him. The friends, the job, my dignity.

"What do you want, Hunter?"

My eyes are brimming, burning to let loose a stream of sadness, loss, guilt, self-doubt that I've carried with me since I left him here all those years ago. And I'm back now. Because he forced his hand in a way that gave our destiny absolutely no other path. I grind my teeth, still trying to keep it together, retain composure. *Like the perfect pretty princess you're always supposed to be.*

Why did he want me back home? Why was it so important he'd lie by omission on the terms of our competition and make me believe I had a shot at a pageant charity, when he knew good and well I'd come home to find it's gone, discontinued, extinct?

And while that thought pains me, the thought that a program that raised me from a tiny junior princess to a reigning national queen and gave me a place to be myself before I knew who that even was…is gone? The fact that all of it is done and over with in this community and other girls won't get that opportunity to shine, all because nobody stepped up after Miss Clara and kept it going? While that pains me indefinitely, what pains me even more is the thought that maybe Hunter brought me back here because he did want me to fail. He does just want the job. It is just a competition, and I am his enemy.

Maybe it had nothing to do with his feelings for me at all.

I couldn't stand it if that were true. I might be able to perform a skilled level of emotional masonry, packing brick by brick into place around my feelings for Hunter and everything we've been through, but I can't stop how much it would hurt if I thought he stopped caring about me altogether. About *us* and everything we've been through.

I need to know.

I step closer to him, brushing away tears on my sleeves and smearing them into the fabric, wanting nothing more than to be held by this man I keep running from. Wanting to stop being so damn fickle with my heart and just let it be. Do what I want. Fuck him, date him, make him mine.

And wanting to know he wants me, too.

"At first, you know, I thought maybe you were in this for both things. The job and the time we'd have to spend together. I let myself think we could be friends and fair competitors. But now? Now I don't know what you're doing to me, Hunter. This push and pull, hot and cold thing you have going on. You spill coffee on me, then save my ass in the interview and try to kiss me in the elevator. Help me with my Jeep and my bags, but then screw me out of a pageant and potential job of my dreams? And now you're here chasing away a nice man who could have been my happily ever after, for all we know—"

"A nice man, Devyn? Garrison is not a nice man. And he is most certainly not your happily ever after. I saved your ass from something you don't even understand. He's distanced himself from everyone for reasons, Dev."

"Oh, my gosh. You are insufferable! Men are all the same. It's all appearances, ego, and who you know." I stalk back and forth. "Well, you know what? People used to talk shit about me, too, remember? But look at me now." I slam my hand on the wall behind him. "Look at me, Hunter!"

His face darkens and his eyes flare with something that looks a lot like anger, but more like something else. Something that makes me hot and bothered in more good ways than bad.

He lowers his voice almost to a growl. I always used to roll my eyes when men would growl in romance novels.

...I get the appeal now.

"Garrison Presley is an animal abuser," he says, looking around to make sure he's not drawing attention. "He's a disgrace to the farming community, Devyn. Not only does he use inhumane methods with his cattle, but he keeps his chickens in those little cages you hate, so come at me if you want, but don't say I didn't warn you."

Oh, my God, he's so fucking hot when he's mad, and I need to rein it in.

"Okay," I grind back at him, trying hard to school the cavewoman attraction I just experienced and get back to the stuff that really matters. Still, note to self...screw Garrison. I hate those tiny cages.

I'm not admitting that to Hunter, though.

"Are you in it for the job?" I finally ask. Because the answer to that makes the difference in everything going on between us right now. "Are you trying to sabotage me, or are you playing fair? What do you want?"

"You."

He looks at me like I'm an absolute idiot who should have already known this. Like it's been obvious.

Like his answer to that question hasn't changed since the beginning of time.

Oh.

We stand in silence, or it feels that way, at least, because I can't hear or think about anything around me right now, and despite the sadness and anger bubbling in the pit of my stomach, there's something more there. It's something good.

And the only thing I really know about it, as confusing as it may sound, is that it comes from Hunter saying he wants me.

Me.

"And I'm just supposed to believe you didn't have any selfish motives? That you weren't trying to screw me out of the job by tricking me with the pageant? How do you even explain that, huh?"

He sighs dramatically—exasperated, it seems—as he yanks at his hair. "The only selfish motive I've ever had was to get you back here, Dev."

I want to believe him. To run to his arms and let him scoop me up, wrap my legs around him and kiss him with everything I've held back for so long, but I can't. Not for the man who had someone to replace me the minute I left. Not for someone who got over pain that still lives within me daily. I turn away from him again and press roughly on the corners of my eyes, willing them to give me their everything, to hold back my tears and keep me from falling apart right in front of him.

I feel him touch my shoulder, soft and slow, my skin heating beneath him. He spins me back around, gently wiping my eyes with his thumbs, then tilts my chin up so our eyes meet.

"If you knew there wasn't a pageant program anymore, I wasn't sure you'd have a reason to come back home. You could have raised money from the city, doing your library readings and women's club fundraisers, or whatever it is you've been doing all these years…it's not like I Google you or anything." He smiles, magnetically attracting my own to do the same. "I couldn't chance it, Dev. Once I saw you in that interview room—*shit*, once I saw you on the street, mad as hell and dripping in coffee, it was over for me. I had to get you back."

"So you made up a reason for me to come back to Pine Forest…to be with you?"

"Yeah. I did." He shuffles back and forth like he's seventeen and picking me up for homecoming, nervous as hell while my dad shines his shotgun, even though he'd never use it on Hunter. He was like a second son. Still, I see glimpses of that boy I remember in the man before me now, and pieces of my heart shift together in ways that feel natural. Even if that does scare me.

Will I always feel this way when I look at him? He sifts his hand through his hair and then holds it out to me like he's decided something.

"Will you dance with me, Devyn?"

I nod, taking his hand and letting him lead me to the dance floor, like we've done a hundred times before. But we were just teenagers then. And this feels more intimate with him than it ever has in any of the memories I recall. I resist the urge to squeeze his palm three times…once for *I*, twice for *love*, thrice for *you*. It was our secret thing. And it feels almost robotic for me when our fingers are entwined like this.

"She Is" by Lady Antebellum plays in the background as we walk to the center of the floor and sway. One hand holds mine, while the other comes to rest on my hip, creating a spark of electricity that makes my thighs tense.

I can't help it. I whimper. Always me whimpering involuntarily. *What the heck is wrong with me?*

He smirks, eyeing me suspiciously. I feel my face flush, wondering if he can read the inappropriate thoughts, or if his smirk has something to do with whatever he and Lemon were whispering earlier, when I was talking to Garrison Presley, King of the Glow Ups.

They may think I didn't notice their plotting, but they are sorely mistaken. I might not know what they're up to, but I know it does involve me.

"Make me a deal," Hunter says.

I raise my eyebrow in question. *I'm listening.*

"If I can sweep you off your feet with one song, you'll get drinks with me and the old crew."

"I don't know," I tell him, backing away. "They don't really like me anymore." I notice Katie Simmons is at the table, too, and she had some words to say to me the last time I was here.

I did flake out on the pageant council the year I left, though, and I may have screwed some people out of references I'd promised to give them for the larger pageant circuits. Katie being one of them. But the rest of them just hate me because of Hunter. Because I left and got out of this town. And they stayed here and believed whatever version of things people think they know.

Whatever.

"They'll like you just fine, Dev. Look how it turned out with Lemon."

I raise a brow, still unconvinced.

"People grow up, and you're the first one to remind me of that, so take your own advice. Let's put the past behind us. Please, Dev?"

"Fine," I say. "If you sweep me off my feet with one dance, I will hang out with your friends—"

"*Our* friends."

"I will hang out with *our* friends, tonight. If your dance moves knock my socks off. That's all I'm promising."

"And I get to call you babygirl whenever I want."

I twist my lips. *Seriously?*

But it *is* kind of cute, and I half like it.

"Fine."

The slow song ends, and "Backroad" by Tanner Adell starts to build in the speakers. I smile because this song always takes the energy up a notch. I used to take some swing classes growing up here, and I surprise myself as I fall into the moves with Hunter, leading me along in a *pas de bourrée* that comes one hundred percent from his sexy, TikTok-famous hips. He's so good at this. I lick my lips, eyeing every muscle in his arms as he twirls me around the floor.

Why is he so good at this?

The way his hips move to the music, and his strong grip presses into my curves as he leads me across the dance floor, it's both sexy and exhilarating. The bass rumbles as he swings me out then twirls me back into his arms where I'm surrounded by his smell. Sandalwood and pine trees. I can't breathe in without feeling him all over me, around me, and all I can think about is how I wish he were inside me.

I gasp as he grabs my neck with his huge hand, a hand that somehow has the power to kiss my whole body, even though it's only in one spot. He's not quite choking me, but he is at the same time. And the messed-up part about that is I don't seem to mind.

I like it.

My whole body likes it.

His fingers curl around my neck, pressing into my flesh, but still offering me protection as he lowers me into the sexiest fucking dip I've ever experienced in my entire life. Our eyes lock while my head is inches from the floor, and my heart thumps in my chest so loud I swear he must hear it. This feels dangerous, raw, *passionate*.

And I want him to consume me.

My skin flushes, electrons and atoms and pieces of the universe itself shooting through me, as he flips me over twice mid-dip and catches me between his straddled legs, pressing the obvious bulge in his pants against my body as he pulls me up by my actual fucking throat…so slowly, and so sensually, that I don't even realize it when I reach the top and I press my lips to his, and my heart falls faster than it ever has before.

Hunter kisses me back, wildly, erratically, and like he hasn't kissed anyone in ten years. I know it isn't true, but I let myself think it all the same. Think about how familiar he tastes. How safe he feels. How he's mine.

He's all mine. He's always been mine. The thought fills my brain, and it's all I can think. *Mine. Mine. Mine.*

Hunter's fingers grip my sides as we grind to the music. He spins me around, so my back is flush with his body, my ass pressing into his hardness as he roams my neck with his hot tongue, and the same word running through my head seems to be haunting his too.

"Be mine, babygirl." *Mine.*

The words fall from my lips before I can take them back.

Chapter 17

Devyn

Hunter spins me around, eyes wide with hope.

"Did you just say okay?"

And that snaps me out of it. *Shit.*

"Nothing official," I quickly amend, and I don't miss the hurt in his eyes when I clarify that little tidbit. But one night of dancing…dancing that made me wish the ballroom was a bedroom, mind you…doesn't fix the hurt I carry with me when we're together. Even if there's also something deliciously electric happening between us.

I squeeze his bicep. His huge bicep.

Shit. Focus! "I'm not opposed to exploring these feelings, but things need to move slowly."

If we're going to let them move at all.

He raises a brow at me, wetting his lips with his tongue as he thinks about my conditions.

"Is this some sort of Cinderella thing? You're not gonna run off on me at midnight and never come back, right?"

I shake my head, tugging at my bottom lip with my teeth so he can't make me smile like he wants to.

Like I want him to.

"I'm not going anywhere. Not yet. And I especially wouldn't leave magical glass shoes behind…have you met me?"

The energy in the air shifts with my promise. Hunter takes his time reading my face. It feels intimate, even though we aren't touching. If you told me Hunter Isaac had figured out a way to peer straight through to my soul, I'd believe you. I've felt him do it before.

I feel him doing it now.

Or maybe I don't know what I'm feeling.

Lust?

You haven't had sex with anyone since Chad-the-soon-to-be-dad. You're feeling lonely. And now the man you've spent the last, oh, fifteen something years fantasizing about, under the darkest layers of your bedsheets, is here in front of you with everything you think you need.

That's the keyword. Think. Is Hunter what I need? I don't know. I just think.

And I *think* I'd be wise to lighten the mood. If we're going to be anything, it has to be casual. For the sake of not only our potential jobs, but everything.

I hold out my hand to the cowboy in front of me and give him a sassy grin. "Besides, even if I wanted to escape you, I don't have a pumpkin."

"But you have a Lemon!"

Like magic, Lemon has appeared before us, and three drinks rest on a tray that, *thank the lord*, look way more my speed than whiskey and whatever the hell is in a pinkie.

"We're about to play some new bar game on Robbie's phone." She hands us the Coronas with limes, and even though I think I should be jealous, seeing as how there is no way in the world Lemon knows my go-to drink is a Corona with a lime unless someone told her. That someone being her new bestie, Shana…that's just the thing.

I'm…

I'm not jealous.

"Oh, my gosh! I'm not jealous!"

I probably look like a lunatic right now, and yeah, I've had alcohol, so someone's going to chalk it up and say I'm drunk, but I'm not.

Okay, I probably am a little.

But that's not why I look like a lunatic.

"I'm not jealous of your relationship with Shana!"

At first, Lemon seems concerned, scooting back and pursing her lips as she inspects my eyes to see just how drunk I might be. I am feeling good, but I'm not that drunk. I swat her away.

"I don't hate you anymore. I just realized it. I don't know what you did to me, but I think…I think the truce healed me." I look at my hand in Lemon's and smile. "I don't think I'm a bitch anymore!"

Lemon and Hunter burst into a fit of laughter. Hunter folds over, holding on to a nearby barstool, and Lemon fans herself as she blows out delicate little jets of air on a, "Hooooo, Devyn, girl. I need some of what you've been getting. Jeremy!" She waves at our friend, *huh…our friend*. "Get me as good as you got Little Miss Whiskey over here. She's a hoot!"

The bar collectively cheers as "Country" by Jason Aldean comes on the speakers and several patrons shimmy their boots to the dance floor. I can't explain how surreal it feels being in this atmosphere. Feeling free. I'm smiling so hard, my cheeks might burst open from the pressure.

I wouldn't be surprised if I were in a dream.

One where my heart wasn't torn from me far too soon, and I never left this little town. This group. There are people here

I care about. Dustin, Jeremy, Lemon, Hunter, Shana…maybe even Robbie and Katie, who knows?

And they call me their friend. They laugh when I'm being a bitch instead of scoff.

They accept me as I am and genuinely seem to want me around, whether I bring the thick accent and cute one-liners, whether I win silver or gold crowns, whether I wear platform booties or dusty old shitkickers. They prefer the shit. They embrace the kicking.

And Hunter. He's…

I try to remind myself of the false promises ripped from within me and thrown out, the sting of abandonment when those voids never felt emptier. I remind myself that Hunter's tryst with infidelity wasn't the only time I felt betrayed by a man who knew the darkest of my secrets. Anytime I open myself to someone I think I could love. Then I learn it's conditional.

Everyone has conditions.

But ten years, I think as I'm pulled through the bar by the grown-up version of the boy I fell in love with before I even knew the meaning of the word. A man who smirks for thousands, but somehow only has eyes for one right now. And it's me.

And I'm his girl. Tonight, at least.

I promised him that much, after all. To try.

The long, wooden table we're led to is carved from red oak, and finished with a unique flair that could only have been done by the same company Dustin's came from. They're almost identical in hue and stain. But I inspected Dustin's furniture once it caught my eye, and there was no company logo or branding. And he practically flipped his own farmhouse from what I saw earlier.

Did my brother do these? That would be a newer hobby he picked up, if that's the case, because I had no idea. But then, I wouldn't know about anything new or old.

Ten years is far longer than I realized. And it isn't only Hunter and my brother reminding me of that.

We scooch into the bench seats and all the way to the far corner, nestled in a darker part of the dining area. I'm glad we aren't too close to the center of the table. The way we're positioned at the angle, it's like our own private space. It's awkward enough being somewhere you didn't feel like you belonged even before you left. But being surrounded by a handful of familiar, yet foreign faces in this little group of Hunter's is panic inducing.

Where did this stage fright come from? It's unfamiliar and unwelcome, and I wonder faintly in the back of my head if these bouts of nerves lately don't corelate pretty damn directly to times when I'm trying not to be fake.

Shit. Shit. Shit.

I've been fake so long I get nervous being me? I mean, it makes total sense. I've always put on a face, an act, a show. And it's never failed to earn me a crown.

Whether that be an actual one or a metaphorical one.

Nobody's ever called me a winner for being just plain Devyn. Is *Just-Plain-Devyn* someone anyone even wants?

Do I want her?

Faces I grew up seeing smaller, younger versions of, surround us. They're all grown up. Smiling. Laughing. It's nostalgic to say the least. And while I feel like half of my emotions are probably drunk-girl feelings, the other half of me knows with experience that a drunk girl's words are a sober girl's thoughts.

Do I like it here? I think I do. So, what does that mean?

I chew on my lip, mulling over the feelings.

Hunter, Lemon, Home.

"You okay there, princess?"

I jump, startled by his words.

"Forever daydreaming." He smirks, pressing the glass bottle to his lips. I watch as he takes a swig, and for some reason unbeknownst to me, but totally *knownst* to my ho of a vajayjay, I continue to watch his Adam's apple push a path along his throat as he swallows.

"I always loved that about you," he says, eyes crinkling at the edges.

He leans in, and my lips part involuntarily, my skin tingling with the proximity of his perfectly sculpted body, so flush with mine. Close enough that his heat is mine. And it's scorching right now. Hunter is infuriating sometimes.

I spend hours choosing my outfits, but this man has the audacity to look sinful as all get-out in nothing but a pair of tight jeans, dirty shit-kickers, and a plain white T-shirt. His sleeves are stretched so tight over his biceps that they hardly look comfortable. I really should rip the cotton from his body and free them.

And run my fingers over the ridges.

I fan myself, turning my face away from him before he can see how he's affecting me. I want him so bad I can't stand to be beside him.

Hunter hooks an arm around me, his fingers twining through the ribbons of hair that flow down my back. I sigh wistfully, leaning into the crook of his arm, my heart skittering with the smell of his cologne and the way his body tightens around mine when he feels me nuzzle in.

He runs light trails up and down my side with his fingers, and a wake of goosebumps follows. They follow everywhere he touches. Down my arms. Over my thighs. I gasp when they move in between my legs, which part for him all on their own, stretching open as far as my jean skirt will allow.

Nobody can see beneath the table, especially with the corner we've somehow managed to find ourselves conveniently nestled into. I turn my head into his neck and bite down to stifle a moan when he guides his rough fingers along the lace edges of my panties, the teasing touch of his fingers almost too much to handle. But the thought of him stopping is almost unbearable all the same.

"Don't stop," I mutter breathlessly.

Reminding myself of why I shouldn't do this is completely useless right now. I don't give a fuck what Past-Devyn has to say about this, Present-Devyn wants this man's fingers to slide approximately one centimeter to the left and make a shit ton of little circles until she comes into oblivion right under this suspiciously beautiful table.

I might be drinking, and I might regret my decisions, but a few drinks do not beer goggles make, and I'm certain right now, as I move my hand over his jeans and make my way straight to the hardness pressing tightly against his zipper, that he's done being cordial about this, too.

I lean closer, licking my lips as he stiffens beneath my hand.

"I'm going to touch you," I tell him. It's not a request for permission, or even a question. It's just a truth we both seem to be living in the middle of.

Hunter nods, his mouth turning up on the sides, and leaning back to give me better access, his eyes roaming my body and lingering appreciatively over my lips, my chest. My heartbeat quickens and flames kick up in my belly, a fire scorching beneath my skin and heating me at my core. He chuckles when I tug my bottom lip between my teeth, unsuccessfully suppressing a whimper.

"So needy," he whispers into my ear, guiding me by my waist into his lap. With his hard body behind me like this and his strong arms holding me down, I have nowhere to go. Nowhere to hide.

But that's okay with me.

There's nowhere I'd rather be right now than precisely where I am.

His hard cock pressing into my ass makes my pussy clench, and he groans, throwing his leather jacket over my lap and fisting my skirt, hiking it up higher as he trails hot kisses across the back of my neck. His fingers feel like electricity with each point of contact, making me hot and static. I could explode at any minute.

And the sexy asshole knows this, chuckling low and sensual, his voice a smoky velvet that pours into my senses with warmth and promise. I gasp, his fingers brushing over my panties and stopping to pinch my clit through the fabric every so often. And the crazy part is, I don't even care what's going on around me. I'm here for this. So wet, and I'm not even a bit embarrassed by that.

It's his fault.

He's done this to me. Turned me into a wild, hungry beast who wants nothing more than to devour his heart and keep it inside of me. To feel him there always, to fill the empty spaces in my soul.

I'm bucking against his lap now, shifting my weight back and forth and wishing he'd *fucking do something* about the ache I just can't seem to sate with rocking alone.

"Touch me." I press the back of my head against his shoulder, whispering the command in his ear, breathy and lust filled. I hardly recognize the voice coming out of my mouth.

He groans, smirking at me dangerously, but then he complies, cupping my entire pussy and using two fingers to juice me like an orange, until I'm dripping all over his hand, grinding against it, and—*oh my, oh God, I want every part of him.*

Where did this Hunter even come from? The last time we were together, it was not like this. I mean, no man has ever been like this…this…*skilled.*

Nobody except the ones in books. That's what he's got. That thirst trap thing. That look in his eye that makes thousands of women subscribe and save. He's a walking book boyfriend. And I am hopeless against that kind of power.

I grind against him harder, rubbing my ass along his erection and wishing we didn't have these barriers between us, like clothing, and…well, an audience.

"Such a filthy little princess," he whispers, kissing down my throat. He places both hands on my hips, guiding me with a rough grip. My pussy clenches because of his words. They're dirty and so…

"Ooh," I moan when he bites my ear, still rocking me along his shaft through his jeans like it's high school all over again and we haven't yet done things under the clothes.

"Only bad girls wear tiny skirts and dance all over assholes to make their boyfriends jealous, you know."

He pinches my clit again, and the sting shoots through my center, settling over my swollen core and sending little ripples of pleasure shooting through me. I rock harder, and he lets out a groan of approval, tightening his hold on my sides, his fingers digging into my flesh in an almost bruising grip.

"That's it, babygirl, rub that dripping little pussy on me. I want to walk out of here stained with your cum all over my jeans, so nobody ever questions whose girl you are again."

Oh, my God, he's filthy.

He runs his fingertips over my swollen center but doesn't

leave them there nearly long enough. I whine in protest, shoving my ass hard against his cock and grinding down.

"So fucking needy." His lips press against my neck as he pinches my clit. I gasp and look around the table to make sure nobody saw, but he only seems pleased with that, chuckling when I clench my muscles in protest to his teasing.

I pull away, worry creeping in that I'm drawing too much attention when I see Robbie flick his eyes our way one too many times, but Hunter pulls me back against his chest, my arms pinned to my sides like I'm in a straitjacket, and it's hot as fuck. I can't lie. It's rough and forceful, and nothing like what I imagined.

It's better.

With his free hand, he spreads me open and pushes his two middle fingers inside of me, and it's more than something. It's everything. I clutch the table and steady myself as he pumps his fingers into me, spreading my juices, and evidence of my clear as fuck arousal, all over my pussy.

"Mmm, see what I mean, princess? So fucking wet down here." He pinches my clit, twisting, playing. Taking his time. Hunter Isaac is the fucking king of thirst traps. He rubs circles around my sensitive bud of nerves, making me moan and buck against his hand, leaning my head back, and closing my eyes.

"Look at you, such a little tease. Letting me put my fingers inside of this tight little pussy in public. But I can't fuck you, can I, babygirl?"

He winks, and yeah, that does it for me. For fucking sure it does. But it's his words that send me over. This is all new territory for me and Hunter.

First of all, I thought I wouldn't ever in my life meet a man who talked like that and didn't exist in the pages of a book. And second of all, the last time I had sex with Hunter Isaac, we weren't old enough to have preferences. We didn't know about kinks.

So, then, how does he know all of mine?

"I like that," I tell him in short breaths as he pinches my clit again. He does it faster, using my cum to coat his fingers so they'll slide around as he squeezes. And suddenly, I'm turning my face to his neck, as I release a shudder into his ear and my orgasm takes over my body. I feel him tense beneath me, his teeth digging into my neck in a rough, bruising bite.

"Mine," he grumbles into my neck. I'm not even sure if he's aware he's said it. And I really shouldn't like how horny that makes me feel.

He kisses my neck, right over the bite he just branded me with.

Because that's what he just did.

He marked me as his and then said *mine.*

We have a lot to unpack when we're sober.

I straighten my skirt and slide off Hunter's lap so he can… adjust. And just like that, we're shifting back into place before anyone at the table even notices.

Maybe. I'm honestly not sure I'd care if they did.

That's a strange thought. That I wouldn't care what people think. *Huh.*

"Well, looky what we got here, y'all," Robbie coos as he shoves his way into the bench seating across from us, followed by Lemon and Katie Simmons, who decides to scoot in on this side next to Hunter instead of beside Lemon. "Who here is *at all* surprised the one and only Devyn Lynn Campell, Mrs. American Rodeo Queen and Southern Belle of my TV and yours, wasn't home a single day and she's already up in Isaac's lap?"

Robbie takes a swig of his beer and gulps loudly, belching and wiping his face on his sleeve. It's gross, yeah, *but it's Robbie,* I think, rolling my eyes and not caring what he says, like old times.

"I'm not surprised." he continues, "Mmm, mmm, mmm." He gives me an exaggerated wink and stands at his seat to gyrate into the air before he's swatted back down by Lemon.

"He's like…really drunk," she says, almost apologetically. It crosses my mind that her apologizing for Robbie's behavior is weird. She's like the mother hen here. Everyone kind of follows Lemon's orders. And I'm still not jealous of her. I smile, thinking about how she saved me from Garrison. Even before Hunter got there, she wouldn't have let me leave with him. She seems to be keeping everyone in line tonight.

I'm starting to see what Shana sees in her. She's good people.

"Shut up, you big ol' goose!" And the way she draws out goose—no, the way Robbie's eyes widen when she says it, like he's terrified she'll spill some tea on him, is bizarre. It's enough to shut him up and sit him down, though, which is good. I really don't want anyone making a big deal out of Hunter and me because I don't want Hunter and me making a big deal out of Hunter and me.

I don't even know if there is a Hunter and me.

See? I knew it would be complicated coming back home. Still, I feel happier than I have in a while.

And that means something. I'm not jealous here either.

That means something, too.

Well, I thought I wasn't jealous, that is. But maybe that only extends to Lemon. My gaze darts down the table, and I feel my nails curling into the bench the closer Katie gets to Hunter. She and Robbie are explaining this smart phone bar game, which is basically just a fancy version of Truth or Dare. And the way she puts her hand on Hunter's arm and laughs when he makes a joke about the background photo on her phone…Nope, still a jealous bitch.

"Excuse me, Katie, right?" I blink at her and smile so brightly, you'd think we were on camera.

She looks at me, wide-eyed and annoyed. She should be. I've known her since we were five.

"Yeah, obviously." She rolls her eyes and waits for me to continue.

I point to Hunter and then back to myself. "He's got plans tonight."

She looks mortified. *Good.*

It feels less than great being a jealous bitch again. But it feels better making sure she knows his plans do not include her in any way, shape, or department store booties form.

Okay, that was harsh, even for my thoughts.

"I mean, your booties are cute," I say quickly, grasping for anything at all to fill the silence and distract everyone from the fact that I think I just claimed Hunter in front of half the town.

But he's not distracted, and the look in his eyes tells me he is more than pleased with my public display of…ownership over him. A thrill of excitement shoots down to my core with that thought, but I have to shake myself out of this orgasm-induced stupor.

What on earth is wrong with you, Devyn? What happened to taking it slow? Casually?

I scold myself internally. Now the whole table has all eyes on us.

"Holy shit!" Robbie says, his eyes as wide as everyone else at the table. Except Lemon. She looks like she's trying not to laugh, shoving her straw in her mouth and sucking like her life depends on it.

"Ya'll are still into each other." He points back and forth between Hunter and me, and even though I should continue to deny it and lean away, I don't.

No, I don't lean away at all.

I taste him instead. He's kissing me. Or I'm kissing him.

And all of a sudden, I'm in his lap for the second time in a ten-minute period.

He's hard. *Because of me.*

I turn, straddling him and winding my arms around his neck as he sifts his fingers through my hair and fists the blonde strands, holding me in place, my head tugged back almost painfully while his tongue lashes out at my mouth, tasting my lips, teasing my tongue, my—

"Ehemmm," Robbie grinds out, breaking our kiss, and the silence I didn't realize we caused. Several sets of eyes stare, fingers point, lips whisper in ears beside them. And they're all looking at us. Lemon says something to Jeremy, and I see him nod, biting his lip to keep from smiling. I'm suddenly very aware of the position I've put myself in, and I frantically search around for cameras before I feel a squeeze and a light kiss on the back of my neck.

"It's okay. You're not in the city."

Miss American Rodeo, whether she be reigning queen, future queen, or past, like me, isn't usually supposed to be seen straddling cowboys in seedy bars and sucking their face off. *Usually.* And I may have been a hot topic for the tabloids when I was in my early twenties. Getting caught in places I shouldn't have been with people I shouldn't caused a lot of drama in my life. People always seem to think they know what they don't.

I feel relieved when Hunter reminds me it's not like that here. Half the people in this town are still living in the 90s. Most people around here don't even have smart phones, and the only paper they get is the *Farmer's Almanac* and the *Pine Forest Courier*, run by the same man who owns all the vending machines in the strip mall.

Yes, you heard that right. The one and only strip mall.

"It's easy to forget Pine Forest doesn't have reporters crawling all over the place when you've been away as long as I have."

Hunter squeezes my shoulder, and I offer him a smile. Knowing he's got my back even when he doesn't really have to makes me feel safe.

Robbie enters our names into the app, and we all wait as it tells us the rules. It's weird being in a time of AI and robots. I remember seeing movies about them as a kid and thinking how insane that culture would be, but here we are, letting a telephone tell us how to play a game older than time.

"Do we really need this thing to explain Truth or Dare?" I complain when the rules seem to drone on forever from his speaker.

Everyone laughs, even Katie, to my surprise. I thought she'd give me the side-eye all night after my display of dominance, which is really what it was, if I'm being honest with myself. I felt like a lioness in that moment, ready to tear her head off with one quick bite if she got any closer to Hunter.

And that, my dear self, needs to be examined by Sober Devyn tomorrow.

"She's right," Robbie admits, squinting as he reads through the first few instructions in his head. He waves a hand through the air. "The rules are the same. Let's just play."

He eyes the table for a moment and then lands his gaze on Katie. Robbie was always notorious for being an ass at games like this, doing whatever he could to make us all uncomfortable.

"Katie May Simmons, I dare you to kiss Hunter."

Katie's lips part on a gasp, and her eyes dart to the side, but not to Hunter.

Nope, to my absolute amusement, she looks at me.

Good girl. I wink at her. Hunter sees this and nudges me, but I don't care. I snake my hand over his jeans and cup his junk beneath the table as he groans a kiss into my neck.

"I don't think that's a good idea," she says, shifting in her seat. Robbie sighs but concedes after seeing her hesitation. Or maybe he senses the lioness too.

"Never mind," he says. "How 'bout Truth? Do you have a thing for Hunter?"

My eyes widen, and I twist my head to face her, but I'm just a split second too late to see her immediate reaction. And I have a feeling the one she's got in place right now is most definitely a mask.

"No," she says firmly.

Hmm.

I narrow my eyes at her, but Hunter's voice in my mind is almost as close as his fingers on my hips.

Breathe, Ponygirl.

It eases my immediate jealousy. *What is wrong with me? Why am I being like this?*

"Your turn, Katie." I keep my forced smile firmly in place. Despite my constant hiccups with bitchery, I realize I can't stop being a bitch if I keep being a bitch. It's difficult.

She nods, seeming to accept my neutrality. "Okay." She fiddles with her tennis bracelet. "Devyn…" She hesitates, breathing more heavily now. But why?

I've seen this look on a dozen women before, and all of them were nervous.

But they were nervous about me. Pageant girls going up against the best around, or interns wanting a big shot at the station, knees knocking together as they'd walk to my dressing room and work up the courage just to tell me I'm their idol.

But why is Katie nervous? I'm certainly not her idol. Or maybe…just maybe, it's not nerves. It's courage. And just like that, she morphs into something different. Her chin tilts up, her back straightens, and she widens her smile.

Oh, Katie is not passing the vibe check.

"I dare you to sleep with Hunter," she says, folding her arms across her chest in a triumphant and, I'll hand it to her, pretty badass move. If I didn't hate her right now, I might want to be her friend.

"Nice try. But you can't dare someone to have sex."

"No, not sex. I dare you to spend the night with him. One night. No sex. That's the dare. Because there's one more rule, you can't have any sexual intercourse even if you want to. I'll put fifty bucks on it." She smirks and turns her attention to Robbie. "I doubt they last an hour."

"What?" Lemon and I say in unison. And I have to admit it feels good that the girl's got my back. I'm not used to that. I'm used to being the one other girls hate. Katie? I'm not sure yet.

"This is a horrible idea, Devyn. We should call Shana and—"

"No."

Hunter's eyes widen in my direction. Most everyone at the table has something to say about it. It's wrong. It's stupid. We wouldn't last a day. We would kill each other. Someone, I think Robbie, says he wants it on film.

Ew.

Then again, it's kinda hot to think about filming myself with Hunter. Laying his TikTok moves down on me, above me, while the world scrolls by and sees he's mine and I'm his.

Stop. Nope. Lemon's right. Bad idea.

"Look," I say, coming to my senses, "on second thought, maybe Lem is right…"

"Whoa, there," Hunter interjects. "Don't I get any say in this?"

"Hear ye, hear ye!" Robbie slams down his beer-bottle-made-gavel, suddenly the drunken grand master of bets and challenges. "What's your input, Isaac?"

Hunter drags his eyes across my body almost as slowly as his tongue across his lips, scorching me internally as he holds my gaze.

"I say we're on. But I want something out of it." He strums his fingers together. "I want more than a night with you. Let's make it a month."

I gasp, and the rest of the table does too. But Lemon smiles.

"And," she adds in singsong tune, "whoever caves and initiates sex first forfeits the charity competition for Classy Country and lets the other one take the job."

At first, I'm flabbergasted. I shoot Lemon a death glare. How could she? I thought we were friends now…truce and all. Why would she do that to me?

But I hear *psst* from across the table, and she winks at me. Not at Hunter. And it's then I realize she's an actual genius. I am not going to cave.

But I'll do everything in my power to tease the hell out of Hunter so he does.

Everyone says I always do things impulsively, but I've thought it over, in the point-three seconds I've had since realizing it, and I've decided this is a win-win for me.

I tease him, he caves before I do, and I get my dream job. It's as simple as that.

In the back of my head, Sober-Devyn shouts things about guarding our heart and feelings and risks, but I take a big swig of my beer and drown that Debbie Downer right the fuck out.

"No problem. I'm in," I tell the group before twisting to face a smirking Hunter beside me.

"Are you sure about this, babygirl?" His fingers brush my bangs away from my eyes, and I shiver. He leans in and kisses my ear, the sensations that ripple across my body each a separate promise of their own that he won't make this easy on me, either. "I know how much you want that job. I'd hate for you to fail because you couldn't behave."

He whispers that last part directly in my ear, and the stupidly sexy asshole even lets his teeth linger, nibbling for far too long to be considered appropriate for a group setting, and leaving behind a hot, wet breath that I want to preserve against my skin so I can feel him there.

When I'm alone.

Thinking about his words…

"*Such a filthy little princess.*"

Can I really control myself around him?

But yeah. I know I can. And I love a good smack talk before a competition, so I take it up a notch, making sure to wiggle my ass down over his crotch very, extremely, undoubtedly purposefully.

"Two can tease, Isaac." I lean my head into the crook of his neck, arching my back as my lips brush his skin, pleased with myself when I see his throat constrict. On and off, I wonder if I can, very well, control myself around him for a month.

In his house. In his bed.

"You daydreaming again?" Hunter moves my legs to the side so he can hold me and look at me at the same time. My eyes bore into his, searching for answers I could just ask him to reveal to me with words, but for some reason, I can't bring myself to ask the questions that would spark them. Even after all these years.

The way our breath mixes, until I'm not sure whose air I'm breathing anymore, takes hold of me, and then I'm kissing him again. Not carefully this time, but wildly. My teeth clank against his, hands roaming over his shoulders, squeezing his biceps and loving how tight they feel when he flexes beneath my hands, craving more when he grabs my throat and pulls me deeper into the kiss, like he's demanding he have total control of every part of it, my mouth becoming thoroughly fucked by his lashing tongue.

"Shiiiiiit. I ain't even got goats that horny, y'all," Robbie observes, slamming his beer mug down on the table and breaking me out of my love spell. "Hundred bucks says they don't just do the deed. These two're fixin' to get hitched by the enda this."

"Deal," I hear Lemon shout, smacking her hand on the table. And I'm not sure if I'm happy or upset she doesn't think we'll get married. I frown, thinking that over. Does she not have faith in our relationship?

But what the fuck am I thinking? We don't have a relationship. I don't want a relationship with Hunter.

We break away from the kiss, both of us noticing we're halfway to losing the challenge and we haven't even gotten to his house yet. And, well, it's kind of true.

"I'm not worried," I lie, twisting around and facing the table again. "I know I can do it, even if I were married to him. I could resist going all the way with him. Hunter, on the other hand, wouldn't last a single night married to me without begging for it."

"Pro'lly wouldn't be able to put up with her bullshit," Robbie chimes in, and he's quickly smacked in the head by Lemon. "Ow."

"What do you mean, I couldn't stay married to you?" Hunter asks. "That'd be just about the easiest fuckin' thing I've ever done." His deep blue eyes roam my body possessively, and the way he makes my nipples hard with the promise in his stare is not just dangerous, it's addictive.

"It's what I've always wanted," he tells me. Straight, honest, and outright.

My breath leaves my lungs with that admission; at how freely and publicly he offers it. Does he mean that?

"Even if there were no sex involved?"

"Yes," he says simply.

"You'd want me for…just me?" I grind my teeth, slipping my finger beneath my hair tie and stretching it tightly, forcing the words from my lips. Words I speak to him alone, "Even though you know I'll never have—"

He nods, cutting me off, and my breath hitches again. "Why?"

"I've always wanted you for you, Dev. No matter what."

I stall. Tears well in my eyes. And even though the sting is real, I will not… *I will not* cry. I'm not ready to let him see what this means to me. It's the one wall I can't lower so freely.

"Do you mean that, or are you just tipsy?" I ask, searching his blue eyes and needing desperately for the former to be so. Wanting to believe the things I've feared for so long might not be true. That I'm not too broken. That maybe there is a future for Hunter Isaac and me, despite the scars that will forever outline our love.

Even though I'll never be a whole me.

And I don't care that the whole table is watching us right now. This is monumental.

I need to know.

"Devyn Lynn Campbell," he says, his blue eyes pinning me in place, brimming with an unyielding truth I can't ignore, "I swear to all the stars in the sky and the mountains that kiss their light that I would marry you for a thousand reasons, and not one of them would be to change you."

"I dare you," I breathe.

Chapter 18

Devyn

A loud buzzing wakes me from my sleep. I groan, snatching the pillow from under my head and shoving it over my face and ears. But the buzzing doesn't stop, meaning it's not just one or two texts, it's calls or something too.

What the hell? I just want to sleep.

I reach to the bedside table, but realize it isn't my brother's guest room bedside table. It's a dresser. And it's just now registering to me how thick this pillow smells of—

Pine and sandalwood. *Shit.*

I shoot upright, throwing the covers off to ensure I am in fact clothed. *Whew!* And then I look to the left and confirm there's no other body in the bed with me.

Okay. You just stayed the night, I tell myself as I scan the room for my shoes and purse.

Just like Katie's dare implied. You stayed the night and slept with Hunter. But not sexually.

I think.

But then again, with the way we were under the booth at Cowboy's Paradise, I'm not gonna say it would be out of the question if we did end up doing…*everything else.*

I fall back on the mattress, groaning as I feel how hungover I actually am. I'm groggy and gross and my head is pounding. I stare at the ceiling. It's tall. A raised, slanted ceiling with a sunroof that takes my breath away. That must be where all the warmth is coming from…the light that spills in with the sun.

How romantic.

I scold myself, clearing away my daydreams. It's time to get up and get the day started. Once I'm up and have some food and water, I'll be fine.

I don't entirely remember last night, so while I'm pretty positive, based on my fully clothed body and lack of, you know… soreness…down there, that we didn't do it, I still feel the need to clear the air on what did actually happen. After the kiss, that is.

Because that's all I remember. Kissing him. In his lap. And then…okay, there was more than kissing. But nothing aside from some handsy stuff.

And then we played Truth or Dare. I jump straight to my feet and stumble to catch myself on the large oak dresser, my brain instantly pounding against my skull.

Yep, still hungover.

I grab for my phone and fumble with the unlock screen for far longer than seems reasonable. But once I've got the stupid thing open, I realize something most definitely did happen.

Thirty-six calls? From Dustin, Mom, Shana…

My heart races as I scroll my call history.

Oh, *my God, what happened? Is someone hurt? Shana's dad, maybe?*

But no, it can't be. Because I've also got missed calls and texts from people entirely disconnected from Pine Forrest. Dad, the Miss American Rodeo Council…*Molly from Classy Country?*

Holy shit. Holy shit. *What has happened?* I scramble to pull up my social media and find something that can help me figure this out. I have one hand manning my phone and the other pulling on my heels…the same ones I wore to the bar last night. Because yes, even among all this chaos, I will still be doing the walk of shame today.

I stall, curling my fingers around my phone. I'm not sure I believe what I'm reading right now. Shoving my foot in my other heel and taking a quick seat at the edge of a…is this a vanity stool? Does Hunter have an elegant as hell vanity made of matching deep oak that goes with the beautiful dresser… that matches a certain booth I got very familiar with last night? Furniture I think my brother made?

I am so totally fucked if I'm not supposed to fuck him when I see stuff like this. I bite my lip, clenching my thighs together, as I will the ho inside me to calm down just a teeny bit while I figure out why I'm getting blown up with notifications all of a sudden.

Also, where *is* Hunter?

I read a few texts that make no sense whatsoever:

CHAD: Congrats, girlie, I'll always remember our special time. <Winking Emoji>

Ew. Why do some men seem super attractive at one point in your life and absolutely disgusting the next? I shiver and scroll on, trying not to get hung up too long on why Chad is even congratulating me in the first place.

SHAY BAE: OH MY GOD, DEVYN…Call me, please. I'm not even mad about last night. Lemon told me you guys are cool. BUT WE NEED TO TALK ABOUT THIS HUNTER THING!!!! OMG CALL ME!!!

Oh, shit. What does she mean by—*this Hunter thing?* I suppose Lemon told her about the dare to stay here for a month. I mean, it's not that bad. Makes sense she'd want to mull it over with me, but it doesn't explain the other buzz going on in my phone. Or maybe that's just the light, pulsing feeling in my head. I forgot how much I hate drinking.

I hover over Dustin's text next, but I don't get far before my phone is ringing again…

Claudette Charbonneau, I read on the screen.

What am I missing?

I swipe to the side and accept the call. At least I know this woman isn't going to sugarcoat whatever the hell is going on and will give it to me straight.

"Um, hi. Good morning, Claudette. How are—"

She cuts me off with a boisterous laugh and a dark little chuckle that ends in an "mmm, mmm, mmm."

"I did not think you had it in you, my dear, but wow. You have blown even me away with your quick thinking and sharp wit. I like you." She punctuates her sentence with nothing but air. A silence she commands simply because she is none other than Claudette Charbonneau, Queen of Southern Fashion and CEO of Classy Country.

I'd love to be as regal as she is. But then I shake my head and push that thought away. I'm still confused.

"You and your"—she sighs wistfully—"sexy cowboy have caused quite the riot."

I sputter at that. Sexy cowboy? Has she lost her damn mind? I look out the window to make sure the world is still out there and there isn't some sort of apocalypse or something, but I just end up taking in the beautiful rows of wheat and pastures of wildflowers, as far as the eye can see. Oh, my gosh. Hunter wasn't joking when he said he had a farm.

But it isn't just a farm to me. It's…it's a kingdom. A

place we used to wander and sneak around when it was just an abandoned building sitting on what we considered *our spot.*

A whole lot has happened on this land…on this exact farm…in this very house. Even if it was just dilapidated boards and crumbled bricks back then. I breathe in deep and try to focus back on Claudette, faintly smelling bacon in the air. I say a quick thank you to the big man above because at least there's bacon.

As I follow the most glorious smell on Earth through the beautifully renovated farmhouse where I grew up romping and rolling about, I home in on a word Claudette just uttered and walk face first into the wall before me.

"Did you…" I stutter, catching my breath as I turn and lean against the wall, steadying myself so I can hear what I think I heard. "Did you just say my *marriage?*" Surely, I heard wrong. But then I put Claudette on speaker as I go back to scrolling through the rest of my texts. The one from Dustin stops me in my tracks, and no sooner than I read what I think I just read, does Claudette speak the very words into existence.

DUSTIN:YOU.MARRIED.HUNTER?!

I swallow my confusion, stalling, pressing the center button on my phone and close my texting app altogether. I'm pretty sure whatever else is in there, whatever other secrets my brain is hiding from me in its post-drunk-girl wisdom, those things can, and probably should, wait until I confirm what Claudette and Dustin just told me.

And bacon can happen first too. Because, at this point, I know something crazy is about to go down in this little town. It apparently involves me, Hunter, and marriage.

Whatever I'm about to face, I am sure as hell getting bacon before it commences.

At this point, Claudette is just going on and on about how wonderful our video was last night. And that just sweetens the pot even more, doesn't it?

We posted a freaking video.

What on Earth is even on the video? Well, that will be the next mystery for me to solve. After bacon. I rub my forehead with my free hand and listen in as she thanks me. But it strikes me as weird.

"What exactly are you thanking me for?" Because I am so genuinely confused.

"Well, your video last night…" I knock my head against the wall. *I have got to see this video.* "It sparked quite a bit of interest from both of your followings. Point blank, your fans are in love with your love! And so is Classy Country. In fact, I talked to the other investors, and we have decided to sponsor a reception in your honor after the charity fair is wrapped up. All expenses covered, of course."

I'm speechless. What in the ever-loving world is going on right now? Did I bump my head last night? I mean, I know Hunter and I were all over each other, but not like… past second base or anything. And I know we made that dare to get married. I just…I can't remember anything past that. And I'm wondering how drunk I really was if that's the case.

From what I can tell, we came home to his house after some unknown blackout period which must have included a…

…a whole freaking marriage? There's no way we'd be able to swing that. He was just as drunk as I was, nonetheless. Details on that to be discovered later. I have a ton of questions.

Anyway, we came home, I'm still in my clothes, and it seems as if we just went to sleep. I've got to be missing something. I curl my hand around the banister, and I feel something hard and constricting press against my finger. My ring finger, to be exact.

It can't be.

But oh, yes, my eyes widen, because it most certainly can. And it most certainly is.

The prettiest ring for the prettiest Ponygirl, I remember, a smile creeping across my face as I take in the woven bits of colorful starburst wrappers that snake around my finger. It reminds me of a time when the air smelled of barbeque and shoes were optional.

"Did you hear me?" Claudette says. "We don't want you to worry about the competition. With the hype and excitement this surprise marriage of yours has caused among the consumers, we are one hundred percent committed to your brand as a couple, and—"

I cut her off, stunned to hear her speak those words. "Did you just say, 'your brand as a couple?'"

"Well, yes, dear." She lowers her voice now and speaks to me in what feels like the most direct and motherly tone I've ever actually gotten from someone. Even from my own mother. My stepmother, too, not that she was ever old enough to be considered my mother in the first place, but I digress…

"We are offering both of you the position. As Classy Country's first ever Co-Marketing Directors of Influence and Outreach. You'd have equal share in the company, and you are both guaranteed the position whether or not you make the most at the charity event. Let's use this platform to propel our brand forward even more!" She lets a giggle erupt from her throat at the tail end of a chuckle, tickled by these events. She's not used to surprises like this, and she…wants us both?

To work together.

"But why?" I ask. I mean, this all sounds amazing. We both get the job. What more could I want? And it's not like I don't want to explore whatever these feelings are for Hunter and all, because there are a lot of feelings, but I get the feeling Claudette thinks this is an actual marriage.

One that wouldn't ever end.

At first, I was kind of concerned it was, too, but now that I see the Starburst ring, I feel pretty confident this was part of our drunken shenanigans…and for show at the bar.

We didn't really get married.

Either way, I think as I rub my fingers across the folds of my paper ring, the one who makes my heart skitter with its similarities to the zebra-stripe gum version that seemed to appear magically in my sixth-grade locker and became a permanent fixture in my jewelry box for the rest of time. It's still there, nestled next to my hospital band—both our bands. I brush a stray tear from my cheek, not willing to let it fall all the way.

It doesn't make sense to tell Claudette. I do recall accepting the staying the night dare. And I am pretty sure Lemon or someone used their dare to amend it for a month. And now that I'm thinking really hard about it, I feel like…

"I dared Hunter to marry me…it was me," I suddenly whisper, cutting off whatever it was Claudette was going on about.

"Well, of course you did, my dear! And well done. A woman's got to chase after what she wants on her own terms."

I stall at that. Hunter is not what I want. "He's…I want him, yes, but—"

"Well, it's all settled, then. We will throw you the reception and wedding of the century, using all Classy Country designs, of course. And you will handle the updates exclusively in partnership with Classy Country and your own social media platforms."

Wait, what? Is that what I just agreed to?

I don't even need a wedding reception. I'm not sure Hunter wants one. And posting updates to our social media about our not-so-real marriage? What the hell just happened?

"Congrats, newlyweds! We'll talk soon. Ciao!" And then she's gone. Hung up and gone.

My eyes are wide, and my mind is still reeling as I shove my phone into my pocket, thankful designers are putting pockets in dresses these days. Life is too stressful to deal with holding stuff just because we have ovaries. Today is the perfect example. Might be doing a walk of shame, but at least I've got pockets.

I make my way robotically down the stairs of the large farmhouse, wishing I could take my time appreciating the work Hunter seems to have put into this little slice of memory, but not having anything left in me after what just happened.

Let's recap.

In the last seven minutes since I woke up, I found out I married my ex-boyfriend; apparently, there's some sort of saucy video about it online that's caused three-point-five thousand Internet users to visit my page since last night, and a competition that seemed near impossible because either way it was reckless, is now over with.

If I had won, I'd have gotten the job and probably wrecked any chances with Hunter based on how awkward that'd be. And how natural it would be to push him away as my competition. And if he'd won, I'd have lost the job *and* lost him. Because, let's face it, he can't settle down. He's proven that before. And even if he is ready to settle down at this point in his life, it wouldn't be with me.

Not when he knows my secret. A secret very few know but will always tie me to him.

In my heart and in my nightmares.

So, what do we do, then?

I'll find Hunter and tell him about the call with Claudette. Find out what he remembers. We can watch this video together and figure out the damage, then make a plan.

We obviously can't stay *married*. Fake or not.

But maybe we can figure a way out of this and both keep the Classy Country co-exec positions if we raise a shit ton of money and keep the followers happy somehow? String them along for just long enough. Maybe come out and say it was all just a big episode of *Punk'd*? Remember that show?

But they'd hate us when we split up…

It's all so messy. I sift my hands through my hair. *What the hell have you gotten yourself into this time, Devyn?*

I rub my temples and look around downstairs. I see an open concept, farm-style kitchen with a beautiful white marble countertop that wraps around into a bar endcap where three handcrafted, wooden chairs are spaced evenly on the other side for seating. I smile, picturing a gaggle of kids sitting there after school and doing homework, chomping on their little apples and peanut butter snack while they go on about sports tryouts or school plays.

My breath hitches when I realize where I've let my mind wander, and a crease forms in my brow that I've come to be unfortunately familiar with. I rub it out, reminding myself I cannot be anything other than what and who I've been made to be.

Regardless of how that feels.

God. The universe. Whatever you believe in—they've got a plan for me.

And even if I wanted him to be, Hunter isn't it.

I put my hand on my stomach, directly over my womb. Right where she'd be if she were still safe inside me.

Our secret.

Our girl.

Chapter 19

Devyn
Eleven Years Ago

Tugging at the hem of my already-too-small sweater, I use my free hand to reach for the big party bowl above the fridge. I know I'm not supposed to reach above my head. The paper even said it could make something mess up with the umbilical cord, but I can't very well tell Mom that.

Because then the cat would be clear out of the bag. Hunter and I would have to come clean sooner than we planned. And that's not happening. Nope, not at all.

He's going to take me to prom, finish up his senior year, get a job on a farm, and then we're going to buy that stupidly perfect little run-down farmhouse out by Piper's Creek and fix it up.

For the three of us.

I twirl around carefully, sufficiently satisfied that the baby is fine from my overhead grabbing since I don't feel anything funky, and hand the bowl to Dustin. He's opening a giant bag of chips and setting them out next to a bowl of dip, a tray of chopped veggies, and about eighteen packs of hamburger buns.

Tonight is the graduation party for the Pine Forrest Rodeo team and their families. Technically, graduation isn't for three more weeks, but with next week being exams and then prom after that, there really isn't another weekend to make it happen, and this year the party is at our house. I'm still not sure why. I hate how many people are about to be here, when I'm feeling less than stellar today. I groan when I smell the chips Dustin shovels into his mouth in handfuls.

"Ew, those are so gross. How can you even eat them?"

Dustin glares at me suspiciously.

"I thought you liked salt and vinegar. One time you even kicked me in the shin when I ate them all."

Shit. I'm so queasy today I'm not thinking straight. But I can't slip up. Dustin cannot know about this yet. He would kill us both.

I run my hand through my hair, casually shrugging like I'm bored with the conversation already. "Whatever. Why are we even having this dumb party at our house, anyway? Robbie's mansion is way more suited for this."

Dustin's face pinches in a sour look. "You know Mom loves any excuse to parade her children around like trained monkeys with no purpose other than to show the world what beautiful and superior spawn she created."

He rolls his eyes, making a joke of it. But we both know it's true. It's what she's done to me with pageants my whole life.

I often wonder if it isn't to distract people long enough that they won't notice the stench of alcohol lacing her words. Won't notice her glaring failures beneath the glow of our successes.

It has always made me sick. But I think the sickness I'm feeling right now might actually be related to the fact that I'm seven months pregnant and not from how toxic a single dose of my mother's presence may be.

Dustin shuffles through the hallway with a plate of raw hamburger meat, and my stomach rolls. I shove away from the kitchen counter and race through the hallway to the small half-bath by the mudroom, stabbing my finger at the lock button on the handle and throwing my body into the direction of the toilet just in time to vomit up the entirety of my breakfast.

Whew.

I breathe slowly for a little bit, trying to get my dizziness under control, but it's so hard when I get like this. I drink plenty of water, and I eat healthily, so I should be fine.

But...I can't tell Mom I'm growing a child inside me. Not until Hunter graduates and gets that house. I know what will happen if not. I'll get shipped off somewhere as soon as Mom calls Dad. They'll separate us...force me to adopt our child out to some family, convince me I'm too young, that we're too young.

But we aren't. We are old enough to raise this baby that we've already decided on our own to love. And I don't care what anyone but me and Hunter have to say on the matter.

I've never felt as young as my age, anyhow. And who wants to be old and wrinkly when your baby is young and requires energy? I've thought through everything, and I really don't care about any of the alternatives. I want my baby.

We want our baby.

And if Hunter is holding down a steady job and has an offer on that house...we've already saved up a quarter of the downpayment as it is by sneaking our money away into a savings account that we convinced old Abe at the feed store into setting up for us. You had to be eighteen, and we couldn't tell either of our parents. Since Hunter turns eighteen in a few weeks, and he's the only one who knows the truth, he said he'd keep our secret. He set up the account for us months ago.

I don't exactly know why. Maybe he understands what it's like to be young and have the whole world tell you how your life will be before you're allowed to figure it out for yourself. Whatever his reason, I'm grateful to him. Mom's a lost cause. But if Dad sees we've already stepped up without them and figured it out, I think it will all be okay.

That's why I can't let anyone know. And Mom is already awful about counting my calories and doing weigh-ins as it is. I've been sneaking as many extra portions of veggies and meat as I can, but it's hard when she gives me the eyebrow of question with each extra spoonful on my plate.

'Every extra scoop is another inch of fabric I must pay for. Don't want to lose to Lemon Perkins on a matter of waist-lines, now, do you?' I can practically hear her say it. She's said it so many times before. But I'm feeding two now, and I really couldn't care less about Lemon Perkins or the damn Rodeo crown when I think about my baby growing inside me.

So I sneak as many as I possibly can. I've managed to gain only three pounds while my baby measures six, miraculously, and the doctor Abel found us at the free clinic in Centerville, just across the tracks, thinks the baby is doing just fine growth-wise. She said at my age, it's normal not to gain much weight at all and just look like you swallowed a basketball. Weird way of putting it, but as I stare down at my baggy Hunter-Hoodie, I'm beginning to wonder if my basketball is big enough.

It hardly looks like a bump at all. It's small enough that my family hasn't even noticed it yet. The doctor said I need to make sure I'm eating enough to power myself and the baby's growing body, but I'm not always sure I am when I get dizzy and sick like this.

I read most morning sickness stops after the second trimester. It feels like mine never will.

But every pregnant woman gets sick. It's times like these when I wish my mother was normal. That I had someone I could share these insecurities with.

But she's not.

And I don't.

So, I shake it off and wipe my face on my sleeve. Steadying myself, I look into the mirror and smile back at the girl in front of me. She's puffy and tired looking, and far younger than she should be while growing a living being inside her, but she's happier than I've ever seen her. Because for once in her life, there's purpose aside from fancy dresses or smiles for the crowd.

There's a whole life ready to be molded and set free upon the world. A heart to shape and hold that comes from both me and the boy I've loved since before I knew the meaning of the word. We might have made her by accident, but nothing has ever felt more purposeful.

Life has never been more perfect.

Chapter 20

Devyn

No, Penelope! You gotta stay with your babies!"

The little girl's voice fills my ears as I'm rounding the corner of the bright red lean-to stationed a few hundred feet left of the farmhouse.

Now that I've had a plate full of bacon and seen the note Hunter left next to it, I'm feeling a tad less anxious about what may or may not have happened last night.

Ponygirl,

Two Rules for today…

1. Don't freak out—we're fine.

2. Wear your hair down again.

When you've had your fill of bacon, and you better eat the whole damn plate, like I know you want to, come find me in the barn.

Don't run, Dev. Please.

Love,

Your Husband

Husband. That word.

Who knew one word could make my body heat from the inside out? And number two on that list? Wear my hair down?

Stupid *sexy cowboy* knows exactly what he's doing to me with this little note.

But I won't run. Rubbing my fingers along the Starburst ring, I let a smile steal my lips before a spontaneous giggle breaks free. Despite how much I hate that I blacked out and don't remember everything that went down with this whole fake-marriage thing, I can't ignore what Claudette just told me.

I got the job. The job of my dreams. And so did Hunter.

How the hell did we manage that?

I walk slowly toward the noises of animals and…the little girl. My spiky heels aren't the best choice of footwear for a farm. I wish I had those old worn-out boots of mine from the blanket chest right about now as my heels penetrate the soil, sinking into the ground with each step. The crazy thing is, I'd normally be concerned about ruining my six-hundred-dollar designer outfit. I'd be as ruffled as Claudette was at the start of my interview. But I couldn't care less right now if I keep these shoes in pristine condition.

I just want to see Hunter. I can't explain much else, but I have an inherent need to see him right now. To find out what he's feeling about all of this. To see if his thoughts line up with mine. To be close to him, most of all.

Frustrated with the sinkhole I seem to be falling into, I lean my hand against the fence and support myself while I yank my stuck foot from the ground. My foot comes loose, but the shoe doesn't. It mocks me, just the tips of the pink opening visible from beneath the mud.

Screw it. I chuck the other one off and settle my foot back down, curling my toes into the soft, squishy mud, and remembering a time in my life when I never knew where my shoes even were, my body always bare and flush with the earth. *My soul connected to something bigger than myself.*

I probably look a bit ridiculous in my bar crawl outfit from last night, mussed up hair, dark circles, and smelling of bacon and Hunter. This is by far my most eventful walk of shame ever. I giggle thinking about that, because the more I'm up and moving, the more I'm positive we didn't go all the way last night, and I let some of that stress drift away with the breeze.

It's been long enough for me that I'd know. Chad wasn't all that endowed, so to speak. With Hunter's specific…package… in mind, I would most certainly be feeling signs.

So, that might mean things between us will be okay. We just have to figure out what the heck we're going to do when Claudette finds out the marriage she's so excited about isn't real.

"You can do this, Penelope. I know you can. Please, sweet girl, they need their mama."

It's the little girl again. Padding my bare feet toward the sound, I spot her lying on the roof of a bright yellow chicken coop. A smile breaks over my face. She reminds me of myself when I was that age. I was always getting into things I shouldn't have, climbing coops and tree stands. She's about eight or nine, maybe. Reddish-blondish curly hair frizzes around her face as she lies on her back and stares up at a white hen she's holding above her. The hen stares back at her, unconcerned that she's being manhandled by a mini human with an attitude.

Is she having a heart to heart with a chicken? I smile at the sentiment because kids are great like that. They don't care if it's weird or if a chicken can't understand them. If it makes sense to them, they just do it.

I wish I could be more like that.

I stay hidden behind the lean-to while I watch her inter-action with the bird. She flips over on her belly and shoves the chicken into her armpit while she climbs down from the side of the coop, using the door latch as a foothold and then hopping the rest of the way down, chicken still in tow. Now, that's a kid who knows her way around a farm.

Wait. Whose kid is this?

My chest is a little tight. My throat, too.

This is Hunter's farm. And the more I think about that, the tighter my throat gets. It shouldn't feel like a betrayal, staring at the little girl I don't even know.

But it does.

I swallow the lump in my throat and shake my head because no, he wouldn't do that to me. He wouldn't blindside me about a kid he's had for nearly the entire time I've been away. Not after what we've been through.

Unless he was afraid to tell me.

If he felt sorry for me.

I think back to the summer I came home before college, and a pang of jealousy hits me as thoughts cascade through my head. The river, the party, the freaking girl he took to that bedroom. Right in front of me, like I wasn't there. Like I wasn't his best friend. Like we hadn't shared a life, and a trauma, and a fucking *child* together. All that pain and sadness comes swirling back, wrapped up in a dark, menacing bow.

But he wouldn't, would he? Last night…what he said. He wouldn't say those things and have a secret kid hanging around he never planned to tell me about. He couldn't.

The girl's bright hair, hair that looks more like Hunter's the longer I look at it, streams behind her in the wind as she skips to the nesting boxes and shoves the bird back into them.

"There! Now, I don't want you comin' outta there 'til you have lots of babies hatching under you. Got it, Penny?" She wags her finger at the nesting box as if the chicken has any idea what words are, and even though her presence disturbs me, mainly because I don't know if she is or is not Hunter's, I feel an acute sense of respect for this child who seems to go after what she wants and has the courage to keep trying.

"If she won't stay on the eggs, you know, you can try letting one of the silkies sit on them instead," I say, creeping up from the side of the coop. She turns to me and narrows her eyes, probably because I'm a stranger. Smart kid. But she inclines her head, waiting to hear more, so I go on, moving a few steps closer so I can take a look at the nesting boxes, too.

And take a closer look at her.

There are eight eggs in the box she just shoved the bird she calls Penelope into, and there's another hen in there beside her laying on her own eggs. Scanning my memories, I think this one is a barbed rock, because it's got those beautiful pencil-etching marks over its wings. The barbed rock is in the box beside Penelope, and she seems content where she is. She has no plans of moving off her eggs anytime soon.

I watch the little girl scrape her bright blue eyes over the other bird, then puff her bottom lip out in a decisive frown. It's obvious she's wondering why the one bird will do what she's supposed to, but the other won't.

A familiar anxiety tenses inside me.

You can't make any living thing bend against their will. She's lucky she's too young to have learned that.

"Why silkies?"

I smile as I see her defenses against me drop a little. Seems she keeps her walls secure, too.

"They are amazing mamas," I tell her, picking up a furry black hen and running my hand down its back. The hen purrs, and I close my eyes, taking in the warmth the creature offers back to me. The chickens always were my favorite. "They almost always adopt the eggs if you give them a chance. I've even seen silkie hens raise a duck before."

She sputters with laughter and complete wonder. "A duck? There's no way! We have ducks…maybe I can convince Papa to let me try it." She picks up another furry hen and holds it above her head, inspecting it, before turning back to me with a grin that's a mix of half grown, half baby teeth. "Whatta ya reckon we'd call a duck baby raised by a chicken?"

"Hmm." I tap my finger to my chin. "What about Chuck?"

"Chicken duck! I like it!" Out of nowhere, she widens her eyes like she's just had the best idea ever. "Tag! You're it!" she shouts, taking off toward the cattle.

"Wait!" I shout back, unable to stop the laughter pouring from my soul as I chase her through the wheat with my toes covered in mud and my hair wild and free, flowing like hers.

No, flowing like *mine*.

Like it used to. And with the wind against my skin and the tickles of blonde tendrils hitting my face as I run through the field with wild abandon, I sense how dead I've been inside. And how alive I feel right now.

"Wait up! You never told me your name!"

"Catch me, and I'll tell youuuuu," she screams, turning to look at me briefly before darting to the side with a quick tuck and roll. With practiced moves, I watch her bounce onto a mini trampoline, using one hand to hoist herself over the fence, and then landing on her feet like a total badass.

I think back to a time long ago, when a boy not much older than this child in front of me jumped over fences and let his scrappy, reddish-blondish hair fly through the breeze, and my heart stills.

I come to a stop at the fence, threading my fingers through the chain-links of the metal and pressing my face to the side while I take in deep breaths. I haven't run that fast in years, but the running isn't what has me breathless…it's her. I tried to convince myself it can't be, but…her spunk, her farming skills, her hair.

And those blue eyes.

I think back to our conversation just a few minutes earlier.

'Maybe I can convince Papa to let me try it.'

Papa.

"Wait!" I shout as she slings a knobby-kneed leg over the side of a massive stallion and gets ready to take off to who knows where, covered in dirt with pine stuck in her hair.

"What's your name? Your name!"

I probably seem like a crazy woman. A strange lady in last night's clothes, strolling onto her farm and demanding personal information. But there are just too many coincidences for me to ignore.

I have to know.

"Your name! What is it?"

She squints, assessing me. Her horse rears back on two legs, letting out a whinny, ready for whatever adventure she's about to take him on. And I watch closely then, as the little girl I've just met, the one with the deep blue eyes that match those of my dreams, clutches the horse's mane and brings him down on all fours again with expert precision.

Precision you only learn if you're raised by a real–life cowboy.

And in a matter of seconds, she whips her head back toward me, lifts her chin to the sky, and breaks my heart into a million pieces with two simple words.

"Ellie Isaac."

Chapter 21

Hunter
Eleven Years Ago

What about Clementine?" I ask, biting back a smile. Dev has turned down all thirty-seven of my girl name ideas, and six of them have been fruits, just to mess with her.

"For the last time, Hunter, we are not naming our baby a fruit. Just look how Lemon Perkins turned out." She wrinkles her nose at me through her reflection in the floor-length mirror of her bedroom, covered in peeling pink flower stickers I helped her put there over a decade ago. She always was destined to be my girl.

Both my girls, soon.

I stand, moving behind my pregnant girlfriend and wrapping my arms around her. My hands cradle her swollen belly, my lips pressing soft kisses behind her ear. She sighs, relaxing and leaning her weight against me, just like I want her to.

"You're so damn perfect, Dev. Holding my daughter inside of you. All swollen and full. You're irresistible." I guide her to the bed, lowering her onto her back and leaving a trail of kisses across her stomach.

"Hunter," she moans, threading her fingers through my hair, and that alone thrills me. I want to make her feel good. She's having so many sick days lately, and my girl's been a badass, putting on a face so nobody knows our secret. Carrying on like she isn't superwoman in disguise, growing a human, winning pageants, going to school like a normal teen.

It worries me she's got too much going on.

We're interrupted by thumping feet running up the stairs and a loud knock, followed by a hushed whisper from Dusty through the door, "It better be PG in there. Mom's on her way up!"

"Great," she says, groaning as she rolls onto her side.

"Hold on," I say, getting to my feet and helping her to a seated position on the bed. Luckily, we still have our clothes on, except for Dev's baggy sweater, which she pulls rapidly down over her baby bump just before her mom comes waltzing in with no knock or notice at all.

I owe one to Dusty for his warning.

"What are you two doing in here?" Mrs. Campbell teases, eyeing the two of us with a smirk that is fuckin' fake as shit because she's trying to be the cool mom who seems like she doesn't care if we were just fooling around, but she's such a crazy bitch that her own daughter is seven and a half months pregnant and so afraid to tell her that she's been wearing extra-large hoodies for the last month and she has yet to notice. I mean, how fucked in the head can you be to not notice your own daughter is about to have a whole-ass child?

I wish we could tell her. I've been part of this family for longer than I feel like I've been a part of my own. That might be an exaggeration, but there's some truth to it. I never had a mom growing up. She died giving birth to my brother Sam, and shit…I'm just lucky I had her for the first few formative years of my development. Because Sam? He's got shit to work through. I hardly recognize him these days.

The Campbells have practically raised me. My old man's been in and out of jail most of my life. Technically, Aunt Sarah has custody of me and Sam, but I don't think he stays there any more than I do. I have a bed in Dusty's room, for fuck's sake. Sam has a few friends he splits time between. Parents don't question the constant sleepovers as much when you're Sam's age, but when you're seventeen or eighteen like me… they just start to feel sorry for you. At least, the Campbells did. Even if Devyn and Dusty's mom is a complete lunatic, she's always served me the same shitty spaghetti and Cheerios she gives her own kids.

Their dad's not too bad, when he's around.

Doesn't excuse the anger I feel when I look into the green eyes of her mother. Eyes that dare to look almost identical to Devyn's, but different at the same time. Darker. Blacker. Like they've lost all their sparkle. And that makes me sad for her.

I focus on Dev, tugging her shirt down over her belly to hide any signs of our growing baby from her mother. *Just a little longer, babygirl. We only have to hide a little longer.* Her mom has always made her feel fat and ugly. A naked, plastic doll nobody could ever love unless it's dressed up and made up. Flawless. Pinching her love handles, making off-handed comments about too many cupcakes or slices of pizza that everyone else eats triple of.

My jaw clenches. I can't wait to take her away from it all. To our little farmhouse.

Just me, my farm, and my girls.

And I'll never let them lose their sparkle. Not in a million years.

"What do you think, honey?" Mrs. Campbell says to me, her eyebrows raised in question.

"I'm sorry. I wasn't listening." I wink at Devyn. "I was distracted."

Mrs. Campbell rolls her eyes. "Oh, Lord, Hunter, you are too much." She swats me like we're friends, getting way closer than I want my girlfriend's mom to be, her hand lingering awkwardly on my arm. Devyn sighs, shaking her head and offering me an apologetic wince. I peel Mrs. Campbell's fingers from my arm. She smells of tequila, and I really hope Devyn doesn't catch a whiff of it before she leaves. Pretty much anything causes her morning sickness at all hours of the day now.

"Distracted?" She laughs, the smell wafting out from her mouth and filling the space around me. I scrunch my nose and back away, but she doesn't notice. She's laughing at what I said. "Distracted by my daughter? This little chunk?"

She reaches for Devyn, to pinch the small roll of flesh hanging over her pants, and all it takes is one beat of nothing before I lose it.

I lunge forward. "Don't touch her!" My voice is thick and commanding, assertive and menacing in a way it's never been before. It's me, the happy-go-lucky class clown. The boy who charms your southern mama and steals a cola from your fridge on the way out.

That boy is gone. The one standing in his place is a man ready to fight anyone, including his girlfriend's own mother, if she so much as touches his girls.

"What has gotten into you, Hunter Isaac?" Mrs. Campbell shrieks, placing her arm in front of her daughter in a show of protection, which is just fucking laughable. She's protecting

Dev? With calorie counting? Reverse psychology? With tanning beds and juice cleanses? Naw.

Hell, naw.

"What's wrong is that I don't appreciate you making her feel like shit for what she looks like or how much she weighs!" Devyn's eyes are glassy with the promise of tears, but true to her nature, she doesn't let them flow down her perfectly made-up face. Anything so her mother still thinks she's pretty.

It's messed up, but that isn't Devyn's fault.

She sniffles, smiling at me, and even though she's sad and confused, my heart soars when I see the sparkle still there in her eyes. It's not dull. Not like her mother's.

Not anymore.

How could it be? We have each other. We have our girl.

For a moment, I let myself live in the bliss that will be our life together, and I smile down at the beautiful, perfect girl in my arms. Not a pageant queen or the star of the dance team, but so much more. The girl who made summer camp magical and Monopoly unbearable. The one who chucked a roller skate at my head for making fun of her ballgowns, but still let me lead her across countless dancefloors wearing them.

The girl who holds my baby inside her. She's mine to take care of now.

"I'm taking her out to eat as much as she damn well pleases," I tell a still shocked Mrs. Campbell. She doesn't do anything, though, just lights up one of her Virginia Slims and throws her satin robe back over her camisole and shorts, mumbling something about the party and what the neighbors will say if the Junior Miss Southern Rodeo Queen isn't there… not Devyn…The Queen.

And with Dustin, it's always The Grades. The Sports. The Reputation. My fist curls at my side, and it's all I can do not to punch a hole in the wall with the anger I feel toward this woman who raised two of the best people I know. And she doesn't even see how amazing they are. She just picks and picks and picks.

"I don't give a shit what they say," I tell her.

But her eyes rear back angrily, scorching me with a fire I wasn't sure Mrs. Campbell even had left inside her. I can take it, though. I'll fight any fire-breathing dragon for the right to save my princess. Forever and always.

"She needs to be back for the party." She points her long, manicured finger at me. Funny how someone can pay thousands for beauty and still be genuinely ugly at their core. She casts her gaze down on Devyn, her own daughter, who she should love and adore no matter what she looks like or what the number on the scale might be, and my breath stills in my lungs, because all she looks…is disgusted by her. And by me.

"You! You are just like your mother," she hisses. "Always trying to save everyone." Her lip curls up in a penetrating sneer, and it stings to hear mention of my mother from such putrid lips. Mrs. Campbell's eyes flare when she hears my sharp inhale, and she digs her talons in deeper.

"What you need to realize, and what your poor mother never could, is some people simply aren't worthy. And they must learn to save themselves."

Devyn gasps, putting a hand to her side in a way that her mother won't notice, but I can feel, being pressed against her.

"Hurts," she whispers into my chest, pressing her face against my shirt. And I'm not sure if it's the pain in her side she's talking about or her mother's words. Either way, we're done here.

I stand, locking eyes with the woman who somehow created the angel currently lacing her fingers through my own and shake my head. I remember a time when she wasn't like this.

Or do I?

"One day," I say, "I hope you sober up and see how amazing your children are. I only wonder if you'll be worthy of their love when that day comes."

I lightly tug Devyn's hand and lead her out the door, brushing past her mother, like the knight in all those books from years ago. Saving my princess from the castle, whisking her away to a kingdom all our own.

Giving her the Happily Ever After she deserves.

We're halfway to the Sugar Stable when Devyn finally speaks. She's been crying softly for about five minutes now since we left her house, the emotions of the fight with her mom finally hitting her, I guess. Or maybe she's just comfortable enough with me to cry. I smile at that thought, but only a little. I can't smile for long when Devyn's hurting.

"Ellie," she says, sniffling and wiping her tears on the back of my hoodie sleeve. I gave it to her to wear when we got in the car because she was cold, and because I love the little humming sounds she makes when she smells it, because it smells like me.

"I want to name her Ellie."

"Ellie." I test out the name. It rolls off my tongue easily enough, and even though I won't tell her this, I was going to say yes to any name she finally settled on regardless of what I want. I couldn't want anything more than my two girls healthy and happy and home…with me. I want us to create a life for our daughter that is filled with love and comfort and happy family memories. Ones that don't include weigh-ins or divorces, deaths and custody fights, social services, and hidden pregnancies.

Fuck, our parents didn't know what the hell they were doing.

And we don't either. But as long as I live, I'll do whatever I need to protect my family. I swear it. I won't be like my dad, a bachelor and a gambler. And Devyn won't be like her mom, broken and lost. And our baby will be loved. Always.

"Ellie." I repeat the name, turning to Devyn in the passenger seat and smiling.

"I love it."

As we pull through the intersection, it feels like we've just crossed a new barrier in our relationship. I can see the sign for The Sugar Stable now, and I can't wait to scoop her up into my lap and get her the extra-large strawberry milkshake she won't admit she wants; the one I know always brings a smile to her face.

But she's not smiling. Her eyes are wide when I look over at her, and she's—

"Hunter!" she screams, and then I see it.

An eighteen-wheeler coming straight toward us…

In the wrong lane.

I grip the wheel, searching, scanning, praying to God for a way out. For a path of freedom. For something I can do, but there's no way out.

My heart is racing to the beat of my thoughts.

My girls. My girls. My girls!

There's nothing I can do but pray. I steal one last glance at the woman beside me, the one who feels like a walking representation of my heart, sitting outside of my body, pleading with me to save her.

To save our daughter.

"I love you," she breathes.

Chapter 22

Hunter

Respectfully, Mr. Campbell, go the fuck to hell." I spit the words into the air, wishing I could stand and face the man on the other end of the phone who thinks he's a damn god rather than having no immediate body to direct my anger toward.

I shovel a heap of straw into Beau's stall, rolling my eyes when I see Lyle's stall is also in need of fresh bedding, a clear indication Ellie hasn't done her chores before taking him out for a ride again.

Ellie.

I hadn't thought about what might happen once Devyn got back home and met the little girl who shares our daughter's name. The one who has stolen my heart and wrapped it up in pink tulle and friendship bracelets for the past nine years.

She didn't replace our Ellie. That could never happen.

But she came into my life when I needed her the most.

When my two loves had been ripped away from me and I was at my lowest of lows.

Yeah, Aunt Sarah, I know…A child will lead the way. I don't think I'd be where I am…be the man I've become—leading the youth clubs, organizing charities, raising millions for people who need it. People who are hungry, small businesses who are failing…I help them now. I have the means to help them.

And my tenacious little buddy, my sweet Ellie girl, she's the singular reason I'm still alive. At the rate I was headed, I could have easily become just like my father.

Like my brother.

I grind my teeth, staring into Lyle's stall. But Eleanor needed me to be her papa, and I needed her to save me from myself.

I took that money, and I won't let myself regret it longer than I have already.

"You gave me your word, Isaac. Nine years ago, when you came to me, a wasted mess with a bottle practically glued to one hand and a boxing glove on the other, still a whole *year* after what happened to my daughter—"

"*Our* daughters." I cut him off swiftly. He may not view our unborn child as a life, but we did. We suffered. We lost. And I'll be damned if he sweeps her under the rug like she never existed. Like she didn't change our lives forever.

Silence fills the line. Silence followed by the sound of his pen drawer opening. I know the sound because of all the years Dev, Dusty, and I spent sneaking around his office, pretending to solve mysteries. I also know the sound because over the years it's always accompanied the smooth wisps of his pen swiping across a blank check.

To ward me off.

It won't work this time. I'm no longer desperate. I'm no longer weak. No longer a child.

And I know down to my bones how I want this story to end.

"You have the same desk." I finally say as I hear the pen begin its predicted scribbles. The sound pauses, and I know I have his attention. "You always were quick to pull out a check and send me on my way. Sweeping secrets under rugs rather than facing them."

"The fuck do you want, boy? You want another half a million to pay for a farm? Done. Want me to match your yearly scholarship donations? Done. In fact, I've done it for years, in case you hadn't noticed…and do you know why? Because your mother was a fucking *saint* when we were kids. She was my friend. Then she died and left you with that asshole father of yours, and I felt sorry for you. Like a damn son to me. I coached your fucking little league, Isaac! Then you went and impregnated my daughter, and I still felt sorry for you. But I feel sorrier for her."

There's silence. Because fuck if I have a response to that. So I just breathe and listen. For the pen to scribble? For the drawer to slam shut? I'm not sure. Maybe because he's the only father I have. Even if he isn't mine.

"You've lived without her for the last ten years, and you can do it for ten more. My little girl has had enough therapy and scars for a lifetime, and I will not sit by while you slice them back open. So, tell me the fucking price, and I'll pay it every damn time, but you better fix this. You will break it off with my daughter, or I'll tell her how you traded her in for a farm and a little girl just like the one she lost."

"*We* lost."

"Do you hear me, Isaac? End this charade before she gets hurt again."

The call ends with a click before I can even process the monologue he just vomited. And I feel like I might vomit, too. He gave me his word all those years ago that if I walked away from her and left her alone, he'd never tell her about my fighting addiction, my stint in rehab, or the fact that I went bankrupt on that farm and the only reason I have it today is because of his loan. A loan I've since paid back but still admit I needed. And by proxy, I needed Mr. Campbell.

Anger and guilt sear me from within, and I pull at my hair. I hate that I ever took money from him. I hate that I let myself get so low that I thought it was the only way. And I regret not telling Devyn any of it, because she wouldn't understand. It would just look like he paid me off to forget about her. In a way, he did; that was his intention, at least.

But it's all bullshit.

I could never forget about Devyn Lynn. And no, I will not be breaking it off with her either. I rub the crisp ring around my finger, the one she made me last night from a white paper straw wrapper, mostly to mock me for her Starburst ring. It's the last thing I remember before I blacked out.

Lemon drove us home. I know that much because she left a note on my kitchen counter that says, "You said we could do things my way. Don't forget that when you wake up mad at me."

Fucking Lemon. I still need to watch whatever this video is that I have far too many messages about. Mr. Campbell didn't seem pleased by its content, which only makes me grin smugly as I lean the shovel against the stall.

Beau's out in the field grazing, and Ellie's got Lyle out there somewhere. I wanted to check in on her before I found Dev, let her know who she is and all. I rub my temples and sigh. There will be no easy way of doing something like this.

"Shit," I say to Peggy the Pig, affectionately named by my sweet girl, like most of the animals on this farm, "I really didn't think any of this through, did I, Pegs?"

"No, you did not," a sharp, familiar voice slices through the air.

I groan, dropping my head and bracing myself for the inevitable lecture. She's two hours early to get Ellie. Which means she wants to chat. And I can only imagine it's about what everyone else wants to chat about today. Me and Dev.

I turn to face her and paste on a smile that I hope will melt the ice inside her soul.

I'll need all the armor I can get for this conversation.

"Katie."

Chapter 23

Devyn

Ellie Isaac.

I repeat the name that I haven't spoken aloud more than once in my life.

A name that lives permanently etched into my heart. Burned there. Branded.

Because Ellie was my only child. Even if her death certificate was signed before her birth. She was my only child, and always will be my only child.

The breeze picks up, and the field seems to come alive with movement. The wisps of wheat pull at the fabric of my dress and the tiny hairs on my arms as I walk through the endless expanse.

When the little girl…Ellie…when she rode away, I ran alongside the fence for what felt like minutes, tears streaming down my face, my heart practically beating out of my chest, chasing the discovery as far as my legs would carry me.

Truth be told, grief does strange things to a person. And

seeing Ellie? Hearing that name leave her lips and fill the air around us…I thought for a moment.

I shake my head. *A ghost.* I can't believe I thought that little girl was a ghost or an angel or…I don't even know what I thought.

The fact is, that little girl lives here on this farm with a man she calls *Papa.* And she's the spitting image. The fact is, I think Hunter has a daughter he's kept from me.

But whose daughter? And how could he betray me like that? Of all the names he could pick for his child, why the same name as ours?

When you're in the country, time seems to slow down. I guess without the honking cars and the constant flashing of computerized ads all over the place, it's easy to settle in with the world, get back on Mother Nature's time. I smile, thinking about the wild strawberry-blonde curls trailing behind Ellie as she rode her horse away. How much it reminded me of my own childhood.

I stop dead ahead when I realize I've walked myself to the old white shed. The one I unashamedly lost my virginity behind. You can call it whatever you want, but we were teen-agers, and there are only so many places you can sneak off to in a small town and go unnoticed by older brothers and angry dads. I laugh, running my hand over the worn handle on the door. Right below it, carved into the wood, is a small heart and the initials *D+H.*

Does it bother me that he named his child Ellie? Kind of. Okay, yes. Yes, it bothers the heck out of me. But what bothers me more is that he *has* a child.

And it's not with me.

I don't know what makes me so damn entitled to know everything about him. It's not like we've been together for over a decade. We're both allowed to have lives apart from one another. I guess it's just being back here and feeling so many intimate memories all over this farm. It feels like a space I can call partly mine, even though that's entirely ridiculous. It's obviously Hunter's farm fair and square, and he seems to be doing really well. I turn the handle and push on the shed door, and a loud creak that tells me this place is in serious need of some WD-40 echoes through the space. The smell is a mix of garage musk and potting soil. I crinkle my nose at the combination and reach into the room, tugging on a metal cord.

When the lights flick on, my jaw drops. It's so cute here. Little beaded curtains line the walls, and colorful gel inserts are shoved onto the light bulbs that cover the rows of tiny, baby sunflowers lining the floors. Some are taller than others, but all of them are still curled into themselves and clearly in their early developmental stages. A smile tugs at the corner of my lips when I spot a wooden sign, painted in lime green and hot pink sparkles:

PROPERTY OF ELEANOR ROSEMARY ISAAC. DO NOT TOUCH THEM OR THEY WILL EAT YOU. YES, THAT MEANS YOU!

Eleanor. Ellie. Okay.

I tug at the hem of my skirt, wishing like hell that I'd worn pants last night. I swat the seventeenth mosquito from attacking my thighs and shimmy my way back out of the sunflower greenhouse that seems to belong to Miss Ellie. Her dad has certainly shown her the ropes of gardening.

It shouldn't make me feel physically ill knowing he's got a daughter he loves and clearly teaches life skills and takes care of. In fact, I want to be elated for him. To scream to the heavens a resounding *thank you* for sending him something he absolutely deserves. He's a good man.

And as much as I wish I could pin my years' worth of heartache on him, none of us handle things the right way one hundred percent of the time. In fact, it's in the times we handle things the wrong way that we usually learn something about ourselves. Just look at me quitting the station. I never would have come home, never talked things over with Hunter, never confronted my past.

The facts are, he lied to me by omission about this little girl. But everything I felt last night was real. And if it was for him, too, then I'm not running away this time just because things are messy.

I'll find Hunter and sort this out. And then we'll figure out what to do about everything else.

Making my way toward the barn, I bring my hand to a place on my body where I seldom let my attention linger. I cradle my womb.

I can't feel the scars through the fabric of my dress, but I know from sheer memory exactly where they live along my skin. Scars are like that…no matter how long they've been there, you'll always feel them.

I love my scars for that reason alone. My Ellie will always be there.

And I'll feel her right there until the end of time.

Chapter 24

Hunter

Before you start on me, keep in mind I haven't had my second cup of coffee yet, and no, I have not watched the video either." I point my phone at Katie and gesture for her to take a seat on an open bench. She declines, naturally.

I wonder sometimes if my niece's social worker understands the meaning of the word "social." We weren't friends growing up. She was a few years younger than me and did rodeo pageants with Dev and Lemon, but she was always shut off to most of us. Unapproachable.

She's pretty and strong, though. One of the smartest people I know. Props to the man—or woman—who manages to thaw her icy heart one of these days. As for me, I happen to be on the receiving end of the ice queen's more lethal powers most of the time. Usually because of rules I'm breaking.

Like arguing with Ellie's principal. But Mrs. Finkelman had it comin'. Ellie only hit the Presley boy because he's a little shit and everyone knows it.

She had a mean right hook too. I grin, proud of my little cowgirl. She's a fighter. Reminds me of a younger version of Devyn most days—fierce, loud, passionate.

I roll my eyes at Katie's blatant disgust as she picks hay from her knitted cardigan and flicks it to the barn floor, checking beneath her heels for whatever it is she thinks she's stepping in.

It's shit. No question. But I don't tell her that.

"If you'll give me a sec, I'm gonna look at the video. I've had three phone calls about the damn thing this morning, and it isn't even nine o' clock." I turn to Katie, the judgmental twist of her lips and one raised eyebrow telling me she knows something I don't.

"I'll spoil it for you to save everyone some time. You're married," she deadpans. "But you remember that much, don't you?"

I nod, letting a slow smile break across my face as I thumb my ring finger. "Yeah, but it shouldn't change anything, right? Whatever we posted online seemed to cause a stir, but why does any of that concern Ellie's placement? It's just a drunken TikTok and a fake marriage."

"Not exactly," she says, smoothing out her pants. "Lemon is a certified wedding officiant. She took a test online last summer for our cousin's wedding."

My eyes widen. "You're cousins?" How the hell did I not know that?

"What? Yeah, I always thought everyone knew that. But that's beside the point." She squares her shoulders and puts her hands on either side of mine. "Your wedding may have been fake, but your marriage—it's the real deal, Hunter."

"You're telling me Devyn and I are legally married?"

She nods. "It needs to be filed at the courthouse, still, but yes."

"You're fucking with me," I growl, daring her to prove me wrong, but praying to God she can't.

I stare ahead, the muscles in my face unable to move in any arrangement except for one that probably leaves me looking like a damn codfish, my mind returning to the first part of her statement.

"Lemon's a minister?"

"Officiant. But aside from that, the video is rather harmless, so you can calm down where that's concerned. It is a bit," she pauses, wrinkling her nose in disgust, "sickeningly sweet. Promises of lifelong bonds and sacrifice." She waves her hand. "Honestly, it was gross. However, the fact is you are now a married man, and that does affect custody matters."

I freeze, my neck stiffening as tension rolls over me. Custody.

I hate that word where Ellie is involved.

"Why does anything need to change? She's always lived with me as a permanent foster. Nobody has ever cared before now."

"Because now that Aunt Sarah is dead, Eleanor's mother has applied for custody review." She lets out a frustrated sigh. "For once."

Anger and something akin to desperation take hold of me, and it's all I can do not to kick the stable door. "Why does that woman get any review at all? She's a horrible human being, Katie. She doesn't care about Ellie. The only reason she would ever care is for her inheritance from Aunt Sarah. Why do you think she's never tried for a review before now?"

Katie shakes her head, resigned, like she agrees with me, but she's spent the last of her resources tryin' to fix it. And the look in her eyes tells me there's not much more she can do. Her hands are tied.

"Look, Hunter." She lowers her voice and chooses her words carefully, like she thinks I'll break if she says something wrong.

I might.

"You've been a father to Ellie since the moment you knew she existed. I'm not giving up on this yet. Why do you think I send her off to all those meet and greets loaded up with pranks and smoke bombs in her pockets? Do you both seriously think you've been putting one over on me all this time? I don't want her adopted out of this family and away from this farm any more than you do. I care about these kids, you know?"

I do know. Ellie isn't the only kid on the farm, in this community, on Katie's roster. She fights for our kids like she was one of them. Because she *was* one of us. It's the same reason I run my farm. To be there and make this town everything it wasn't for our generation.

"This is why I became a social worker. But the truth is, the system is shit for cases like yours and Ellie's, and with Sam's prison sentence extended to life," she pauses, offering me an apologetic smile as I wince at the sharp, factual, way she presents that information to me. I know my brother will be in prison for life, but hearing it never gets easier. It makes me sad for Ellie, but she's better off without him.

And she's definitely better off without that woman called her mother.

I tense, raking my hands through my hair and tugging in frustration at the precarious situation we're in. Katie goes on.

"The courts will try to place her with the closest biological parent of sound of mind and clear of issues. Right now, the courts are favoring parental rehab so children can be placed back with bio parents long term." She frowns, shaking her head. "Even years after the child has been removed from care of that parent."

I can't listen to this.

My heart is so loud, I think it's possible I'm outside of my body entirely. Floating around in another time and space where down is up and wrong is right. And only then would it make sense that the courts would think sending Ellie to live away from me is even within the realm of possibility.

Katie grabs my hand and squeezes. It's not normal for her to offer anyone comfort, but she does. Because she knows how horrible that possibility would be, and I start to falter. A tear runs from the corner of my eye, rolling down my skin, and that's when I let the dam break. The water rushes in. Floods over me. I lay my head down on Katie's shoulder, slumping over her tiny, five-foot-four frame, and cry.

"I can't lose her."

I don't know how long she lets me cry on her. It's likely she'll go back to being standoffish next time she sees me, and we'll never speak of this moment again. I'd prefer that, I think. What with the crying and all.

I pull away from her, using my sleeve to wipe the mess that is my face, and snort so loud even the pigs give me a look.

"Thanks, Kate."

"Yes, well." She pushes her glasses back up on the bridge of her nose with one pointed finger, reminding me of a British nanny, and it makes me laugh. I wish she had some kind of magical powers in that bag of hers. An umbrella with the power to smack some sense into the guardian ad litem and steer Ellie far the fuck away from Cruella De-Mom would be handy.

She takes a seat on the empty bench and pats the spot next to her, surprising me, because I thought she just came here to break bad and peace out, but she's got more to say.

So, I sit.

"Like I said, I'm not giving up yet." She pulls out an iPad and stylus that she clicks and scrolls around for several moments. "You and Devyn got married last night, no mistake."

I groan and rub my forehead. "I know, I know. I fucked up. It just—"

"Let me finish, please." She clicks her tongue, like I'm one of the kids at the group home who won't listen.

"Yes, ma'am."

"You got married. And you are the next closest living biological relative, who isn't in jail with a life sentence, aside from Eleanor's mother, who has a hefty record and history of drug addiction."

I nod, following so far, but still unsure of where she's going with this. I'm still not her damn mother. I'm not even her father. I'm her uncle. How do I compete with that kind of biology?

"But if she's been clear on drug tests and out of rehab, isn't that what you're saying? That the judge will still favor the mother?"

"Well, there are several case studies that would confirm the courts favor a strong, healthy, two-parent home with any biological relative regardless of whether that person is the mother or father. It can be a grandparent or even an uncle…if they're married and both upstanding people."

"Are you saying that being married makes me the better option?"

Katie's lips slide into a sly smile, one of the first I've ever really seen reach her eyes. A smile that says she's found a loophole she's confident she can use to win.

"That's exactly what I'm saying. We have a strong case already since you've raised her from birth and have taken all the parenting classes adoptive families are required to have undergone. We have a very good shot here, Hunter."

I holler, scooping Katie up and earning several swats and yelps from her in the process of spinning her around in celebration. "We're going to win this, aren't we? For good!" I yell, setting her down and hugging her tighter than I imagine she's comfortable with.

But I can't help it.

"You're the best, you know that? I don't know what Ellie and I would do without you on our side."

She stiffens in my arms, but then settles into my hug once she realizes I am not letting her out of feeling emotions for once. I've seen this woman twice a week or more for Ellie's whole life, and this is our first hug.

"Thank you," she says, politely peeling my arms from her body. "I appreciate your candor."

I laugh. *God, this woman needs to get out more.*

"Now," she says, looking to me with all the seriousness in the world, "you need to tell Devyn."

I sigh heavily, backing up and nodding. I turn away, mulling over the ways to break this to her when our relationship is already fragile enough.

"How?" I ask Katie, hoping she's got more magic up her sleeve for today, but she's used it all up. No spoon full of sugar for me.

I just have to confront the woman I love. Tell her I've been raising my brother's daughter for the past nine years, that she's everything in the world to me, and keeping her with me could hinge solely on her decision to stay married after one drunken night back together and a damn *dare*?

With our past.

I close my eyes, rubbing at my temples as I pace in the barn, my boots wearing a path beneath my feet as I think.

"I know this is complicated." Katie straightens her cardigan, dusting the hay from her backside as she stands. She pauses, and I see a rare smile curve up on one side of her face. "But the way the room comes to life when you and Devyn are together is something I've never quite seen before. And that kind of love is what Ellie deserves."

Beau comes trotting through the field, a whinny echoing through the open doors of the barn. Brooklyn must be riding him since Ellie stayed next door with her last night. I peek out the window and see Lyle trailing behind, Ellie riding with damn near perfect form and laughing like a song my ears can't get enough of. There's no way I'm letting them take her from me. I'll tell Devyn. I just need to figure out how.

But what if she thinks I lied to her again? What if she thinks the only reason I did this was for Ellie's sake and she runs? I could risk losing her *and* Ellie. My stomach seizes with the idea of it. I can't let that happen. *I can't.*

On the other hand, Devyn was the one who initiated the marriage dare. And it got us both the job we've been after, so it's not like she isn't gaining something by staying fake married.

But it isn't fake.

Katie supposedly has copies of the napkins we signed. I pull out my phone as the text pings to see the copies she said she'd send me. It's miraculous that Lemon was sober enough to pen down the legal jargon so thoroughly…but still. It's there. Both our signatures. And Lemon's. In pink pen and signed with Devyn's lipstick kiss.

My stomach tenses. Devyn might not be okay pretending if she knows it isn't pretending.

Turning on my heel, I grab the brushes and tools I'll need to help Ellie get the horses cleaned up from their run and ready for lessons before I pop back in to wake Dev. I smile, imagining this could be our new normal, as I make my way through the barn and toward the sound of laughter.

But it isn't Brooklyn with Ellie.

It's Dev.

She rides into the barn.

On my fuckin' horse.

And if the sight of my woman bareback on my horse doesn't damn me straight to hell for the sins I want to commit against her right here in this barn, then I don't know what will.

Not just my woman…*my wife.*

Fuck, I like the sound of that.

Devyn's hips sway with the motion of Beau's canter, her smile stretching from ear to ear as they trot behind Lyle and Ellie. And she wears her hair down.

Fuck, Dev.

"What a perfectly good boy you are, Mr. Beau," she baby-talks to him. Her blonde hair whips from one side of her body to the next when she lifts her head to the sky, laughing and smiling brighter than the summer sun when he seems to neigh in response. I chuckle; my horse is such a damn flirt for Devyn. I'd swear he might just remember her.

She doesn't see me yet, as she dismounts Beau, kissing his nose like she's visiting an old friend.

And I like that. Watching her fall back into her element in Pine Forest is like a drug. I can't seem to get enough of her wonder and nostalgia as she makes up for lost time with the place she remembers, her practiced movement around the horses as she pads along in filthy bare feet with her heels dangling from her fingers, evidence enough that you can't take the country out of the girl.

The animals are eatin' her up, and I don't blame them one bit. Hell, I'm jealous of my own damn horse as she runs her fingers through his mane.

But this wasn't how I was going to introduce her to Ellie.

"You're awake." I stride toward Devyn, giving Beau an

affectionate pat. He nuzzles my cheek, demanding attention. Devyn breathes in audibly and gives me a look I can't quite place. But she's not angry.

Her eyes swipe to Ellie and one eyebrow raises at me in a silent question. A sad smile ghosts across her lips.

"You've met—"

"Ellie?" Her smile falls then, taking pieces of my heart along with it. I don't want to hurt Devyn, yet I always seem to be the source of her pain.

"I'm sorry, it isn't—"

She stops me, placing a finger to my lips and meeting my stare dead on.

"Don't you ever apologize for that little girl. You've done a damn good job, from what I can see." She swallows, saying more with her eyes than words ever could. It kills me that she never lets those tears out, even after all these years. That hasn't changed. I see them on the tips of her irises, glowing, shining, daring someone to break the impenetrable wall that holds them back.

"I've missed you so much," I say. But I'm not as strong as Devyn Lynn. My walls do break.

I let my tears fall as I tug her close, and we mourn the loss of a life together we never got to live. A child neither of us properly grieved. A child who was *ours*.

When I pull away, and she wipes the tears from my face with painted thumbs that look something like sunflowers, I feel the pieces of my life click together. A movie playing out before me with only one possible ending ever in mind. Perfectly plotted and planned.

My destiny.

And this time I'll do whatever I have to do to protect it.

Chapter 25

Devyn

She's not my biological daughter." Hunter paces the living room as I sit on the arm of a Bordeaux and cherry oak recliner that matches everything else in his house with Pinterest perfection. I guess when you film a lot of your content in your own home you want it to feel neat and put together most of the time.

I try not to post too much of myself on my page. It decreases the times I get drawn to looking at myself and picking apart one thousand and two things I can't stand. I learned long ago it's best not to pay attention to photos or video clips of myself, so I try to post group settings and events in fun, artsy ways instead.

I lost several thousand followers when I quit the station and stopped posting selfies. Eye-opening is what that is.

But not as eye-opening as what he just told me.

"Of course, she's yours. Hunter, you don't have to sugar-coat this for me. I hung out with her all morning. She looks like you, acts like you, has your last name, and calls you Papa. She's—"

"Samuel's."

He watches me carefully as I take in this new information. A swift breath of air releases from my lungs and escapes my lips, as relief floods over me. But he frowns, and I try to take it back.

It's too late. And my blatant relief is over the very thing that might be causing him pain.

"I wish she were mine." His eyes meet mine, and his message is loud and clear. This is still very much his child, father or not. "Devyn, I don't want to scare you off." He grabs my hand, toying with the crease of my Starburst ring where yellow joins orange. "But she's mine. I'm hers. We're a package deal."

"I understand," I say, linking my fingers with his. "And I'm not running yet, am I?"

I surprise myself with that revelation, because a whole lot has happened in the last few days, and most of it revolves around Hunter and this life I didn't even know existed a week ago. A life that feels so ingrained in me that there's no way I've been away from it for this long.

I'm not ready to leave it behind, either.

He has a child. A niece, I correct myself, watching as his eyes bore a hole into my soul, waiting for something more. I can live with that.

"What happened last night," I say, switching gears, "I know we were drinking, but I wanted all of that to happen. I needed you to know that."

He smiles a shit-eating grin that's so damn smug, I wish I could take my words back just to give him hell longer.

"Oh, I know." He licks his lips, leaning in and getting dangerously close to my ear. "My jeans from last night are covered in how much you wanted all of that to happen, remember?" I shiver, hating that he's right and loving how downright *slutty* it makes me feel, which is a whole new kink Hunter has seemed to unlock that I didn't know I had.

I swat him away, lifting my body from his lap and turning to put my hands on his shoulders as I tower over him. "Excuse me. We are taking things slow, Mr. Isaac. You just sprang some soap opera level news on me about a secret daughter, and then basically all but molested my ear, so I feel the need to point that out."

I stand and walk away, giggling quietly as I hear him groan. He follows me to the kitchen, spinning me around to face him, his hands on my hips like electricity in my veins.

"Call me Mr. Isaac again, wife." He leans in and presses a light kiss to the corner of my lips, and I can't help the smile that pulls at the edges of my mouth even when I'm trying desperately to make it do the opposite.

"Oh, my gosh, you can't say that." But I'm practically melting into his arms and shoving my neck into his warm, languid kisses as he tongues and bites and all but fucks the skin on my neck. I back up, holding him closer and angling to give him more access to all parts of my body as heat takes over and claws its way through me.

"I'm gonna fuck you so hard once you let me." His teeth scrape my earlobe as he pulls away, sending pulses to my center with every swipe of his hot mouth on my body.

I want him all over me, inside me, on top of me. I want him everywhere. I grind my body against his, and he picks me up by my butt, hoisting me and wrapping my legs around him. His hand pushes between us, and his fingers brush my clit.

"Feels so good," I moan as I press my body harder into his and rub myself over his fingers until I can feel the slickness from inside me seeping out all over him, and fuck if this isn't the hottest thing I've ever done. I want more.

I want so much more with Hunter Isaac, and I don't even know what more there is.

But a voice in my head keeps saying we need to protect ourselves. We need to take this slow.

"Stop," I gasp. And he stills, instantly pulling his hand from between our bodies and bringing me back down to the floor, eyes wide with worry.

I feel so fucking embarrassed for that. I made this so damn awkward.

"I wanted that," I assure him. "I did. I just…I think I need us to slow down a bit longer before we pick it back up to whatever that level is."

He smirks, and I can feel my cheeks turning pink. "I'm so awkward. I'm sorry." Spinning around, I place my hands on the counter. The immaculate, beautiful counter he almost fucked me on.

It would have been just as good as any fantasy I've ever had, too. He would have spread me out, and I'd probably hang off the edge a little, and—

"You okay there?" he asks, breaking me out of my daydream, yet again.

"Yeah," I say, heaving a wistful sigh. "I am, but I'm also hungry, and you have a whole lot more to tell me, so let me cook you something and we can chat. Take things slow." I gesture to the stool directly in front of the island, making sure to state my boundaries loud and clear. I'm not sure if that's to him or to myself, but it's been stated all the same.

"I got it, Dev." He smirks. "I told you, I'm only gonna fuck you hard once you let me. Consent is very sexy." He winks then moves to the other side of the counter, sitting at the barstools I imagined our non-existent children sitting at only hours ago. Only, that's no longer true. He does have a child who likely sits here and does homework.

I smile at that.

"Okay, husband," I tease, spinning to the fridge and opening it wide, "you have ground turkey, soy sauce, green onions. Do you have honey?"

"In the pantry." He smirks as he watches me skip around his kitchen in search of utensils, and I smile brightly as I take the ingredients to the counter in front of Hunter, because I'm obviously putting on a cooking show for him if I'm gonna do this.

I laugh at his skepticism, eyeing me suspiciously.

"No offense, Dev, but since when do you cook?"

"Since a while. I have secrets, too, ya know."

We stay in the kitchen for roughly an hour, and he tells me all about his pride and joy.

Eleanor Rosemary Isaac.

It turns out he named her after her maternal grandmother, Eleanor, who was the only one of her mother's family to show up at the hospital for her birth, not long after our own Ellie died. "Something about that name felt...fated to me, Dev. I can't change how it happened or why. I took one look at her, and I knew her name was Ellie."

Ellie's mother, it so happens, was a drug addict, too doped up to even fill out the birth certificate or any other paperwork when she was born and taken back to the state penitentiary shortly after they got her detoxed.

She never asked about Ellie again after that day.

Here he was, a nineteen-year-old boy, fresh out of a heartbreaking relationship and the loss of one child, and he was responsible for his teenage brother's daughter. He was the next best choice, along with his elderly Aunt Sarah as a licensed foster care provider and unofficial co-guardian.

I can't imagine the kind of responsibility he was faced with in just a matter of seconds.

I watch him as he tells me his story, the way his face changes and morphs as he goes from happy memories of baby Ellie and her first steps and pony rides, to scarier times like meet and greets with her biological mother after she was released from prison.

I want to know what Sam did to earn a life sentence at sixteen. To be wrapped up with a teenage drug addict he ended up impregnating. But I know what it's like to be from Pine Forest well enough, and I can tell Hunter isn't willing to talk any more about Sam or Ellie for a while.

I get lost for a little while in dancing around the kitchen to whatever music Hunter has streaming, but it stops abruptly when his phone rings and he takes it off Bluetooth for the call. It turns out Ellie's social worker called to say she's made arrangements for Ellie to stay next door with the family who has respite care certifications until she can come by and get my fingerprints tomorrow. I didn't realize what sort of ripples I was creating being here with Hunter and Ellie, and the weight of the situation officially hits me in the chest.

But I can't run, I remind myself. New and improved, less of a bitch, Devyn doesn't do that anymore. She faces her anxieties with logic.

Hunter comes back and inhales dramatically. "It smells amazing, babygirl."

I blush; I can't help it. I've always wanted this moment. The one where my husband walks through the door and smells what I'm cooking, and I'm all swoony as he takes me into his arms and dips me for a kiss.

"You're daydreaming again, wife." He winks, moving behind me to the fridge and squeezing my ass on the way. I yelp, giggling as I search the drawers for silverware.

"You cannot keep calling me wife." I point a butter knife his way. But I obviously hope he doesn't stop.

"I'll stop calling you wife when you stop cooking barefoot in my kitchen looking far tastier than the meal I'm meant to eat."

"You are so bad," I say, smiling from ear to ear and biting my lip to keep from letting him get the satisfaction of saying I did so.

"It honestly does look good. Smells good, too." He peers at the stovetop, where I've just placed the meatballs to cool and am arranging the rice and veggies on our plates. "I might have to let you cook for me more often."

"Don't get too carried away. I've only done like three Fresh Doorstep kits so far, so I'm not exactly swimming with skills yet."

"Fresh Doorstep. I knew it was too good to be true. You're a fraud, Mrs. Isaac." He takes me in with darkening eyes when we both realize what he said. The room is thick with our desire, and I'm not stupid enough to deny that's what this is.

Pure, animalistic desire.

"Shit!" I suddenly remember. "I need to call and cancel my subscription before they renew! I won't be home for two or three months. It's just gonna sit there rotting."

"Why don't you just send a neighbor to grab them for you?"

"A neighbor?" I blink.

"Yeah, I'm sure someone would want to make the meals that are already scheduled to deliver."

I shake my head, almost too embarrassed to look him in the eye. "I don't know any neighbors."

"A friend, then?" he asks, raising an eyebrow that tells me he's not gonna let this one go. "Someone who lives near you who you could text?"

I turn away, pressing my fingertips to my stinging tear ducts, and he pauses, reaching across the counter and placing a hand on my shoulder and spinning me around. My eyes burn because I don't like to confront pieces of me that are less than what they should be, but he squeezes my shoulder, and I don't feel so alone. Not with Hunter.

I just can't figure out if that scares me or not.

"Don't you have any friends in the city, Dev?"

"Look, I just worked a lot when I was on the news, okay? Went out with work people if I did things. It's not a big deal. Can you just hand me my phone?" I point to the end table behind him by the recliner where my sunflower and daisy phone case glitters in the light, and mentally lock my walls back in place around parts of me that feel far too raw and exposed for how new this is.

Hunter creases his brow but complies, reaching over to grab my phone which seems to be lit up with notifications, from what I can see. Probably more Pinterest wedding boards from Claudette and Molly. They've been texting them all day long, and I'm honestly about to tell them it's a fake marriage just to get them to back off for a few hours.

I wish I would let myself loose on Hunter. My mind and my body are telling me two wildly different things about what I should and shouldn't do with him, but he looks like a god sitting at his bar in his house on his farm and calling me his wife.

I'm hopeless.

Hunter finds my phone and squints down at the notifications, a sly smile spreading across his face that gives me pause.

"What is the Obscene AF Book Club?"

My face pales. *Shit. No, no, no, no.* That is not a corner of my phone he should be on.

"It's nothing!" I shout, practically leaping over the counter at him, and earning an even deeper grin as he raises one eyebrow, drawing his hand back so I can't reach it, and scrolling on.

"Well, nothing, as you call it, is texting you left and right. You got another man I should be worried about?" His eyes gleam as he scrolls through what I know with one hundred percent certainty is not another man, but worse. A complete cesspool of debauchery. Mortification falls over me in boundless waves.

Rightfully so. Because that chat group? It's not for normal books. I slide around the living room, waiting for the perfect moment to snatch my phone back.

"My Internet friends and I read books and chat about them. It's nothing," I say, getting close enough to touch the hem of his T-shirt. But as soon as I do, he twists his body around and flops to the couch, holding up a pillow shield while he reads on.

"Interesting. So, you do have friends."

I roll my eyes. Maybe it's better to use reverse psychology on him.

"Whatever." I cross my arms over my chest and assume nonchalance. "It's probably nothing. Sometimes we find a new book and the text chain just goes off for a while."

"But why is it obscene?" he teases, still scrolling. When I realize my reverse psychology very much isn't working, I dart around the corner and yank the pillow shield from his hand.

"You really don't want to know, I promise. Just give me the phone."

"Oh, I don't think so, Little Miss Perfect." He holds the phone closer, and his smile suddenly widens, his gaze shooting to mine.

"Dev, are you one of those book girls?"

His darkening stare could pin me to the wall, and I really wouldn't mind. If he stares at me like that for the rest of my life, I'll stay pinned wherever the fuck he wants me.

Holy shit.

"You're thinking filthy fucking things when you make that face and stare off into space. I just know it."

His teasing words snap me out of my fantasy.

But is it a fantasy if he's offering it up on a silver platter? *It could be a reality if you let it.*

"No! I mean…well, yeah, I guess."

His smile twists. "This is golden. You're into those kinky Shades of Sex books, aren't you?"

"Oh, my God, that's not the title of those," I scoff, maneuvering around the side table. "Look, you really don't want to read that. If you think those books are bad, you aren't ready for what's lingering in the depths of my Kindle. Promise." I shake my head, unable to stop the heated blush spreading across my face, as he lies back into the pillows and kicks up his feet, waving one hand while the other stays clutched to my phone like it's the morning paper and we're in a fifties sitcom.

"You go finish dinner, wife. Leave me to my research. I need to see what I'm up against so I can be your happily ever after."

"I don't think you're gonna like what you're up against." I snort, tongue in cheek.

"Hold the fuck up." He sits up suddenly, eyes wide and serious. "You're telling me that you, and thirty other women you know, have read *Stuffed by The Mashed Potato Man*?"

"And liked it." I smirk proudly.

"*Auctioned Off to My Alien Stepbrothers*? What the hell, Dev?" He shakes his head, looking back and forth between me and the phone in disbelief. Laughter breaks free from my body and fills the room.

"They're not as bad as they sound, honest. Most of the time, we just read the crazy ones to have something to joke about all day long, but other times…" I shake my head and whistle through my teeth. "I gave the mashed potato one four stars, not gonna lie."

"You've gotta be kidding me."

"Nope, that spice was spicin'."

Hunter loses it, bent over the counter, laughing so hard his face is turning red, and I'm laughing too because, fuck it. If I can't share my weird kinky side with the man I feel most intimate with, then who can I?

My heart stills at that thought, and I smile, running my hand through Hunter's hair and kissing the top of his head where it rests on his arms along the counter. His laughter settles, and he pushes up to his elbows.

"Who knew our sweet little beauty queen would grow up to be a closet freak?"

"Don't make fun! At least I'm reading, Mr. Thirst Trap."

He rolls his eyes, but I'm not done convincing him.

"Next month, we're reading a lovely holiday romance about redemption and giving."

"*Claiming Santa's Lap*?" He points to my screen. "I can already tell you that one doesn't have a happy ending." He pushes himself up, rounding the side of the counter and closing me in against it, my back flush to his chest, his breath so hot and inviting against my skin that I lean against him, begging him to press his lips to my neck.

"Why not?" I gasp as he sucks at my skin.

His kisses grow deeper, his free hand threading through my hair and sending pleasure between my legs. He pushes my cheek down against the counter, running his hand down my body, kneading my curves and squeezing my flesh like he can't get enough of it. His hand rides lower, until he's brushing the back of my thighs and fingering the hem of my dress. I gasp when I feel his fingers trace the edges of my panties, but I rock into them all the same. I want nothing more right now than to submit to him. Whatever it is he wants to do to me, he can have it all, as long as he never stops his touch. His tongue swipes against my ear, teasing and biting until I'm moaning, arching my back to give him better access because *God, I just need him to touch me,* and then he lifts his hand and slaps it hard against my ass.

"Santa only comes for good girls."

Then he tugs my skirt back in place and walks away.

Chapter 26

Devyn

"Spill it! How's the sex?" Lemon bounces up and down in the booth, adding a fourth sugar to her coffee. That finally explains where her energy comes from.

"Shhh! My brother owns this little gem, did you forget?" I search the Sugar Stable for any signs of Dustin, but thankfully, I find none.

"Yeah, yeah," Jeremy waves me off, "big scary brother, we got it. Now, give us the details. What's better? Isaac eyes or Isaac thighs?"

"Oh, my God, Jeremy, you can't say stuff like that in public!" Shana turns bright red. I giggle, noting how nothing seems to have changed with her pretentions since childhood. Still, even she looks at me expectantly.

I hate to disappoint the peanut gallery and all, but there is no story to tell yet. I mean, there's been a whole lot happening, that's for sure, but it's been exactly what I asked for… slow and steady.

The thing is, I didn't realize slow and steady with Nearly-Shirtless Nick, the Internet famous cowboy, would be such a damn tease. Between watching him teach kids how to bottle feed baby goats and filming videos where he quite literally humps a tractor, my vajayjay has some demands.

"We haven't had sex," I tell the group, which consists of Shana, Jeremy, and Lemon. My *friends*, I guess. That brings a smile to my face, having actual friends again.

I squeeze Shana's hand and turn to face her. "Thanks again for being so understanding about the other night, Shay. You didn't deserve what I said. I wasn't right, and—"

"Stop apologizing," she says, pursing her lips and scolding me about it for the thirtieth-something time since I got here.

I can't help it. I feel horrible. I will apologize to her for years, probably. If the time I was rude to the Home Goods manager two years ago still haunts me in my sleep, this will for sure. To be fair, everyone knows BOGO strictly implies free, unless otherwise specified, so it was absolutely false advertisement. Still, I may have been less of a Devyn and more of a Karen that day. And I can never un-Karen that moment in my brain. Par for the course with an overthinker.

"I'm thrilled you two are on good terms again and all," Lemon interjects, "but can we perhaps circle back to the main itinerary?" She blinks at us, waiting for me to say something more, but there's nothing more to say. She rolls her eyes. "What do you mean, you haven't had sex?"

Jeremy snorts, shooting me a look that needs no words.

"I mean we haven't had sex. We were broken up for a decade. It's not like I can just spread myself wide open for him after only a few days just because I'm…horny," I say, exasperated. But I'm not sure if it's at them or at myself, because I'm right there with them, wondering how the hell we haven't ripped each other's clothes off and broken a few bedposts by now.

"It's my fault," I whine. "Believe it or not, I asked for this. I told him I wanted to take it slow, and ever the gentleman he always was, he's been listening to me." I frown. "Being respectful."

"Mmm, hate that for you," Jeremy says.

It shouldn't feel like a problem, but it does. I let out a much-needed sigh, giving in to my friends and letting it all come tumbling out. "He hasn't even grabbed my ass all week. It's like the very day I told him I needed to slow down, he just…he listened!"

Everyone laughs, even me. Because it's absolutely ridiculous.

"What am I supposed to do, y'all? On the one hand, I want to take it slow and build back what we had. Take our time. He has a kid, for goodness' sake." I narrow my gaze, looking each of my friends in the eyes. "A kid who I'm still mad at all of you for not telling me about."

"Hey," Shana says, "I tried on the phone and at the bar. You didn't even let me get my drink order in before you stormed outta there like a madwoman." She looks around the table and lets out a heavy sigh, leveling her stare at me. "And none of us wanted to tell you about her before that because…we didn't imagine you'd ever come back, Devyn. Not me, your brother…honest truth. There wasn't any point bringing you back to those crippling memories. You were in such a better place…or so we assumed."

"Point made." I sigh, stirring my water so the ice clinks against the glass. "On the other hand, I have spent the last six days waking up to him making coffee…shirtless, and like, I'm not trying to buy into the thirst traps or anything, but I'm jealous as hell of those stupid haybales. I wish he'd throw *me* against a barn wall for once, ya know?"

"You have it bad." Jeremy pats my hand across the table.

"But the good news," Lemon interjects, "is that you both want it. So just take it."

"It's not that easy. I don't feel right sleeping in the same room as him, not with Ellie living there. It's not fair to her. I'm just some new fling in her eyes. She doesn't know about our past," I tell them, leaving out the part that really drives me crazy. That I'm not sure how long Hunter and I will last. That I don't want to be another woman coming in and out of Ellie's life. I know what that's like, as a child of divorce. I won't be that to her. "So, what am I supposed to do? Sneak into his room like we're teenagers at the lake? Besides, things are good right now. We've been catching up and addressing things we really needed to address between the two of us. What if sex messes it all up and we go backward?"

Nobody seems to have an answer for that.

I didn't think so either.

"I'd just do it," Lemon says, leaving Shana to roll her eyes.

"Of course, you would. You're impulsive to a fault. You're the reason they're married to begin with," Shana says.

Lemon gives her a strange look that I file away for later, because as much as I want to trust her, and I think I do, I still have a hard time trusting anyone. Let alone someone who turned the pageant community against me after I lost my baby. As if losing her wasn't enough, people I cared for suddenly didn't care for me, all because I wasn't what they thought. I wasn't a perfect, pretty, good girl. I was a fake.

Good girls don't get pregnant in high school.

Not in Pine Forest.

Lemon clears her throat, breaking me out of my head.

"All I'm saying is it's only going to get worse. He's going to get more attractive, more naked, and more thirst trappy, so bang it out and go from there. It's not like you can't take things slow emotionally and still avoid driving yourself crazy with need in the process."

"She's got a point," Jeremy agrees. "Don't hold yourself back just because you're worried about being a ho. Everyone knows the Ex to Ho Ratio states the longer you've been apart from someone, the sluttier you're allowed to be. You have chemistry, history, probably even algebra. We don't know. That's the point. Only you know. So, ho it up, girl. Get your slut on if you want to."

"Maybe you have a point. But it doesn't help my other problem. I don't have a way to raise money for Classy Country's charity without a pageant. And even though they don't care about the competition anymore, I still feel like there should be a pageant. Like old times."

"Would it be hard to start your own?" Shana asks, ever the voice of reason.

I shake my head. There's so much to do to get a pageant program up and running. Not only that, but there aren't any participants.

"We'd need actual kids for that." In a small town like this, where everyone works blue collar jobs, half the girls who'd want to join wouldn't even have after school transportation. "Clara had a carpool system that made it manageable for parents."

Lemon thinks, tapping her long, painted fingernail to her chin. "I got it!" she exclaims, tossing her hair back over one shoulder, eyes gleaming. "What if we hold practices at the farm? We could use Hunter's recreational bus. It already takes a load of kids to his property after school for his Farm to Friendship program, and there's a pavilion he uses for town events that's usually vacant unless it's bingo night. I'm sure he wouldn't mind us throwing some girls in there for a few weeks."

"Farm to Friendship?" I ask, my forehead creasing as I look around the table at Jeremy and Shana. But they don't seem surprised. "Is that the name of his little rodeo group?"

"Little group?" Jeremy sputters. "Dev, his program is not little by any means. It's the top non-profit youth farming program in the region."

"What?" I ask, rearing my head back and leaning against the booth. "He has busses and everything?" I look at Shana for confirmation from my oldest and most loyal friend. She offers me a small smile.

"Remember when you asked me about the renovations to the town and the bar?"

I nod.

"Well, that was Hunter." She blinks. "Hunter Isaac practically *is* the town. He's everyone's hype man and a gracious benefactor of the small business in town. He grew up, Dev."

I swallow the hard knot in my throat, blinking at my friends, speechless. How is it possible that one person can change so much?

But my heart swells with pride, too, because I'm not sure how much of that is change and how much of it was always there inside the boy I've always loved. The kind one who read me stories before I could make out the words, the brave one who defended me at parties, the genuine one who held my hand and spoke of a day where our kids would never want for more.

He never left.

I did.

But I don't run from my problems anymore. This new Devyn doesn't do that. She faces them.

"Let's do it," I tell the others. "Let's start us a rodeo pageant!"

Chapter 27

Hunter

"Where does the scary witch go?" Devyn shouts down to Ellie from the gallery overlooking the living room. Strands of blonde hair fall across the witch doll as she hangs her head over the railing, holding it in front of her face like a mask.

"Boo!"

A joyous scream followed by a loud set of giggles fill the house, and I haven't been able to put my finger on what it is about that sound that makes everything in the whole world feel right. But it damn sure does.

It feels better than right.

Not just Devyn being here in my space but being part of my family. And it's the way she is with Ellie.

They're inseparable.

In a few short weeks, she's taught her to make pancakes from scratch, albeit they weren't the best tastin' things I've ever had grace my palate, but the two flour covered chefs who made 'em were the cutest pair I ever saw.

Then there was the movie night I wandered in on yesterday when the sun went down. I was greeted with handmade paper tickets and a bowl of popcorn at the door, and it didn't stop there. They even made little macaroons and had a blanket pallet ready to go on the living room floor.

And each night, they spend time in our old shed, underneath a setting sun, making magic with nothing but a pair of smiles and a room of sunflowers.

This girl.

My girls.

My eyes gather up a shine that I tell them must be the onions I'm chopping for the pot roast, but I know good and well it's not.

I think it's pride. Maybe relief. That such different parts of my life could come together so seamlessly.

"Hey, Dev!" Ellie shouts, running up the stairs two at a time with a tub of Halloween decorations. I smile at her use of the nickname and walk to the pantry for the potatoes.

Ellie's voice travels my way, telling Devyn about the various *Nightmare Before Christmas* figurines we've collected over the years, so I wash up and join them upstairs while the meat thaws in the microwave, not willing to miss out on this time with…family.

"This one is my favorite." Ellie shows off her Zero, the ghost-dog ornament meant to hang from the Halloween tree.

"I've never heard of a Halloween tree." Devyn shoots a smile my way.

"We started it when Ellie was two. The first time she met her mother." It's sad, but I smile, unable to do anything but that when I look at the growing nine-year-old before me and still see the roundness in her cheeks that was there in the baby I swore to protect when my brother failed her all those years ago.

She's growing up so damn fast. "Ellie wasn't even old enough to watch *The Nightmare Before Christmas* that year, but she saw that dog at the pharmacy after a very long day, and trying to pry it from her tiny little hands was never an option. So, Zero came home with us."

Ellie runs to my side and squeezes me in a big hug, turning to Devyn and handing her another spooky ornament to hang on the tree. "Want to add one?"

"I'd love to." Dev wipes her eyes. I nod to the tree when she looks my way.

"Go ahead, babygirl," I say before it can register. Up until now, we told Ellie the marriage was a silly, fake game for our work, like an acting gig, and that we're just old friends. She's been staying in the guest room. I mean, it's not a lie. But I haven't told Ellie how I feel about Devyn. Or about our past.

"Babygirl?" Ellie whispers, one eyebrow raised.

She giggles when my eyes go wide, and I sputter to respond.

So much for the innocence of youth.

"Don't try to hide it, Papa. I think she likes you, too."

She throws me one of my own damn winks, dropping bombs and skipping off to Devyn.

Kid is way too smart for her own good.

"What's this?" Devyn's voice is a marvel of questions. Ones she already knows the answer to.

I don't even have to ask what she's found.

I know.

"Oh." Ellie's brows pinch, shooting me a suspicious glare. "That one always goes up front and center." Papa's…friend made it for him when they were kids." She pauses, eyes widening as she puts the pieces of my stories together in her nosy little brain, and then she cocks her head at me and the corner of her mouth curves up.

This little shit.

"He doesn't get to see that friend anymore, and it makes him, like, really-really-really sad, so he puts this up every year. You know why?" She throws a sly look at me over her shoulder.

"Why?" Devyn grins.

"So maybe his friend will know it's there somehow and know he hasn't forgotten. Right, Papa?"

She pins me with her stare, hope shimmering over smiling eyes as she re-examines Devyn and me.

Unable to control my own eyes any more than I can the beat of my heart, they meet Dev's, the green portals to her soul shining like emeralds, curious and beautiful.

A treasure.

Because that's what she is to me. She's a gift, meant to bring this family together, and that's clear to me in this moment, even if she does look at me with mistrust somewhere deep within.

She holds up the little crocheted pumpkin she made me in Miss Henley's middle school home economics class. The one I pretended to shove in my backpack and forget about, because you don't acknowledge crushes from your best friend's middle school sister in the ninth grade. You just don't.

But I kept it in my nightstand.

I never told Devyn about the pumpkin before our breakup.

This is likely the first time she's seen it in the twentysomething years since she made it. As a little girl.

And here my own little girl is, spilling some of my deepest secrets to her, saying words I've wondered how to say for a decade in a short, simple breath.

Smelling her orange scented perfume in my bathroom, hearing her laugh fill my home, seeing her traipse around in nothing but spandex shorts and an oversized T-shirt.

My T-shirt.

I've got it bad for this woman. But I've respected her wishes. I haven't touched her since she stated her boundaries.

If she wants to take things slow, I will be the slowest of the slow. I will be a sloth.

And yeah, it might kill me bit by bit to watch her sway that round little ass around my farm in dirtied-up Daisy Dukes and not smack it a time or two, but I'll do it. Even if I am pretty sure she shakes it around more than normal when she sees me, just to call me on my bluff.

But I'll do anything to earn her trust and keep her. Even if it does mean being hands-off.

A nagging feeling in my gut reminds me that her days of trusting me are over if I don't tell her about Lemon's marriage stuff soon, but I plan to. It's just not the right time yet. I can't scare her off or have her thinking I've been with her for any reason other than because I love her.

Because I love her.

Yes, it might benefit the custody, but that isn't why I sought her out. She's gotta see that.

I'll get her to see.

Because what I want more than her body, more than marriage, more than some stupid fuckin' job…is her heart.

She breaks our stare and walks to the tree, hanging the pumpkin in the very center where Ellie shows her, then turns to me, a smile curving her lips.

"She hasn't forgotten."

Chapter 28

Devyn

"Alexa, connect to Devyn's Galaxy and play Motivation Mix," I shout, picking up a fifth sock from the living room floor. Warmth settles over me in the form of a rare, genuine smile. Ellie and Hunter toss their socks at the end of the day almost identically. All of it solidifies my notion of who they are to one another. Hunter very much is Eleanor's father. And she's got him wrapped around her little rebel fingers.

"Playing Motivation Mix," Alexa replies. I marvel, still in disbelief that I'm living in a place so fancy that there's built-in surround sound through the whole house. He's certainly impressed me with his renovation of the farm. Of the whole town, really.

Dustin did try to tell me.

Dustin. Who still isn't speaking to me because I 'always rush into things' or whatever.

I roll my eyes, sashaying to my phone to shoot a quick text to my brother who made it very abundantly clear, via a

213

long series of voicemails, that Hunter and I were the most impulsively stupid people he knows, and he wants no part of the "shitshow" he predicted.

Like he's not the one who told me to admit my feelings. I huff a frustrated sigh that blows my bangs away from my face as I type.

It's time he stopped sulking about it. Hunter and I are together. It's been almost a month now, and it doesn't seem like a fake marriage. Not anymore.

Truth be told, I miss my brother. I've only seen him twice since I've gotten home, and once was when Shana and I blindsided him at the Sugar Stable on his birthday with a cake. Thankfully, Shana knew what time he'd be there, her dance studio being directly across from it and all. Maybe I can get her to tell me when he's in and just blindside him at work again.

On the other hand, only two visits with my favorite and only brother is just not gonna cut it. I'll simply have to use my little sister powers. Splinter my way under his skin until he has no choice but to deal with me.

DEVYN: Are you still mad at us?

DUSTIN: …

DUSTIN: Just Hunter.

DEVYN: That's not fair. It takes two to say I Do.

DUSTIN: We had an understanding. "Ease into it" doesn't mean "Marry my fucking sister."

DEVYN: I'm a grown adult. You don't get to have "understandings" about me with my husband.

DUSTIN: If you keep saying husband, I will vomit in a bag and mail it to you.

DEVYN: Husband.

<Dustin has blocked your number>

I smile, sliding the phone back onto the bookshelf. He's too easy. My splinter is already working its way in, and he doesn't even know it.

Dustin will come around. He just has to see Hunter and I are…different now. It hasn't been long, but it has at the same time. We're falling into a routine together. Ellie, too.

Tomorrow, we post our first couple's video. We've posted a few on our own pages over the last few weeks, mine about the pageant program, and his…humping an excavator…anyway, this will be the first cohesive one with 'glam,' as Hunter calls it. Beats me. The most glam I use on my posts are those free filters that make you glittery. Miss American Rodeo and Channel 5 curated most of my content before now, and it feels a bit eye opening. I've never considered the work that goes into these influencers' posts when you realize they do it all from scratch.

Hunter has a friend coming by to film, since Dustin's still being a grump and all. I know it's eating away at him, Dustin being mad. I also don't think he likes having to advertise our relationship online like this. It makes my brother that much more skeptical about our intentions with this marriage thing, but we both agreed we would do the bare minimum for the job.

Neither of us asked for the shenanigans; it just happened this way.

In other news, Hunter's been working with his group on two rodeo challenges for the fair. We decided to combine our efforts. Marriage perks and all, like filing taxes together, right? And we're doing one event.

Together.

The first ever Friendly Farms Fair, my pageant and his rodeo being the main events. We've met with the interested families a few times already, and now we just have to figure out a stage of some sort here on the farm grounds.

It's a good thing the property is huge. I'm not sure how

busy this place gets in the spring and summer, but the number of kids and parents coming to and from youth lessons and events is mind-blowing.

And I think the truth I'm finding is I love it here. I love being married to Hunter Isaac. Even if it is fake.

There's at least five times a day when I wish it were real.

He makes me feel safe, effortless, like when we were kids. Everything with Hunter is perfect.

But it isn't all the same.

He has this way of taking something totally ordinary, something perfectly imperfect, and bringing out the beauty and vibrance from within.

Like burned ravioli.

"It's pan-charred," he'd told Ellie, so it would seem like I'd done something special. In moments like that, it's his inherent, natural chivalry, wrapping me in a tight embrace and promising the world.

This man has me under a spell, and I know why.

I'm beginning to trust him.

For once in my life, I'm trusting someone. And isn't it crazy that it's the one person I always trusted before? Wholeheartedly. Full circle.

I love him.

It's not cliché, either. It's precisely what Jeremy said. The Ex to Ho Ratio…minus the ho part. The longer you've been with someone, the easier it is to love them, even if years have passed between the conception and the rekindling of that love. And If I'm being completely honest with myself? I don't think that flame ever died for us.

It got dim, but never gone for good.

Like any fire, it just needs to be fed.

I grab the Swiffer from the hall closet where I've seen Hunter tuck it away and begin tidying the floors. With the film crew coming tomorrow morning, and the pageant meeting I'm holding with my friends that same afternoon, I feel the need to make this place look like the beautiful piece of art Hunter has crafted it to be. I feel somewhat prideful of the home he's made. And something about being in it, cleaning it like it's mine, too.

All of this feels right.

My cleaning spree continues, as I spot a pink fleck behind the couch. I lean over to see if it's Ellie's missing sock, leaving my butt sticking straight in the air in my tiny dance shorts.

"Gotcha!" I say to myself, triumphantly snatching up the rogue garment. But before I can right myself, his voice stops me.

"When I prayed for Heaven on Earth, I didn't think it would come in the form of your backside stretched across my couch."

Heat and lust spread across my body in sharp waves as I shoot upright. His voice seems to kiss the tips of my nipples, the hardened points poking through my—I look down, taking in my appearance.

His shirt. I put it on earlier without realizing.

Okay. I one hundred percent realized and loved every damn minute of smelling like him all day.

His eyes meet mine as I turn to face him, and his lips curve just slightly.

"Is that my shirt?"

His voice is rich, a thick, heated tease. I shift on the couch, pressing my thighs together to relieve the throbbing pressure building between them.

"Yes." I bite my bottom lip, watching his eyes narrow on my tight, hardened nipples pressing against the fabric where the words Pine Forest Rodeo are spelled out in green. He presses his lips together and shakes his head, his eyes undressing me where I kneel on the cushions. The way he watches me, like someone just popped the hood to a vintage sportscar…it's intoxicating. It makes me feel alive.

I want him to watch more. I sit up straighter so there's no mistaking what I'm pressing against the shirt that covered his own chest only hours earlier. The one that smells heavily of sandalwood and pleasure. The one I snagged when he wasn't looking, so I could feel like he was on me even when he wasn't.

He groans in approval, tilting his head and running his teeth over his bottom lip as he inspects me.

"You haven't the faintest what this does to me, do you?" He licks his lips, stepping so close that my body yearns for him. His breath mixes with my own, hot and needy. "Seeing your naked body draped beneath my clothes?" He fists the fabric, tugging me closer so our torsos are flush, my nipples rubbing against the fabric and sending chills across my skin.

"What does it make you want to do?" I ask him breathlessly, hating how cliché I sound, but hoping to God his answer is to shove me face down against this couch and take me from behind, slap my ass again like he did before I put the brakes on the sexual side of things. And fuck it, I don't care anymore. We did things slowly. Slow was great. We talked over our problems, and we seem to be loving life together so far, but I can't take it anymore. I can't stand to be in a room with him, admiring his muscles with my eyes and never tracing them with my fingers, listening to him say he loves me and not climbing in his lap to say it back.

Unashamedly and irrevocably.

And I'm tired of waiting for the other boot to drop.

Hunter cups my cheek and kisses me, but as soon as it begins, it's over. My heart protests with each quickening beat, but he backs away, a light sparking in his eyes, like he's remembered something very important, and a sly smile curves his lips.

"It makes me want to respect your boundaries."

"Seriously, Hunter?"

But before he can reply, Alexa cuts through the air.

"Playing I Seriously Miss Hunter Playlist."

Oh, my God, this is not happening.

My gaze darts to the shelf where my phone is nestled and about to expose years' worth of secrets to Hunter, but his eyes beam.

"My God, Dev, your phone is a goldmine full of secrets, isn't it?"

His smile grows, and all I can do is bury my heated face into my hands as Jung Kook's "Seven" bursts through the surrounding speakers. Hunter's eyes widen in recognition, laughter pouring out of him endlessly, as he swings his hips and gyrates to a song that promises him I'll be fucking him not one through six…but seven days a week.

On a playlist that is about missing him.

And that's a recent song. I can't even lie and say it's an old playlist. I meet his gleaming eyes and turn away as quickly as I can.

"Oh, Ponygirl, you don't get to hide from me that easy." He twirls me around, but I keep my other hand over my face, like a child at a scary movie. I don't want to look him in the eyes, don't want him to see I'm half smiling.

He pulls my hand off my face and replaces it with his lips crashing down on mine while he sways us across the floor in time to the music, our tongues doing a dance of their own.

I rest my head on his shoulder, enjoying the caress of his fingertips along the hem of my Hunter-shirt, brushing my thighs, teasing me until I'm a wet, dripping mess in his arms.

"To be fair, the edited version just says 'loving' you seven days a week."

I'm sure my cheeks are pinker than the sock I threw to the floor. I remind myself to grab it before I do laundry, like a total housewife, and not exactly hating that idea.

Of being his *real* wife.

"What'll it be, then?" he asks, a playful twist to his lips. "Do you want to love me or fuck me, Mrs. Isaac?"

"What if I want to do both?"

I close the distance between us, cocking my head to the side and twisting my smiling lips.

"Are you being coy with me, *wife*?"

My breath hitches as he places two fingers beneath my chin, lifting my lips to his in a total panty melting move that there's no way he's not doing on purpose, and I say a little thank you prayer for my personal thirst trap before I flutter my eyelashes.

"I think you know what I want, *husband*." I trace the collar of his shirt and lean in for a kiss, but he stops me, putting a finger to my lips.

"Nah, that's not gonna cut it," he teases. "You wanted me to take things slow, and you had no problem being explicit with me about what you didn't want then. Don't deny my right to hear it come straight from those pretty little lips of yours now. Tell me what you do want, Dev."

"You're kidding, right?" I cross my arms, but he isn't budging. He just runs his tongue over his bottom lip and throws me back that same cocky smirk I fell in love with.

Stupid smirk.

He really is gonna make me say it.

I roll my eyes as dramatically as possible just so he knows how I feel about his little game.

But I must admit, there's something extremely sexy and empowering about having total control over my body and desires.

And knowing he'd respect that entirely?

"Tell me what you want, Dev."

It's everything.

"I want you to fuck your wife."

Chapter 29

Hunter

Remember what I promised?"

I slam my body against Devyn's, shoving us against the inside of my closed bedroom door. I worry I'm too rough with her, but the way she tilts her body to form around mine feels far from a protest.

Her green doe-eyes may look innocent, but the way she's using them right now should come with a warning, fluttering those long eyelashes like fuckin' Bambi. Begging me to cut the romance short and fuck her senseless, that's what she's doing.

But all I offer is a devilish smile.

That's not what's happening tonight, babygirl.

I want to take my time.

And what she doesn't know is I've been doing my research. I read a few of those smutty books she likes. What I learned is, well, for one, there is a concerning amount of hockey smut on her Kindle, and I'm not sure she even likes hockey, but aside from that, some of it was actually...

Okay, it was way fuckin' worse than the hockey.

Monsters, stalkers, mafia kidnappers, the list literally does not end.

My girl wants to be thoroughly fucked.

"What I told you…" I remind her, gripping her by the soft curves of her ass and hoisting her legs over my shoulders. My cock jumps like it's got a brain of its own with every sexy little whine and moan that falls from her lips, throbbing as I take her in, spread wide open, and only the faintest tease of black fabric between my mouth and her lips. "…is that I was gonna devour this pretty little pussy once you let me."

"I thought you were going to, and I quote, 'fuck me hard,' so, which is it?"

Fuckin' brat. Just for that, I spread the flat of my tongue over her fabric-covered pussy lips and hold perfectly still, letting the heat of my breath make her writhe around my face.

"Gonna do whatever the fuck I want. Now, wrap your legs around my head and be still."

Devyn cries out when I slide her Spandex shorts to the side and my tongue swipes over her swollen clit, tracing circles in a firm, steady motion, centering on one spot in particular when I notice her moans grow longer and her fingers dig into my hair, shoving me down harder. And I love that. Seeing her grow in her confidence. Take what she wants. Let me in.

"That's it, babygirl, show me how you want it," I say, barely able to get a word out for the haste in which my tongue aims to work her opening.

She bites her lip, shaking her head like she's embarrassed.

"Don't be shy," I mumble against her pussy, greedily lapping up the juices that flow from her as she rides my face through her dance shorts, my hands digging into the flesh of her ass in a grip so tight, I worry I might bruise her. But she urges me on, bucking her body across my lips, riding my tongue while she moans my name.

"I love this pussy, you know that?" I ask, shoving my beard into her wet folds and shaking my head back and forth until she's moaning again and rocking against my mouth for more.

"I'm coming!" she cries, tightening her thighs around my head and pressing her swollen flesh against me.

"That's it, babygirl." I suck her clit, running soft circles around it with my tongue as she full on fucks my face in the sexiest way imaginable, and I draw her orgasm out as long as I can. "Look how nicely you come for me. Such a good girl."

She gasps, whipping her head up and getting to all fours on the bed, a wild gleam in her eyes that's just what I hoped I'd find.

"Did you just call me a—"

"I did." I smirk, watching her shift her thighs back and forth on the bed. And then I see it again.

My shirt.

"But I reckon I was mistaken." I circle the bed while she follows me with her eyes, licking her lips so they're wet for me. I groan, rubbing my cock through my jeans at this goddess before me who dares to look this fuckin' sexy in my goddamned bed.

In my goddamned shirt.

"A good girl wouldn't traipse around a grown man's house half naked under his own damn shirt like a fucking tease, now, would she?"

She gasps, puckering her lips in a way that, under any ordinary circumstances would be completely un-sexy, but when she does it, it just makes me wonder how those plump, glossy lips would feel wrapped around my cock.

My grin widens as I take her in, crawling toward me on the bed, because in some fucked up way, the more I talk to her like this, the needier she gets, her body and her eyes begging me to claim her, no matter what else happens.

Fuck, she's so beautiful leaning into her kink. Asking for what she wants.

Her lips twist in a playful smirk as she kneels before me.

"I like it when you do that," she says, running her hands across my skin, lingering just above my cock until my breath hitches with her closeness. I almost come on spot when she wets her lips with that hot little tongue and blinks up at me obediently. "Please call me a good girl again."

I groan, palming the front of my jeans. She's unreal, this one.

"Or what?"

I tweak her nipples through the T-shirt, and she moans, arching her back into the mattress.

"Please," she begs.

"Look at you, begging me to call you kinky little names from your filthy books." I fist her hair, and a surprised sound comes from the base of her throat, making my cock twitch. I twist it around my hand and tug until she has no choice but to crawl to me on all fours to the edge of the bed. I yank her head down until it's pressed against the mattress, and I worry briefly if it's too much. I don't want to hurt her, but I'm so fuckin' into this if she's into this, and she certainly seems fuckin' into this.

"Yes! More!" she cries, swiftly addressing my concern, and I wonder if it's inappropriate to thank the lord for moments like Devyn Lynn Campbell's plump, wet lips hovering inches from my cock.

"Does my good girl want something to suck on?"

"Yes," she gasps, her mouth popping open in surprise at my question, hips grinding into the mattress as she begins to push herself up, but I stop her, keeping pressure on her head and holding her down. My cock gets harder every time she gasps, her little moans so sexy that each one could be the final straw that causes me to lose my load right here, before I even get inside her.

"Stay down and keep your tongue out," I command.

"Okay," she replies, doing exactly as I say and earning a rub of my hand down the front of her face. She leans into it and moans.

"Good girl," I say again, shoving two fingers into her open mouth, fucking her face like I intend to do soon with my cock. And it only sends her rubbing herself with her free hand.

God, she's so into this.

I'm so fucking into this, too.

I slide my fingers from her mouth, dragging them across her lips before I kiss them, sucking them into my mouth like I own them. She can't take them from me ever again.

She moans, wiggling her ass that's still stuck straight up in the air because I told her so.

She lives for the praise. I guess she always has.

And if that's what she needs, that's what she's getting.

"Such a good little slut, ass out, pussy up, just the way your husband likes it." She moans immediately, rocking her hips back to me, asking me to touch her without using words. My cock responds, jutting forward.

I release my cock from my pants, jerking from hilt to tip and using the spit from Devyn's mouth to coat my shaft while I watch her writhing against my sheets. Devyn opens her mouth wider, her tongue fully out and ready, waiting. Her eyes swirl with desire, and I tug harder as my own desire takes hold of me. I want to see them widen as I fuck her there. I slide my length across Devyn's wet tongue and into her throat, fucking her mouth while I lean over her and slip my fingers back under her shorts to finger her needy cunt, bucking up against my hand until she's so wet, her arousal seeps through the fabric and over her skin.

"More!" Her muffled words spill out from around my cock.

Pulling out of her mouth, I get behind her on the bed and admire how well she behaves, and how much I like this dominant roleplay.

Isn't that what it's called? I've learned plenty about it online and even spent a summer learning bondage rope skills from a friend of mine who owns a club in the city. It was mainly so I could do sexy rope tricks in my TikToks, but some people practice it the way my friend does. As a form of this…dominant play. I never felt comfortable enough with a woman to try it.

Devyn whines when I pull my fingers from her, pushing her butt up in the air.

"Someone's impatient." I laugh, slapping her ass through her shorts.

"Need you," she whines, turning over her shoulder to meet my eyes.

"Then take off this shirt and booty shorts combo you keep teasin' me with," I growl, fingers gripping the edges of my T-shirt that she's taken hostage in the best way possible, but she pauses.

For too long.

"Devyn?"

Chapter 30

Devyn

My arms take up motions all their own, shooting down and covering my waist, where the elastic of my shorts secures around my body.

They're high rise. Like all my bottoms.

Because I can't stand to see it.

My scar.

My eternal reminder of the day I lost my baby.

I finally turn around, looking up at Hunter while I finger the line that stretches across my stomach in a thick, solid chunk, longer than a C section scar and thicker than one too. Because mine slices both ways. Up and across.

The first slice up was a wooden shard from the electrical post about as thick as the blade at the deli, the recovery nurse told me later. It shot through the car after our impact with the Mack truck ricocheted our vehicle violently off the shoulder, the pole coming down above us and the sharp, broken edges piercing right through me.

I passed out then. I didn't get to see the blood.

Or the wreckage. There are times I wonder if I'll ever remember the in-between. And worse times when I think I do. But the brain fills in the gaps for you, the doctors told me. What I think happened is most likely the fear, a nightmare in my mind, not unlike most dreams. You make parts up based on things you've seen or heard in real life.

I hope that's the case. Because the dreams I have don't seem like ones God would ever allow to have occurred.

And yet.

Don't go there, Devyn.

I didn't hear anything after the screams that filled the car as Hunter and I held on to one another, praying for protection.

If we'd landed only centimeters to the left, the post would have punctured my heart. I'd have died.

Maybe our baby would have lived. I haven't forgiven God for the way he answered my prayers that day. Not yet.

And truth be told, I don't think I'll ever believe when someone says 'everything happens for a reason.' I'm not sure that's true.

I think everything just happens. And maybe things will come of it, or maybe they won't.

But here we are together again, leaving me to question all I know.

I wring my hands, dropping them from their place of protection around my waist, turning toward Hunter and forcing my body to calm. This isn't just anyone I'm being intimate with. My scars are his too, and I want desperately to share everything with him right now.

My soul. My mind. My whole body.

Even my scars.

He senses my hesitation, his brow drawing inward as he reaches for me. But I don't shove away. I take his hand, letting him tug me closer, into his embrace, his warm arms, wrapping around my shoulders and his lips placing soft, supportive kisses on my shoulder blade.

"I don't have many great experiences with intimacy," I admit, unable to meet his eyes. I keep my face forward, his touch on my body grounding me, bringing me complete peace to talk about this without the anxiety that normally seizes me when I do. He squeezes me lightly, a gentle nudge to go on.

"Once they see my scars, it gets awkward. They say things, and I can't brush them off, and then it's just over after that. It ends almost immediately in that moment."

As much as I wish I could pretend Chad was just a horrible human, he wasn't so bad. I mean, yeah, he was conceited, but most people in the city are. He was still a decent guy.

But it always feels the same. Once I'm finally willing to be vulnerable about my past, the scar itself is either too much for them to handle, or it becomes too much once they realize what it means.

I'll never bear them any children of their own.

A doll with a broken body doesn't last on a trophy shelf. Even with the shiniest crown.

"Who made you feel like shit about your scars, Dev? You tell me names, right now." He grinds his teeth, his eyes burning so fiercely I believe he would actually take those names and do something with them.

Is it normal to be horny about that?

It's probably normal.

It's definitely hot.

He cups my cheek and kisses me as if there's no time left between us, immediately searching my eyes.

"Calm down, Alpha Male." I smile, fingering the hem of my shirt, riding it up inch by inch. "Just because you read a bunch of my books doesn't mean you need to go un-aliving all my insensitive exes. Even if it would be a major turn-on."

"It would be, you say?" He grins.

His eyes follow my movement as the shirt goes up my torso and over my neck, exposing the upper half of my body, and the top portion of my vertical scar. I brace myself for the weight of the world to crash down, but there's nothing.

No sound.

No cringe.

No scowl.

No widening eyes of disgust, or furrowing brows of sympathy, or words of rejection to spark tears that spill over pillows of tomorrow.

All I see is love in his eyes.

I toss my shirt to the floor and peel the shorts down my waist and thighs, earning a groan of approval from Hunter when I'm totally naked before him.

My horizontal scar, from the emergency abdominal hysterectomy, is now exposed to him for the first time.

The scar that stole our child.

I lean back on the bed and for once in my life, as intense of a moment as this is, full of dredged-up memories and sadness, I don't feel broken underneath the stare of a man.

He sees all the pieces of me, and he's every bit a part of them.

The past, the history, and the wounds.

The faults that bind us together, and the scars that forever seal our love are etched across my skin like a story. One only he and I can finish.

He runs his tongue over his bottom lip, just how he knows I like it, and goosebumps ripple across my skin when he hums into my breasts.

"Wanna taste every inch."

He swirls his tongue around my nipple, and pleasure rushes to my center, sending my hips rocking against his body. A low growl rumbles from his throat, and I can't help but wonder what that sound might feel like in other places on my body.

Reading my mind, he lowers his kisses, leaving one hand to pinch my nipples to points up top, while he teases his mouth down my stomach, licking and sucking at the skin above my scar lines.

My breath hitches when he nears it, but my center still throbs for his touch. I don't want him to stop. And what's even crazier, the feelings that normally come in these moments—the rejection, the guilt, the pain—aren't present right now.

It's just me and him.

Devyn Lynn Campbell and Hunter Isaac, the boy I've always loved.

From top to bottom, he places purposeful kisses across the once-marred flesh, but it isn't until he reaches the top of the vertical scar that touches my ribcage, that I feel his tears. He leans his weight into me, his head sagging as quick tufts of air release from his lips, breath blowing across my skin, and arms wrapping around me in an apologetic hug that says volumes, without saying anything at all.

He's crying. For me.

For her.

For all of us.

I sift my fingers through his reddish-blond hair, and I'm reminded of the other little girl.

The one we didn't lose.

The one who came into our lives at different times but needs a family. The one who stole Hunter's heart and is fast collecting mine along with it. Suddenly, seeing this through is more important than my pain, my past or my scars.

Because scars are meant to be reminders, not barriers. Not walls we put up to keep others out, but roads we map to find our way.

I kiss the top of his head.

"I love you, Hunter Isaac. And these scars are devastating, yes. I'm reminded of that day every day because of them. But they represent our past, and right now the future seems more intentional than I ever imagined."

"You're something else, Ponygirl."

"If I'm a Ponygirl, then let me ride you already," I tease.

And that's all it takes before I'm thrown to my back and the heavy weight of Hunter's wide frame is pressing down on top of me, his mouth roaming every inch of my neck, making his way to my chest, caressing my nipples with his tongue as he rubs his hardness against me. My body lights up, still needy from before, and when he shoves my breasts together and covers both nipples with mouth at the same time, my entire pussy quakes.

"*Fuck*," I whimper. "Please, fuck me."

"You better behave," he warns, spreading my legs open for his access. He wraps one hand around his thick shaft, pumping up and down.

I watch.

How could I not?

He fists his erection in front of me, slowly and sensually. Putting on a goddamned show and he doesn't even realize it, all while his gaze roams my body, his brows creased in deep thought, like I'm a battle map in a war room and he's figuring out how he'd like to conquer me.

That's my Roman Empire.

And fuck, if it's not sexy as hell.

But I'm too turned on, and I want him inside me, *now*.

"Are you abiding by the 'look, don't touch' rule?" I twist my lips playfully. "Because if so, I do not plan on behaving."

"Is that so?" He chuckles, biting down on his bottom lip and slowly releasing it as he leans over my body and lines up with my opening. "I better give the princess what she wants, then." Without hesitation, he shoves his cock inside me and thrusts deeply to the rhythm of our heartbeats. Fast, hard, and heavy. I clench around him, enjoying the fullness of each thrust.

My head knocks into the nightstand, a testament to the force with which this man fucks me. Rough and animalistic, like he isn't even in control of it anymore.

He grabs a fistful of my hair. "So fucking perfect." He yanks my head back with each thrust, but he's careful in his roughness, knowing just where to ride the line of pleasure and pain. I feel wanton, used, but mostly…worshiped.

I'm a goddess who has the power to make this man bend with my body alone. To say filthy things to get me off. *To fuck me just how I like.*

"I'm glad Ellie calls you Papa," I whisper into his ear, wrapping my legs around him as he drives into me deeper and harder than before. He groans, and I know he's close, his teeth biting into my shoulder when he exhales, cradling his body around mine tighter with each thrust.

"Why's that?"

"Because I like the idea of calling you Daddy."

I lick the shell of his ear, gasping when he pushes in hilt deep and throws my body into pure ecstasy. He hits my G-spot dead center, and I come, digging crescents into his skin with my fingernails while he groans, pumping and spilling himself inside me and sending me over the edge until I see actual stars. The ones dancing across my vision as my orgasm takes over my body are almost as bright as the real ones spilling in from the skylight above our heads.

And for once in my life, imperfect feels right.

My heart flutters when I take in that I don't immediately want to cover my scars back up. I lie beside Hunter, letting him touch them instead.

Because something big happened to both of us just now. And the meaning of these scars doesn't feel secular when Hunter is here to share their burden. Not when he's by my side to kiss away the pain.

"Daydreaming already?" He smiles, placing a soft kiss to the corner of my mouth. I laugh, rolling onto my belly.

"Ew. You made me messy." I sweep my legs to the side and do an awkward mermaid-sit, staring at him expectantly, you know, waiting for a towel or something in the least attractive moment of human intimacy culture, but he just cocks a brow and snorts in response.

"You seemed to like the mess I made just fine when you were calling me Daddy," he levels, stalking back over to me on the bed and placing his thumb under my chin. I look up at him, my heart already pounding so hard, my ho of a vagina can feel it inside her. I'm hopelessly taken by Hunter Isaac, and as spent as I am, with this man, I could go again all night long.

So, I let my lips pop open of their own accord.

He smirks knowingly, a cocky-ass grin that seems to sweep over his face like a sexy leather coat, before he shoves his thumb in my mouth, surprising me with how willingly my body responds to his commands without my brain needing to be involved in the slightest.

"Suck," he says. It's not a request.

So, I obey, running my tongue along the length of his thumb like it's a cock I can't get enough of. Sucking, swirling, tasting it and wishing like hell it was the real thing all over again.

"That's what I thought," he says, tilting my head to the side, inspecting my jaw line as his lips curve up dangerously. "Since you don't like my messes between your legs, I'll put them right here sometimes. But only when you're a good girl, Devy."

I gasp, his eyes shining with promise when he pulls his thumb free and wipes the wetness across my bottom lip, dragging its plumpness to the side before it pops back into place.

"I'll get you a towel, princess."

He winks, heading toward the bedroom door, swinging his hips and giving me a private, X-rated show of his Internet famous swag.

But then he pauses, arching his brows and whipping his head around.

"Do you hear running water?"

Chapter 31

Devyn

The chickens too?" Ellie whines, throwing her bucket to the ground and stomping toward the coop. "I already cleared out the sheep and horse stalls."

"Well, remember how much shit you got yourself into next time you try to flood a guest room," Hunter shouts as she storms off, her strawberry hair whipping angrily in the wind.

"I can't believe she flooded your room." He whips off his hat and runs his fingers through his hair, like he does when he's stressed out.

"Cut her a little bit of slack. She's only nine, after all."

"Almost ten. She knew better." He shoves his hat back on his head and looks like he might storm off just like she did, but I take his hand and he sighs, releasing more than stress into the air. More than flooding. And even though I wish he'd let me all the way in, to whatever else is plaguing him, I know what it's like to live with scars.

I won't press him. Instead, I rise to the tips of my boots and kiss his forehead. He releases a deep breath and curls his arms around me, resting his chin on my head, and I can only hope he'll open up to me all the way when he's ready.

"I don't know what got into her. She keeps insisting she was only helping me." He scrunches his brow. "It doesn't make any sense. She likes you. Like, really likes you. She all but gave me the go-ahead the night of the Halloween tree."

"The Halloween tree?" I peel away and meet his eyes, my heart swelling with happiness. He's been falling for just as long as I have.

Now it's my turn to cast him a cocky smirk.

"Why, Mr. Isaac," I tease in an over-the-top southern drawl, "that was nearly three weeks ago, was it not?"

Hunter Isaac, the bad boy next door, blushes, and I absolutely love it.

"I've never not been sweet on you, Ponygirl."

I bite my bottom lip to keep the pair from pressing against his and forgetting what it is we're doing out here in the first place.

"Do you suppose I could talk to her? Woman to woman?"

"She's only nine."

"Almost ten," I say with a pointed finger to his nose. He scrunches it at me. "I hate to break it to you, Hunter, but that is not a little child." I point to the coop a few yards ahead of us where a tall, gangly 'tween sticks out of the wood, her brightly beaded anklet decorating a stray, barefoot limb of painted toes.

"That is a little lady right there. You better face the facts before they face you. She's smarter than you're giving her credit for."

His face scrunches up, like he's appalled at the thought. Of her growing up, most likely. Most parents make that face when you say, 'Oh, wow, she's gotten so big,' or similar customary phrases. Sadly, I can't say I get it.

I don't understand what it's like to see your baby grow up in front of you like he does.

Doesn't mean I can't help him out where a woman's touch could make all the difference, though. Doesn't mean I don't want to.

Desperately so. She's grown on me in a way I can't describe. I think because she's Hunter's, I feel closer to her.

"Let me talk to her."

He smiles, softening and letting some of the stress fade from his face. "Go ahead," he says, lowering to kiss me long and deep before he retreats to the stables.

I make my way to the chicken coop, my boots working in tandem with the land, unlike my heels all those weeks ago. She knows I'm there before I can announce myself, Hunter's kid and all, and the uncanny similarities between the pair has me, once again, in awe of the fact that he raised this young lady. On his own.

"You were right," Ellie says on a low sigh that's void of her signature pep.

I follow her voice to the far back of the coop, where she's crouched next to the nesting boxes from the inside. I suppress a laugh. It's not that I don't take her seriously, but she's a kid in a coop, and I can't not giggle a bit at how adorable she looks snuggled up next to the hen we call Polly. She's a gorgeous black silkie, and my eyes dart to Ellie's in question, one she answers with a click of her tongue and another deep, long sigh.

"I put Polly on these eggs two days ago, and she hasn't left them since. Except to eat and poop, which I did witness on account I slept in here on Tuesday." She runs out of air explaining and sucks in a quick breath that makes me laugh out loud. "Then our duck laid an egg, and I stole it. It's been under Polly for a whole day, and she's just sittin' on it same as her other two, even though she didn't lay it. Even though it doesn't even look the same as her other eggs."

The passion behind her eyes runs wild, her curiosity and wonder coming in never-ending waves. A scientist. A lady. A girl who is screaming for answers.

"I reckon we're gonna hafta call him Chuck, huh?" She lifts her chin, eyes shining like bright blue sapphires against the night sky, and I confirm what I already suspected, that she absolutely does not hate me.

Still.

"Why did you flood the guest room, Ellie?" I ask. Plain and simple.

When I was a kid, everyone was always trying to sugar-coat life for me. Make it dazzle and shine, so the moment was never dull, conflict always controlled, but all it does is harbor disappointment that breaks loose years later like a cannon, all-encompassing and aimed to kill.

No, honesty is always best.

"I was trying to make you sleep together," she mumbles.

"*What?*"

Does she know what she just said?

I must show every range of questions across my features because Ellie bursts out in a fit of giggles and then claps her hand over her mouth, clearly understanding a whole lot more than her Papa thinks she does because she says, "Ew, no! I didn't mean that way. I mean, like…well, you're in love, aren't you? And if you're in love, you won't leave. Guests leave."

"And just so we're clear…you don't want me to be a guest?"

She nods.

"I want you to be for real married to Papa." She climbs out of the coop and down the ramp meant for livestock and not sixty-pound pint-sized cowgirls, landing on the dirt with a thud and darting her little eyes up at me. "If you're for real married, you'll stay. And if you stay…" She trails off, widening her eyes and turning her head away in determination.

A determination I can read with every fiber of my being. Because it's me through and through. Somehow. Even though she isn't *my* Ellie, not really, she shares this with me all the same.

I can tell. She won't let me see her cry.

I twirl her around and guide her to the nearby bench where we sit. "If I stay…maybe what, Ellie?" I ask, eyes locked on hers as she struggles to hold back the tears building within them. "I don't like to cry, either" I admit, holding her stare. "But we don't have to. We can let the tears sting and burn together as long as we want, because we don't have to do anything we don't want to do. We don't have to love the hand we're dealt just because people say we should. And we certainly don't have to be okay."

She nods, her nostrils flaring. "If you stay, they won't make me leave." She closes her eyes and breathes in deeply, then watches the silkies, deep in thought. How does one explain the huge emotions sparring within when they've only had a decade to learn them?

"Penelope was a shitty mom," she finally says, looking at me sharply to gage my reaction to her language, but I don't budge. I may not be her mom, but if I were, I wouldn't care if she threw a curse word in there a time or two if it helped her express how she's feeling, and Hunter would think the same. Somehow, I inherently know that.

"Go on," I say.

"She didn't want to stay with her babies, even though that's literally the only thing she had to do. She had one job, and she didn't care enough to do it. I thought maybe it was her eggs, but I tried different eggs, you know? But she wouldn't do it. Until you came along and said to try the silkies, so I did. Polly."

She inclines her head toward the coop, referring to the bird who remains affectionately stationed atop her eggs—and of course, the duck egg—with no signs of leaving.

"Polly loves those eggs, Dev. She stays on them like her life depends on it."

I quirk a brow. "Yet you still seem so frustrated."

"Why can't Penelope do it, too?"

She kicks her boot at the dirt, and chunks of mud and debris flake off into the air, and we watch it fall. She gasps as bits of it hit her arm, then she looks back up at me with apologetic eyes.

"It's okay. You can cry if you want. Or you can kick the ground. You can be as angry as you want about the things you feel in your heart, Ellie."

She pauses, shoving her face into my gut and locking her tiny arms around my waist, letting the tears fall freely like she hasn't done it in all her life.

Maybe she hasn't.

I comb my fingers through her hair, pulling the tear-drenched strands away from her cheeks and forehead, and wrapping her in an even tighter hug as we rock, back and forth, in a way I don't think either of us has ever experienced as a mother or a daughter.

"You know, I had a Penelope, too. In real life."

She sits up, wiping her face on her sleeve and pulling her knees to her chin. "You did?"

"Yup," I say, letting it hang in the air, an unfinished answer.

"Did you ever get a Polly?" she finally asks, looking ahead at the pinkening horizon.

"No."

I look into the eyes of a little girl raised by the only man I've ever loved. A little girl with so much tenacity and promise. An innocent child who was born, not of her own choice, but because two system-failed teenagers didn't know another way. A child who is only alive and healthy today because the man I'm madly in love with chose to make it so.

A child I love, as crazy as that may be.

And I know, right here and now, why my life has led me to this moment.

Why I never got my Polly.

So, I tell her, the girl who stands here, asking me the same things I begged of the world before her.

When I was her.

"Because I was meant to be a Polly."

Chapter 32

Devyn

First thing's first," I tell Lemon and Shana, strolling through Abel's store with a grin plastered on my face, the familiar scents of pine and feed, portals to my youth. "I need to find me an Abel and get a big ol' hug."

Before I can't.

My heart swoops to my stomach for Clara, another integral role model during my formative stages, someone who looked out for not just me, but all the kids in Pine Forest. I run my fingers over the hand-painted sign by the wall of carts.

Live, Laugh, And Pray There's Not Shit on Your Boots When You Walk Up in My Store!

Everything's the same here.

"I have ten years of hugs to make up for," I whisper, almost to myself, but Shana hears. She grabs my hand and squeezes.

"I'm sorry you didn't know about Clara sooner."

"How do you always know what I'm thinking? It's honestly spooky, Shay." I shake my head.

She laughs, tugging me down the aisles, but her tone evens when she turns to me, and we stop mid-aisle. "My dad doesn't have long, you know." She twists the tie of her hoodie in her free hand, a nervous habit a lot like my hair tie. But she's done this little thing for as long as I remember.

"I'm sorry. About your dad," I tell her, veering us to chat more privately by the boots and apparel. "I know what it feels like to lose your whole world, Shay. And I'm sorry I haven't been here while you've been dealing with losing yours. I have not been the best friend I should be."

"Devyn, stop."

But I won't. I'm not going to let her give me an easy out on this one. She always will because Shana is just that brand of beauty. But it's not fair, because I'm not off the hook…not in my own heart, at least.

"No." I give her a pointed stare. "I've been a selfish bitch these last few years. I hated my past. My scars. Shay, I hated myself. I tried to be a check in all the boxes on everyone else's lists for so long that I became a person so unrecognizable to myself that I just…I hated her. And she wasn't in a place to be someone for anyone then."

"I know, Devyn," Shana says softly. "That's what I'm trying to tell you." She smiles, nudging me with her elbow. "You never let anyone get a word in, ya know?" We laugh, resuming our walking again when Shana turns to me, a curious glint in her eyes.

"I won't be losing my whole world," she says, "when he dies."

She says the last word with such finality and confirmation that it haunts me. The resignation in her tone. That he's dying, matter of fact. Just like that.

And I know she has to do that because he *is* dying, but it's so much to handle. The way she's been doing it with such grace since is astounding.

To have such confidence in the future, even when the present seems clouded.

"I used to be scared," she says, plucking a Frisbee from an end-cap. "Not knowing what would come next can be crippling, mentally, so to speak." She looks up, and I nod. It can be. "When he dies, I will truly be alone out here in the world. Not an orphan, right? Because those are kids. Just…something like it. But this last year, the town has poured their love around me. Hunter, Lemon, Jeremy…you…among others."

She presses her lips together in a smile that reaches all the way to her eyes and pulls me into a hug. She squeezes so tight we both might burst. It's exactly how it should be.

"I've missed you, bestie. You are all my world. My life is just beginning. And yeah, I might be alone once he's gone. But I'm alone with the best group of friends I could ever ask for."

She pulls away, still grinning. "That's what I've been trying to show you. Life might get crazy around here, but the people haven't changed since you left. And when it comes down to it, a more loyal group of people doesn't exist, Dev." She brushes her hair behind her ear and links arms with me. "We all want you to stay. Even after the fair, I mean."

I'm gut punched, and simultaneously elated, loved, accepted. But more than anything, I feel a deep sense of dread. Not dread for staying, not at all. Dread over the simple idea of leaving. Up until that moment with Ellie in the coop, I hadn't even thought of it.

It's been a week since that day. A week of bonding with a man and his daughter, knowing what it is she wants from me. Who and what she wishes I were to her. To her papa. A family who welcomes me in and fills the empty spaces of my heart, all the cracks and crevices, until I'm whole again. And it's not just the sit-down dinners celebrating a proud little girl's new racing records, or the perfectly sinful evenings under the sky-light when my body isn't my own.

It isn't even the familiarity of the roads or the thrill of the pageant and starting something new.

It's the whole shebang.

It's home.

"Thanks, Shay," I say, stifling my emotions before they do something crazy again like show. I exhale quickly and whip my head around, scanning the warehouse.

"Let's find the old man," Shana says, bumping hips. I'm glad she understands my cues and knows I've had enough feelings for one moment. She also knows how important it is for me to see Abel, whether I leave or stay.

"Rumor has it he can tell you the future, you know?" I grin as Shana giggles, hooking her pinky in mine. She and I started that rumor in sixth grade. Doesn't stop me from believing it to this very day.

The whole town has a sweet spot for Old Abe, and I am no exception.

"He'll be happy to see you. He's rather nostalgic these days."

"These days? He's always been like that."

Lemon snorts behind us, and I feel bad because I honestly forgot she was there. I break away from Shana and open the space between us. Lemon notices and chews her lips briefly before twisting them into a smile and launching forward, linking her arms into Shana's and mine.

"You'll see. By the way," Lemon says, "I know it was you two who started that rumor. When you wanted me to believe the puppy shampoo would make my hair grow longer." I burst out laughing, and Shana whips her focus to me, concerned, but Lemon just clicks her tongue and rolls her eyes.

"Come on, Shay, it's totally fine. I don't hate you guys. Anymore."

You'd think her calling my best friend by the nickname I created for her would tick me off coming from Lemon, but it doesn't.

We pass through the aisles, and it's as if nothing's changed, yet everything has all at once. Just like with Cowboy's Paradise, there's no denying this is Abel's feed store, but it's brighter, newer, even sturdier. The drop tile ceiling is freshly re-installed instead of flaking from above and making that tapping noise every time it slings against the vent when the heat kicks on. The floors are painted red and blue to match the lettering on the sign out front. Hell, he's even got security cameras in the corners.

Things here have been taken care of and renovated, like every other local staple this little town has. A free smile slips across my face with the knowledge that this is likely because of Hunter.

My Hunter.

"Is that little Devy Lynn I see in my crystal ball?"

Abel's deep cadence crackles through the air and peppers me with joy and familiarity. It's as if his laughter was designed for that purpose alone, and it's proven so when my eyes meet his and I see the curve of his rosy, Santa Claus cheeks holding up wire rimmed glasses that must be the same damn pair he wore all those years ago, the red paint on the rims worn and faded.

He chuckles, elbowing the gumball machine for old time's sake and lifting the flap to pull out a single sphere.

"You always did like pink best, if my old memory serves me right. The littlest Campbell with the biggest personality." He puts the gumball in my hand and closes his fingers around mine.

"Welcome home, Your Highness." He drops my hand and bows to me with a wry smile.

"Oh, knock it off, Abe, you old goose. You don't need to go bowing for me." I swat at his arm, but as gently as possible. It doesn't escape my notice that he's got a funky gait about him when he walks or stands or, really, anything he's doing. He doesn't use a cane, but as I peer over to his desk area, a smile pulls at the corners of my lips.

"You still have that damn stool, Abel? You don't want a new one?"

He huffs and waves his hand. "I'll have you know that stool has done me plenty well. No use recreatin' the wheel."

"It's leaning on one of the legs," I point out, which only seems to earn me a scowl.

"I heard a rumor, you know. I tend to hear these things, being the center of everyone's world and all," he teases with a wide grin.

"Oh?"

But he doesn't elaborate. He just grins like a proud grand-parent, laughing at me when I huff in protest.

"Oh, come now, Your Highness. You know I don't spread gossip. I only collect it."

I roll my eyes at the old man and look over the tops of the shelves for Lemon and Shana, but they're off looking for stuff on the list Hunter gave us.

Rope, zip-ties, cables, bolts, and duct tape...

Honestly, the list sounds like something he might need to tie up a victim, not build a stage. The thought sends an unnecessary thrill straight between my thighs, and I snap the hair tie on my wrist to bring myself back down from Hunter La La Land or whatever the hell this place is called where pure unadulterated fantasy and lust live rent free in my mind.

"You're blushing." Abel chuckles, turning and hobbling back to his stool. I follow him because I feel the very instantaneous need to correct him.

"I am not blushing."

"You are."

"No, I'm not."

He whips back toward me, impressively fast for his age, and cocks an exasperated look my way, a rumpled loose-leaf paper held tightly between his left fingers that he clings to while he speaks.

"You and Mr. Isaac are insufferable. You have long since been destined for love, and yet you fight it so relentlessly. It's a miracle you've even been given the chance to choose again."

"Choose again?" I furrow my brow, leaning over the counter and picking at the glue on the edge of his laminated *No Returns* sign.

"Well, of course. Why do you think you're here, young lady? Everyone has a choice. Every choice has a purpose. You can choose love, or you can choose whatever else exists out there." He turns away suddenly, shoving his crumpled papers back into the desk drawer before glancing my way, brows pinched with sadness etched over his features. "But this is important. Be prepared to live with the consequences of your choice. Should you choose the alternative, you may not be led down this path again."

"What's the alternative?"

I honestly don't know.

If Hunter is the first choice, is Not Hunter the other?

Not Hunter means Not Ellie…Not Lemon and Not Shana.

Not Home.

Still.

What if I'm Not Sure.

"Earth to Devyn!" Lemon snaps her fingers in front of my face and laces her arm through mine. "We got the rest of the items on the list. We just need to load the lumber. Robbie checked us out already on lane two. Here's the receipt incase Hunter needs it for write-offs."

"Write-offs. Right," I mumble, looking around for Abel, who seems to have mysteriously vanished into thin air, his stool leaning right where he just was.

Wasn't he?

"Where did Abel go?"

"Dunno." She shrugs. "Hobbled off that way. Something about his papers. You know Abe."

"Right."

Because I'm a blubbering idiot who daydreams in random places and doesn't even notice people moving about in front of her.

"I think I'm confused."

Lemon eyes me with concern and pulls me down the plumbing aisle where we lean against the model toilet bowls.

It works, I guess.

"What are you confused about, hon? Is it Hunter? The pageant?"

"It's everything," I admit. "I didn't know about Ellie."

Lemon frowns. "I know…we should have told you sooner, but we didn't think you'd understand until you met her. And it wasn't our story to tell. Hunter's been a saint to this town for years. He raised his brother's kid as his own and provided a place for all the other kids to thrive. He created scholarships, business loans for mom-and-pop shops, even a community garden. Pardon me for saying it like it is, babe, but your man has grown the hell up since you were last here, and it's okay if that freaks you out a bit. It's all right if you take your time to get to know the new man he's become. And it's normal if you're feeling cold feet about being a mother."

"Mother? I didn't say anything about me being her mother." My eyes widen. "Did I?"

Lemon shoots me a knowing glare. One I imagine older sisters use on their younger siblings when moms aren't around to do so properly. I wouldn't know. I had an older brother with a hot best friend who snuck in my bedroom window instead.

Shit. Why does my mind always come back to that like a damn default screen?

"You're thinking about him again," Lem points out, and I concede, sighing heavily and leaning onto her shoulder. Sitting here like this, it feels like Lemon and I truly are friends. Then the Lemon I recognize is back, teasing.

"Oh, poor Devyn. Wins Miss American Rodeo, garners thousands of followers online for sponsorships and news station appearances, basically gets insta-famous and comes back home to find an older, sexier, financially stabler version of her high school sweetheart with whom she falls wildly in love and lives happily ever after...oh, poor her."

Suddenly, I'm laughing out loud until my abs are sore. Lemon laughs, too. Wildly, loudly, and ceaselessly, bringing Shana back to our corner of the store, staring like we've grown two more heads.

"What the heck happened to you two?" She rolls her eyes, but her grin says it all. She's thrilled to see her two best friends becoming, dare I say it, best friends.

"Y'all are right," I tell them when our laughter finally settles into a silent, shared smile. "I'm in love, head over heels, with Hunter Isaac *and* his daughter."

And I want to be her mother.

I don't speak those last words out loud, though. Not yet.

Something inside me still screams it's too much, too good to be true. But I will say one thing.

"I'm staying."

Shana and Lemon tackle me to the floor in a hug, and we laugh all over again, until our faces are numb.

Riding home, we blast Shania Twain, hollering the lyrics to "Man, I Feel Like a Woman." I marvel at the rows and rows of sunflowers, fields of wheat, rolling hills and haybales for miles to come. The smell of manure is thick in the cool, fall air, and the chill on my face as I let the wind whip away at me through the open windows of the truck is telling of an approaching winter. Crisp. Exciting.

Magical.

"I've been thinking about something. Ellie told me Katie keeps trying to place her with other families because Hunter isn't married. But right now, everyone already thinks we are. What difference would it make if we just, I don't know, made it legal for the sake of him winning custody. It's not like we couldn't change it later once he's fully adopted her, and maybe we wouldn't even want to…I mean the way things are now, I'm not sure I wouldn't—"

Lemon stops me. "Katie does not want Ellie with other families, Devyn. She has purposely been working with Hunter to sabotage any potential foster matches while he fights for custody, just so you know. She's on your side."

I couldn't have imagined that would sting so much coming from Lemon. I mean, I understand she's Katie's cousin, but she knows so much more about this than I do. So much more about a girl who feels like my responsibility. Not hers. And that's crazy, right?

That she feels like my responsibility?

But I don't care. That is how it feels.

"I was just feeling like Hunter and I had this whole new level of trust, but he hasn't told me anything about her custody placement other than it's been up and down. Ellie's revealed more to me than Hunter has, and I get the feeling he isn't telling me the stuff that truly has him in knots."

Shana clears her throat, gripping the wheel with white knuckles and elbowing Lemon. Lemon, who is awkwardly wedged between Shana and me right now, stiffens suspiciously, but I go on.

"If we were for real married, as Ellie put it," I smile at the memory, "Hunter would have a better chance of full custody, don't you think?"

"Oh, boy, we have to tell her," Shana suddenly blurts. "I can't keep it secret anymore."

"Shut up!" Lemon hisses. "It's not your secret to tell, it's—"

"Tell me what?" I snap at them both.

But before I can get my answers, Shana slams on the brakes and the truck comes screeching to a halt. She pulls to the shoulder and flicks on her brights, illuminating the field so we can see—

"Ellie?"

Chapter 33

Devyn

My first reaction to what I see ahead is to snatch someone's kid up and demand to know why he hit a girl. My breath left my lungs at the sight of Ellie's blood smudged cheek and mussed up hair. But when I see the other kid—the one with the busted lip and two black eyes—I remember gender equality and all.

Ellie looks much better than the other guy. She might have even started it.

"What the hell happened here?" I whisper to Ellie. She's standing oddly close to the boy who seemingly hit her. Unless she hit him? Maybe some other bully beat them both up, and—

"Jon-a-than," she drawls out the syllables, a whip of her neck assigned to each, glaring at the kid through narrowed slits in her eyes, like she aims to cut him with the sound of his own name.

Savage.

But…no. It's also wrong.

It's something Bitchy-Devyn would have condoned, but that doesn't make it okay. Even if I do feel a tiny streak of pride at her competitive nature. Instead, I scowl at her as she continues, a silent plea for her to take it down a notch.

She does not, of course, take it down any notches.

"His father is the reason! If he wasn't a no-good, animal-hurtin' son-of-a—"

"Stop sayin' that!" He clenches his fists by his side then huffs incredulously at the moon. "Dang it, Ellie! I helped you free the calf, didn't I? We're even!"

My brain circles back to past conversations with Hunter, talk of Ellie getting into fights with a boy at school. It breaks my heart that she's going through so much all at once. Custody, bullies. Kids can be downright mean.

I should call Hunter right away. I know I should.

A smarter person would.

But after what she trusted me with the other day, the bond we share is…well, it's just that. It's a bond. It's fragile and it's new. And I want to help her.

"You stole this cow?"

Neither of them answers, so I go for the weaker looking of the two. No offense to this kid over here, but he looks like the one who'd crack in an interrogation, and I know for a fact Ellie will be keeping her lips sealed as long as she feels she needs to.

Because Hunter and I would have done the same damn thing.

"Is this your dad's cow, Jonathan?"

He nods reluctantly. But only after shooting a quick glance to Ellie and waiting for her nod, confirming what I'd suspected. She's at the heart of this little heifer-heist.

"We're going to call your papa after we walk Jonathan and his cow back home," I tell her, patting the baby cow on the nose. He's a cute little thing, but not worth throwing punches over.

Ellie huffs and puffs about the cow going back, but I hold up my hand.

"Whatever excuse you have, violence is never the answer."

"How do you know he didn't swing the first punch?" She arches a brow, testing me, but I've got her number. Can't bullshit a bullshitter.

"You look like you had a seasonal nosebleed, Ellie," I say, turning my attention to Jonathan next, "and he looks like he barely survived the Hunger Games." Jonathan scoffs, puffing his chest a bit higher to prove me wrong, but quickly pulling back in on a wince. Ellie scrunches her nose when she notices.

"I'm sorry I hit you," she mumbles, kicking at the ground in front of her. He swings his head up to meet her eyes and she cringes, taking in his bloodied face. "…again, that is. I'm sorry I hit you *again*."

"It's okay. I haven't said the nicest things to you at school. About your, uh…bio dad. I didn't mean it when I said you're just like him. You're not."

They stare at one another for a moment, a visible under-standing forming between them, and it's awkward as hell. It's honestly more of an A and B conversation, but they're still only children, so I'm just chillin' in the background of Boy Meets Fist over here…*chaperoning*.

But I'm absolutely uncomfortable, and I really want to get this kid back home and call Hunter.

"Ehhhemmm," I finally manage, deliberately loud.

They break their weird staring contest, and thank the lord, because I am not prepared for whatever level of parenting that is.

Jonathan bends down to wipe the mud off his jeans. I wonder how long Ellie had him pinned before he gave in. Maybe she should be in wrestling and not rodeos?

He wipes his bloodied lip on his sleeve, and Ellie offers him a handkerchief she slides from her beltloop.

"It's fine." He waves her off. "Gives my dad a reason to remember I exist."

He whispers that last bit. So quietly I almost don't hear it. But I do.

This is why Hunter started his farm, isn't it? To give these kids a safe space to exist, so someone is always there for them, even if home isn't perfect.

I fall in love with him that much more, without even being in his presence. How could I not?

His influence is all around us. It's present right now, before my very eyes, in this little girl. A daughter who wasn't meant to be his but is in every sense of the word. I see it when I look into her matching blue eyes, yes, but I also see it right now, as she turns an enemy into a friend, wearing her heart on her sleeve.

Believing in second chances.

The wind whips around us, the goose bumps spreading across my bare arms reminding me it's getting late. Lemon and Shana, who have been searching for a first aid kit in Lemon's mess of a truck, end up finding only one of those crack and pop ice packs, which I obviously offer up to Jonathan, seeing as how *Million Dollar Baby* over there barely has a scratch.

They agree to stay parked while I walk the kids…and cow…back, the headlights from the truck illuminating the path ahead.

"Should I call Katie?" Lemon shouts as we're starting up the hill, but I shake my head.

"I imagine Hunter will want to deal with this himself." *Without the involvement of Ellie's social worker.* Whether she's Lemon's cousin or not, she's still someone standing between Hunter and Ellie's permanency, isn't she? "Besides, it sounds like they've worked out their differences. Right, you two?"

The kids share a look before nodding.

"Good. We'll walk you home, and then, Ellie, you can ride home with us. You have a lot of explaining to do later. Don't even think I'm covering for all that." I gesture to the mess that is poor Jonathan's face.

He smirks, looking up at Ellie every so often. "You know, I'd rather beat your barrel time than your face."

Ellie snorts. "Dream on, Pres. You'll never beat my time. Not with the way you flop around going into the turns."

"I don't flop."

"Yes, you do. And your horse is scared to death you'll fall off. Why do you think he sticks his nose up every time you go into your turns? He's slowing down for you." She rolls her eyes, chewing her bottom lip. If I had to guess, which I obviously do, I'd say it's to force back the smile threatening to steal her face.

Pres. Not sure where the nickname came from, but I wasn't born yesterday. Ellie likes this kid. And he likes her. And that honestly explains a hell of a lot where their fighting's concerned. I wonder if Hunter has noticed this detail.

He wasn't much older when he first called me Ponygirl.

It would certainly help him to understand things from her perspective. And what Jonathan said about her being like her bio dad? What Ellie had said about Jonathan's dad abusing animals? There are some underlying issues here. And maybe it's good we're getting them to work it out.

I reach for my phone, but Ellie stops me.

"Wait, you can't! Not yet. Papa will be furious about the fight, which isn't even a problem anymore, and Porkloin will get lost in the mess of it all. And just *look* at him." She motions to the admittedly emaciated calf who I guess is named Porkloin. "His dad's got the poor thing chained up to a wall day in and day out. He's not even feeding it the farm-grade stuff either. It's a diet not even fit for raising veal, and they don't offer permits for that in this zone, even if he wanted to!" She breathes in, exasperated, pleading at me with a light in her eyes that begs to let them do this. Let them take this cow back to our farm and treat it right. I can see very clearly that is all the world to her right now. Even Jonathan's got his hands clasped together and swollen lip jutted out.

"Fuck it," I whisper, earning dual looks of shock from *Ocean's Eleven and Under*. "Give me a break. This mom stuff is new to me." I sigh, but I realize about twenty seconds too late what it is that I just said.

Out loud.

To Ellie.

I suck in a quick breath, not because I want to take the words back, but because I truly mean them.

And there is no going back.

She stops walking and turns to face me.

"Mom stuff?"

Blue eyes that match the only other pair I've ever loved lock onto mine in question. I can profess my love to Hunter through and through, but this is the real moment when I decide on something I can't run from. This isn't just Hunter asking me to stay. Or me knowing inherently I've never stopped loving him.

It's Ellie.

My chance to choose again.

I want this life with Hunter and Ellie.

I choose her.

I choose this.

"Silkie stuff," I say, meeting her bright blue stare. And it happens, I watch the light fill her eyes as the tears fall from mine.

For happiness.

She beams, throwing her arms around me. Blood, snot, and tears fall from her face and coat my clothes, but I couldn't care less about any of that.

She needs me, and I can be there for her.

Even if we didn't get the chance with our own child, I'm being given a chance right now to be something to someone who desperately needs me back. More than one someone.

A family. *My family.*

Purpose bubbles from within, filling me with something I didn't know I needed. I tried filling it with parties, sponsorships, and influencer banquets, with fancy dresses and designer heels. I even tried filling it with success, which only made me emptier somehow, but nothing compares to the feeling I get with this little family here in Pine Forest.

With *love.*

We march our way through the field, calf in tow and my checkbook in my purse, ready to bargain.

It occurs to me that we're walking up a familiar bend. A ranch house with a clearing I remember from parties years ago. But who even owned this house back then, and who does now? An uneasiness churns in my gut as we reach the porch steps.

"Jonathan," I call. He twists around, hand on the rail, and I take a moment under the glow of the porch light to really look at this kid. Blue eyes, tan skin, blond hair…

"Is your father—"

The door swings open, and I instinctively shove Jonathan behind me with Ellie and Porkloin. I feel oddly protective over all three of them right now, and I can't explain that, but I'm rolling with my heart and my head these days, so here we go.

"Well, if it isn't my own personal Highway Ho-Down," Garrison Presley slurs, leaning on the doorframe. "Didn't think pretty little buckle bunnies like you made house calls."

He grins, but it isn't a nice one. It's a sloppy one. A drunk one. And as he peers behind me and takes in Jonathan's and Ellie's faces, and the livestock in tow, it morphs into something else entirely, and I wish I'd called Hunter after all.

He and Lemon tried to warn me about him, saying he's changed since we were kids. He seemed normal enough to me in the safety of the publicly lit bar, but right now, he feels more like a stranger than the happy-go-lucky party boy I recall.

A drunk stranger, who sees his bloodied-up child, a stolen farm animal, and me in between.

Shit. This was not covered in fake wife OSHA training.

"Garrison, look, before this goes any further—"

His smile shifts as he takes in the scene, and I'm suddenly shoved to the side as he barrels down the front steps, kneeling before Jonathan and inspecting his face.

"What's that little bitch done now?" he spits, whipping his head toward Ellie, who's standing unashamedly proud in front of Porkloin. It's a protective stance, and I wonder how she got to be so brave. Her papa would be proud of her, not limiting herself to cower in the presence of someone as toxic as Garrison Presley.

Ohhh, Pres.

"She's a kid, Garrison. If you have something to say about her, you can speak with Hunter or me, the other adult here, instead of my—" I stutter to call her whatever she is to me, unsure of what she'd want, but also feeling a strong mama bear urge to claim her as my own. So, I just do.

"My child."

"Your child?" He quirks his brow, entertained by this more than I'd like him to be, especially with how pungent the stench of whiskey is coming off his breath. Reminds me of my childhood, and I hate that for Jonathan. At least it doesn't seem like Garrison wants him hurt. Or hurts him at all, for that matter.

From what Johnathan said, he just gets ignored.

I'm not sure if that's any better. But I can guess the alcohol is part of it, because that look Jonathan has in his eyes, is one I know all too well.

I could crawl inside it and live through the same lenses without ever having left my own body at all. We're the same, he and I.

He and Ellie.

And Hunter.

We're wounded children in need of someone to guide us. Lost souls who find comfort in friends…and family in sacrifice. I'm only just now learning those things about myself.

Ellie steps forward, those glossy eyes burning like we both let them, refusing to let our tears be seen by anyone less than worthy. "That's right! She married my papa, and that makes her my mother, too."

"Oh, really?" Garrison coos, his voice sing-songy and unhinged, both menacing and mirthful, sending an uncomfortable prickle across my skin. His perfect lips stretch over his sinister face, and it's devastating how handsome one can look when they are full of so much hate.

"You can tell your *papa*," he puts the word in air quotes, "that your real fuckin' father cost me everything! Caught the whole thing on fire." His eyes burn with terror as his memories take hold of his words, a mix of agony and slurs.

"He watched the love of my life burn, burn, burrrrn. Diddde ever tell you bou'that?" He looks Ellie in the eyes, but he says it right to me, piercing me, a sharp blade, pinning me in place as I listen and twisting deeper as he goes.

"Samuel wasn't only a killer. He was a thief. And from the looks of it, so's his flesh n' blood." He nods to Porkloin who cowers behind Jonathan, shaking, the mere sound of Garrison's voice a threat to the creature's sanity. My fists clench at my sides. I have had it with this asshole. I don't know what the hell he's spewing about Sam, but I'm over this.

These are kids.

This is a living, abused animal.

And he is fucking drunk.

I step forward, red waves pulsing across my vision, my fight or flight responses kicking fully into gear.

And I lose it.

I swing my arm, landing a punch square in Garrison's jaw. He stumbles back up the porch, and I feel my knuckles pop… or his tooth? I've never actually hit someone before, so I don't know the dynamics of it all, but God, that effing hurts. I pull back my own hand in shock, and Garrison uses that spare moment to grab my wrist and pull me up the steps, slamming my back against the wooden door, the cold metal of the door knocker digging into the back of my head.

"You like it rough?" he whispers, the sour tinge of alcohol invading my senses and making me retch. "Ah-ah," he says, squeezing my cheeks, cradling my chin in a bruising grip. "I know they want that damn cow. I'll let 'em have it forrra' price." His hips press into my pelvis, keeping me immobile while he trails his free hand down my side.

"Dad, let her go!" Jonathan screams, moving to rush the steps, but Ellie is so much wiser than her papa gives her credit for. She throws her arm out in front of him and keeps him back. *Good girl.*

"Don't," she says. "You don't know what he'll do to you."

"Why do you care?" he asks, and Garrison huffs a laugh at that, his eyes still roaming my body possessively, licking his foul-smelling lips. It's disgusting. I knee him in the balls, and it gives me a split second to turn out of his hold, although he still has my wrist. I wince in pain as he digs his fingers deeper around my arm.

"I care because this town is crazy," Ellie snaps at Jonathan, still holding him back, in a bear hug at this point, as he threatens to break through her hold. "We have to take care of each other, right?"

And it breaks my heart that she gets it too soon. That Jonathan gets it too soon. But I'm proud of her. Pride that seeps into me and coats me in an armor I need desperately right now, pushing me.

Yanking my arm free from Garrison's grip, I march back toward him and use my new position to shove him to the wall while he's still groaning about his ball sack. That's the thing about ball sacks. Vaginas can take a literal pounding, but a single tap to the balls sends men to their knees in agony.

And like, let us not forget that God makes no mistakes and all. That was a design choice.

"Now, I'm buying your cow or I'm telling the cops you drunk assaulted me. You pick."

"C'mon, Devyn, all I wanted wazaa lil' of that sssweet sss-southern pie you flash all over the TV." He licks his lips again, and I hate the sight of him, so I slap him once across the face, and I watch as the blood drips from his lip.

"Who assaulted who now?" He grins, pushing his weight back against me and striding ahead, backing me against the wall once more.

"Please, let's calm down and talk," I try, but he's no longer fighting me with his weight. He's falling against me, using me to hold his body up, and he's shaking.

Is he crying?

He slumps against my body with most of his weight, and I struggle to hold him up. He pushes until we're against the wall and he's hugging me in a way that's not sexual in the least. I'm more of an anchor for him right now.

"Gone. Sheeee's gone," he cries. Goosebumps prick my skin, and I lower us to the deck floor, resting atop the welcome mat as he hangs across my lap, heaving tears and gasping between gargled words.

Jonathan approaches from the left and kneels beside me, a sad look ghosts his face. "Let's get you inside, Dad."

He tries to pry his dad's arms from my shoulders, but Garrison snaps back, almost feral, alcohol holding captive any semblance of lucidity. He slips in and out of the present as he grips me tighter.

"No, you can'ttttake 'er from me!" My heart races, and I don't know what to do. He's clearly not the sexual predator he seemed a few minutes ago, but he's something quite possibly worse now. It's a kind of trauma-based hallucination.

He needs help. But he's unpredictable.

I need to get the kids away, most importantly. Adrenaline pumps through me, and I pray to God for whatever strength he gives all those women who lift fallen trees off their babies on YouTube as I attempt to wiggle free.

Garrison tightens his hold, sobbing and combing his fingers through my hair, and as much as I try, I can't overpower him.

"Get Lemon and Shana!" I shout to the kids, finally realizing I can't do this alone. I don't want to do this alone.

I crack, tears of frustration finally breaking over my eyes and rolling down my face. "I don't want to do it alone!" I scream, shoving all my weight against Garrison's drunken form, but it's no use. He's twice my size.

The kids take off down the drive, but they stop in their tracks and begin to wave and jump when a honk sounds in the distance and a bright pair of headlights come charging up the rolling hills.

Not Lemon's truck. This one is a rusted, ugly, white Ford that I've never been happier to see.

Hunter launches himself from his truck, slamming the door. His eyes darken as he takes me in, pinned beneath Garrison, and his lip curls up, seething.

"Gary! Get the fuck off my wife!"

Chapter 34

Hunter

Papa!" Ellie screams, running into my arms. I squat beside her, raking my eyes over every inch of her tiny body to make sure, but then—" Anger burns from within me as I take in the blood on her face.

Garrison has smartly shoved away from Devyn. I was about ten seconds shy of beating his entire fuckin' body through his own damn door if he hurt a single hair on her head. And that's how I feel again when I see the blood on my little girl's cheek.

Blood that was put there by his son.

"Your boy do this to my daughter?" I spit at Garrison, peering around a sickly calf to get a look at the Presley boy. It's always that same boy. But my feet stop their crunch along the gravel when I see he's covered in bruises and cuts worse than hers.

"Ellie?"

"She did it to him," Devyn says. I don't miss the way she clutches the railing. He's scared her shitless. From the looks of it, he's been in one of those drunk throes he finds himself in once or twice a month.

Crumpled on the steps, tears and dirt coating his swollen eyes, red-faced and shaking.

He thinks his wife is burning alive.

Because of my fuckin' brother. I clench my fists so hard I wouldn't be surprised to find blood on my palms when I open them.

None of it gives him any excuse for who he's become. It just…it is why he's become this person. The reason our families have never aligned.

Why he can't stand the sight of my kid. Or his own.

Not after what Samuel did.

A low growl forms in the base of my throat, and I force myself to look Ellie in the eyes.

"Did you beat up the Presley kid?"

She nods, and I curse.

"This is just what we need right before custody." An assault to the mayor's great nephew under my guardianship. I can't lose Ellie. And even though this is all a technicality, and I'm surer than shit the kid deserved it, I can't condone this behavior either. I'm no better than Samuel if I don't steer her in the direction she needs to break the generational curses that stain us.

She's supposed to have everything we couldn't.

How can I give her that if she's not under my care?

My heart pounds in my chest. Anxiety? Fear? I'm certain it's both, but I can't rein it in. I'm broken when it comes to Ellie.

I can't go through the loss of a child again.

And no, it's not fair to blame anyone for this, but somehow, I do.

I blame her.

I blame *Devyn*.

My eyes roam the scene wildly. Bloodied children, stolen livestock, Garrison-fucking-Presley, drunk and throwing accusations at my nine-year-old, who is already walking a tightrope frayed to bits when it comes to social services and their rules. My mouth foams. Words are coming out, but it hardly feels like I'm the one speaking them. Words that sting.

"How could you let this happen?" drops from my lips.

"*Me?*" She gapes. "I showed up after all of this happened. I'm helping."

"You think this is helping? Coming here to rub it in Garrison's face that she hit his kid? Right the fuck before a placement hearing." I glance at Garrison, but he's barely coherent. Drooping against the frame of the door. He won't be conscious much longer.

I've seen him do it before. At least he won't remember the fight. And if that's the case, maybe we'll still have a shot at covering this up before it reaches Katie. Or worse, the fucking mayor.

"You should have called me the second you found them so I could warn you against coming here. And alone?" I wring my hands through my hair, pacing in front of them. "Do you even know what could have happened to you, Dev? To both of you?"

Her eyes flare in shock and then flick to the ground. They stay there, and I know that can't be good for me, but I gotta sort this other shit out. I'm a father first. I don't have the luxury of playing it safe where Ellie's placement is concerned.

"Gary," I say, stalking forward and pulling him up by the shirt collar to look me in the eyes. He's a sloppy mess, but my heart still tenses. I get it.

He's me, before Ellie gave me something to live for.

But Jonathan? He stands far away from his father right now…holding Ellie's hand.

I've missed some serious parts to this story.

Devyn wraps her arms around the kids, and I know instantly I've made a mistake. Hell, I knew it before I even spewed those words at her. I take in the tears streaming down her cheeks. Ones she very rarely shares with the world.

But there they are.

Because I hurt her.

She's been here dealing with something Ellie got herself into, something that wasn't even her responsibility, and I wasn't here for that. She put herself in harm's way with a drunk farmer she barely knows for my daughter.

And all I did was let the custody battle blind me from seeing how close we are to being something more than Ellie and Me…or Me and Dev.

It could be *us.*

And I may have messed it up in one solitary moment.

I groan as another problem rises to the surface of my mind. I can't leave Jonathan here with Gary tonight. He's wasted. Lucky for me, or unlucky for me, I'm not sure which, he's too wasted to protest anything I say.

"Your boy's stayin' at my place." I nod at Jonathan, bending down and sniffing the air to see just how much his father's had. A lot.

"You can get him tomorrow when you're sobered up. We're gonna talk then. You hear me?"

"She's gone, Isaac. Jusss fuckin' *gone.*"

I know who he means, and I feel a tug at my heart.

Gary and I are one and the same. He lost someone much like I did. Too soon and much too fast.

Guilt creeps over me, and I grind my teeth as I shove my arm underneath him. I gave up trying to help him years ago. I tried to get him to see he's got a damn son to live for, just like I had Ellie. But how do you get someone to see what's right in front of them if all they ever do is look behind? I know all too well where this path Garrison is on could lead him, and I can't bear to think it's all because of our fucked-up family history. Not when I see his son, the same age as Ellie, begging him for more.

He needs help.

I breathe in, lifting his heavy frame.

I'm going to help him.

"I know. I know she is," I tell him, hoisting his entire body over my shoulder with Jonathan's aid and easing him into the house.

Jonathan gathers an overnight bag, and I take the private moment to look around. It's not dirty, but it's not clean. Not dark, but not bright. There's food and clothes and furniture.

But it's missing something.

Hope.

Something Ellie brings into my own home. That bright, shining sense of wonder and possibility that Devyn's since enhanced.

I deposit Garrison's limp body on the sofa next to a picture of Annabelle, a beautiful woman with brown hair and the voice of an angel. When she'd sing at church, Gary couldn't look away, always braggin' to the rest of us that her voice is as good as her cookin', and her cookin' is as good as her lookin'. They were so in love, they'd barely popped out the first kid before she was carrying their next.

Samuel's my younger brother. I think I'll always feel a sense of responsibility for the things he did that plague so many, because no matter what you do in the present to right it, the past is always the past.

And the dead don't return.

I make sure there are no candles burning before we turn out the lights and go home.

Chapter 35

Hunter

One thing about Devyn is you know when she's pissed. And right now, she is really fuckin' pissed. At me.

"I'm sorry." I grip the steering wheel tighter. "I shouldn't have blamed you for what happened back there. I just…there're things I haven't told you about yet, and I—"

Devyn whips her neck to face me, nothing but narrow slits where her bright round eyes usually appear, and she cuts me off with that look alone. The words she says after sting, but the look on her face when she says them is heartbreaking. I've wounded her. I've betrayed some of the trust we've carefully built back up.

And I watch as she painstakingly slides those concrete slabs back in place, the invisible ones she wedges between us when it's too much to face skin to skin. The ones she thinks I can't see plain as day.

I see you, babygirl. I've always seen you.

"You blamed me. Do you know how bad that hurts?" She grits her teeth to get the message out, but it's her eyes I'm still stuck on, the shining orbs that are so close to spilling over, I might see it again this time. Two times in one night I will have made her cry. I've fucked up.

"You don't understand what power Garrison holds in this town, Dev," I whisper, checking the rearview mirror to see Jonathan staring out the window. I don't want him to hear me talk about his dad. A conversation like this one is better off happening later. At home. Even if Devyn doesn't understand that.

"Can we talk about this when we're home?"

"Your home, you mean?"

Her words slice me open. I've come to think of it as our home. Of her as my girl.

Of us as a family.

"It's *our* home. And I was wrong to make you feel anything to the contrary." I hope she can read my eyes the same way I can hers.

Do you see me? I beg her with my stare.

"This isn't the first time these two have had problems, and Ellie is one strike away from getting in serious trouble for it. I panicked when I saw you brought the evidence of their fight right to the very person who could act against her."

"All I was trying to do was help her out of something she got herself into when nobody else was there to do it, Hunter. She was hurt. And scared. Hell, they'd already made up by the time I got there. We were just taking Jonathan and the cow back home when we found Garrison."

I grab her hand and cock my head slightly toward Jonathan behind us, and Dev gets the message. She stops, maneuvering her words away from Jonathan's living demons.

But she's still my girl. Tough and unrelenting. So, she gives it to me all the same.

"You haven't even asked about the cow." This part is loud enough for the kids to hear.

"What the hell's the damn cow got to do with this?" I ask, earning twin groans from the back seat and a look of pure outrage from Devyn.

"You know what?" she says, threading her hands through her hair and facing forward again. Away from me.

I don't like it.

"I've been assaulted, frightened, and blamed enough for one night," she drops her voice to a whisper, "but what I'm madder about is that little girl back there, she needed me, and I tried to do the right thing in your absence, but what you seem to be implying is that I should have stayed out of it. No matter how close we've grown, no matter that the whole town thinks we're one big married happy family and you've asked both Ellie and me to go along with this. But it's not my business, right? Because she's not my kid? And by those standards, Hunter Isaac, this isn't our home…it's yours. I'm just a part of it you made some space for."

My heart breaks the way they say it does in all those books she reads. It's not a metaphor. I feel it, the tense pain between each crack that splinters through my chest at the thought of her not belonging right here with me. With us.

"That is not at all how I feel, Devyn. I love you. This whole place is made better because you're here. Because you're *you*. I don't just want you in my world, Dev. I need you in it."

I look back at the kids. We've been whispering, but fuck knows they heard every damn word from the looks on their faces. And they have been through enough tonight. Most importantly, I need to talk to Devyn about stuff Ellie doesn't need to hear. It's time to come clean about everything if I don't want it all to come crumbling down on me.

I put the truck in park and turn to the kids. "Can you two get settled in with some leftover pizza in the kitchen while we talk?"

"No!" Ellie snaps, and I angle my shocked face to meet a spiteful glare. "I'm not going anywhere until you two make up. You can't blame Devyn for something that's between me and Jonathan and our own fists."

"You mean *your* fists," Jonathan interrupts, gesturing to his bruised and bloodied self, and earning an exhausted sigh from Ellie.

"Anyway," she rolls her eyes and continues, "we already forgave each other." She shoots a glance at Jonathan to let that sink in again, and I try not to laugh. She'll be all right.

"It wasn't her fault we stole the cow, either."

"Ellie, the house," I grind out. But she only bucks back at me, holding her chin up higher and daring me to make her leave. This is what happens when you raise a strong-willed kid. I rub my temples and exhale, relenting because I haven't the strength to fight her tonight.

"Hunter, you and I," Dev reaches back and links pinkies with Ellie, smiling, "and Ellie. We've become a family. And I can't spend every single day with this amazing child who belongs to the man I love and not feel like she's a daughter to me. But tonight felt very much like you against me. Will that be what it's like? Will I be an outsider, no matter how I weave myself into all of this?"

"No, Dev, not at all." I sigh, not knowing how to best explain it, but I have to try. "That's just the thing, she isn't your daughter."

Her mouth pops open, and I can see the pain there. Pain caused by my words, but I can't lessen that pain for her. I can't even do it for me. And if she wants this, with us, with me and Ellie, then she has to know that. None of this life comes free from pain.

I lean closer, cupping her cheek to soften my words so she'll hear them for what they are. They aren't meant to hurt her. They're just facts. Facts we unfortunately don't get to ignore as Ellie's guardians.

"I don't mean that in the emotional sense," I tell her, pulling my hand down to hold hers over the console. "But in the straight, legal, factual sense that I have never gotten the luxury of ignoring where Ellie is concerned, there are things you don't know that you aren't thinking about. Things that—"

"Well, maybe if you'd tell me! Trust me with all these secrets you guard so closely. I tried to be a sounding board for this earlier in the week and you brushed me off. I get that you don't feel like you can totally open to me about everything, but I wish you'd see how much I've had to lay myself bare to be able to trust you again. Fuck, Hunter, *Lemon* knows more than I do. And what the fuck happened to Garrison while I was gone, huh, the fuck *was* that?" She braces herself on the center console for support. "I can't do this if we don't trust each other enough to share life's problems. Lord knows we aren't done facing them."

She's right.

I haven't trusted her. She found out about Ellie on her own, she has no idea about her father, and worst of all, I still haven't told her about the fact that our marriage is—and could stay—very real, if she wants. Because I've been so worried about if she doesn't want that. And what that could mean for me and Ellie. This whole time I've been trying to bring her back into the folds of Pine Forest and work her into my perfectly crafted life, assuming that was enough because of love.

But she's been in complete darkness.

She's sat and timed Ellie's skills with Lyle, increased our score for trivia nights at Sugar Stable tenfold since joining our team thanks to all her random news facts. Hell, she's even building up a pageant program with one of her oldest rivals.

She's been there for us even after I revealed a secret fucking kid and has made no plans to move back home after the fair.

"Papa?" Ellie says softly. "I'm…not your daughter, either, you know." She scrunches her little nose as she says it. I don't know if she's trying to soften the blow, or if she's just now hearing how that sounds for the first time.

"No, I could never be Samuel, and I'm sorry, but that's a good thing, Ellie. You are who you are because of what you come from, and you can't change that, but you can use that power in any way you like. I used mine to make a life for us. Me and you. But there was a time when I almost didn't. I almost used it for an early ticket to my grave. For fighting. To satisfy my anger and fear."

She sniffles, and I know she won't want me to see her cry, she's a lot like Dev that way, but I look her in the eyes all the same, because everyone is getting the truth from me tonight.

No more secrets.

"Even if you aren't my daughter by technicalities, you are mine because there's a place in my heart that you fit indefinitely. You started off as my reason for healing, Ellie. But you've become my reason for being. And I will never stop fighting to make sure you stay right here. Exactly where you belong."

Ellie throws her arms around me from the back seat, burying a tear-streaked face into my shoulder.

"I love you always, Eleanor Rosemary. I promise I'll make this right for us," I whisper into her hair. This time, only she can hear me, and she nods, trusting me to do just that. To make it right, to earn back Devyn's love *and* her trust.

She sniffs, wiping her face on her sleeve and nodding twice.

"Thank you for helping us rescue Porkloin," she tells Dev, then flicks her focus to me and raises a brow before directing her attention back at Devyn.

"Even if you aren't my mother by technicalities, there's a place in my heart that you fit *indefinitely*."

She hugs Devyn from behind, winks at me, and scoots out of the truck, hopping from the bed with a crunch of gravel beneath her boots as she runs after her friend.

Message received, loud and clear.

Chapter 36

Hunter

"You know what's funny?" Devyn asks as we walk side by side to the stables. I tell myself it's to tend to the horses before bed and not because we have some serious shit to get through that doesn't concern either of those kids in there.

Somehow, Devyn's beauty only enhances when she's mad, but I won't tell her that. If I did, it would only distract me from what we need to talk about, because when her eyes go dark green like they are now, I willingly lose myself in them every damn time.

"What's funny?" I follow her gaze to the stars, and we both smile when one shoots across the sky. "You have to make a wish before you answer that."

"I wish we could go back in time," she whispers, then laughs, letting her head hang low. Our eyes meet, and I want to tell her I want that, too.

But it would be a lie.

"Dev, I'm gonna tell you a lot of things tonight. And you might not like me afterward, so before we get into that, let me just say that I'm gonna be very honest with you. No more lies."

She nods, watching me while I tug at my beard. God, why is this so hard? Fuckin' vulnerability and shit. I fuckin' hate it, but this has to happen, or…I can feel it in my gut.

She'll run for good this time.

"I don't wish we could go back. Not the way you do. And if this is going to work, you have to know that. None of this—" I wave my arms around the stables, rows and rows of horses people trust me to board. The best of the best in Pine Forest. "—the community, the scholarships, the town, *Ellie*…None of this would be here if I hadn't lived the alternative first."

If you didn't leave me.

"The alternative?" she gasps, backing away, but I take her hand, holding on and praying to God she never makes me let go.

"When we lost her—" I pause, the words pricking my tongue like pins. "When you left, my heart shattered. But you have to understand, Dev. You were alive. And that's all that mattered. If I could have gone back to that day and picked myself over our baby, if I could be the one trapped beneath the wreckage, I would have. And I let myself drown in that knowledge. What you don't know is that…for the time you were gone, you were better off without me."

Devyn lifts her chin, but she's not shutting me out. She's still listening.

"That same grief is what made me worthy of you again. To be worthy of what fate had in store for me with Eleanor. So, I don't wish it never happened. I'd do it all again if it led me here. To her. And you."

She blinks up through soft, rolling tears, and a sad smile falls into place. It's one that tells me she understands.

I lean in and wipe her cheeks with my thumbs like she did to mine a month ago in this very barn, when she learned about a little girl she never got to love, but was raised in her image nonetheless. I cup her face in both hands.

"The only thing I want now is a second chance with you, Dev."

Her pink-tipped fingers, fresh from a girls' night manicure she had with Ellie, snap the hair tie on her wrist. She brushes me off lightly and shakes her head, sagging onto the bench and running her fingers through her hair before resting them on her lap.

"You say all that, but you make it seem as though you never fell out of love with me, like we were destined all along, but here's the thing. I came back to visit…to talk about it, several times that next year, and you looked plenty over me then when you were getting under all of Lemon's friends. You pushed me away, just like you're pushing me away now."

She tugs the hair tie again, snapping it twice this time.

"It feels the same, Hunter. I'm letting you in. I've rearranged my whole world to be with you. I'm even learning to parent a little girl who has the same name as a child we almost shared, a level-headed, brave, and perfectly beautiful young lady you've spent years raising on your own, but I am just now learning to love."

She twirls around, looking at the barn, inspecting it like she's seeing its intricacies for the first time.

"You say you want me to be your wife, but what I need to know, Hunter, is if you want me to be her mother. Because I don't think I can be one and not the other."

She swallows, twirling the hair tie around her wrist, and I hate myself for making her doubt her place. For causing her this worry. She sniffles, and my heart breaks as I stare into glossy, green eyes. "You're a package deal, isn't that what you said?"

Fuck.

"Dev, of course I want you to be her mother. You have no idea how much I want that. From the start, I—"

"Then what's with the secrecy? What aren't you telling me that has you all twisted up? And what has Garrison Presley got against a nine-year-old girl that makes you think he'd use a little playground scuttle against her? It's her custody hearing, isn't it?"

Really? I blink at her, exhaling quickly and pressing my lips together in disbelief. It's uncanny, this woman's ability to pull information from my brain like a damn siphon.

"I knew it," she hisses, chewing her bottom lip. "What does Katie say? What are your chances? You know my dad can pull strings if you need him to talk to someone in—"

I cut her off. "No! I cannot ask your dad to help this time."

"This time?" She inclines her head, arching a brow.

Shit.

"Look," I hold my arms out to the sides, "this is part of the stuff I wanted to tell you about, but I had an order to it, and now it's all mixed up. But fuck it, here we go."

She eyes me suspiciously and settles back onto the bench as I pace across the stable, my boots kicking up straw and dirt as I go.

"After you left, your dad was afraid you'd come back when you turned eighteen, which we can now confirm he was right about."

"Hunter, do not tell me that your ignoring me had something to do with my father," she seethes, and I know she's not going to like the rest of it, but I can't change the truth.

"I needed help. I was…" I run my sweaty palms down the front of my pants as I think of how to word this. "I was sick, Dev. I was drinking straight through the night and into the next week, skipping work, cussin' out anyone who'd hire me just so they'd turn around and throw me out like…" I exhale a heavy sigh and shake my head, finally speaking it for the first time. "Like the trash I thought I was."

"But you still drink now. And you're okay doing that?" I'm used to this question. I did stop drinking for years after my treatment, but that wasn't the problem for me. I guess I'm lucky in that way. Garrison, not so much.

"Drinking wasn't my addiction." I swallow, unable to keep my gaze from darting to hers every few seconds to gage how she takes this in. "I did it, don't get me wrong. But it was just pre-game for the main event."

"Which was?"

"Fighting."

"Fighting?" She scrunches her nose. "You mean like punching and kicking in little Speedos kinda fighting? You were addicted to fighting people?"

I shrug. "You make it sound like it's not a thing, but it's a thing, okay?" I grin at her. I have no idea how she can make talking about something I usually dread opening up to anyone about feel light, but she does. Something about that sweet little southern drawl she thinks she doesn't have.

"I'm sorry. I just don't understand, I guess. Was it dangerous, what you were doing?"

I nod.

"Underground fighting was taking over my life. I was intentionally throwing fights for money, a paid punching bag for guys twice, sometimes three times my size, so they could rise in the ranks. So I could take that same money and throw it into another fight and do it all over again. Some nights, I could get two or three fights in before I blacked out. I lived for the nights I was so black and blue that the pain seeped into my dreams. Because those nights, I wouldn't dream about you… with a pole protruding from your bleeding womb."

I huff, realizing how messed up that sounds out loud.

"I used to think of those as the good nights."

Devyn squeezes my hand again, and I squeeze back to let her know I feel her. She doesn't have the words, but she cares like nobody else ever has.

Except one.

"Your dad is the reason I'm not dead, Devyn. That's the honest truth."

"My dad? He's always hated you."

"Not enough to watch me waste away, I guess."

She tilts her head, crossing her arms over her chest, and I can see the moment the pieces click together for her as I tell my story, one she's long overdue to hear.

"You had been gone a few months. Samuel was in with some shady people, moving heavy amounts of product from the city." I let out a deep exhale. It still shocks me what people will do for money. Power. Security…even my own brother. I swallow the grief, like always, and go on, noting Devyn's fingers lingering closer to mine, our pinkies nearly touching. Her eyes shine; that's how I know she feels the same things I feel. She knew Samuel. He isn't just some blank-faced felon she can count off in her mind. No, like Dustin and a few others who grew up with Sam, Sammy back then, she understands. Probably asking herself the same question I have.

What went wrong?

Difference is, I've had time to think about this. I've had nine years to figure out that it's all interconnected. We're bigger than we think we are. Each one of us.

And when a community isn't together, when people don't build the world up for what they want to see it be, we have nothing.

Samuel had just that.

Nothing.

Except a felon father, a dead mother, and a brother who was drowning himself in grief.

I was his best hope. And I let him down.

I move my hand the final few inches it needs to trail my fingers across her knuckles, and when her eyes swipe up to mine, I lean in and kiss her, just once, before I face forward and prepare for battle.

That's what telling this story feels like, a battle. One where nobody comes out unscathed at the end, fresh wounds opened and rubbed raw, each time the words leave my lips.

But our hands stay together, and when she squeezes once for I, twice for love, and three times for you, it feels easier to say what I need to. I'm not plagued with guilt and riddled with the fear of a grown man who's lived and lost.

I'm a young boy, skipping along a stream, holding hands with the girl who reminds me of sunshine and makes me want to pick flowers for days, if it will only make her smile.

I want to marry this woman all over again.

I kiss her, wishing I could stop the story and lean into her, replacing the words that leave me with the taste of her sweet tongue against mine.

"I could taste you all night long," I tell her, watching her chest turn pink in the moonlight that spills through the barn. "But you showed me your scars, and it's time I revealed mine."

I kiss her again, biting her bottom lip as I pull away, and she nods in understanding.

"One day, Sam was busted during a deal. He led a chase through some back roads connected to the interstate." Devyn grips the edge of the bench, her eyes a mirror of mine, clouded with fear and sorrow. Wrapping her in my arms, I hold her tight, my chin resting atop her head as I stare forward, my own head projecting images across my mind of the night I didn't see, but only know of because it's fact.

There was a police report. A jury. Witnesses.

And a defendant who couldn't possibly be my baby brother. I thought.

"He led the chase onto Garrison's property, where his pregnant wife was working."

Devyn's hand curls around mine and squeezes.

"Samuel swerved, but the car behind him flipped into a shed, and the whole field went up in flames."

"No," Devyn gasps.

"Sam was okay," I choke, but a sob starts at the base of my throat, hoarse and thick, the words a sticky tar, forcefully peeled from inside me.

"According to an officer who was pinned under his vehicle and later rescued, Annabelle Presley was alive, too, trapped beneath a wooden frame that splintered from the shed when it exploded." My fingers dig into my own palm as I see it in my mind. Annabelle, beneath those wooden splinters, trapped like Devyn. And what followed…

My brother, Annabelle, flames.

I've gotta speak the words if I'm ever going to be free of them. To be sure they don't wedge an even darker place between the woman I love and myself. So, I fucking do.

"Rather than save her," I spit out, holding Devyn tighter for support, "Samuel used Annabelle's last precious minutes to smash into his trunk and rescue six duffel bags of his precious *product*…one after the other after the other, until they were all laid in a neat, protected line outside the wreckage."

I hang my head low, my voice barely a breath.

"Annabelle's screams rang through the air."

I loosen my hold on Devyn and exhale. My voice cracks. "She burned alive."

"Sammy?" she croaks through a cracked sob. "*Samuel?*"

She can't believe it any more than I could.

It's still the truth.

"His girl was part of it. They planned to run off with whatever was left, but ended up arrested at a gas station later, two counties over."

My teeth grind, my head shaking as I relive the hearing all over again. The images of Annabelle Presley's scorched body on a fifty-two-inch projector.

Fuck! I slam my fist against the wall, not giving a shit about the pain, but summoning it. Wanting my fists to crack and bleed. But Devyn grabs my wrist and tightens her hold, cradling it until our fingers twine, and I meet her teary-eyed stare.

"That's all Annabelle's death bought them, fifty miles of getaway." A sob rips from my throat, and I turn to face her. "How could he do that, Dev? Sammy."

She pulls my head to her chest and holds it there for a moment as I breathe, keeping time with her heartbeat, steadying my own. I've never released this information to anyone before, and I can't stop now. Not while I'm sharing with someone who knew the Sam I did.

"I have to keep going." I sit up straight and brushing my face across my sleeve, the reassurance she provides being exactly what I need to get this out in the open and off my chest.

"Sam's girl was arrested with him that day. At six months pregnant. That's why Garrison resents her."

His child died, while Samuel's lived.

"Ellie," she gasps, eyes wide with a new understanding of a reality that never should have been.

I nod, our eyes meeting squarely for the first time since I started the story.

"I became legal guardian to a newborn baby as a nineteen-year-old, with an addiction to fighting, gambling, and a one-bedroom rental by the tracks, Dev."

"What did you do?"

"I called your father," I admit, rubbing the back of my neck. "I didn't know who else to call. He had money, resources, I don't know. He was my fill-in father growing up. Nobody ever came to my career day, but your dad had no problem claiming both me and Dusty when he'd show up in our classroom. My boys, he'd call us. Until I got you pregnant, crashed that car…everything was my fault, Dev." I turn back to her, shaking my head. "I know that. I've always known that."

"Your fault?" She whirls on me. "Hunter, me getting pregnant was not your fault. In case you're forgetting, I all but jumped you that day in the shed. The hearts carved on that weathered wood out back are proof of that. And the crash?" She shakes her head. "The other driver was drinking, for Christ's sake. You can't seriously blame yourself for someone else's actions."

"Don't you? I should have swerved sooner. I could have—"

"You wouldn't go back and change it, right? You said that yourself." She lifts her chin, holding me hostage with her stare. "So, stop going back in your mind and blaming yourself."

I take in her serious face, scrunched brow, pursed lips, and flushed cheeks, all lit by a glowing green gaze.

God, she's beautiful.

I huff a solid gust of air, knocked in the gut by all that is Devyn Lynn Campbell.

"I'll agree to anything you say because you're so pretty," I tell her, earning a swat to the chest. She stands to pace the floor, wiping her tear-soaked face across her sleeve.

"So, my dad helped you with Ellie, how? Got you a custody lawyer or something?

"Not exactly. Custody wasn't on the table. The best Katie could do for us were long term foster care rights, providing Aunt Sarah act as a co-guardian, when she was still with us, which I took.

"Your father bought the farm. Told me he'd give it to me outright if I finished rehab for my—" I stop, blowing out a stream of air, but it's okay. *She sees me. She knows me.*

"—my problems. There was this special family program for non-drug and alcohol related addictions. It was outside of town, but Katie fudged some details on the paperwork and your dad may or may not have paid the right people not to care." I smile, a laugh even escaping me as I recall the yellow wallpaper peeling from the entryway. "It had dorms with kitchens, like a shelter, sort of. Ellie and I stayed there for a few months while your dad sent people to clear out the old barn and renovate it just enough to pass as livable by social service's standards. Then, once he found out how low those standards actually were, he had a team of people come in to make it livable by Mr. Campbell standards."

I chuckle, thinking about how he'd barely toured the first floor of the farmhouse with its caving ceilings and moisture damaged flooring before he snatched Ellie from the Pack 'n Play and refused to let us stay there until his 'people' came by to fix the place.

Devyn smiles, and I realize she's mimicking my own expression. This is the one part of the story that is somewhat laced with happy memories.

"He came to visit once or twice. Checked up on Ellie."

Devyn's eyes widen, and she stands, walking across the room. I stand, too, my voice carrying through the barn.

"Once Ellie and I moved in and fixed it up, we turned it into a real farm. I paid him back as soon as I could, but he had one caveat."

"*You will not speak to my daughter. Ever again. Do you understand? If she comes to you, you will make it very apparent that you are no longer interested. Whatever you must do to convince her, you do it.*"

I take a deep breath and dare to steal a glance at her. I step forward, taking her hands in case she tries to run.

I wouldn't blame her.

"I was the caveat, wasn't I?"

I don't answer that. She already knows.

"Dev, I never wanted to keep secrets from you, but there's more to this. And now that we're being open about everything, there's more to tell you that I—"

Her lips crash against mine, arms wrap around my neck, her tongue snakes its way into my mouth and tangles with mine. I think she's claiming me, and that makes about as much sense as tits on a bull, because it dawns on me, as I stand here opening myself to her completely, that for the last ten years I've done nothing but lie to the woman I desperately love.

A woman I don't deserve to feel in my arms, her curves pressing against my body, her hands slipping under my shirt.

Fuck.

But then she pulls her face away, lowering off her tiptoes and resting her cheek against my shoulder. My arms automatically wrap tighter around her.

"All this time, I thought you stopped loving me," she says, pressing close.

"I could never stop loving you."

I kiss her again, savoring this goddess of a woman who stands here before me while I lay myself bare to her, and still sees me as the man she did before.

"But there's more. Since coming back—"

"You don't have to tell me everything right this second, Hunter, but thank you for finally letting me in."

She looks up at me, then, worrying at her hair tie.

"Wait, that time I came back, and you were with those Valley High girls?"

"I didn't have sex with them," I admit to her in a rush. I've hated letting her think that for years, and I'll never forget the hurt in her eyes when she opened the door and I let her believe she was replaceable.

The truth is nobody could ever replace Devyn Lynn Campbell. Not in my bed and never in my heart.

"I wanted to tell you about rehab and Ellie, everything. The second time you came back, I tried. I had almost worked up the courage to come clean about your dad, about the lies or the fact that I hadn't been with anyone but you, since you. But you took one look at me having drinks with Lem and Katie at the Sugar Stable, and you were back in the city the next day. You never came back after that, Dev."

The moonlight spills in from the barn doors and illuminates her from behind. Like she's an angel. She's been gone so long, when I first saw her on that street corner, I thought she might be. Much too beautiful to be a ghost from my past, but an angel? They're eternal. *Just like Dev.*

"I thought you'd never come back to Pine Forest."

She looks down, and I tilt her chin back up to look at me. "I don't blame you for that either, Dev. I figured you were happy in the city. You were Miss American Rodeo, for fuck's sake. You were on the news every morning with a bright, beautiful smile on your face and in the tabloids at parties having fun like you're supposed to in your twenties, not raising a child and fighting an addiction like I was. You were better off without me."

"No," she says, laughing into my shirt and…

"Are you smelling me?" I smile.

"Yes," she says, sighing wistfully. "It's just, we both thought we were fine without each other all those years, but it's only because we were convincing ourselves the other person was better off without us. Neither of us wanted that. You don't find that funny?"

"No, I find it depressing."

"But what about Ellie's custody?" Devyn suddenly remembers, and I groan. There's still a lot to talk about, and that kiss earlier made me want to do anything but talk.

But this is life. This is adulting and this is partnership, and this is…our relationship. A relationship that, up until two months ago, I didn't even think stood a chance of existing. My lips curve into an undeniable smile as I mull that thought over. The thought of a relationship with this woman. As my wife.

I steer us back to the bench, and we go over the cow story. I smile at Ellie's bravery, her ability to stand up to her bully and hold strong to her morals. I couldn't be a prouder papa, even if she did throw the first punch. *We'll work on that.*

I explain to Devyn the ins and outs of our custody issues, never realizing how freeing it would feel to have someone to share these burdens with.

And we have our fair share.

I curl my lip in disgust even thinking about the woman we'll have to deal with at the next hearing.

"Her bio mother only wants her for her inheritance. Every one of us kids got something from Aunt Sarah when she passed last year, and since Samuel's sentencing has been extended to life, Ellie gets twice as much. Hers and Samuel's."

Devyn nods in understanding, but pauses, scratching her head. "If it's Ellie's inheritance, how would her mother even be able to use it? Even with custody, it's still pretty strict."

"That won't stop her." I shake my head angrily. "She'll find a way. Regardless, I can't let her become responsible for Ellie."

"I've been meaning to ask you about that."

She stands, twisting the hair tie on her wrist in circles.

"Ellie said if we were for real married, you'd have a better shot at getting full custody. Is that true?"

I wince. This is where I was headed next, but telling her feels like it could break this new understanding we have. Still, the truth is what we need. I know that now.

"Devyn, the day after Truth or Dare, I found out that Lemon wasn't very honest with us. She played the part of wedding officiant so well in the TikTok video because she is a wedding officiant."

Her eyes pop open wide, but she's not angry with me. It's the exact opposite as her grin forms, stretching to meet her eyes.

"You're smiling." I shake my head in disbelief. "I thought for sure you'd be mad, but you gotta understand, Dev, I wasn't trying to lie, I just…needed more time."

"Time for what?" she asks, hands on her hips, every bit the sassy little cowgirl I fell in love with all those years ago.

I take a step closer. And then another. Until we're face to face again.

"Time to make you fall in love. With both of us," I add. "I was worried you'd run if it felt too permanent, not just with me, but with Ellie specifically."

"Run?" She laughs. "Hunter Isaac, I'm never running from you again. There's too much FOMO going on from the one decade apart for me to even consider ever leaving. I swear to God, if I go in one more store and see your face hung on the wall like a damn saint, I'll barf."

A laugh breaks free of my face and tumbles around her own as she wags a finger at me.

"No, you've done enough for this town. It's my turn to be the center of everyone's attention in Pine Forest." She winks, twisting her lips into that duckface I love to kiss right off, and a smile spreads across my own face at that. At her ability to crack a joke and lighten even the most serious of moments.

"So, you'll stay 'for real married' to me, then?"

"Do you dare me?" she teases.

"Fuck, babygirl, I'll beg if that's what it takes."

She considers that for a moment, chewing her bottom lip and tapping her chin to fuck with me. And God, that part of her has always turned me on.

She leans closer, and I can smell her lip gloss. I love that I know what it tastes like already, vanilla cupcakes, but I still lick every bit of it from her face when she presses her lips to mine. I devour them, my tongue diving in when her lips part for me, claiming the spaces around her breathless moans. We pull apart, and I watch her blushing chest heave up and down as a smile curves over her lips, wet and bruised from my kiss, breathless and breathtaking all at once.

"Okay then, husband, I'll be *for real* married to you."

She grins, while happiness and relief consume me. I take my woman in my arms and swing her around before setting her back on her feet and pulling a piece of paper from my pocket.

"This is the certificate Lemon left for us. We just need to file it with the court, and it's official. Although it hasn't stopped me from using it as leverage against Catherine, Ellie's bio mom. She doesn't know it's not filed yet."

"I get it now, why you were worried about the fight. If Garrison wants to press this up the ladder with his uncle, that can't be good in the family courts with Judge Owens presiding. They're practically best friends, Mayor Presley and him. But it didn't seem like Garrison was as concerned with Jonathan's eyes and lip as he was with…Annabelle?"

"Yeah." She's right. "He needs help. He was in rehab with me, but he never stuck with it. We had a class together…grief and loss…he was my…*fuck,* we bonded over losing an unborn child. He was my friend, Dev." I flick my gaze to hers and see the same sadness, a sympathy we both share with Garrison. "But he's so twisted with his own grief he lets it out on his animals, on his farm, he resents anything to do with Pine Forest because none of it matters without her. It was her dream, his farm, and he hasn't tended to the fire-fields since she died. Doesn't seem he's tended to his kid, either." I frown. "His mentality altogether is…self-destructive." I sigh heavily, my own realization sinking in.

"Maybe you can help him," she says, snapping the band again.

"Why do you do that? Snap that thing on your wrist?" She stops, her lips forming a small "O" shape, like maybe she didn't think I'd noticed this habit. It's cute she thinks I'd miss anything about her, as if she's unremarkable in any way.

"It's a therapy technique I was given after the crash," she says, inspecting the frayed, black elastic around her arm.

"When my mind fills with things that seem uncontrollable and crippling, I snap this. It gives me back some of the control. It's hard to explain, but it's like my mind focuses on the sting because I told it to, and not on the things I obsess over."

"They taught you to shock therapy yourself in counseling?"

"Um, I guess you could call it that," she says, chewing her bottom lip.

So often I find myself jealous of this woman's teeth for their proximity to her mouth, and I can't control it any more than I can the weather. I reach out and run my thumb along her bottom lip, popping it free of her bite.

"I want to suck on this," I say, and I feel the breath leave her lips as she gasps. "Can I?"

"Yes," she says, her gaze wandering to the mounted rack along the stable wall that holds rows of thick farming ropes, and my smile widens.

"I want to show you something that requires full honesty and trust for both of us."

She eyes me cautiously, like prey.

And fuck if I don't like it.

I come to life around Devyn. The things I want to do to her body are as sinful as they are endless. But I'll ask for forgiveness another day.

I reach out, tweaking her nipples through the fabric of her shirt. She lets out a sexy little sigh, and my cock instantly grows in response. I roll my thumbs along the hardened points until she drops her head, pleading for more of my touch, and I take advantage of what she offers as she arches her body back into my hold.

She tastes like oranges, as I kiss her bare collarbone, sucking and licking the skin as she moans my name. I pull away, watching the skin across her chest react to where I sucked in soft red welts, and I shoot my gaze back to the ropes lining my walls and groan, imaging how perfect she'll look, wrapped up and coming all over my finger, binds pressed tightly against her soft flesh, as she takes her pleasure from me.

Fucking beautiful.

"Do you trust me?" I ask.

"I do."

Chapter 37

Devyn

I know what we went through tonight was a lot, to say the least, but I'm happy about that.

I'm heartbroken for Samuel.

His life wasn't easy when we were kids. He was so much younger than Hunter, too, just a year behind me, when their father started those awful benders, night after night away at an unknown bar in some other town. Envelopes would overflow from the letter box and fall to their doorstep.

I could never imagine what that felt like, being alone for weeks. Staying with friends. Never knowing. Never having any control or say in the matter.

Nobody would know where to find him. Not Hunter. Not Samuel. Not Aunt Sarah, who would swoop in to help every few years, but get pushed back out by their father when he'd return with a need to prove he'd change this time. Said his kids didn't need her handouts.

But it doesn't excuse what Samuel did. Or…what he didn't do.

He didn't save her.

And Hunter bears those scars for him. I could see as much in his eyes. He blames himself for his brother's actions, just like he blames himself for the actions of a drunk driver who wrecked our relationship and our dreams all those years ago.

I won't let him do that anymore.

Being back in Pine Forest has been hard for me, too. I had the memories and trauma shoved into a box in the farthest corner of my mind, packed beneath layers of bricks. Entire shelters. All self-constructed to keep me from remembering. From thinking. From...feeling.

And without even knowing it, I've been doing precisely the thing I've always resented, but I've done it to myself. I made my life sparkle so I'd never feel the pain. But I still felt it. I felt it every day then, and I feel it every day now. I trace my scars over my clothing. I don't need to be naked to feel them. Much like being with Hunter, we are more than skin deep.

And I don't need anything more than faith right now to know that.

The jagged parts of life, the parts that don't sparkle, were things I needed to feel. Not to move on, but to *carry* on. To see the big picture.

A brother who let me tag along led me to a best friend who showed me love and something bigger than myself.

A tragedy that knocked our lives off balance led to years of twists and turns we never could have imagined.

And a job interview, a turn of fate, led us back together.

To a little girl who needs us now. And isn't that what we talked about all those years ago, lying under starry skies behind an old shed?

We promised each other the world as we held a life between us.

And what I've learned is that mine can't exist without Hunter Isaac in it. Whatever that may mean.

My ties to happiness aren't woven from career success or fancy offices. And they most certainly aren't related to winning a competition, or pleasing anyone who thinks they know what's best for me.

Mom, Dad, Dustin…those people's opinions matter, but the only singular opinion that can change my fate for me is my own.

"Always daydreaming."

I jump at Hunter's voice and turn to face him as he swaggers in, my back pressed against the barn wall.

"The kids are asleep." He pulls the doors shut and slides a lock in place from the inside.

My eyes instantly whip up to his, a thrill running through me at the thought of being locked up, with him…or, from the looks of those ropes…*by* him.

"Just in case they wake up and come out here," he says with his signature wink, "they'll have to knock, and we'll have time to—"

"To fuck me?"

His eyes flick to mine, a hunger there that I feel all over my body. He stalks forward, but he doesn't speak, teasing me with his eyes as he trails his fingers down the rows and rows of coiled ropes that line the wall.

I clench my thighs, my heartbeat taking up new residence in my clit and pulsing relentlessly against the lace of my panties just beneath my shorts.

Hunter seems to consider his roping options for an eternity, driving me absolutely mad, the muscles of his back flexing in show as he makes his selection. My arousal drips down my inner thighs, and a whimper escapes my lips when he wraps a thick cord of red rope around his clenched fist.

First and foremost, why is that so erotic? My pussy throbs, and I can't stand it. I need him on me, in me.

"If you don't tie me up or rub that shit on my clit pretty soon, I'll take my merry ass to the wall of doom and do it myself."

"Ohhh, look at what we got here." He chuckles, his lips curving up to meet the devious gaze in his eyes. "The Princess of Pine Forest, throwing out ultimatums before manners. Seems like I need to teach you."

"Teach me what?" I ask, licking my lips.

He retrieves two other ropes and a…riding crop.

"To say please." He stalks forward, straw rustling beneath his boots as he comes closer, invading my space and kicking my legs apart with his knee.

It surprises me, and a giggle slips from my lips as I'm knocked off balance, but he catches me, meeting my eyes with a promise in his own that says we're going to do this.

A second chance at life together.

I lurch forward, crashing my lips to his. I want him inside of me *now*, and I hardly realize it's me when a moan breaks free from somewhere inside me, as I rock my body into him.

"So dirty," he mumbles, laying the flat of his hot, wet tongue over the front of my neck and gliding it across my chest as he backs me to the bench, lowering me inch by painstaking inch until I'm lying down, writhing as he leans over me, caressing me with his mouth in a way that heats me from the inside out.

"Thought you were gonna be a good little girl for me, but you just can't help how fuckable you are, can you, Devy?"

Oh, my God. The dirty words on his lips coupled with my childhood nickname send me over the edge. He hasn't even touched between my legs yet, but it's all I feel, pulsing, throbbing. My thighs slam together, trapping his knee between them, and I grind my body against it until I'm coming and cursing. He smirks, licking the shell of my ear with his whisper.

"Do you feel better now?"

I nod, twisting my lips as an embarrassed smile pulls across my face. But he wastes no time. He slides his fingers into my hair and hoists me up, bracing me from behind and bringing me to my feet, angling my head so I have no choice but to look into his eyes. Eyes that could open to the blue sky above us and I wouldn't even know the difference.

"Good. Because what we're about to do requires you to stand perfectly still, and I can't have you coming all over my pants the way you like to while I'm tying you up."

"Tying me up?" My voice is thick and husky, and I lick my lips, unaware of where this ho inside of me comes from, but embracing her all the same as I throw a coy smile his way. "I thought we were going to play out your fantasies, not mine."

His eyes darken, as he curses beneath his breath.

"Fuck. Take off your clothes." His eyes rake down my body as he scrapes his tongue across his lips.

Slowly. Tantalizing. And I'm pretty sure when he does it, there's a button that presses against the swollen bud between my legs.

It drives me wild.

Goosebumps prickle my body while I do as I'm told, removing my blouse, then my shorts. Next go my black bra and hot pink lace panties that earn an appreciative groan from Hunter, who's standing there in his full clothes watching me with a hunger I don't think I've ever seen in a man's eyes.

My heart thumps wildly as I bend down to remove my pink cowgirl boots, the ones I had Dad ship me from the city after my heels met their maker in the muddy fields. I pull one halfway off, but Hunter stops me, his voice a thick command that settles in my core.

"Leave the boots." A curve tilts his lips. "I want you spread open, covered in mud, and ready to work, like the Good Lord intended."

Oh, my God, the filth that pours from his mouth is sinful. And I can't help how turned on it makes me feel all the same. I want that, too. I want to be tied up in front of him, put on display for him, to do whatever he wants. To take the pressure of all that away from me.

To own my body so I won't have to, if only for this moment in time.

"Don't speak unless prompted, do you understand?" I nod, but bite back my laugh. And yeah, don't get me wrong, normal Devyn would show this cowboy a thing or two about where I can shove these pretty little shit kickers when I'm told what to do, but normal Devyn has clocked out and gone home for the night. This is the Ex to Hoe Ratio thing…Jeremy is on to something. Because why else would I agree to something so controlling, taboo, and…

Who am I kidding?

It's sexy and kinky and I want it.

Hunter takes my wrists and places a soft kiss on the inside of each, maintaining eye contact all the while. He carefully arranges my body, positioning me face up on the bench, my thighs hanging open, straddling either side so my boots are flush with the dirt.

"You did something bad, Dev. Do you want to know what?" A shiver of delight passes over me, an excitement I can neither quench nor explain as he unbuttons the cuffs on his sleeves, rolling them up to reveal his muscled forearms. He lowers his head to just above my center, and I want his mouth on it like I want air.

"You called me Daddy," he says, his eyes hard and menacing. He plays the part so damn well. If I didn't know any better, his shift in energy would scare me, but I do know him better, and all it does is make me wet. He groans as he drags his fingers over my leg, where it drips down my thigh, coating his fingers in my desire.

"In those books you read—" He rubs his hands on my thighs, going higher with each hitch of my breath, until he's mere inches from where I want him to be, his gaze scraping over me possessively. "It means he's the Dom, doesn't it?"

I bite my bottom lip, averting my eyes, but he uses his other hand to grab my chin between his thumb and forefinger and whips my focus back on him.

"It does," he says, "and I decided I like it."

He stands tall and circles the bench, tweaking my nipples and tugging my hair on his circumnavigation of my body. I could tell you it feels degrading, but it's hot as hell, and all it does is make me insatiable, my desire soaking my Spanx right through.

"I like the idea of you falling apart under my command. Submitting to me."

I moan when he twists my nipple, just lightly enough not to hurt, but rough enough to make me need him, crave him. I rock myself against the bench, and he coos.

"The only words I want to hear from those pretty lips of yours are *Daddy* and *Sir*," he says firmly, tugging me closer by the same nipple he has yet to release. He holds it, possessively. Like it's his.

And I'm so turned on in this moment that I'd agree in an instant if he'll promise to put it in his mouth and run his tongue around it like he did inside my mouth earlier.

"Yes, Daddy," I tease, rolling my eyes and earning a slap to my bare pussy, and I can't help the moan that pops from my lips in response. It feels so good, the pleasure that comes just after the pain.

He moves behind my head and positions my arms by my side and brushes light trails over my breasts, placing a kiss behind my ear. I shiver in anticipation. Wanting and needing so much more than he's giving.

"Be patient." He swats my wiggling hips. "This exercise isn't about lust. It's about trust." He rubs the rough, singed edge of the rope along my nipple, drawing the tiniest bit of pain with pleasure.

I whimper, bucking my hips up involuntarily, and he laughs. He begins binding my arms to my sides with the rope, coiling it around me as he holds my body in place against the bench.

"These are a nylon-hemp blend. We use them for cattle and horses because they are strong, yet soft. Good for lassos," he says when he gets to the tops of my shoulders. "You know what lassos are for, right, Ponygirl?"

My brows pinch together. "For stray cattle?"

"For the ones who run away," he rasps. And I can't tell you why that turns me the fuck on, but I buck my hips up so high that even he can't help but chuckle as he holds me down.

"Just like wranglin' a bull, aren't you, babygirl? You gonna break and let me ride you?"

At this point, he's bound my arms from the boobs up, and now he's working his way back down, making sure to coil the remaining red rope around each breast. It's not so tight that it hurts, but it is tight enough that they're pulsing. That same heartbeat that was visiting my clit earlier has shot its way to the tips of my reddened nipples, blood rushing to them with the force of the ropes and begging for someone to suck them, lick them. God, I would do anything if he would bend me over and fuck me senseless right this instant.

Maybe this is the patience he was talking about, I think as I struggle against the ropes. He stops coiling, lifting an eyebrow in question.

"If you want me to stop, just say…" he thinks briefly, "…
sunflowers, and I'll stop, okay?"

"Okay—" I start, but he swats his riding crop down on my
swollen breasts, and I cry out in ecstasy. Not sunflowers, but…

"Yes! More!"

The pain is intense, shooting through my nipples and over
my blood-rushed body, but the pleasure comes after in soft
waves, washing over me and somehow stimulating my pussy
simultaneously.

I lick my lips, panting. "I mean yes, sir."

"Good girl," he purrs, running his hand down my body
and cupping my pussy. He palms my clit, rubbing circles around
while I buck into it, searching for the pressure that will send
me spiraling again, but he stops, drawing his hand back up.

"Patience, Dev."

I whine, but I'm not done playing his game. If I wanted
to stop, I'd say *sunflowers*, but that isn't what I want, is it? I
want him to tease me. I want him to touch me. I want him to
have total control over my body because it feels good. Because
giving it over to him means I don't have to live in the reality of
overseeing all that is…*me*. If only in the here and now.

It feels like hours while he slowly wraps me in length after
length of the nylon cords. Somehow, he knows perfectly how
to do the twists and ties that seem extraordinarily detailed and
specific, and a sliver of jealousy slices into my gut.

"Hunt—I mean, Daddy?" I ask, biting my lip, and he groans
in response. I can see the way his cock hardens beneath his jeans,
revs up when I speak those kinky words. He likes it just like I
do. "How do you know how to do all of this…" I can't exactly
gesture down my body since I'm literally bound by the arms,
but he gets my insinuation anyhow, cutting off my question.

"Shabari. It's a form of rope tying. It's not always sexual.
It's…a type of meditation. An art, even. It's about transcending."

"Transcending?" I tease. "Since when did you become so spiritual?"

"Around the same time you started snapping that hair tie, probably."

My heart goes still for a quick beat, giving space for pieces of his to fit back in, and we both fall silent as he makes work of securing me with pretty twists and intricate loops.

He continues wrapping my body. This time, a beautiful X shape is fashioned across my midsection, leaving my belly button and pelvis exposed. He uses two green ropes to tie along the bottom of the Xs and around my hips, hoisting me so my pelvis is suspended in the air a few inches above the bench while he tugs a thin pink rope through my…*butt crack.*

I gasp, giggling because it tickles like crazy, but he swats my ass and lowers me back down, my thighs coming to either side of the bench, and he lays me down and kneels in front of me, right between my spread legs.

My pussy is on full display. And the cold night air against my skin on all the patches the rope doesn't cover has my body shivering, my nipples poised, and I can feel my need for him wetting my skin the longer I wait, drenching the wooden bench beneath me when he breathes in my scent and growls appreciatively.

"I'm going to line this pretty pink pussy with matching pink rope. It's going to push your lips together real tight while I play with you, until you're begging me to split them back open with my cock." He licks his lips, staring at me dripping before him like a fucking buffet. "You'd like that, wouldn't you, pretty girl?"

"Yes, Daddy!" I cry, desperation and need taking over me. But I still have to wait.

Painfully, minute after minute ticks by on the damn cowboy hat clock on the wall that I plan to smash with the heel of my boot when this is over because it's making my anticipation ten times worse. And the whole time, Hunter stays perfectly silent.

Aside from his groans and grunts of approval every time his fingers brush the wetness beading from my labia, practically weeping to be fucked. He's fully bound me from neck to hips, my legs held open by two ropes he's fastened to the bench and my ankles, and just to be clear, if I don't get fucked soon, I will die. I will literally die. So, I tell him this.

"Hunter, I am going to die if you don't—"

He chuckles, his heavy body easing on top of mine, as he lays long, languid kisses over every inch of my exposed skin, summoning pleasure from every nerve ending I possess, pinching and tugging at various spots in the roping as he goes, snapping it against me and making tiny, painful scratches over my body. It only seems to make the pulsing in my breasts and my pussy more intense, like a balloon, tight and eager, stretched to its fullness and in danger of popping with just one quick prick.

That's all it would take for me, just one prick. I try not to snicker at the double meaning and fail, earning me a swat to the pussy that only spurs me on.

He's so hot laying into this kink. I tilt my hips up as high as I can while still bound to the bench by my ankles, and Hunter stands again, backing away, inspecting me.

"You can't stand not being in control, can you, princess?"

"No," I grind out, straining against the bindings, even though I kind of like them. I'm enjoying being this secure, and it's exhilarating being at his mercy. "That's kind of the point of the hair tie. It gives me control of the pain."

"And this will give you control of the pleasure." He grabs his riding crop from its spot on the bench. "You will count each strike. And when you've had as much pain as you can take, I'll fill you with pleasure."

"You'll fill me with something, I hope."

He huffs, shooting me an incredulous glare.

"Jesus, Dev, we're doing a sexy thing…could ya just—"

"Sorry. Continue." I blink my doe eyes up at him and wink. "*Daddy.*"

He shakes his head at me, smiling as he swats my pussy again, but this time it's with the riding crop, not his hand. And it stings.

But…do I like this?

I close my eyes, moaning softly as his fingers rub soft, feather-like circles over my plumped-up pussy lips between the hot pink roping. It feels heavenly, the soft caress over the stinging pinpricks of before.

"That's it, babygirl, lean into it," Hunter purrs in that rich, Internet thirst-trappy voice of his. It's not exactly a fake version of his own, but it's more exaggerated, sexier for show.

Fuckable, as he puts it.

"Are you ready to count?" He strokes the crop, scanning my body. I nod, squeezing my eyes shut and waiting for him to begin.

But he doesn't, so I open my eyes to Hunter's stern look of disapproval, and I have to suppress a giggle from slipping past my lips again when I realize why.

"Yes, Daddy," I say.

And now he begins, leaving only a heartbeat before snapping the riding crop over the bottom of my left breast.

"One!" I cry, sucking in breath through my teeth to hide how much it hurts. It surprised me, but then the soothing tickle of the leather as he trails the crop softly over the assaulted skin is enough to send ripples of pleasure to my pussy. I stretch my legs to test the give on the ropes that have my thighs held wide, but they don't budge. They were tied up by a cowboy, after all, and that thought sends an electric shockwave down my core. I'm at his mercy.

Pain strikes down on me again before I can grip reality, and this time it's to the skin just below my belly button. I buck my hips, a whimper falling from my vocal cords, unashamedly asking for more, faster, lower.

"Two, three, four, five," I call as each strike finds its own place on the bits of skin beneath the bindings. I wonder if, when this is over, I'll have marks in all directions, a mix of webs and welts, of pleasure and patience and pain coming to one.

Like life.

"Six, seven," I scream, each strike getting progressively harder, the eighth and ninth peppering my hardened nipples and causing me to writhe beneath my bindings, the nylon straining against my skin and rubbing my clit just the right way if he'll keep his body pressed against me for just a moment longer. I moan, bucking with what little give I can, but he moves his thigh where it's been resting against the bench, relieving me of the pressure I was receiving and making me scream, my body wishing it could be free to climb him like an animal.

"Fuck me, please!" I shout, followed by a *smack*.

"Ten!" *I* cry out as his riding crop flares across my clitoris, my pussy exploding with electricity as he drops the crop and, thank the lord, gets to his knees, slides a knife from his boot, and slices the ropes from my body like a package, which, to be honest is hot as hell, my man, inspecting my body, kissing my scars, licking my swollen breasts like he hasn't had an ice cream in all his life and my chest is a full on hot fudge sundae.

The absolute skank inside me slips free, and I hardly recognize myself, leaning fully into this kinky game of predator and prey.

"*Please*, Daddy," I moan, rubbing my nipples and biting my bottom lip. "I was so good. Won't you split me open with your cock?" I twist my lips up, playfully, and he growls in response, grinning dangerously at me and yanking me free from my hot pink bindings before shoving inside me all the way to the hilt. I gasp, the fullness inside me leaving little room for air, and he groans from deep within.

"Such a little slut. So fucking wet for me." He sucks the skin on my neck and leaves absolutely no room for me to confuse him with a gentleman when he hooks my knees over his shoulders and finds a whole new angle to fuck me from that has me literally gushing, squirting…

No, this is…I'm squirting. Oh, my God!

"Hunter!" I gasp, embarrassed, but also…it feels so good. My body clenches, every bit of pleasure exploding through my center as he hits the spot that keeps me coming over and over and over again. I don't want him to stop. "I'm getting it all over you. I didn't know I could do this…" I trail off, looking down with wide eyes at the mess seeping between us, but he groans again, squeezing my hips harder. He doesn't stop. Just throws an incredulous laugh into my neck while he continues to thrust into my G-spot like it's his last chance to fuck me ever again.

"I love you, Devyn Lynn," he growls as he finishes inside me, tensing and hanging on to me while he rolls his hips slowly for several beats, all the while laying soft kisses across my chest. With that, how could I deny it?

"I know," I tell him as his exhausted body collapses atop my own. I wrap my arms around him and tug him close as our hearts find a way in their own erratic rhythms to beat in time.

"I love you, too, Hunter Isaac. Now and always."

Chapter 38

Devyn

That's not possible!" I hear the shouts filtering in from the floor level of Hunter's farmhouse. It sounds like he's on the phone, but I can only hear half the conversation from my spot under the blankets of his bed.

Something else is going on.

"I'll get us some muffins," Ellie says to someone. My guess is Jonathan. "C'mon." Footsteps canter away, followed by the swinging screen door from the kitchen.

"I don't care what that random woman has to say about her maternal rights. She didn't care about Ellie when she was pregnant with her any more than she does now, or she wouldn't have been born addicted to that fuckin' stuff that put her and my brother behind bars in the first place. We had to wean a newborn from drugs, Katie. You were there!" He curses, slamming what I presume is his phone onto the marble countertops…*ouch*. There's a big pause before Garrison chimes in.

Wait, Garrison's here? I sit upright in the bed and scooch my ear closer to the door, looking around for a pair of sweatpants.

"I'll call my uncle if that will help with Ellie's placement. What we talked about this morning, about my problem…I want what you said, Hunt. To be free of it. I'll take Jonathan and be on our way until the, uh…" he clears his throat and lets out a long breath, "…the meeting later. And if it's okay, I'd like to apologize to—"

"My wife," Hunter's voice cuts in, sharper than I think he really needs to when Garrison is clearly offering to help with something that has to do with Ellie and her mother, but then again, drunk or not, Garrison did go too far last night. And it sounded like it's not the only time he's had those throes. He needs help.

Which is what Hunter promised to give him. He's going to be his accountability partner for meetings. Someone who can mentor him when he has an urge and needs help. But only after we help him get his house in order.

Lemon and Shana already agreed after I texted them what happened. We are all going to help our old friend get his life on track. In a way, it's like what my dad did for Hunter all those years ago. Because people deserve second chances.

Hunter's phone rings again, and he curses.

I pull a Pine Forest Rodeo hoodie and sweatpants set over my body and tug the strings as tight as they will go because they're Hunter's, and I look like I got swallowed by a polar bear no matter what I try. Shrugging at my reflection, I slip into some socks and pad down the hallway, stopping when I hear Hunter groan again.

"It's not about that. Okay, well, if I'd known it was being moved up sooner, maybe I could have it filed, but—"

"Is it the marriage license?" I ask, running down the stairs in a breathless plunder. "Is it? Do we need to file it?"

"It's too late," Hunter says sharply, but it's not really at me. It's directed into the phone.

Most likely at Katie, and I feel bad for her too. She's on our side. I didn't know how to feel that kind of faith in people before moving back home, but I feel it inherently now. Faith in Katie. In Pine Forest. In us.

"We'll do it. We'll look like the better option. Tell Katie I'm on board," I urge him, wrapping my hand around his arm. He looks down and into my eyes, an apologetic shake of his head spearing me in the heart.

But he doesn't give up that easily. Neither of us has given up yet. Not when everything we had was ripped from within and between. And not now.

"Don't shut me out, Hunter. Let me help you. Please, tell me the full details."

He sighs and shakes his head, running his fingers through his hair like he does when he's thinking, and he seems to agree with me that he did, in fact, say there'd be no more lies or secrets where our relationship and Ellie are concerned.

"Katie, can you fill her in?"

"Right. Your marriage license, a napkin as it is, well, it isn't valid until it's filed."

We all wait. I mean, I kind of get it, but I also don't.

"If it needs to be filed, then file it, right?"

"Filed, meaning it needs to be turned into the courthouse and signed by a judge. Depending on the appointments and schedules…it could take you weeks to get in with the local justice. Our courts are still overbooked from closings last fall." She sighs. "I don't even understand how her mother managed to get pre-trial waived in a matter of days."

"Shit," I whisper. "So, Ellie's mom could get custody of her because we can't get this legitimized soon enough? Is that all?"

"Um." Katie clears her throat. "Well, it's kind of an all or nothing situation, Devyn." I roll my eyes. She can't see me, and that's probably for the better because Hunter raises his brow at me, and I just shrug. Can't ask me to stop being bitchy *and* judgy. Give me *something*.

"I get that, Katie Kat," I say into the phone, "but I can take care of it by…noon. Can you buy me until then? When did the thing get moved up to?"

"It's tomorrow at eleven a.m. in Courtroom B of the Juvenile and Domestic Building. I'll have a little side room booked for prep. Bring the signed document to me there as soon as you can tomorrow. I'll be there all morning. It's our best hope."

She finally stops talking, and I remember she isn't an Alexa recording. She sounds so robotic, it's hard to tell.

"Got it," I say confidently, because I do.

I know exactly who I need to talk to about this, and it seems like there are many other issues from the last decade concerning this very person. And that same person is going to help me fix them.

After a few minutes of toothbrushing and scrambling for cuter clothes, I throw on my cowgirl boots, smiling when I think about what those boots were a part of last night.

I am in love with Hunter Isaac. And soon I'll be married to him. But first, I need some help from my big brother.

Chapter 39

Devyn

Make no mistake, if there was something shady done behind my back where both parents were involved all those years ago, my big brother, Knows-What's-Best-For-You-Dustin, knows every bit about it.

And if I'm correct, he's just the person to get Dad to change his mind and help us.

I adjust my hair into a long braid down one side of my body. This way, I feel every bit the brave knight, set out on her hot-pink steed to save the princess from the fire breathing dragon, or in this case, the custody hearing. Which feels uniquely similar.

There's a metaphor there I'll explore when I have the time, but now I'm feeling the sweet taste of victory as the gravel crunches beneath my tires in Dustin's driveway. This time, there's no heels to click and clack across his perfect suburban walkway. I really can't help but stare in awe over my brother's entryway herb boxes, though. Gosh, it's so cute.

I shake my head. *There's no time for marvels of wonder, Devyn. It's showtime.* I march up his stoop and whip the screen door open only to find—

"Shana?"

"Devyn! What are you doing here?" she spurts, red-faced and stumbling down the stoop, backing toward her car that I didn't notice parked on the curb until just now.

"What are *you* doing here?" I counter, but before I can get an answer, she's shoving her body into her car and shouting something about stupid pancake recipes and new pointe shoes.

"What?" I practically shout over the loud screech of her old clunker. But she's off, leaving dust in her wake.

Odd.

But then I turn back around and see another surprise guest. Suddenly, anything involving Shana and the pancakes is put on the back burner.

"Mom?"

My mouth gapes. My hand stills on the door handle. I don't know if I'm supposed to cry, or run, or smile…so I just freeze.

"Sit," she says. She's smiling, and something about that feels off. I try to remember a time I saw it look the way it does right now.

Genuine.

And she wants me to sit. Beside a woman I haven't seen in a ghost of time.

Stinging droplets dance around the domes of my eyes while we do nothing but stare at one another. Her smile is wide and her eyes crinkle in an unfamiliar way.

Lovingly.

"What have you done to our mother?" I call out to the kitchen without breaking eye contact, hoping Dustin will hear and come save me. The last words I ever spoke to her ring loudly through the room. So loud, I squint at her in question.

Can't you also hear how loud it is?

But she can't, of course.

That's how trauma makes you crazy.

"I'll never understand how God could let someone like you be a mother, but take that away from someone like me."

"That's because even He knows you aren't worthy."

That's what she'd said back then.

I lean away, examining the woman who looks like a different version of my mother. A cleaned up, polished version. One with thoughts of others. Kindness. The one who only let herself out in glimpses when we were children.

She seems different now.

"Sober," she says, as if reading my mind. I shoot her a glare, and she just winks, patting the sofa for me.

But I don't sit.

Until I do.

"Hey, I wasn't expecting you, Dev." Dustin walks in from the kitchen, out of breath and wiping what looks like flour from his hair and shirt. I eye him suspiciously, but he shakes his head at me, sending white powder peppering my dress.

"Mishap with the KitchenAid when I was training my new hire." He finishes brushing off his shirt and wipes his fingers on the towel in the pocket of his apron. "What are you doing here, Devyn?"

I huff, turning to Mom, who is…still smiling in a genuine way that freaks me the fuck out, to be frank, but okay, I'll allow it. I turn back to Dustin and crank my neck to the side, blocking the Alien-Abducted-and-Replaced-By-An-Imposter-Mom from my vision, because that's too much to confront right now, and I direct my attention to my brother, who is acting equally weird today.

I need to get on with this. I don't have time for weird

family reunions where everyone smiles deceptively. I have a marriage to consummate.

I mean, well, we did that part. Can't ignore the little markings that are barely noticeable to anyone but myself along the soft parts of my wrists and forearms from the rope last night. I realize I'm blushing physically and mentally, and snap myself back to the present.

"Did either of you know about Dad giving Hunter money after the crash and making him swear to push me away?"

Dustin's eyes widen, as do my mother's, and both their jaws drop as they look between one another. And that confirms it. Everyone was in on it.

"Okay, so that's a yes, then."

"Look, Dev. You were almost killed. And you were depressed. And Hunter was…Samuel and Hunter's family were going through some times. We needed you in a safe place where you could heal. Not here where you'd spiral again."

"Oh, so you guys decided without me? Just shipped me off with Dad to an all-girls school on the coattails of the crash, the death of my baby, and Mom and Dad's divorce, and hoped it would be Princess Diaries and Happily Ever After? That I'd just go on winning pageants and making a new life for myself away from it all? Packing it into boxes and stacking them so high I'd never see through the bullshit?"

I stare at Dustin and Mom as their faces twist. Going from something of judgment to a place that suggests, dare I say it, sympathy. And damn it, I'm latching on while they seem to be listening for once.

"My baby had just died. Hunter's and my *child*. A child we prayed over each night from the moment we realized what we'd gotten ourselves into, holding hands in a crying bathroom stall at the very high school you drive past each day. Your core memories of it might be from rodeo championships or class elections, maybe even just the boring bits like study hall or exams, but mine are from whispered rumors behind locker doors, too snug gym tops, and a pink plus sign on a plastic stick, in a dimly lit bathroom stall of the second-floor ladies' room that Hunter was never meant to hold me in. He and I *needed* each other. And we always will. You understand that, right?"

"I do now." Dustin tugs me into a big brother hug that feels snug and protective, just right.

"You smell like my brother," I say, laughing.

"You don't use that line on your husband, do you?" he teases, and I swat his shoulder and shove him away.

"Call him my husband one more time and I'll vomit in a bag and mail it to you," I tease back, raising an eyebrow. "I'm still waiting on that package, bro."

Dustin laughs, offering up a coffee to Mom and me. We both decline in the same way, a soft toss of the air with our hand. It's kind of a bitchy move now that I'm seeing it in action.

No wonder! I want to tell her she's the reason I'm a bitch, but I think that might make me, also, a bitch. So, I'm evolving. I smile, keeping my newfound knowledge to myself and effectively breaking the cycle.

As soon as Dustin settles into a spot on the chair beside me, I let it all out. I manage to explain why I need their help to convince Dad and his lawyer buddies to legitimize the certificate before tomorrow's hearing, but it's actually Mom who surprises me.

"Devyn, I wasn't a great mother to you. I won't apologize. But I will say this." She scoots to the edge of the sofa and leans into us. "Before I cleaned myself up, I was blind to how lucky I was to be a mother. Especially to the two of you. And you will make great parents who listen and put others first one day. Both of you." She nods at me and Dustin, perching on the edge of the loveseat. "That being said, I know about Eleanor. I have watched Hunter raise her for many years now. He always said he'd be better than I was, than his dad was. And you will be too, Devyn. You have always shined brightly. I just couldn't see it past my own darkness."

I force a smile and nod. It's not totally fake, but I'm also not going to throw myself around her and tug her close from that alone. It's not enough for me to say we're okay. It's not an apology that encompasses the years of pain her actions caused me.

So, I don't say okay.

But that doesn't mean what she said doesn't warm places in my heart that I believed were frozen for good. Ones a sad little girl carved out of herself and shoved in a shoebox, to hide from the world. From her own self.

My mother's words, whether I want them to affect me or not, open that box. They may not be enough to heal the carved-out parts of me that took years to break, but they are a start.

So, I do take her hand, and I give my mother what I can offer.

I nod.

She nods back.

But we do not cry.

"Let's call your dumbass father, now," she finally manages, and Dustin and I share a look that tells me we agree on one thing. That sounds a lot more like the mom we remember.

Dustin dials up Dad and puts him on speaker on the coffee table.

"Son," he clips, short and forced. Mom rolls her eyes immediately, and I chew my bottom lip to avoid laughing. She hates that man insurmountably. "Do you need something?"

"Yeah, Dad." Dustin sighs. He hates talking to our father, and he avoids it like the plague. You can tell by the shake in his voice. Anyone who deals with Dad on a regular basis knows not to wobble. He hates a weak backbone if he perceives one.

I wince, sensing the lash-out coming before it even does.

"Well, spit it out!" he booms through the phone, and I puff a deep gust of air from my cheeks impatiently, which has Mom rolling her eyes again. Anymore and they might fall from her head.

"Dad, let's cut the crap," I finally say, because I can't stand the incompetence. No offense to Dustin and all, but I'm sure Dad appreciates my clarity more than this shuffle of false pleasantries. "I'm gonna send you a marriage license on a napkin and you're gonna get your friend Randy to approve it over some cocktails at Morgana's in three hours, okay? I already made the reservation. Please, Dad?"

Dustin shakes his head and rolls his eyes, unable to hide the smile pulling across his lips when his eyes meet my mom's and they both break out into a low snicker at my antics. "*Daddy, pwease,*" Dustin whispers in the background, sending Mom bent over in silent cackles and slapping her thigh.

I struggle not to laugh at myself. It is a little ridiculous that I can still pull out these kinds of stops, but if I must use the Daddy's Girl card, I will. Ellie's placement is on the line. I've done it for new stilettos; I'll do it for this.

"Dad, I really need you to help me. I'm in love with Hunter, and if we don't get this filed, he could lose his daughter. Just have Randy sign it and put it through on his little court laptop we've all seen him toting around the country club, and all will be well."

Silence. My heartbeat picks up. He needs to agree to this. I don't have a plan B. I groan, looking over to Dustin for help, but he just shrugs, unhelpful as ever. I scoff at him and turn to Mom. Thankfully, for once in my life, she offers me a smile and a firm nod of camaraderie.

"Gotta be firm with your father," she'd always told me when I wanted something as a kid. I have to say, at least they prepared me not to be a pushover in life, whether that kind of thing is healthy for a developing child's psyche or not.

Be firm it is.

"You can cut the bullshit, Dad, because I know all about you helping Hunter and swearing him off way back when, and don't think I'm not going to circle back to that once I know this marriage thing is straight."

He sighs, deep and heavy…contemplative. Mom taps her foot on the tile, as Dustin keeps eyeing the kitchen.

"Oh, for fuck's sake!" I shout, surprising everyone around me. "I'm a grown-ass woman! Let me make my own damn decisions and stop worrying about my future. I'm worried about right now. And right now, nothing matters but a little girl I can't fathom living without, who needs a paper you won't give me."

"I'm trying to keep you from making mistakes I made. You can be anything in the city, Devy. You're in a box out there. You're my little girl."

"But, Dad, I can't be anything in the city. You can, but there's one thing I can't be there. I can't be happy. And that is the most important thing of all, isn't it? Isn't that why you moved yourself out there and followed your own dreams?"

"Yes, but being a parent to a child who isn't yours could be…"

"Magnificent. It's magnificent, Dad, and it's exactly what I want."

I try not to be affected by my mother sitting across from me for the first time in ten years, with tears of happiness flowing down her face…for me.

"All right," Dad says, "I'll get Randy to sign it. We'll upload it to the court site, but it won't show up as filed until the clerk updates the listings next week."

"That's not soon enough, Dad. The hearing is today."

He sighs, the creak of his desk chair sounding through the phone. He types something out on his keyboard and a few clicks later offers a satisfied grunt. "Randy's got an online notary. I'll send you a certified PDF to print. Give me an hour."

"Thanks, Dad." I breathe a huge sigh of relief.

"Don't mention it," he says gruffly. But he lingers on the line, a question clearly on the tip of his tongue. "Devyn? Will you tell him something for me?" He groans again. "Your *husband.*"

A smile spreads across my face, my cheeks giant shining bulbs at how happy I feel to finally have my father's approval, after all these years. I look at Dustin, who is also unable to keep his teeth hidden for this moment, and he nods at me, too. So does Mom.

"Please tell him I'm proud of him. Of both of you. I thought, you know, as your father…you never want to see your baby girl the way I saw you suffering. I was supposed to guard you from these things, the dark parts of your life, but they found you anyway. On your own time. And for that, my child, I was wrong."

"Dad, stop. You don't have to—"

"No." He cuts me off. "I do. You will be the best mother, Devyn Lynn, because you have the biggest heart. You shine, not despite the darkness, but all the way through it. Go, win this. And fight for that little girl."

Chapter 40

Devyn

And just like that, Devyn Campbell became Devyn Isaac. With a swift flick of a painted finger on a mouse hovered over the word *Print*.

The paper's still warm, and the pep in my step is probably evident to everyone within a mile, as I practically leap over the stoop and sashay to my Jeep, throwing kisses behind me in the wind to my brother and, weirdly enough, my mother.

I have won twenty-seven titles since I was in middle school. All of them came with sparkling tiaras and glorified titles like Princess or Queen. I was given the trendiest diets to follow and the prettiest ballgowns to model. I was even provided with the finest education in the city and a built-in fan base to follow.

But happiness isn't in career success, reputation, or crowns.

The most beautiful smile is still held up by the same set of jaws. And mine were clenched. Maybe even wired shut.

It doesn't matter if it was by me or anyone else. The fact is you can't lie to yourself. You have to be *you*.

The fact is, with Hunter and Ellie…

My mouth opens, and it sings.

I rev the engine, the rumble beneath my bones filling me with a sense of urgency. I throw on my playlist, *Can't Stop Me Now,* and I know in my heart everything up to this point has been for a reason.

In my heart and in my gut, I feel it all shift. Today is a new beginning for all of us.

My tires glide across the road, hugging the parts that matter and adjusting to the twists that require give. I smile because Hunter had these aligned and rotated for me when he took it to his friend's shop. He paid for all the extras of course, causing me to become infuriatingly more attracted to him. But I didn't want it going to his head.

I searched everywhere for the bill. Even called up the shop to ask what he'd paid so I could sneak it back into his wallet, but they wouldn't tell me. My grin widens.

Hunter and I go back so far that the whole town has been rooting for us from the get-go, and I hadn't even noticed. Lemon with the not-so-fake marriage, Katie for allowing it to go on despite her pretty serious conflict of interest with being Ellie's social worker, and don't even get me started on Shana for being complacent as all get-out for the goody-goody she usually is.

But sometimes you don't know what you need like your friends do. And that just warms my heart further. The fact that I have such amazing people around me. Ones who love me for me, the bitchy parts and all. And ones who want to see me succeed, who see the best parts of me, despite the worst ones.

They tried to point me in the right direction even when I wasn't ready to see the way. That's friendship.

My heart soars almost as fast as the numbers on my dash, and I glance down, relieved to see that even though I'm pumping it hard and fast to some dub-step instrumentals I have no idea the name of, I'm not speeding.

Just three more miles until I reach the courthouse.

Katie is there today, preparing, and I want this done and filed before Ellie's bio mom even wakes up tomorrow morning.

The marriage certificate and ticket to Ellie's freedom sit directly on the seat to my right, and nothing has ever looked more intentional. I clench my hands tightly around the steering wheel, ready to get this done once and for all as I fly past Mullins Road and—

Crash!

I'm jolted.

I hear the screeching of tires, feel the scraping of metal, smashing of glass, the impact throwing me to the side faster than I can blink.

The sound reaches me from within, bursting from my eardrums, and the beat of my heart pounds with the same intensity as the song that plays on repeat through the speakers. My body curves unnaturally upward, the air rushing from my lungs like it was stolen. It fights its way out of me, clawing the inside of my throat, and my body cracks, smacking hard against the interior of my Jeep. I distantly gather that we must be upside down.

Blood rushes to my head as time slows, and my neck whips violently to the left, smacking my skull against the window. We're rolling.

I feel the pain in every nerve ending upon impact as my brain thrashes within the crevasses of my skull, and the fullness lulls my head from side to side with the direction of the vehicle. It's fuzzy. Everywhere I look I see blood, slowly dripping down my forehead, into my eyelashes. Sticky. Thick. Paint from a barn door before the summer rain, spattering, dripping from the sky.

For a fraction of time, it's just me, the air, and a floating paper that represents my purpose.

That, and the beat of my heart.

The car falls to its side, my vision in and out in colors and pain, and it's not exactly slow motion, but it is long enough for Abel's words to run through my head. *A chance to choose again.*

And I chose them.

Even if that chance ends today, with my last breath, I have no regrets. I'd do it all over again. I know what Hunter means when he says that now. I'd choose the time spent with Hunter and Ellie all over again despite any heartache life throws my way.

Because in the end, that's choosing the most important thing of all.

It's choosing individual moments you can't replace. It's choosing the here and now, even if those things are hard and scary.

Imperfect. Or *broken.*

It's choosing to make them whole again with love.

The earth shifts in an instant when the car comes crashing down to the pavement, the shards of metal, glass, and plastic exploding like fireworks across my vision. And I know nothing in this moment other than the abrupt smack of all-encompassing pain, as my body slams hard against space and time.

And there is only darkness.

Chapter 41

Hunter

Beep, Beep, Beep.

The machines hooked up to the woman I love are too familiar, and it's near impossible not to feel transported to another time, in this very hospital, with the similarities.

The damn *waiting*.

"Open your eyes for us, Ponygirl. We need you," I whisper from the rolling chair I've nestled as closely as I can to the hospital bed. I'd climb up in there and snuggle her the way I know she likes if the nurses didn't keep checkin' up on her every five seconds.

It's comforting to know they're here and paying attention, but it's concerning that they need to be with her so often.

None of that is surprising when you consider the way she was brought in…who knows how long she had been injured prior to being cared for. Katie never got the paperwork Devyn was on the way to bring her. It didn't take long before the sirens reached the courthouse, and the judge ordered a recess since the opposing counsel never made it to the courthouse either, stuck behind the wreckage like half of town.

The other car was damaged too, and the passengers unconscious like Dev. The doctors informed us as of yesterday that if she'd continued to bleed any longer, recovery might not have been a possibility.

At this point, they say her recovery is entirely up to her.

"Stay with us, Ponygirl."

Ten Years Ago

Beep, beep, beep.

The beeping is loud, but it gets quieter as we run alongside the gurney. I get one final glimpse of her, one last squeeze of her small, limp hand before I'm forced to stop. I hang alongside the counter and shout past the guards stationed by the ICU doorway.

"Dustin, text me as soon as they say something, please, man!"

"I will," he yells back. "Hey, she loves you, even if she can't say it right now. We all do. You hear me?"

I grind my teeth. That's what he says. But Mr. and Mrs. Campbell said the opposite when they blamed me for the wreck and all but shoved me out of the way as soon as they got here.

Like she isn't mine and I'm not hers.

He walks backward now, jogging almost, turning his head back to check he's still following them as he shouts his last words to me, words he can say all he wants, but I'll never agree with.

"None of this is your fault."

Then he's gone. The doors swing shut, and I watch my best friend follow his parents and the medical team as they wheel Devyn away from me.

My heart thunders, my fingers gripping the edges of the nurse's desk that blocks me from going farther than this spot right here. The beeping in the distance that fades to nothing the farther they travel down the winding hallways of the hospital mocks my patience.

Helpless, that is what I feel.

I said I'd protect her, and instead I may have ended her life. And not just hers. Our daughter's.

Tears fall from my eyes, hard and fast. Our little girl. Gone in an instant.

I shut my eyes tight and hunch over the counter, my sobs waning to nothing more than slopping hiccups over a drenched sleeve, until a nurse comes and puts her hand on my shoulder.

She's older, maybe sixty. I wouldn't know. There aren't many older people in my family who stuck around long enough for me to ask their ages.

I wanted something different for our daughter. For us. I wanted to be that family man who hosted breakfasts with Santa and fall festivals on the farm for the whole town one day, with my family by my side, passing on generations of togetherness. Something I never had. Might never have again.

I wipe my face on my other sleeve, but it's right soiled too, so I just yank the whole thing off and ball it in a wad, tossing it to a seat by the water cooler.

The kind but militant woman offers me a tissue, and I take one, wiping my face and moving to an empty set of chairs. She sits in the one opposite me and waits patiently, her lips pursed, and hands clasped over one knee.

"Well," she finally says, "I don't know about your girl-friend's injuries because I'm not involved in her medical care. And I wouldn't tell you if I could due to HIPPA constraints," she adds with a wink, "but I do know anyone traveling down that hallway needs the staff's full attention. Do you understand what I'm saying?"

I nod, taking a few more tissues from her, and then just grabbing the whole box when she arches an eyebrow at me. She wants me to calm down and stay out of the way. That much I do understand.

But she hasn't left yet.

"Well, are you going to tell me about her or just sit there and sulk privately?"

I snort at that. I never had a grandparent around, and Aunt Sarah was never this blunt with me about anything, but I imagine this is what she'd be like if my mom's mom were alive right now. Mom had a bit of sass to her bite too, from what I can remember. And maybe that's what has me opening up to this strange woman I just met.

"She was pregnant," I say, watching her face soften. "The baby was…they couldn't save her when they pulled Devyn free." I pause, recalling the long shards of metal and wood, the whole chunks of vehicle and signage imbedded into her middle. Grief pools over me, so I slam my eyes shut. But the grief is there too, seeping into thoughts and private moments that are supposed to be just for my brain and the thoughts I choose to think.

It sliced through her womb and up her chest. I've seen it. It's burned into my mind like a curse.

"What if they can't save her?" I grind out, crying to the nurse…Rosemary, her badge reads. But it doesn't matter her name. For what it's worth, she's a stranger in a waiting room. And I'm just the fuckup boyfriend who wasn't allowed to go back with family.

"Things don't always work out how we imagine they might," she says sadly. But that's not supposed to be what the wise old stranger says in the story. The fuck? Where's the encouragement or words of sudden understanding?

Where's my solution to all this?

"So, what? I do nothing? You don't understand. It's my fault. It should be me on that table dying!"

"But you aren't," she says, "and what you do with that is entirely up to you."

Present

Beep, *Beep, Beep.*

Devyn's machines haven't stopped beeping since I got here. But I'm told that's a good thing. It measures her breathing. She's been out of it for two days now, concussed.

The doctors say she sustained a traumatic brain injury. Along with a total shoulder tear and several minor injuries that needed stitching.

She's stable, and I feel a wave of relief wash over me every time I hear that word.

But she hasn't woken up yet.

I won't forgive myself if she's not the same when she does. I'm the reason she was on the road. Again.

"I'm sorry," I whisper, brushing soft yellow strands away from her face. A deep cut runs from the top of her ear to the bottom of her chin on the right side of her face now, and I count the stitches.

Ten.

That's just the one side. I feel another round of tears welling up in my eyes, and I wonder how much a man can cry before he depletes his sources. Is there a limit?

There never seems to be one for my tears, nor her scars.

I know she can't hear me, but I need to get the words out of my head, so they'll stop their torment, even if I'm the only one who ever hears them spoken. Speaking them aloud makes them real.

"This is my fault."

"No, it's not," Dustin's voice blares in from the hallway. I turn, giving him a look that tells him I'm not in the mood for anything even remotely related to sarcasm, and he nods as I rise for a hug.

"It's not your fault, Hunter. You're my best friend. She's my sister. I don't want to see anything happen to her any more than you do, but I also can't sit by and watch you blame yourself all over again for something you had no control over."

I back away from him and scrub my hand down my face, shaking my head in disagreement.

"You say that, but the only reason she was driving there so quickly was because of that marriage license, and you know it. And the only reason for that was me."

Dustin shakes his head. "No, my friend." He smiles sadly, wrapping his arm around me and hauling me out toward the hallway. "The reason for that was not you. The reason is right there." He points his finger into the waiting room where Ellie is waiting anxiously on the small bench by the fire extinguisher, her legs crossed at the ankles where her foot bounces uncontrollably.

"Papa!" She cries when she sees me, running into my arms and knocking me off balance as I wobble to catch my footing on the slippery white floors.

She wastes no time, wiggling her way out of my hold and throwing me a look of alarm, her eyes red-rimmed and shiny, and my heart breaks even further for the pain she feels.

I feel it, too.

"Let me see her!" she says, running into the hospital room, shoving her way through anything and anyone in her path until she gets to Devyn. We run after her, Dusty and I, but she's too fast. We're only to the doorway by the time she's pressed her body against the gurney.

She leans on her tiptoes to see, and gasps when she takes her in. She's pale, stitched up and bruised, lying unconscious on the hospital bed, lips cracked and dry, hooked to those fucking machines.

I feel the grief drape over me like a coat, the guilt a searing belt, secure and snug as my head rings terrors through my skull.

She's barely alive again. Because of you, she's barely alive.

And I can't bear it. I swing my arm out in front of Ellie and scoop her into my arms, holding my hand over her eyes.

"You don't have to look. I'm so sorry." But she shoves away.

"I need to look, Papa."

Her red eyes burn, pleading with me, and she's right. This child standing here who was once just a handful of flesh and bones, not even mine, handed to me in a room much like this.

She didn't even have a name.

A tear rolls free, and I nod at her, this young woman before me now. One who stands tall and brave for what she believes in. Who is not asking but *telling* me what she needs.

"Okay," I agree, releasing her.

The room falls silent, except for the beeping of the machines and the soft padding of Ellie's footsteps across the tile floor.

Dustin stands by my side, his arm around me, as we watch Ellie approach the bed, her miniature boots scuffing the sterile floors with chicken shit dirt clods in their wake, and a smile tugs at my lips, just slightly. Devyn wouldn't have her hospital room any other way.

I notice that Ellie a bouquet of sunflowers in her left hand, and her tattered up diary in her right that she doesn't bother setting down as she hoists herself onto Devyn's bed, crawling in beside her and snuggling her, just like I wanted to do, and that brings a smile to my lips.

They fit so well together like that, my two girls. Cradled together like it was always meant to be.

Please, God, make her well.

It's the only thing I can manage when I see the two most important pieces of my heart outside my chest like this.

"Devyn, you can't leave us. You have to wake up, do you hear me?" Ellie whispers, kissing Devyn's cheek softly and shoving herself up to a sitting position.

"You were right about the sunflowers," she says, sniffling through tears and snot and wiping her arm across her face. "It didn't matter if it was blue or green or even yellow light. It didn't matter about the soil or the water." She holds the sunflowers up as if Devyn can see them, and a spastic laugh bubbles from her throat. "No matter what I did to the baby sunflowers in the shed, the minute I transferred them to the fields with full sunlight, they all bloomed. They just needed the right conditions."

She leans over on her knees and lays the sunflowers down on the table beside them, settling back down next to Dev, and I realize minutes later that my eyes are blurry because I'm crying. Full out. Watching an interaction that could be their last.

God, it can't be their last. I say prayer after prayer while I watch them.

Please do not let this be their last.

"You were right about Jonathan, too. He does like me." She makes a face that's a mix of disgust and excitement and squeezes Devyn's hand. "Just like you were right about the silkies and the ducks, Dev. You were right about it all."

She starts to cry now, softly at first, but soon it's picked up to heavy waves of tears until she's gasping, hyperventilating. "Please, D-evv-p—please—wake."

"Maybe you should take her out of here," Dustin suggests, but I'm already one step ahead of him, leaning in toward Ellie to scoop her back up, but she swats me away.

"*No, Papa, no!*" she screeches, yanking her body away from me and curling her fingers back around the edges of the hospital bed. She drapes her body over Devyn and sobs into her. "You have to wake up, Devyn. You have to! You were right! Polly is a better mother because she's there! She wants to be there! That's what it was all along."

"Ellie, please, baby, you need to give her some space to heal. Let's just—"

"No! She's going to wake up. She's gotta wake up. Wake up, Devyn! Wake up! You're my silkie. You're my Polly. Wake up, please. *You're my Polly!*"

"Eleanor!" I scream at her, grabbing her by the shoulders and shaking her so she snaps out of it and hears me. She quiets, her eyes wide, lips trembling as she shakes, her breath coming out in short, rapid spurts.

I look into her eyes, wild and full of fear and that same grief that plagues me.

"Breathe," I tell her.

And she does.

We breathe together just like that. Next to Devyn. We try to match her breathing.

Soon, I'm cradling Ellie while we wait for Devyn to wake, all of us breathing together. And in a way, it's soothing.

"It should be me in that bed," Ellie suddenly says, which has me sitting straight up.

"Why would you say that? It couldn't be further from the truth."

"I heard Uncle Dusty tell the police officers she was taking a paper to the courthouse for my custody. I know about the marriage certificate too. I listen in on just about every meeting with Katie, just so you know."

"You aren't in that bed, though. You know that? Devyn made a choice and had an accident. But do you think she would have made another choice where you were concerned? Because I can tell you she wouldn't. She'd choose you, Ellie. I know that about her."

My strong-willed wild child stares back at me with eyes full of questions. Ones it's my job to teach her the answers to. Ones I need to face myself.

Because you can't just place blame on yourself, sulk, or wonder what would have been. This little girl in my arms is proof enough that you never know what lemons life will throw you…or in this case, what bit of life *Lemon* will throw at you.

Go figure, Devyn isn't lucid enough for me to tell her that pun and swat me for how stupid it is, but maybe this is how we come full circle.

Or maybe the circle is never filled because it's not over. Life isn't done throwing us curveballs or turning our worlds completely upside down. Fate might have some hold on us, but what we do in the bits in between that fate is what makes us stronger, wiser, braver. And if we're lucky, it makes us happier.

"Life doesn't always work out how we might imagine, Ellie." I wipe her tears and repeat the words spoken to me so long ago, words that held very little meaning until now. "But what we do with that fate is entirely up to us."

"You really did get spiritual, didn't you?" a weak voice rasps, and we both jump.

"Devyn!" Ellie shouts, leaping from my lap and wrapping her arms around Devyn's neck, straddling her. "You're awake! I knew you'd wake up. I just knew it!"

Her eyes scrape over to meet mine, accompanied by a smile that warms my heart.

She's okay.

"I heard what you said, too, Ellie." She runs her hand across Ellie's cheek, smiling.

"And if I'm your Polly, *you*, sweet girl, are my Chuck."

Tears fill their eyes, and even though it's something I thought I'd never see, both of my girls let them roll freely, willingly.

"Is that all right with you? If I become your mother? If we become a family?"

"Yes!" Ellie shouts, jumping up and down on the bed to the point I have to remove her for Devyn's safety when an IV pole gets knocked over and the day nurse comes bustling in shouting curses our way.

"Oh, she's awake! Doctor Bennett!" She turns to us, inclining her head and clicking her tongue. "She needs to be seen by the doctor now, okay? We'll call you two when she's clear for visitors." She smiles impatiently, shooing us out the door.

"Ponygirl," I call to her before it shuts. "You're prettier than a princess. You're a queen."

She laughs, a slow, weak laugh, but it's a laugh, nonetheless. A vessel for hope and a new beginning.

And it's beautiful.

Something like a birdsong or a ride on a midday trail. Like the light on a lake that ripples with the water when your fishing pole gives. Like rain on a summer garden and blossoms on trees.

I look at Ellie, her hands curled around thick, sturdy stems that hold the bravest, brightest flowers in the field, and I smile.

We just needed the right conditions to bloom.

That's what we are.

Something like sunflowers.

Something like *us*.

Epilogue

Devyn

S top wriggling so much!" I swat Hunter, who's twisting around on the barn bench, arms bound to his sides by bright blue rope that I put there personally. I smile ear to ear and offer him a curtsey, pleased with my work.

"The student has surpassed the teacher," I tease, skipping joyfully to the rack and plucking a riding crop from the very center.

"Don't you even think about it, babygirl." He groans, but I notice the lilt in his voice. It says *do fucking think about it, babygirl*, so I raise a brow at him.

"Sunflowers?"

He shakes his head, sputtering a laugh before angling to face me, seriously, smolderingly, so fucking hotly…*is hotly a word?* He's doing it. He's doing hotly regardless of its vernacular validity, and fuck if I'm not frothing at the mouth for it. Does his lip lick thing only do it for me? Or are all the women who watch these thirst traps turned on by my man's lip licking?

A selfish, jealous, animal part of me wants to round them all up and let the pigs live off their carcasses, because he's mine.

But I'm not like that anymore. Living a bitch-free life is amazing, by the way.

I still can't tell if it's more that I'm living bitch-free, or if I'm just around people who tolerate the real me. The latter is more than likely. But if that's the case, then damn, I'm one lucky cowgirl.

"I'm not saying fucking sunflowers, and you're not leaving me tied up, you little tease. You and I know very well people will start showing within the hour." He rakes his eyes over my body slowly. "Unless you want 'em to watch."

I swear, he knows what this does. Every inch of skin he sets his gaze upon flares to life with electricity that I'm quite positive he saves up and magically zaps to my core when he winks.

But I eye the door to see our trusty lock is in place, and I'm on him. My lips are crashing against his, my teeth snagging over skin, my tongue tasting anything I can until he's sensing what I want and taking over, making my mouth personal grounds for his tongue to do whatever the hell he pleases. He dances inside me, and with his lips and tongue alone he makes me clench my thighs, rocking my clit against his belt buckle and the gathering of blue rope that comes together in a loop at his core.

"Untie me," he rasps, bucking his hips up as I grind down, giving me the friction I need to build up my pleasure as I ride him.

"Or what?" I ask, licking my own lips this time, pleased that I taste him there. I bend down to taste more. My tongue trails over his collarbone, sliding between the ropes to the salt lingering on his skin, the sandalwood of his aftershave wafting through my senses and making my toes curl in my boots.

Thank the Lord for skirts, because they're convenient for moments like this, when I unclasp his belt buckle and slide his jeans off his thick, heavy… *God, I want you on top of me…*

"Stop lookin' at me like you need a meal and cut the ropes so I can fuck you right."

"Okay," I surrender breathlessly, scrambling off him and snatching up the safety scissors we keep close by during these rope play sessions of ours. They've become a ritual of sorts that I don't hate one tiny bit. But I admit I prefer to be the one under his prowess. That's the real reason I cut him loose.

The nylon ropes come billowing down his body and land on the floor without a sound, at least not one louder than my beating heart, and in an instant, I'm thrown to my back, his hard, thick body on top of mine.

"Hunterrr, fuuuck," I moan.

"Filthy little wife has a filthy little mouth, does she?" he purrs, his eyes smirking to match his mouth. He knows how to make me insatiable. Always has. But over the years, he's also learned a trick or two, like the way he swipes the flat of his tongue across my neck, licking and sucking slow circles lower and lower down my chest.

I go limp for him, his kisses becoming liquid gold over my skin, wrapping me in a veil of pleasure, his hands tweaking my nipples, giving me spurts of pain and pleasure as he slides my panties to the side and lays a hot, wet, kiss by my ear.

"Can I fuck you, babygirl?"

"Yes!" I cry, bucking my hips and urging his entry, moaning and shouting his name and screaming my love as he enters me again and again, my body molding to his, my clit pulsing with electricity, and my mind reeling with desire, with hope, with *love*.

I cry out as my body pulses, climaxing with the pleasure. He continues to pump into me, his hardness teasing my insides until I'm moaning uncontrollably, my lips snagging across his shoulder and biting down as I come around his cock.

"Look how good you take me," he coos, slowing his thrusts and massaging my throbbing G spot as he does. "Pretty little wife came all over me, but we have a problem, don't we, babygirl?" He thrusts deeper, dragging another moan from my lips. "Because you don't like my messes, do you?"

I gasp, looking up from under sweaty bangs, and I watch his eyes darkening as he pulls his cock from my pussy, lowers me to my knees, which traitorously comply, and releases his hot, sticky seed across my lips.

My pussy hums, my body sizzling as if it could reignite just from the act alone, and it's simply not fair for him to hold that kind of power over me, so I do one better. I stand naked before the only man I've ever loved, and I lick his seed from my lips. I lean in, cupping his balls in my hand, and lower my head, taking his entire length into my mouth, coating him with his own cum and sucking him down, until he's hard all over again.

"I think I cleaned it up just fine, don't you, Daddy?"

He gapes, reaching out to tickle me to submission, most likely, but we're out of time when the barn door sounds with three tiny but firm knocks.

"Ya'll better stop yer kissin' and pissin'! The whole town is on their way, and that scary preppy-clothes lady is in our livin' room drinkin' tea without sugar." Ellie pounds the door three more times before we hear her boots scuff through the dirt as she skips away.

Hunter and I share a look and then burst into a fit of laughter, still tangled in each other's arms and legs, and I know nothing in my life has been wrong.

Even when it wasn't easy to see.

This is where I'm meant to be. Forever and always.

But we do have to get this show on the road. And we have a surprise for Ellie.

We leave the barn and watch as she skips ahead of us to the amphitheater and events arena Hunter and I unveiled the plans for at the fair in November. She's grown so much since then, and it's only been a month. But she's still the awkward kid in overalls, holding nails while her papa builds things like this beautiful community-use structure from the ground up.

Right from the vision in my head.

We go together like that. My vision. His passion. And Ellie, the glue to keep things sticking right where they should.

Besides, we need each other. Can you imagine me swinging a hammer? *Thank you, no.*

I'll fill the space with talented young people who need a place to shine, though. That's more my area of expertise any day.

I'm proud of Ellie for tonight. She's the unofficial hostess of the First Annual Rodeo Talent Show, a non-profit we hope will raise money for teenage mothers of Pine Forest, a new program we came up with together in honor of my story and her own. Together, we decided no teenage mother should ever think drugs, gangs, or hiding your pregnancy from your family are the only ways to turn. Now they'll have another option, a chance for hope, and what they do with that is entirely up to them.

Soon, the crowd is fully seated, and I can't help but swoon over my husband and marvel at his and Dustin's hard work as the hand-crafted stage with beautifully stained rafters of red oak are unveiled for the whole town to see.

A collective awe is heard from the field, and it makes every bit of planning and effort worth it. I see why Hunter has made enhancing this town his life's work.

I look over at Claudette, Molly, and yes, even James, who is chowing down on the corndogs we're peddling up and down the aisles, and I shake my head. There was a time not too long ago, in their very office, at that first interview, when I heard Hunter say something about his "life's work" and I mocked him for it.

Sure, back then I didn't have the full scope of things, but still. I was dismissive of his 'life's work' because I didn't get it. I couldn't see what was right in front of my face; you can't wish for more and never seek it out. And sometimes, even when you seek it out, you don't find it.

That's when you have to create it.

That's what Hunter has done here. What we've done with this amphitheater on a smaller scale. He's turned this town into the place he wanted it to be when we were kids. He's turned our upside downs into right side ups. And even though we officially told Claudette we were pulling out of the collaboration with Classy Country and setting out to start our own non-profit ventures, they've still sworn to attend every event we throw and gave us their full support.

Claudette may have been devastated she didn't get to plan the wedding of the century, but she'll get over it. Hunter and I aren't those kinds of people. We don't need the fuss; Lord knows we've had enough.

Besides, everyone I'd want to invite on a day like that is already right here, surrounding me in my own back yard.

"Ladies and gentlemen!" a very high-pitched, 'tween voice shouts through the mic. *Remind me to teach her to use a microphone properly.* "You have all lucked out, because you are in for a magnificent night of talented cowgirls and…less talented cowboys!"

The crowd hoots with laughter, swatting their jeans at her sass, and I can't ignore I'm one of them. My smile is spread so tight across my face when I watch her on that stage, I think it could split open if I move another inch.

"First off," she continues, "when Devyn Lynn Isaac—that's right ladies, *Isaac*, so don't be sending my papa any more of them lacy underthings in the mail, now. It's getting old." Another round of laughter sounds from the crowd as Ellie twirls and curtseys how I showed her before clearing her throat dramatically into the mic.

"When she told me she was doin' a talent show, I was worried about how much talent this town actually had, and I'm sorry to say, we didn't find any, but we did the best we could, so…enjoy this show instead!" She swats her leg as the crowd laughs on.

"All right, I'm kiddin', ya'll. Now, I know what yer thinkin'. 'But, Ellie, why aren't *you* dressed to compete if it's about being the most talented?'" She smiles, tilting her head sarcastically back and forth as we laugh. Kid's a natural.

"And the answer is…You have to be dumber than a doornail if you think I'd be caught dead wearin' a stupid dress and dancin' round a stage like a princess. No offense, Dev."

I smile and shake my head at her.

She jumps down off the apron of the stage and lands like a cat, on both feet, and the crowd falls silent as she raises the mic back to her mouth and looks up at the camera, her face displayed largely on the projector screen behind her so all can see on the live stream when she says, "But I'm sure as shit gonna shoot the gun that starts the competition, y'all! Now let me hear you *holler*!"

The crowd goes wild, applause, full-on standing ovation and clapping for none other than our Ellie girl.

Our girl.

And I couldn't be prouder. That's why this is the moment

I share a quick look with Hunter, and we rush from the wings to the apron and jump down to meet her in the pit.

"Ellie," Hunter says, taking her free hand and holding mine in his other. The cameras filming, as our whole town, our *family*, watches.

"Devyn and I want to tell you something. As of today, you are officially ours, sweetheart."

She arches her neck, her eyes wide and sparkling, a question on her lips.

So, I answer it, "It's for real, *Chuck*. Forever and always."

"I knew it!" she gasps, throwing her arms around me and then Hunter.

"Who knew you could keep so many secrets at once?" she asks him.

"Secrets?" I query. "As in plural?" But when I turn to Hunter, he's down on one knee. Ellie smiles brightly, her cheeks turning red, her eyes wild, as she jumps up and down clapping her hands excitedly.

"What's this? We're already married."

"Oh, let him do it, Dev!" Ellie cuts in. "It's so romantic."

I shoot a glance at the crowd and roll my eyes, sending them erupting in laughter.

"But I already have a ring, remember? And I like my Starburst one just fine."

"Okay, then." He shrugs. "I'll take back the handcrafted rose quartz gemstone inlaid in a platinum band of diamonds."

"Oh, my God! No, you won't!" I shout, grabbing for the cute pink box with the perfectly dainty bow and opening it to reveal just what he said it would. My eyes reflect in the sparkles of the jewels, almost as beautiful as the family who chose it for me.

"It's everything."

Hunter shakes his head.

"No, it's not. I'm looking at everything right now, and it looks a lot like my two girls in my arms, surrounded by the people we love."

And he's right. That is everything.

The talent show, the friends, and the family.

It's perfectly imperfect.

And after the crowd disperses, and it's just our close friends, we all settle by the bonfire and laugh about the parts of the night that made us feel something, whether it be big or small, happy or sad. We laugh and cry together, as a family should.

I stare at the fire for an unknown time, until my eyes start to see shapes of orange and red when I blink, and I know it's time to rise from Hunter's lap and take myself to bed.

Ellie's long since put herself to bed, Brooklyn's nestled in a sleeping bag on her bedroom floor, and Jonathan is decidedly in his own bed at his own house despite his and Ellie's protests that he should sleep on the couch so he could hang with her and Brooklyn longer. I shake my head. Those two are just like us when we were kids. Better to keep a firm eye on that. But as I'm stretching and preparing to say my goodnights, Dustin eyes me wearily, and I notice him picking at the wrapper on his beer bottle. A nervous tic of his from our teen years.

"Shana and I have something to say," he says suddenly.

Shana and I?

I slide my eyes to my best friend and tilt my head. She was there the day I went for the marriage license. She averts my gaze and turns to Dustin, and it doesn't escape my notice when she places her hand over his. And squeezes.

"Oh, my gosh, you're dating?"

"Not exactly," Shana says.

"We're pregnant."

If you want to read Shana and Dustin's story,
don't miss the next book in the Pine Forest series:

Something Like Sugar
(Coming Soon)

As a thank you, please enjoy a teaser chapter to follow.

For updates, sneak peaks, or to follow my publishing journey,
subscribe to my newsletter at *www.elsiebeabooks.com* or
connect with me on social media. For professional inquiries,
please email *elsiebea@elsiebeabooks.com*.

Thanks for taking a chance on something close to my heart.

Something Like Sunflowers.

XOXO,

Elsie

Chapter 1

I kid you not, it was ten inches long," Lemon stage whispers to Jeremy from across the table, holding up her arm for reference. "The size of my forearm. Tell me how I was supposed to say no to the tour bus after that."

"You weren't." Jeremy puckers his lips, shaking his head as he slurps down a low-fat chocolate shake.

I sip my drink, too, letting my long, dark curls hang haphazardly in front of my face like a little shield, my cloak of darkness to hide the crimson blush spreading across my chest with each growing moment they contemplate which other items might be longer than this rockstar's...*penis.*

I suck in a breath through my nose and blow it out through the red plastic straw, admiring the steady height of the bubbles I'm creating in my root beer float.

"You okay, Shay?" Devyn nudges me. We've been coming to the Sugar Stable a lot since she moved back home a few months ago and started the pageant program. Seeing as how rodeo pageants used to be a huge tradition in Pine Forest before Miss Clara passed a few years ago, and Dev is a former Miss American Rodeo queen, the news of her starting the program back up spread like wildfire. It's becoming extremely popular, to say the least. So many dancers from my studio want to participate that I somehow got roped into becoming a board member too, even though my only experiences with pageants are helping my best friend perfect the dances for her talent portions over the years. Aside from that, I've only ever been a spectator, watching Devyn do her thing.

Not that I don't like being a part of the pageant board.

I do.

It's basically Lemon, Jeremy, and Dev, and I love being with my friends. Usually.

If I'm being honest with myself, I need any distraction I can get. That's the real reason I'm here.

So that I won't be *there*.

Only today it's not as reassuring as I'd like, because while we're supposed to be discussing costumes and whether we should hire a seamstress or have the girls fundraise to purchase catalogue outfits like we do in dance, we seem to be discussing the…male anatomy, and its relation to Lemon's latest one-and-done.

I sigh to myself, blowing hair strands up with the force of my breath as I contemplate why it bothers me so much that she's always this vocal about her sexuality.

It's not like Lemon isn't a grown woman. She's allowed to have…trysts, I guess you call them. And I'm not slut-shamey, by any means.

But it's, like, how is everyone so open to all of this?

One minute you're a teenager, and its taboo to even think about taking off your bra, and the next thing you know, you're twenty-six and everyone you know has an OnlyFans.

"Am I the only one who doesn't want forearm sex?"

"You said that out loud," Devyn says, squinting her eyes and pressing her lips together.

Crimson Blush, meet Entire Body.

I can't stand to meet her eyes, embarrassment washing over me like a cold shower. Harsh. Instant. She's looking at me in a way that…

"You feel sorry for me. Oh, my God—" I watch my best friend bite her bottom lip and scrunch her nose.

"You do want forearm sex. I knew it." I push my drink away and scuttle my knees up to my chest until I'm hugging them under the fabric of my hoodie, swiftly tugging my hood over my head and tightening the strings until only my nose and mouth are visible through the opening.

"Shana," Devyn says, shoving my hands off the hoodie strings and loosening the fabric from around my face. "There." She smiles, making me look her in the eyes while she speaks, and not at Jeremy and Lemon who are pretending they don't see us—and doing a really crappy job of it—sliding their gazes our way every few seconds as they have, what I assume, is a fake conversation.

I roll my eyes at the theatrics, but a warmth surrounds me despite my mortification, because their stupid little act means something, at least.

They care.

I do have fantastic friends, even if I am the innocent, good girl of the group.

"I don't want to have sex with a forearm, just so we're clear." Devyn offers me a sincere smile.

Jeremy, who is miraculously now paying attention, places his hand on mine from across the table. "I don't think it would be satisfactory for my, um, *preferences*, either," he says, biting his lip to keep from laughing at his own implications. A giggle slips free from my lips at that, and I let myself appreciate just how understanding my friends are of my…

I don't know what you call it.

Innocence, I guess.

"Do you feel better now that you know Lemon is the only ho of the group?" Devyn asks, shooting a devious wink at Lemon and making me laugh even harder. Lemon rolls her eyes, but she smiles at me with gentle concern.

"I didn't mean to make you feel uncomfortable. We all experience things at different times and levels…" She drones on, trying to explain to me how I'm not the odd woman out, when I know for a fact that I am the only twenty-six-year-old virgin in the world.

Okay, a bit dramatic, I know. Probably not the world, but like, of all the people I know, at least.

And my friends aren't even privy to that little detail.

They just think I'm conservative, secretive about it all, but the truth is, the last relationship I had was before Dad got sick four years ago. And even then, I was so new to love that I had barely even kissed the guy. Scott was his name, not that it really matters.

He could have been Jim or Timothy for all I recall. He was just a man I met and felt…well, truthfully, very little for. Just like the ones I'd met before him. There was never that spark that told me to lay it all out on the line for someone other than myself.

To be bare. Physically and beyond.

Scott got over me after a while, when I wasn't ready to do more than first base type stuff, and it just fizzled when I moved back home with Dad.

Lemon's been with us for a year now. Well, the home health team she works for has. They take care of Dad around the clock. The retirement he won't ever get to use is paying for it.

And really, I'm not needed at home when they're around to care for him.

I'm just there on my off time, hoping he'll have a good enough day to sit up and talk, considering myself incredibly blessed on days he's well enough to crinkle the edges of his eyes and offer me a few lines of Shakespeare. When he can muster the strength. The good days.

Lately, there have been fewer good days.

And he doesn't need me there hovering over him to die. He might not be alert enough to tell me that right now, but I know my dad. I know how he feels about this. He doesn't want me to watch him wither away. He's too proud.

But how can I turn my back on him now? We're all each other has.

That in itself should be my red flag, though. We're all each other has. I have nobody else. No family. Just me.

I should be jumping at the idea of going out to bars with my friends at night and meeting strangers for sex with limb-size penises, right? Well, maybe just hot dog size to start, because that sounds a bit much.

"You can't sit around an' fuss over your old man forever. Promise me you will find connection outside of caring for me. Find someone worthy of your dance, my sweet Shaker. Cowards die many times before their deaths. The valiant taste of death but once."

It was almost three weeks ago when he said that.

The last good day.

So, what's my excuse? Even my dad's like, 'Yo, go get laid,' in more or less those words.

And it's not like I mean to be a virgin. I just am. How do you even explain that to people my age?

I was a very focused teenager and an even more deter-mined college student. I was always at rehearsal perfecting my craft, my love of dance.

I didn't have time for sex.

And now I'm so far behind that any real relationship-material kind of guy I meet is going to expect I have at least some idea how to do things I have exactly no idea whatsoever how to do.

Do you do sex? Or have it?

See? I don't even know.

It doesn't help that Lemon is going way farther into this than I need right now. I appreciate it, but it's not exactly helping to hear about her perceived lesser sexual acts. She's trying to make this one seem vanilla, but it's just revealing how very few things I know about intercourse.

What even is a cock ring? Oh, my God, I know zero things.

"It's fine!" I say, cutting her off, because she starts going on about her first time giving oral, and I do not need to hear that.

Or maybe I do.

My friends all look at me expectantly, like they want me to tell them more of my…feelings or something.

The thing is, I don't share those.

Feelings.

I have far too many of them running around in my brain all day, and if you ask me, they are extremely demanding little suckers that I simply have no time for and must squash beneath my feet. Literally and figuratively.

Doesn't matter which ones. Sadness, fear, guilt, anxiety, passion…*lust.*

The only time I let myself succumb to those things willingly is when the music takes over and my body feels them for me.

When I dance.

So, I dance as often as possible. I danced my way through a state college scholarship, on to a master's degree, became a dance teacher, and bought my own studio with my earnings.

It's all I ever wanted.

I used to think it was all I'd ever need.

But when the studio closes, and the girls take their sparkling tulle and giggling voices home with them, I go home too.

And there aren't friends or fun, and certainly no forearms waiting for me.

There's the only family I have left.

Dying.

"We're going to Cowboy's Paradise, if you wanna join." Lemon smiles at me from across the table, breaking my awkward silence.

Jeremy scrolls his phone, checking to see which of the bartenders are on shift tonight. Not that it matters, since he works there, knows them all, and will find out in a matter of minutes when they arrive. And Devyn, falling quickly into a cute little mommy role since caring for her ex's…and now *not* ex's niece of a daughter—it's a long story—shuffles the cups around, picking up paper straw wrappers and putting them in a neat little pile for the man bussing tables tonight.

Her brother, it just so happens. Okay, it doesn't just happen. He owns the place. He's like, always here, thankfully.

I mean, not thankfully. Did I think that?

Dustin Campbell is the tall, quiet, bad boy down the hall in all my teenage memories. Better known as my best friend's older brother.

He's owned the Sugar Stable since he graduated high school two years ahead of us. He started here when he was just fifteen but quickly worked his way up to shift leader. He was always one of those silent, hardworking types, and it's hard not to admire that his perseverance is what got him ownership over something like this, the local hot spot milkshake bar.

He went from busboy to owner, even after a quick stint in juvie for standing up to a bully in his tenth-grade year. It was only a few months, but when he got out, he was somehow even better looking than before. He kept to himself, did rodeos, worked, and stayed far away from gossip or drama… unlike most people in this town.

And here he is, still making shakes and checking on customers like he's one of the little guys even though he doesn't have to. Because he cares about this place from the ground up. He's worked every part of it, and he understands the business at its core. He knows how to make something he loves and cares about thrive, and he isn't afraid to get his hands dirty for it.

It reminds me of my dance studio, just across the street.

My studio is my life.

My one true passion.

Other women my age might care about contour makeup or the latest water bottle and leggings crazes, but my obsession comes in the form of beats and melodies that get stuck in my head until my brain commands my body give them physical life.

I tap my foot, even now, listening to the rhythm of the milkshake machine running as strong, muscled hands move the metal cup up and down the spinning rod, spreading the cream around the base until it's smooth and dripping from the spinner.

I don't realize I've been staring at Dustin, his forearm muscles, of all things, flexing with each extension as he twists the metal rod free from the machine to wipe it down, until Lemon turns her head and widens her eyes.

"You're totally staring at Dustin, aren't you?"

"What?" I snap my head back toward her, frantically eyeing the table to make sure Jeremy and Devyn are still locked in conversation and didn't hear that absolute mistruth that just came out of Lemon's mouth.

"I am not staring at…" I drop my voice and cut my eyes over to Devyn and then back at Lemon, "…*him.*"

Lemon's eyes widen to round saucers, but only briefly before she smiles mischievously.

"Noted." That's all she says. And I have a feeling that's bad news.

But I wasn't staring at Dustin.

Was I?

Am I now?

Shoot!

"I think I'm just going to hang out here and look up some music for the recital choreography," I tell my friends as Lemon eyes me suspiciously, a purse to her knowing lips. I plead with her under a scrunched-up nose poking through my hoodie hole. I just want to be in a hole.

But to her credit, she doesn't press me. It's Devyn who does.

"It's October," she argues, "and a Christmas recital, Shay, come on. Hang out with us. You might just meet the perfect forearm, for all you know."

"Oh, my God, you did not just say that." I groan, shaking my head.

Sometimes my friends can be so…loud.

They're more open about things I am so very closed about that you might as well say I'm mummified to them. Like sex, for example. I'm wrapped up, in a box, under a curse, and sealed in an underground tomb kinda closed-off to that.

But Devyn knows this and squeezes my hand to soften the blow. "I know you have a lot going on right now. And that's exactly why you need to let loose sometimes. Meet someone who makes you smile. You don't have to hide in your hoodie all alone, Shay."

Lemon and Jeremy have gone to pay and are talking with Dustin at the counter in order to give Devyn and me this moment, and I appreciate that. Everyone here knows my dad is in his last few months, just living at home.

Waiting to die, I think again, that single thought practically a leech feeding off my mind at all times.

And I guess they all feel sorry for me.

I don't even blame them. I feel sorry for me.

Shana Holiday, the last of her kind.

Like a dumb, young adult, dystopian novel where I find out I have hidden powers, or a fated mate, or some sort of duty and calling to save all of mankind like my ancestors always planned.

Then at least there would be a reason for my fate.

For my solitude.

But there's not.

It's just Shana Holiday, the last of her kind.

Even my friends can sense my doom. So, meeting someone right now? A relationship? Someone who makes me smile, as Devyn put it…that's just not in my cards. It's not part of this story, because it isn't a story.

There is no romance through-line.

It's just reality. And the reality is my dad is dying. I am a weird, emotionally stunted ballerina who only feels in song and loves in movement, and things like *smiling someones* and love… that's another person's story. Not mine.

"I'll see you tomorrow," I tell her, noting the feeling of disappointment coming off in waves with the downward turn of her frown, and the guilt that indicates I put it there. She walks away, and I watch her stop by the register at the door to peck her brother on the cheek before she turns away.

Something I should have done before he saw me.

But I didn't.

And my body pays the price as goosebumps break across my skin in masses, my heart beating a wild, allegro storm, like the wings of one thousand butterflies live inside me.

The way his eyes kiss mine from across the room makes me feel something that has me scooping my laptop into my bag and darting from the Sugar Stable, across the street, and into my studio as fast as my legs will carry me.

Because I felt something just now. And I can't un-feel it. Can't unknow it.

When Dustin Campbell looks at me, it makes me dance.

Acknowledgments

From the bottom of my heart, thank you to everyone who supported me during this journey.

To my husband, K.P., for being the sails to my windy whims, for breathing sunshine into my darkest days, and for steering me through every storm, even the ones I create on my own. Your support and faith in my writing, and the love you exhibit to our family on a daily basis, mean the world to me.

To Truly and Guy, for your smiles and laughter. For your experiences and goofy one-liners as you discover the world. Ellie wouldn't be Ellie without the two of you.

To my McCauleys, for showing up to musicals, beauty pageants, and voice recitals. For reading my angsty teen poetry and for clapping even when the student directed showcases were almost always weird. Thank you for fostering my creativity before I knew how to foster it on my own.

To Cary, for being the inspiration behind every sassy best friend I could ever write, and for trying out different poses with your tall husband so I know how to block them in scenes.

To Anthony, AKA Tall-Husband, for your participation in the aforementioned events.

To Allie, for being my non-stop supporter. Even when my dreams seem outlandish, you're always there to be my hype-girl.

To Lori L., you may have been Mommy's Mean Friend, but I'm so happy I inherited your love. Thank you for believing in me as I painted the dragons into existence.

To Lesa, for keeping the kids when I needed quiet days and for not reading the spicy scenes in this book, hopefully ever.

To Kelly M., for reading every one of my stories from the beginning, even when they were cringe and fan fictional. You are my biggest cheerleader, and I wouldn't have started this journey without your encouragement.

To my alpha and beta readers, Kelly L. and Elizabeth, for your constructive criticism, your passion, and your thoughtfulness.

To my street team, The Bea Hive Babes, Bookstagram influencers, ARC readers, and PR team for pushing my content and making my book launch a success. I could not do it without you volunteering your platforms and time.

To A. Locke, for being my unofficial mentor, for accepting that I will pop up in your inbox periodically for advice and for going out of your way to provide it. You've created worlds and stories that inspired me to share my own. You taught me it was possible.

To Ramona Miahi, your proofreading skills and final suggestions were the cherry on top, and I'm so happy to have you in my corner.

To Molly Donohue, for jumping on board and designing a cover that could rival the romcom industry's finest. It warms my heart to work together again after all these years, from the stage to the page. I can't tell you how insane it is to watch you take my super vague ideas and turn them into the cover of my dreams. Your art is essential and beautiful, just like you.

To Lori Whitwam, I'm a lucky girl to have had you on my copy-editing team. I apologize for every italicized word you had to highlight, gosh there were so many of them, and I thank you immensely for teaching me that inanimate objects cannot sweep one's body or burn like flames. I'll remember for the next book, as I picture tiny brooms, promise.

To Kimberly Hunt of Revision Division, for taking a chance on a debut author with half a manuscript and pages of ideas. This novel wouldn't be the polished product it has become without your eye for detail and story structure, and I can't thank you enough for teaching me along the way and seeing the potential in the final product even when it was at its roughest.

Lastly, to my readers, for taking a chance on a new author and reading my words. Of all the books you could have picked, I'm so grateful you chose mine. By purchasing my novel, you allow me to keep spreading love and hope to as many as possible.

Thank you for choosing
Something Like Sunflowers.

About the Author

Elsie Bea is a contemporary romance author from Richmond, Virginia. She lives 'out in the sticks' with her incorrigible husband, crazy kids, and a gaggle of dogs, chickens, and ducks. When she's not reading or writing, you can find her singing and dancing through her kitchen and spending time with family.